ST. MARTIN'S
PAPERBACKS

U.S. $
CAN

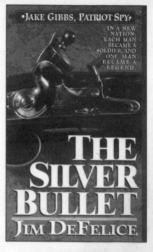

•JAKE GIBBS, PATRIOT SPY•

IN A NEW
NATION,
EACH MAN
BECAME A
SOLDIER, AND
ONE MAN
BECAME A
LEGEND.

THE SILVER BULLET

JIM DeFELICE

**LOOK FOR
THE SILVER BULLET
BY JIM DeFELICE —
BOOK 1 IN THE EXCITING
JAKE GIBBS, PATRIOT SPY
SERIES!**

ISBN 0-312-95635-5

9 780312 956356

50599>

LIBERTY FOR
THE COLONISTS
HANGS BY AN
IRON THREAD—

PQG850479

THE
IRON
CHAIN

JIM DEFELICE

Author of *The Silver Bullet*

THE IRON CHAIN

JIM DEFELICE

St. Martin's Paperbacks

NOTE: If you purchased this book without a cover you should be aware that this book is stolen property. It was reported as "unsold and destroyed" to the publisher, and neither the author nor the publisher has received any payment for this "stripped book."

THE IRON CHAIN

Copyright © 1995 by Jim DeFelice.

Cover photograph by Edward Vebell.

All rights reserved. No part of this book may be used or reproduced in any manner whatsoever without written permission except in the case of brief quotations embodied in critical articles or reviews. For information address St. Martin's Press, 175 Fifth Avenue, New York, N.Y. 10010.

ISBN: 0-312-95635-5

Printed in the United States of America

St. Martin's Paperbacks edition/November 1995

10 9 8 7 6 5 4 3 2 1

INTRODUCTION

About a year ago, my uncle discovered some old manuscripts in the root cellar of an eighteenth century farm he owns in upstate New York. The papers purport to document the adventures of a heretofore unknown Revolutionary War hero, Jake Gibbs. A member of George Washington's Secret Service, the Philadelphia native handled a wide range of duties during the war, from spying to sabotage. The son of a wealthy merchant in the apothecary or pharmaceutical trade, Gibbs was educated in England and served briefly as a secretary to Sir Guy Carleton, later the governor of Canada. In his early twenties during the war, he seems to have been part man of action, part scholar, part lady–killer.

During some of his time in what is now New York state, Gibbs was accompanied by a wily if portly Dutchman, Claus van Clynne. While not officially a member of the Secret Service, this worthy gentleman provided valuable service to his country, though he seems to have gilded much of it with complaints about everything from the state of swordmaking to the weather.

The adventures portrayed in this book directly follow the foray into Canada and New York City described in *The Silver Bullet;* indeed, the action picks up the day after that book ends. While I have "translated" the original eighteenth century manuscript to make it more sensible (and less tiring) to contemporary readers, I have not changed anything essential, and fully trust that my version is as historically accurate as the original. Modern names have been substituted in several cases for clarity, and on the whole I have shortened the original author's verbosity by two-thirds.

Despite his few attempts at appearing neutral, I think it's fair to say the writer was a committed Whig, and more than likely a member of the Sons of Liberty. Thus we must occasionally make allowances for his exaggerations and prejudices toward the American Cause.

This story takes place over the first three days of June 1777. It was a critical and difficult time for the American revolutionaries. Washington had just survived a desolate winter and was trying to regroup his pitifully small army in New Jersey and the Hudson Highlands. Despite strenuous recruiting, he had not quite eight thousand barely trained and ill-equipped men; the British, in contrast, had four times that number and a good portion of the world's strongest navy in New York City alone. In Montreal, a large army of Englishmen, Loyalists, and Hessians was being mustered for an invasion south toward Lake George and Albany. The superior arms and training of the British forces would today be considered "force multipliers" that would make the odds against the Americans overwhelming.

If the British armies in New York City and Canada could unite in New York's Hudson Valley, the war would quickly be lost. All that stood between them was an iron chain on the Hudson—and the redoubtable Mr. Gibbs.

—Jim DeFelice
Chester, N.Y.

One

June 1777

"You will honor me, sir, by raising your hands. You need not touch a particular cloud, but you will stretch in that direction or suffer the most dire consequences."

"And what consequences might those be?" harrumphed Claus van Clynne, settling his hands alongside his baggy russet coat as his gelding took a short, nervous pace to the side.

"I should not like to shoot you." The man locked his knees astride the gray-dappled horse blocking the path and flicked his coat back to reveal a well-polished flintlock pistol, cocked and aimed in the Dutchman's direction. "I must say, though, you would be an easy target, with so large a belly."

"Even the robbers take airs these days," complained van Clynne, who still made no movement to comply with the stranger's command.

Jake Gibbs, sitting on a black mare next to him, silently cursed his companion's obstinate nature. On the one hand, van Clynne's prickly sense of honor, not to mention his stubbornness, often proved valuable in difficult situations. On the other, it occasionally led him to annoy people at entirely the wrong moment, with difficult consequences.

"Claus," said Jake, holding his long arms out in a show of complying with the stranger's directions, "perhaps the gentleman wants to discuss the state of affairs in the countryside." He stretched his hands so high that his shoulders strained the rough gray-brown cloth of his coat.

"At gunpoint? I tell you sir, as a practitioner of the conversational arts, gunpowder makes for very poor grammar."

Jake smiled apologetically at the stranger, and moved his left hand down to shade against the late afternoon sun. The man had come upon them at the juncture of two narrow and extremely obscure lanes northeast of the old New York road in southern Westchester. Van Clynne's irritation was undoubtedly compounded by the fact that he had boasted a few minutes before that not more than three people in the entire province knew this shortcut to White Plains, and that he and Jake were as likely to meet an African unicorn as a criminal.

The country here was euphemistically known as the Neutral Ground, meaning that in addition to being patrolled by both American and British forces, robbers and thieves felt any traveler was fair game. Which specific category the stranger fell into remained to be seen, but was in certain important senses irrelevant.

"State your allegiances quickly," he told Jake, "or I will dispatch you to a more leisurely world. And you—" Turning back to van Clynne, he reached his hand behind him and retrieved a second pistol from a holster behind his saddle. "I advise you not to spur your horse, as you were thinking of doing."

"A mind reader, too," complained the Dutchman.

"We are merely travelers like yourself," said Jake smoothly, easing his hands down. He brushed a piece of dust from his brown breeches to emphasize his nonchalance, and kept his tone as calm and friendly as if a baker had happened upon him and asked if he wanted bread on the morrow. "Were you waiting for someone?"

Jake guessed from the stranger's handsome pistol and horse, as well as his aristocratic manner and clothes—not fine, but fresh and unstained, which was the significance—that he was allied to the British; generally the people with money here chose the king's side of the conflict. But this was not necessarily inevitable, and while the man was obviously waiting for some confederate whose identity was unknown to him, there were a thousand explanations possible.

And no time to hear any of them—the faint click of hoofbeats sounded in the distance, and Jake realized there was as good a chance as not their interlocutor might decide to shoot them when he learned they were not his appointed guests.

"I will ask the questions," said the man. "Who are you seeking?"

"We don't seek anyone," said Jake. "We have concluded a piece of business in New York, and now are traveling toward some friends."

"You are rebels, then," said the stranger, who by using the word *rebel* as good as told Jake that he was loyal to King George.

"By whose definition are we rebels?" asked van Clynne indignantly. His loud voice drew the stranger's attention and momentarily loosened his aim.

God, thought Jake as he slid forward on his horse, grabbing the pistol hooked into the front of his saddle in the same motion, I've been with the Dutchman so long I actually know what he's thinking.

However frightening that was—and the reader would have had to spend a solid week listening to van Clynne's complaints to truly appreciate the fear—it was not an emotion the patriot spy dwelled upon. The weapon in Jake's holster was kept loaded and ready; a smooth, simple gun without ornamentation, it was nonetheless accurate and deadly, even when fired from its sling. It could not actually be called sweet, as its kick was surprisingly heavy for its size. But this heaviness was in direct proportion to the speed and power of the round ball it discharged—a ball that struck the stranger square in the throat.

The jolt of a gun being fired so close to her head was too much for Jake's mare, and the poor beast bolted down the road as if the devil himself were after her. The patriot spy, off balance, fell to the side, an arm just missing a good smack from the horse's foreleg and then the ground. Jake's six-foot-two frame twisted across the back and side of the animal, desperately trying to adhere, while his long hair flew madly above, a guardian angel suddenly jostled from its post.

The horse's speed had been an asset earlier in the day as Jake and van Clynne rode north through East Chester, dodging British patrols and outposts, but now it was a distinct liability. The animal followed the winding road-way, dodging and cutting back with its curves as Jake swam against the wind and the mare's momentum to bring her under control.

The patriot had never been reckoned a horseman in his youth—his priorities were elsewhere—but he had ac-quired a certain proficiency during the last two years of war. That and his natural strength won out in the end, and when the mare felt the strong hands once more pull-ing evenly on her reins, she began to calm. They had traveled more than a quarter mile in her madness, but Jake's only new injury seemed to be the loss of the ribbon that tied his hair into a ponytail—his tricornered hat had been lost nearly a week before.

As for old injuries, both his shoulder and knee vied for attention. They had been hurt the previous day in New York City, and thus warranted some indulgence—he rubbed both before setting back up the road to see where van Clynne was.

As it happened, the Dutchman was not far from where Jake had left him, though under somewhat different cir-cumstances: He found himself in the middle of an alto-gether uncomfortable parlay with two horsemen who had galloped up from the rear and ordered him to dismount.

"I thank God for your arrival," said van Clynne, "for otherwise I should be as dead as my friend." His attitude was in remarkable contrast to his previous manner; he practically bolted from his animal and made a great show of being agreeable.

And there is nothing so agreeable as a Dutchman being agreeable. Van Clynne took off his large, Quaker-style beaver hat and twirled it around in sympathetic gestures as he praised the two horsemen. Each was equipped with a heavy musket, a deadly weapon, granted, but not terri-bly accurate from the back of a horse. The Dutchman took no obvious notice of this drawback, praising both as timely saviors. He bowed and scraped until even the king of Araby would have been impressed.

"A tall man, obviously a villain, ambushed us and demanded our money," said van Clynne when he finally decided he had sweetened the dough enough to insert a piece of meat. "My brave friend resisted—and now we see the sad consequence of valuing gold above all else."

Frowning, one of the gunmen jumped down to inspect the prostrate body. "It's Johnson," he said to his companion.

"Johnson, yes," said van Clynne. "A fine man. Noble and of a philosophical nature. A great loss."

The man on horseback deepened his frown. "How do we know you didn't kill him?"

"Kill a friend? Didn't you see the criminal ride off? You were upon us so quick, I half assumed you were avenging angels, here to take the killer to hell."

"John, if he was riding with Major Johnson—"

"Let's let our guest explain himself, Esmond, before we jump to any conclusions. The woods are filled with traitors."

"Esmond, now there is a handsome name," said van Clynne, holding his silvery gray hat to his chest. "Is it Dutch, by any chance?"

"Not that I know."

"A pity," he said.

"Step away from your horse."

Van Clynne took the rein in his hand. "I merely want to make sure he stays with me. A fine animal, but not too trustworthy. A bit like a rebel, no?"

"And how do you know we're not rebels?" demanded John.

"Come, sir, I would think our loyalties are above question." Van Clynne reached for one of the bags tied to his saddle. "I have always sworn firm allegiance to the king. If you wish, I have some papers that will clear me of any suspicion. Though I would hardly think that necessary under the circumstances. Indeed, there was a time when a Dutchman's wink, let alone his word, was his guarantee—"

"Shut up and show us your pass before I fill your mouth with my musket."

"If he was with Major Johnson—"

"Quiet, Esmond. What is your name, criminal?"

"Claus van Clynne, Esquire, at your service," said the Dutchman, taking the bag in hand as he bowed and waved his hat in a grand gesture of introduction.

Van Clynne's tone had suddenly turned from sincere to sardonic, but the Tory on horseback had no time to respond—a bullet whizzed from the nearby woods and caught him on the side, pushing him forward on his horse.

The author of the shot was none other than Jake Gibbs. The Dutchman had caught sight of him creeping into position in the woods, and endeavored to attract the strangers' attention with his prattle while Jake prepared his assault. But even the most elaborate tactical plan carries with it a flaw, and here the shortcoming was quickly apparent—Jake was armed with only one pistol, and having fired that one, was defenseless as the dead man's partner turned and confronted him with his musket at close range.

The man was so intent on pulling back the lock to shoot that he hardly noticed van Clynne still fussing behind him with his hat and bag. As he settled his aim, the Dutchman dropped the leather sack and flung one of the items it had contained—an Iroquois tomahawk—head over handle. With the sharp flap of a hawk descending for the kill, it flew directly into the Tory's head, slicing it asunder.

Two

Wherein, the American lines are reached and crossed.

"You see now, sir, that fashion can have its utilitarian side," said van Clynne. "My hat distracted them sufficiently for me to remove my weapon unobserved. You could not have done that with your customary tricorner."

"The only distraction that mattered was my shooting them," Jake said testily.

"Hmmph," said van Clynne. "I was ready to attack well before then, but waited for you out of courtesy. It would have been impolite to deprive you of a share of the glory."

"Uh-huh."

"I should remind you that there were two tomahawks in my bag. Frankly, I could not understand your delay in firing; I thought my tongue would rot with its praise of that villain King George."

"I was waiting for you to torture them with an explanation of your economic theories, Claus. They would have run for their lives and I wouldn't have had to waste the powder."

"Mark me, sir." Van Clynne's round face grew bright red, his cheeks puffing above the thick yet somehow scraggly beard that grew beneath his mouth and chin. His nose pinched and pointed northward, and his thick brows furrowed above his eyes. This was a sign that he intended to speak with great seriousness, as was the velocity of his finger as it rent the air. In truth, the Dutchman would declare that he always spoke with great seriousness, but

as he always spoke, some pronouncements were naturally
more serious than others.

"The philosophy of Adam Smith will be revered for
generations to come," van Clynne declared. "You, sir,
should have sympathy with his theories, as they are most
fitting for a democracy, and provide the basis for the
overthrow of this heinous taxation system imposed by the
mother country."

"Revolutions are things of the heart, Claus, not the
head. A man feels he must be free before he can explain
it."

The Dutchman sniffed at the rebuke and followed his
usual tactic when checked, which was to change the subject. "You fuss with those dead bodies so much I would
think you an undertaker's son, rather than a druggist's."

"If I had a shovel and we were across American lines
or better armed, I'd bury them properly," said Jake,
standing back from the fence where he'd propped the
three dead men. In truth, the tableau was a shade grotesque; if not for their gaping wounds and blood-stained
clothes, the men might be sitting down to a roadside tea.
He unrolled his sleeves and despite the lingering heat of
the spring day pulled his coat back over his shoulders.
"We'll have to send the first patrol we meet to do so.
Even a thief deserves to be properly buried."

"We'd best continue on our way before we're in need
of the same service," warned van Clynne from his horse.

None of the dead men carried a shred of paper indicat-
ing who they might be or what they were about. Under
other circumstances, Jake might have decided to spend
some time finding out. He suspected that Johnson was a
British or Tory agent, waiting for other traitors; capturing
their accomplices would be a good day's work. But Lieutenant Colonel Jake Gibbs, secret service agent assigned
temporarily to the Northern Department of the Continental Army, had more pressing responsibilities. He was
to return to Albany in six days and report to Major General Philip Schuyler, commander of the Northern Department of the Continental Army, that General Sir William
Howe had no immediate plans to come north on the
Hudson River.

The reason he had no such plans will be familiar to those who have followed Lieutenant Colonel Gibbs's previous exploits. Gibbs and van Clynne had just succeeded in foisting themselves off on Howe as messengers from General Johnny Burgoyne, telling him Burgoyne did not wish him to proceed north. While this was directly contrary to Burgoyne's grand plan for ending the war, the American agents had managed to completely convince Sir William. As the elaborate strategem has been described in detail elsewhere, we will skip over it here, saying only that had Jake and van Clynne failed, General Schuyler would have abandoned Albany. Indeed, he would have had little recourse but to give over the entire Hudson Valley to the British, thereby splitting the states in two, and leaving New England and the Revolution to be strangled on the vine.

While the author has grown reflective, Jake and van Clynne have mounted their horses, taken the others in tow, and continued north on the road toward White Plains. Jake has retied his hair with a spare piece of black cloth found in one of his companion's copious pockets. There was mention of a rental fee amounting to two pence per day, with interest compounded on the fortnight; the reader has fortunately missed the lieutenant colonel's somewhat scatological retort.

Jake soon had more considerable matters to ponder. He noticed that his mare's right foreleg was giving her difficulty; she had strained herself during her panicked flight. After switching to the gray-dappled stallion so lately owned by Johnson, the two patriots moved forward at a slower pace, hoping the mare could be saved.

Van Clynne in the meantime expressed various opinions, mostly in the form of complaints, about the state of the American economy, which had become subject to wild inflation and artificial shortages, cheating honest businessmen and providing opportunity only for scoundrels. Why the Dutchman fit into the first group when he so easily and consistently made profits the second would envy was not adequately addressed by his theories, though Jake would be the last to point this out—it would only encourage van Clynne to speak at greater length.

Within fifteen minutes—at about the point where the squire was running down the beaver trade—they came upon a party of American pickets, who had set up a post on a wooden bridge over a tributary of the Bronx River. The men wore tattered hunting shirts; if these had been originally cut from leather, they had long since transmuted into a thinner and foreign cloth. Their breeches were not in much better shape, well worn and in a few cases patched; in others, simply torn. Their hose was nonexistent, and it would cause a grave injustice to the language to call the items on their feet shoes. But their weapons were in good repair, and the soldiers themselves cheery enough, as soon as Jake identified himself and his companion as patriots in search of the men's captain.

The troops were Rhode Islanders from Colonel Israel Angell's regiment. Angell was an old acquaintance of Jake's, and this information was warmly welcomed by the captain, an amiable sort found bending over a kettle a few yards away. The man had built his fire by the roadside, announcing his post with a simple stick mounted by a blue ribbon. He had a stump for his desk, and a log for his seat, but nonetheless exuded the air of one naturally born to lead.

"Can I offer you some Liberty Tea, gentlemen? I've added a few herbs I found by the roadside to the usual sassafras. I think it has quite a unique flavor."

Jake and van Clynne exchanged a glance.

"I make it a habit never to drink Liberty Tea after the early morning hours," blustered the Dutchman. "I, er, it keeps me awake."

"I'm not thirsty, thank you," said Jake.

"You're missing a treat." The captain poured the water and its steeped herbs into a crude tin cup and held it to his mouth. He took a sip, winced, then set it down. "Too hot," he said doubtfully. "I'll have to let it cool. Now, gentlemen—your business."

"We are messengers," said Jake, producing a piece of blown and colored glass the Sons of Liberty had given him in New York as an identifier. The captain fingered the clamshell-shaped glass briefly, then handed it back.

"And your destination?"

"I can say only that I am working for General Schuyler. Ordinarily, I am assigned to General Greene."

The captain's expression, wary and soured by the tea, lightened immediately. Rhode Island's Nathanael Greene was well regarded by many in the northern army, and certainly all who came from his state. "Have you seen the general recently?"

"No," said Jake. "We have been on this assignment quite a while. It is a trifle, though there have been moments of interest here and there."

"The general's leg is better?"

"The general's leg has been injured since his youth, so I hardly think it could get better," said Jake. He smiled, acknowledging the cleverness of the trick. The officer's extra bit of wariness was well justified in these woods.

For his part, the captain guessed from Jake's bearing if not his rough farmer's clothes that this guest was not a mere civilian pressed into service or even a disguised enlisted man, as Jake's ambiguous responses were meant to suggest. The officer was wise enough not to press the matter on the one hand, and on the other to treat the stranger with careful respect, even offering his log to sit on. Jake declined the honor.

Van Clynne accepted with a happy grunt.

"Colonel Angell is in Peekskill," the captain told them after ordering a detail to bury the men they had left down the road. "He spends every moment haranguing for supplies. There are shortages of everything."

"What sort of thing does the army need?" van Clynne asked, stroking his beard.

"Anything and everything. Shoes, shirts, boots especially. Food—I believe I would give half my inheritance for a pound of salt. I have not had salt with my dinner for three months at least."

"There is money to pay for these things, I suppose?"

"There is a shortage of funds," admitted the captain, "but surely not so severe that money could not be found if these items could be provided."

More inviting words had seldom been spoken to the Dutchman, who immediately began computing how a profit might be patriotically turned.

If anything, the captain understated his troop's condition by half. Many of the soldiers marched out barefoot, with tattered clothes and not even insignias of rank or unit. There was no shortage of gunpowder, only because there was not enough of it to be issued to a soldier except for a specific duty—a surprise attack would find much of the ammunition under lock and key. Worst of all, any honest rating of the American troops would put these Rhode Islanders toward the top of the men assigned to guard the Highlands—many of the other units were either militia or as green as the sprouting hills around them.

"We had hope when Old Put came in," said the captain, referring to Major General Israel Putnam, one of the heroes of Breed's Hill and a beloved leader of the American forces. General Washington had put him in command of the Highlands two months before. "He has done much, but it is an awesome task. Rumor has it," the captain added in a lower voice, "that there is a plot afoot to destroy the iron chain stretched across the Hudson north of Peekskill."

"Destroy it?" demanded Jake indignantly. "How?"

"If I knew that, we wouldn't be sitting here talking about it, I assure you."

The chain stretched across the river on a diagonal from the shore below St. Anthony's Nose to a point just above the Polpen Creek. It was the key to the defense of the Highlands and the rest of the Hudson Valley, as it kept British ships from coming north. Without it, no part of the valley—not Poughkeepsie, not Newburgh, not Kingston, not even Albany—would be safe. Indeed, were the British navy and its formidable marines able to sail blithely up the Hudson, Jake's recent mission to fool General Howe would be rendered useless. Upper New York could be taken in a hairsbreadth by a tiny fraction of the available British forces, and the vital supply link between New England and the southern colonies would be severed. Massachusetts, Connecticut, Rhode Island—all would quickly starve to death. The Revolution itself would surely follow.

"The chain itself is formidable," said the captain, "but our other defenses, and the men . . . "

Here the officer shook his head, as if his pessimism were a physical thing that had formed on his tongue, and by clamping his mouth he might change the entire situation. He smiled, tried boldly to continue, though his voice was still forlorn.

"Things are difficult for us, with such short supplies. Morale has fallen sharply; even I despair at times. The British have been recruiting men from the countryside as rangers, and it has been difficult to stop them. I have no doubt the man you killed was a recruiter."

"Good riddance, then," said Jake.

"Yes. But there will be more if our situation doesn't improve. Even my own men are tempted to desert."

Jake received this sobering sentiment silently, realizing that though the situation was difficult, Angell would not have a man under him who would truly despair no matter how dire the circumstance. Van Clynne, on the other hand, took offense, and proceeded to upbraid the captain, telling him he was a soldier in the greatest army ever assembled, a fighter for Freedom, a defender of all that was holy and then some.

"Your friend sounds like a member of Congress," the captain told Jake.

"You'll have to forgive him. He hasn't had any dinner."

"I have only dry biscuits to offer you myself. But there is an inn not too far from here, owned by a fellow named Prisco. An agreeable sort—if you told him you are on your way to Schuyler, I daresay he'd advance you the price of a good meal."

"We are well acquainted with Justice Prisco," said Jake. "In fact, that is our destination, since we hope to stay the night there."

And more, perhaps, as Prisco's inn was the same where Claus van Clynne had fallen in love not a week before. Sweet Jane—but perhaps it is better not to burden the reader with her portrait at present.

The Dutchman, having gained an understanding of the overall need for supplies and seeing firsthand the severe effect on morale, had already resolved to assist in remedying the situation—especially as he realized a ready profit could be made. Thus he was now all the more anxious to get to the inn and see Jane—whom he would entrust to make certain contacts on his behalf with merchants further north. He mounted his horse and sat nodding and clearing his throat while Jake spent an inordinate number of seconds bidding the captain farewell.

The gray-dappled stallion Johnson had so graciously bequeathed the patriot spy was a large, well-mannered beast that accepted Jake's long legs gracefully. It was a powerful horse, and would gladly have broken into a gallop if its new master had wished. But Jake, ignoring van Clynne's continued complaints, kept the pace slow to ease the strain on his injured mare, following behind. Despite the Dutchman's shortcuts—there was not a cow path in the state he did not know, nor a route he could not cut by five minutes—night had covered them with a heavy blanket of darkness before they reached Prisco's. The innkeeper himself greeted them in the yard between the large but simple frame tavern and the adjoining barn, used by Prisco as the stable. He had just come from checking on his assistant and some horses.

"Well, well, Mr. Gibbs. And the redoubtable Squire van Clynne," said Prisco, holding up his torch. "My niece will be glad to see you."

"And I her," admitted van Clynne, an uncharacteristic shyness suddenly entering his voice—and tying his tongue.

"Judge, my mare has hurt her leg," said Jake, dismounting to show him. "I'm afraid she'll be made into some soldier's dinner."

Prisco—Jake called him judge because he was the local justice of the peace—examined the animal with a gentle hand.

"I do not think the injury is that bad," he concluded. "We shall nurse her back to health if you can spend a few days."

"We have business north," said Jake, "but I would be obliged to you if you watched her for me. I will pay for her feed."

"All she needs is a few days' rest. New shoes, too," added the innkeeper, examining them. "It's difficult to find a smith these days; all the good ones and most of the rest have been put to work on the chain. But Elmer's lad should do a passable job." He called to his stableboy and turned the horses over to him.

"Does this horse look familiar to you, Judge?" Jake asked as his stallion was taken.

Prisco's round face turned quizzical as he studied Johnson's horse. Neither it nor its former owner were known to him, but he confessed that this did not necessarily go for much.

"My politics are well known. Few British spies have the audacity to announce themselves, though I daresay they have darkened my halls. It is hard to tell these days who is friend and who is foe," added the keeper, who had to stretch himself considerably to pat Jake on the shoulder. "Come now, I've just tapped a new barrel of ale."

"I've thirsted for it all day," said van Clynne, leading the way.

Three

Wherein, Jake plays a portentous game of chess.

William Shakespeare earned much praise by comparing his mistress to a summer's day. Three times as many accolades would be won by a poet who could compare the object of Claus van Clynne's desire to some natural wonder, as the metaphor would be wilder and the language further stretched. Ovid's metamorphosing and Homer's blindness would both be put to strong use.

Or to place it another way—sweet Jane has proven her patriotism under fire and has many other fine qualities, but alas, physical beauty is not numbered among them. Her nose does not quite fit her face, her eyes are off-line, her legs off-kilter. She is sweet, she is brave, but she is decidedly plain.

Do not suggest this to the Dutchman. Nay, admit no impediments to his true love. Once inside the inn he made straight for the summer kitchen, where he found the girl laboring over a plum pie, her homespun dress clinging neatly to her skinny hips and her mobcap tied with a light blue ribbon the Dutchman had left during his last visit. The words they exchanged, the looks—the pie had not half as much sugar.

Jake, meanwhile, took up a corner in the inn's great room not far from the fireplace, which was lit even though it was a warm night. The polished wood-paneled walls glowed a soft red with reflected light and warmth. The patriot spy reached up and plucked a large pewter tankard from the recessed shelf near his chair, appropriating the largest drinking vessel in the place.

But he filled it with Prisco's mildest cider. In truth, Jake had earned a bit of rest, and did not have a pressing agenda—the distance to Albany could be traversed in a third of the time allotted, if he cared to do so. It would be natural for the lieutenant colonel to relax with a full helping of the fine brown ale Prisco was noted for. But a condition of wariness pressed upon him, and restlessness as well. The Rhode Island captain had lit a hot fire of concern in Jake's breast, and not for the first time in the war he worried that he could not do enough to help his cherished Cause to victory. Thus he studied the crowded room and its contents carefully. The sturdy chairs and chestnut planks beneath them seemed to hold no secrets; at first blush, neither did their occupants.

These were the usual assortment of characters one finds along our highways. There were, naturally, local farmers talking politics and sopping up ale and cider; a traveling mechanic, who in conversation revealed himself to be something of a cross between a wheelwright and carpenter; a trading merchant or two, with an ear out for a likely deal. In the far corner of the room, two men with white beards and bare pates were hunched over a small but well-scrubbed pine table, playing checkers. The old fellows had been similarly occupied the last time Jake and van Clynne visited the inn; they pushed their pieces along at lightning speed, as if rehearsed.

Jake got up to stretch his legs and stood by them thinking perhaps it might be diverting to engage in a game. He also thought these ancients might have an idea about the identities or business of the three men he had earlier dispatched to Pluto's vale.

"I wonder if I might play the winner," suggested Jake, pulling up a chair near the old men.

Neither man answered. The game was almost over, with red about to have a third man queened—an oxymoron that nonetheless gave him a crushing advantage. Two moves later, black was cleared from the board. The combatants regrouped, changing colors and ignoring Jake.

"Next game then?" he asked hopefully, trying to appear solicitous.

When there was no acknowledgement, he decided the old geezers must be hard of hearing. Jake was about to wave his hand between them to get their attention when he was tapped on the shoulder by a man whose vigorous manner made his frame appear taller than it was, indeed, taller instead of shorter than average. About his own age and dressed much as Jake in the rough clothes of a farmer, the fellow had a quality in his smile that immediately invited a person to like him.

"You look as if you would like to play draughts," he suggested.

"I thought I might. But these old fellows seem to be in a world of their own."

"Perhaps you would play a round with me. I've just borrowed a set from the proprietor."

"Gladly," said Jake, who called for a refill as the stranger set up the game on an old keg near a drafty window at the side.

"John Barrows," said the man, sticking his hand out over the game board.

"Jake," answered the patriot spy.

If the fact that he had given only his first name bothered Barrows, the farmer didn't let on, plunging happily into the competition. The match proceeded quickly; the stranger was not very good and Jake had four queens on the board before his drink arrived. But the man was nothing if not stubborn, staying in the contest until the bitter end.

"Draughts is not my game," he confessed. "Now chess —there's a game for me."

"You play chess?" asked Jake. "I haven't played since I was in London."

"Yes, I play—I wonder if the keeper has a set," said Barrows. He jumped from the chair and went to find Prisco, returning not only with a set but with a candle to provide better light.

Jake's guard by now had eased; he decided to enjoy a game with his new companion and draw him out on the local situation at his leisure. It was not often one found a chance to play chess these days.

To make conversation, he told Barrows he'd come

down from Fishkill—which was true enough, except that it omitted his recent foray in New York City. They exchanged some other pleasantries and minor bits of gossip. The man said the neighborhood leaned to the Whig side, though there were plenty of people like Beverly Robinson who still held with the king. Jake supplied only bare hints of himself, pretending to be traveling on unspecified business.

Their chat was curtailed by the quickness of the game: Barrows's skill once more proved less advanced than his enthusiasm, and Jake had his king pinned before twenty moves had passed.

"Another game?" he asked.

"Surely," said Jake, changing sides and even offering a pointer or two on technique and opening.

For naught. Jake won this game in sixteen. He was surprised when Barrows requested another chance at revenge.

"All right," said Jake. "Would you like a handicap? I can play without my castles."

The man's expression, which had been jolly enough considering the circumstances, turned positively delirious. Were there no candles or fire, his teeth alone could have lit the room.

"I believe that would be welcome," he said. "Very welcome."

Jake had never seen anyone so ecstatic over a game of chess, not even in Parsloe's, the London hangout of Andre Danican Philidor and the rest of the English chess scene. Amused, he began moving his pawns forward in haphazard fashion, deciding that he would give his companion a double advantage.

This proved unnecessary. Jake had made only four or five moves when he realized that his opponent's game had improved sharply—so much so, in fact, that it was like facing an entirely new man across the board, a man who not only had a two-rook advantage, but had Jake's picket of pawns in deep trouble. It was Breed's Hill all over again—the redcoats, or in this case the white pawns, had charged ahead into the line while the patriots waited. Finally, the muskets opened up—a bishop slashed, a knight reeled, and Jake stood as naked as Gates on the battlefield. He struggled to pull his pieces into a protective cordon, wielding his dragoons and rangers as Washington had when he retreated up Manhattan Island, but it was no use; as brave as his men were, they were outnumbered and quickly overwhelmed. The game ended with queen pinned and king checked—as should all wars.

"The handicap was your undoing," said the man graciously, extending his hand to Jake as he pinned the queen.

Having unmasked some portion of his true skill, Jake expected Mr. Barrows would now ask if he wanted another game, with a small side wager to keep things interesting. The patriot spy was just deciding whether his game was strong enough to take up such a challenge when his opponent surprised him once again, taking a small, carved junk or pipe from his vest and asking if he would join him outside for a smoke.

"I like to get a good breath of fresh air in the pipe as I smoke," said Barrows. "It is an odd habit of mine, but I believe it enhances the flavor of the leaves."

Jake gave a glance to the corner where van Clynne and Jane were occupied in a curious courtship ritual involving the communication of spirits through the ether. The pair appeared so enmeshed as to be dumbstruck, gazing into each other's eyes with less intelligence betrayed on their faces than on that of the average duck. Such a sight alone was enough to send Jake running outside for a smoke.

There was a second factor. Jake had noted during the last match that the man's hands were not so calloused as one would expect from a farmer, especially with the heavy plowing and sowing not long completed. It was a possibly significant anomaly.

"What did you say your name was?" asked the man as they reached the porch. Though of less than average height, his shoulders were wide and his muscular legs stretched his breeches tight.

"Jake Smith," he said smoothly, trusting that the natural tone of his voice would allay doubt about the common alias. There are, after all, a great number of Smiths in the world, even if there are a greater number claiming to be them.

"You were in London."

In that instant, Jake's loose suspicions became a definite theory—this Barrows was a Tory, and an unusually bold and clever one.

Jake drew smoothly on the proffered pipe and nodded his head. "Yes." He handed back the pipe and self-consciously pulled his hair back into its ribbon, as if nervous. "Before our troubles."

"These are difficult times, aren't they?"

"It's the righteousness of the rabble that is so shocking."

"Careful, sir, or you'll give yourself away."

Jake realized the man was no ordinary Loyalist, content to keep his politics covered until the local tide turned. Barrows must be a recruiter working behind the lines, as accomplished at his job as at his chess game.

But he was no match for the disguised patriot spy, who had played out this sort of drama thousands of times before. Jake whirled around with an oath and started back inside, as if he took the man to be a patriot trying to start an argument with him.

"Just a second, sir." Barrows touched his arm lightly but firmly. Jake was a tall man, well built; Barrows's head came to his shoulder. Still, the Tory was powerful, and his touch betrayed more than simple self-assurance. "Let us be frank with each other. My name is not Barrows, it is Busch."

"If you're looking for trouble, I'll oblige," said Jake, still playing the offended Loyalist. "I've had enough from your rebel brethren these past weeks, running me off my land."

"Where was that?"

"Near Fishkill," lied Jake.

"So you've come down from there."

"I told you that before. I am not a liar."

"You rode along the river?"

"What is it to you?"

"You passed the chain, I assume."

Even with his mask so firmly drawn over his true self,

Jake felt an involuntary flutter pass through his stomach. He nodded.

"Did you see the defenses there?"

"I did not ride close to the shore. I have no care for the rebel army, one way or another."

"In these times, it is difficult to know a man's heart from his words," said Busch, his tone still suggestive. "One may profess his allegiance to one side or the other, and yet be lying about it."

Jake now had his opening and drove for it, as if he were leading a team of four horses with a full company of men behind him. His companion van Clynne could not have closed a sale so deftly.

"It's all so easy for you and your ilk, papering over things with your bogus law and your rump committees, but you've left a great deal of the country to starve, and all because of your foolishness," Jake said hotly. "Where do you think this will end but on the gallows? And this year, too—note the sevens, sir, the gibbets. I for one will be glad. Tar and feather me, if you like—I've nothing else to lose."

"Careful, careful," said Busch soothingly. "Calm down. You've quite mistaken me."

"How is that?"

"If you've had enough of things as they are, meet me here after the others have gone to bed, at 2 A.M. Say nothing to the keeper. He is a committed rebel and will put you in jail as soon as serve you an ale. Think it over, sir," added Busch, smiling as he took a step toward the tavern door. "Perhaps it's time you took your fate in your hands, instead of leaving it to others."

Four

*Wherein, the scene is moved to New York City, in
anticipation of meeting a most despicable character.*

With darkness coming on and the inhabitants of
Prisco's inn repairing to their beds, we will shift our scene
temporarily from the bucolic if troubled hills of the Hudson Valley to the lit streets of New York City. We are
searching specifically for a covered chaise, making its way
from the shadows on the west side of the lower island,
across the precincts laid waste by the Great Fire, toward
a mansion that sits atop a hill on the east side of the isle
overlooking the Hell's Gate.

The carriage's finely carved wood panels and polished
brass fittings are a fine example of British craftsmanship,
imported directly to the city two months prior by its
owner, who tonight sits alone in the cabin, contemplating
the hard twists of life that have brought him to America.
Less than a year before, he enjoyed all the prerogatives of
London's leading surgeon and man of science. But in that
achievement lay the root of his downfall: the experiments
that had helped him reach his position—of necessity performed on live subjects—had given certain small and jeal-
ous minds an opening; it was only because of his personal
service to the king that he escaped prison and much
worse.

Major Dr. Harland Keen was not a melancholy man,
and so his reflections did not have the hard-edged bitter-
ness one would expect from so recent an exile. Nor did he
plot a return to London society; he had had quite enough
of it, and in many respects was glad of the ocean between
him and his former home. Still a man of independent

means, the doctor had a wealth of knowledge stored in his brain and a rapacious hunger for more. It was a hunger that the New World, and his position in it, promised to fill.

Major Dr. Keen arrived without fanfare at the mansion in question. This large brick house formerly belonged to a member of the provincial congress, who expressed his confidence in the American army as well as his political preferences by fleeing the city the day the English invaded Long Island. The house had since been occupied by General Henry Clay Bacon, the head of British intelligence services in America, and more ominously, the king's representative of the Secret Department.

It would not be surprising if the reader has not yet become familiar with the workings, or even the existence, of the Secret Department. By far the vast majority of people who have had occasion to deal with them have done so only as their mortal victims. The department, consisting solely of men with close personal ties to the king—and dark tints upon their past which place them utterly within his power—exists only to carry out missions of such nature that all other branches of service, military and civil, shy from even mentioning. Every member of the department is a trained assassin, with additional talents besides; while each man has another, legitimate duty —Keen is employed by the Admiralty as a doctor—his first allegiance is to the department.

Bacon felt so secure in his position and person that he employed but a single guard at his front door. This was no mere soldier, however, nor even a delegate of a distinguished unit such as the Black Watch. Bacon's man had been personally recruited from the southern tip of India and dressed in the peculiar blankets of his native land. His oversized hands had the strength of ten men, and his powers of sight and sound were said to be enhanced by mantras known only among the Hindoo. Locked in his grip was a giant blade ordinarily found only in India; it ran the full length of his prodigious leg and was twice as wide as his immense thigh. Sharper than the razor a barber would use to shave his favorite customer, its balance was so perfect that a single finger placed in the middle could support it.

Dr. Keen nodded at him as he passed through the doorway, smiling at the curved sword; the doctor's own weapons of choice were infinitely more subtle.

Bacon was waiting in his study. Formerly the dining room, the general had converted it because he thought entertaining a frivolous and unnecessary occupation. The large windows stood over the water; he liked to look up from his work and stare through them, sometimes for hours, as his mind prepared its dark designs.

"Doctor, you're late," he told Keen without rising from his desk or changing his gaze, which was directed at the window.

"Excuse me, General, but I was detained by Lord Admiral Howe. He wished me to attend to a medical problem of his."

"Syphilis again?" Bacon spit the word toward the glass. He thought little of either of the Howe brothers—Richard "Black Dick" Howe, the admiral in charge of the fleet, or William, the general in charge of the army. To Bacon's mind—and indeed he was not alone in this opinion—the entire British command structure was laden with incompetents and dandies who relied on politics for their positions.

Keen, as was his wont, said nothing. It happened that the ailment was a cold, but mentioning this would bring only a snort of derision. In Keen's judgement, Richard was an able leader and a far different man than his brother William, even if he, too, was soft on the colonists.

Bacon's contempt did not extend to Keen. The white-haired gentleman with the very proper cut in his powder blue suit and the fussy gold-tipped cane had a hardened, vigorous body and a mind sharper than a fusilier's sword, and Bacon knew and appreciated this. Every piece of the doctor was as balanced and premeditated as a fine watch. The frilly handkerchief he kept up his sleeve, for example, was in fact a deadly weapon—a small bladder secreted inside contained a powder extracted from *Convallaria majalis.* The general had witnessed the powder's effects—immediate convulsions, a paralyzing stroke, and a painful, lingering death. It was an apt weapon for this man, refined from the beautiful lily of the valley, which appeared so innocent yet struck so viciously when probed.

"I assume, Sir Henry, that I am not here to continue our game of chess."

"There are more important matters to be attended to." Bacon made a slight motion with his head, by which his visitor understood that he was to sit in the large chair to his right. It was a concession of honor—there was a bottle of Madeira on the table next to the chair, and Keen knew he could help himself if he wished.

The doctor sat but did not drink. He was quite aware that this raised his commander's opinion of him.

"I have a difficult problem to be unknotted," said Bacon, finally turning his gaze toward Keen. As he continued to speak, a blackened hand seemed to spread over his face; this was an unfortunate birthmark, which became more prominent during moments of great concentration or stress.

The mark had given rise to the nickname "Black Clay" at a very early age. To use it in the general's presence was to risk great wrath and possibly death, but the sobriquet was commonly applied behind his back. Many a man who knew it thought the name referred appropriately to his soul.

Major Dr. Keen was not among them. He saw a person of superior intelligence hampered by the difficulties of his upbringing and his illegitimate birth—for Keen was well aware that Bacon was the bastard son of King George II, unacknowledged half-brother to the present king.

"I only appreciate difficult problems," said the doctor mildly. "An easy task would be boring."

"There was a young man in the city yesterday named Jake Gibbs. He called himself a medical doctor and said he had attended Edinburgh."

"Attending such a school would allow him that honor."

"You have met him?"

"I have not had that pleasure."

"I thought all doctors whored together."

Keen said nothing.

"My men think he is merely an apothecary, though they speak highly of his cures," continued Bacon. "In any event, he has a remarkable intelligence and is widely traveled; a five-minute conversation with him would prove the point beyond any doubt."

"I accept your judgement."

Bacon permitted himself a wane smile. "He claimed to be in the service of a Dutchman named Claus van Clynne, a man of money and property. This van Clynne seemed the embodiment of all that is wrong with the race, but perhaps that is my chauvinism."

"I don't believe I know either gentleman," said Keen, his statement implying the question: Why are they important?

"The Dutchman delivered a message from General Burgoyne to Sir William Howe aboard ship yesterday. The message has been checked and authenticated, naturally. Sir William thought it a bit pompous to have been sent by Gentleman Johnny"—Burgoyne's nickname was practically spit from Bacon's mouth—"though frankly I find it not pompous enough. In any event, the contents are not of immediate interest. But in delivering the message, the Dutchman claimed to have uncovered a plot in our dispatch service, involving a Major Herstraw."

"Another stranger to me."

"A good thing, as he is said to have worked for the rebels."

Keen adjusted one of the gold watch chains on his brocaded yellow vest. He considered looking for a traitor in the messenger service somewhat beneath his level of skill, but an order was an order. "Where was this Herstraw last seen?"

"It's not him I want you to attend to. The Dutchman made some hints to me that he was a member of the Secret Department."

"A Dutchman?"

Bacon frowned, fully in agreement with Keen's prejudices. "The king has, on occasion, used foreign agents on missions of elimination as a temporary expedient. I am personally acquainted with the disappearance of a cardinal that was associated with the workings of an Amsterdam native. Nonetheless, to meet this man—he possesses a certain crude ability, but one would sooner take him for a stage clown than an agent."

"There are ways to validate his identity, I assume," said Major Dr. Keen.

"It is not easy. I would have to send someone to London, and then have certain questions asked, which could lead to difficulties. Nonetheless, it will be done, if you fail."

As Keen was sworn to carry out any mission assigned or die in the process, this was an unnecessary if subtle threat. But the doctor was too mannered to respond directly.

"What hints could he have made?"

"He possessed a knife," said Bacon, almost as an afterthought. "He managed to show it to me discreetly."

The knife Bacon referred to was a long, thin-bladed weapon with a ruby set into its ornate hilt. The stone was modeled after one of the crown jewels and was the department's signifier. A member of the brotherhood was given the dagger at the moment he was assigned a specific task, and it was returned when the job done. There were less than two dozen such knives in existence; to possess one was as sure a sign possible that a man was a member of the small, bloody coterie.

"But you are suspicious nonetheless." Keen had never heard of a member of the department being impersonated; indeed, the very nature of the organization and its members made that unlikely. The knife was impossible to counterfeit and would be guarded to the death by its possessor. Still—a Dutchman?

"I sent a man with them from the ship in New York, after Howe released them. He was merely an intelligence agent, but he was a very good one. I had him pose as a member of the Sons of Liberty." Bacon lifted a small, mangled piece of lead from the top of his desk and stared at it. The metal had once been a bullet; it had been removed from his leg by Keen several years before in London. "The man's body was discovered today in the ruins of the rebel powderhouse that blew up last evening. If this van Clynne was a rebel, then he alerted the rabble and had the man killed."

"But if he is truly a member of the Secret Department, you would expect him to have killed the man, and blown up the powder stores in the process. It would be his duty if the fellow stood in his way."

"There is something in my soul that weighs the first possibility as much greater than the second," said Bacon. "Or I would not have called you. I have learned to trust my suspicions, and act on them."

"A difficult problem, indeed." Keen's hand reached involuntarily for the flask of wine on the table next to him. He caught himself but took up the bottle anyway, ignoring Bacon's ironic smile—the general would be congratulating himself on knowing the limits of his underling's willpower. "Where was this Dutchman going?"

"He said back to Burgoyne, though of course that might be merely a cover story. He couldn't divulge his mission, even to me."

"Assuming he's authentic."

Bacon shifted in his chair, then looked back out the window of his study into the blackness of the night. Unlike Keen, he longed to return to England; he longed to be truly recognized and acknowledged. But he had even less chance than the doctor of seeing his native shores again.

"I want you to locate him and settle this for me," Bacon said without changing his gaze. "Find his assistant as well, Gibbs."

"And if they are rebels?"

"I would think they have much information that would be useful. Your methods of extraction would be called for."

"Naturally."

"After that—Gibbs should be killed outright, as long as it can be done in a painful manner. But this Dutchman— to impersonate a member of the Secret Department is not something that can be punished by simple death."

"There is a venom of a snake found at the tip of South America I have long wished to experiment with," said Dr.

Keen. "It can be used to paralyze portions of the body quite selectively. I know of no antidote."

"Your first target should be the man's tongue. He talks enough for a shire's worth of parsons."

"Perhaps we should experiment on him, regardless of his allegiance."

Bacon's expression did not change. "I would not want a member of our department harmed. But if he met with an unavoidable accident, well, even that would be understandable, depending on the circumstance."

Keen nodded.

"If they are what they say, I would not like anything to happen to our Dr. Gibbs. I would consider recruiting him myself—he has a sharp mind."

Bacon gave Keen a brief but precise description of both men, their weapons, and their clothes, then turned back to his desk. He reached into a bottom desk drawer, where he retrieved a small wooden case. Using a key that hung from around his neck, he opened the box and removed a thin, ruby-hilted knife, his fingers caressing the gem gently before laying it on the desk.

"You are to leave immediately," said the general.

"I would be comfortable doing nothing less."

Five

Wherein, Jake proves his loyalty to the wrong cause.

From the instant on the porch when Busch pocketed his pipe, there was little doubt in Jake's mind that he would forgo his chance at a full night's sleep and keep his appointment with the Tory. While Busch's questions regarding the chain may not have been related to any specific plot against it, the importance of the waterborne defense meant no chance could be taken. Besides, an opportunity at smashing a traitors' nest was not presented on such an attractive platter every day. Jake recognized in the man's smooth manner a particular ability that could do the Americans great harm if not quickly checked.

He realized, however, there was a chance this small detour could delay his moving on to Albany and General Schuyler, who was awaiting word on Howe's intentions. Not to mention the fact that there is always a possibility in secret operations for misfortune, and even if Jake were to consider this night's mission but the light amusement of a few sleepless hours, precautions must be taken.

And so he pressed upon van Clynne the importance of his continuing on to Albany in the morning, with or without him.

"On what grounds am I being abandoned? Have I not done good service?" demanded the Dutchman, standing in the middle of the upstairs bedroom where Jake and he had been led. "Who helped you escape New York City?"

"As I recall, it was the Sons of Liberty. You spent the passage sleeping."

"I had been knocked unconscious, sir, having taken a

blow in the line of duty. My head, as it were, was put to an important use by the Cause, diverting a villain's attention. Undoubtedly my intervention saved you, and this is the thanks I get—to be cast aside like an unwanted scrap."

Van Clynne had taken off his breeches and hose, and stood before Jake in his shirt and a pair of brilliant red drawers. These last were a rather remarkable item, as they included not merely a portion to cover the legs, but extended to the chest as well; a hibernating bear was not so warmly covered. But we will leave the fashion discussion to others more versed in the science.

"I'm not abandoning you, Claus. Someone has to go on and deliver the message to Schuyler that we have accomplished our mission."

"While you stay here and take all the glory. Surely, sir, I deserve better treatment. My competence is beyond question."

"Who questioned it?" Jake turned to the small stand where he had set the candle, and blew it out. It was not quite midnight, and he intended a brief nap for refreshment. "When you leave in the morning, take the Post Road north. Don't delay. I should catch up with you by Fishkill, or perhaps Rhinebeck."

"We're an inseparable team," protested van Clynne. "I thought you intended on seeing your good friend General Putnam on the way."

"I'll see the general soon enough," said Jake, lying back on the bed. Except for his boots and outer coat, he was fully dressed, and had his loaded pistol in his right hand—he hated to be surprised while sleeping.

"I was hoping you would introduce us."

"So you can arrange a sale of supplies?"

"And what would be wrong with that?" asked the Dutchman indignantly. "The Cause is suffering—the condition of the soldiers in this neighborhood is shameful. Surely we must all do our part. Those of us blessed with special gifts for the acquisition of needed supplies would be doing a tremendous disservice to—"

"Quiet now, I want to catch a few winks of sleep. And try not to snore tonight, will you?"

"I don't snore, sir," blustered van Clynne, removing his shirt. "I am a Dutchman, and a fervent patriot."

"Who never let profit come between him and his country."

"Just so, sir, just so, though you meant the words in jest. Enterprise is critical to the survival of our freedom."

"I'll catch you on the Post Road," said Jake, "and if I miss you I'll just ask after the best beer in the country."

"You will easily be led astray. And then our arrangement will be forgotten," said van Clynne.

For perhaps the only time since they had met—many days' worth of severe difficulties and harrowing dangers, to be sure—Jake detected true fear in the Dutchman's voice. Besides his patriotism, van Clynne's strenuous efforts on behalf of the American Cause were motivated by the hope that they might win him the return of his family estate, which had been stolen years before by an English usurper.

"Don't worry about your property, Claus. I'll make a full report to General Washington on your behalf."

"The matter is urgent," said van Clynne. "Especially as I intend on marrying."

"Congratulations," said Jake, closing his eyes firmly. "Now get into bed and be quiet."

"There is no need, sir, to play the enthusiastic reveler," said van Clynne. "I know you are only trying to find my good side. Besides, we have made no formal announcement of our intentions. Your congratulations are premature."

"You haven't told Jane yet, in other words."

"Marriage is a delicate thing to a Dutchman. It proceeds by stages. In any event, it is not the matter presently under discussion. Breaking our partnership at this point would be ill-advised; my services in routing these Tory criminals would be quite invaluable."

"True," said Jake, changing his tactics if not his posture. He sorely wanted some sleep. "But who would believe a Dutchman, let alone a squire such as yourself, to be a Tory?"

Van Clynne could find no argument there, nor would Jake let him, as he continued.

"My success depends entirely on them thinking I am a traitor. Now that is a game I have often played, but yourself—who would believe it?"

"I convinced Sir William Howe. And your General Bacon."

Jake made a dismissive spitting noise at the mention of the first general's name, but at the second his reaction was quite different. They had indeed fooled him, but by the thinnest hair on an aging cat's paw.

"Regardless, I am the officer in charge here. As I have said before—"

"An expedition has but one commander. I would like to review the election where you were selected," grumbled the Dutchman, picking up the bedcovers in tacit surrender. "The ballot was definitely loaded. This is bad precedent for running a country, believe me, sir. There is need for more Dutchmen among your congress; then we would see what a revolution ought to be."

Despite his continued complaints or perhaps because of them, van Clynne soon fell fast asleep—and within a half hour his snores could have been confused with the sound of a grist mill taking on rough wheat.

Jake gathered his rest fitfully. A quirk of nature allowed him to go for several days on barely a few winks, and he rose well before the appointed hour, cleaning and inspecting his single officer's pistol and his four-barreled Segallas pocket pistol to make sure both were at the ready. The latter weapon was a rarity in America, with four barrels placed in pairs before two separate locks; once charged, the top set could be fired and then the barrel works flipped so the second pair could be used. It was an ingenious arrangement, and if its small bullets were useful only for close work, the miniature pistol was nonetheless a prized possession.

Besides the guns, Jake carried a long, elk-handled knife that had been given to him by a special friend, a French half-breed trapper who had helped him escape from Canada a week before. His greatest weapons, however, were his resourcefulness and gilded tongue, both of which he expected to put to the test before the sun broke over the hills.

When the large clock in the great room downstairs struck 2 A.M., Jake put his jacket over his waistcoat and snuck from his room, creeping down the stairs. The rest of the house was slumbering peacefully; the only noise came from the echoes of the Dutchman's loud snores against the rafters.

The rendezvous was quickly met; Jake was but three steps from the door when he heard a hissing from the side of the house. Busch stepped forward, and together they gathered their horses and rode off up the road.

They had gone but a short way, completely in silence, when Jake heard the low nicker of a horse in the woods nearby. He was just turning to Busch when two mounted men appeared from the shadows, guns drawn, and demanded to know their allegiance.

"Why?" demanded Busch.

"Because we asked, simpleton. You—what side are you on?"

"What's it to you?" answered Jake, his voice harsher than Busch's.

The patriot spy assumed that the ambush had been staged to test his loyalty, and so determined to play his role more freely than he might have otherwise. When one of the men—who fairly reeked of rum but was otherwise difficult to discern in the darkness—held out a pistol in his face and demanded again which side he was on, Jake drew himself straight in the saddle and declared for King George.

The response was the soft but definite sound of a pistol being cocked.

"Say your prayers, Tory."

"Which prayers would you like to hear?" Jake asked his tormentor, who edged his horse so close to Jake's that their necks touched. His companion remained silent, sitting on his horse opposite Busch, near the side of the darkened road.

Even as Jake asked his question, he realized he had mistaken the situation. This was not a stage play—the men holding weapons on them were aligned with the

American side, though the hour and the rum indicated they were not regulars.

"You are interested in our money, not our politics," said Busch evenly. "Don't add murder to your crimes."

"It's not a crime to kill a Tory," said the man holding the gun at Jake's head. He nonetheless interpreted Busch's words to mean that they would comply, and his tone lightened ever so slightly. "Hand over what you've got, slowly. And we'll see if your lives are worth saving."

The man started to lower his pistol so he could accept the travelers' gold. Jake's officer's gun was in the front holster of his saddle, near the horseman; it was impossible to get it without being seen—and shot. But at the first sign of trouble he had slipped his right hand into his shirt, and managed to conceal his pocket pistol in his fingers, away from the man covering him.

He was unlikely to have as large an advantage as this again. While Lieutenant Colonel Jake Gibbs did not like harming anyone connected to the American Cause, these two men had already declared themselves criminals, and the patriots would be well rid of them.

He dove down across his horse, flinging his left boot upwards into the flank of the thief's animal with such a sharp kick that the horse leaped sideways, stumbling backwards and losing its balance. The man's gun went off as he fell to the ground; by that time, Jake had fired two of the Segallas's small but deadly bullets into the bulky shadow before Busch. He aimed for what he took to be the man's shoulder, hoping to wound but not kill him. The man fell back in a tumble, his own pistol firing errantly.

Busch drew his gun from a front holster but Jake pounded his stallion's side and got the animal in motion, reaching over and pushing Busch's along with him. The Tory's aim was disrupted and he missed the thief, who by now was rolling on the ground in pain but not mortal danger.

The threat diffused, Busch and Jake thundered down the road. It was soon clear they had not been followed, but they galloped another half mile just to be sure.

Busch's two-cornered hat had slipped from his head

but landed in his hand during the brief battle; when they stopped, he examined it carefully before turning his attention to Jake.

"Are you all right, Smith?"

"Yes, I'm fine."

"You saved us both, I daresay." Busch's voice was grateful, and yet not panicked; he could have been talking about having preserved a few quarts of milk from spoiling. "The villain's bullet grazed my jacket." He showed Jake the damage, a light singe in the otherwise strong cotton that crossed directly beneath the left shoulder, perhaps four or five inches removed from his heart. "I thought they'd gotten my hat as well. I would have preferred that; I'd much like an excuse to buy a new one."

"You're lucky to be alive."

"I can't recall a closer scrape," admitted Busch. "Did you fire two shots from a pocket pistol?"

"It is a gun I bought in London some time ago," said Jake, holding it up so Busch could see. There was a new moon and the tree-covered road was particularly dark. "Made by Segallas. I do not believe there is another on our whole continent."

"It is an admirable weapon," said Busch.

"Who were our friends?"

"The rebel criminals call themselves Skinners, though they are after more than mere animal skins, that you may believe."

"Are they soldiers?"

"The law does not draw a distinction between rebels and plain criminals," said Busch, patting his horse's side gently before spurring it onward. "But no, not in the sense you or the rebel congress mean. These men use the war as an excuse for their depravity—as, unfortunately, do some who fancy themselves Royalists. Come—we have much to do tonight."

Busch's pace precluded further talk. Jake realized that he could not have staged a better incident to gain the Tory's trust. He also saw that his initial assessment of Busch had, if anything, underestimated him. A lesser man might have well been flustered by his brush with death,

nor would it have taken too much ego to insist on returning to finish the thieves off. But Busch had both overcome the shock of the close call and realized the men
held little real threat to his ultimate mission, whatever
that might be.

He was also man enough to admit the truth of the
roving bandit gangs and their allegiances, which many a
hot patriot would not.

Three miles north, the Tory pulled up his horse's reins.
They had arrived at a crossroads undistinguished from
hundreds of others in the surrounding countryside. Jake
had only a vague idea of where they were, a mile or so
from North Castle and not far from the Kisco River.

"We'll rest here a bit," said Busch.

"So what are we all about, then?" Jake asked.

"Come now, surely you've guessed after our encounter."

"I'm not in the habit of making guesses."

"Well, Mr. Smith, what are you in the habit of?"

"I have only good and sober habits," said Jake. "I am
God-fearing and looking for work, if the truth be told. I
have no money."

"I wouldn't worry about that," said Busch. He pulled
his horse around to look down the road. The stars shone
as brightly as they could, but the neighboring vicinity was
still dark and shadowy. "I know from your actions as well
as your comments that you are loyal to the king, and a
brave man besides."

"As are you," said Jake.

"Indeed, I am a bit more," said Busch, his voice instantly acquiring an elevated tone. "I am Captain John
Busch, of his lordship Earl Graycolmb's own Loyal Rangers, working with His Majesty's Marines to defeat the
rebels in the Highlands. I am recruiting men, such as
yourself, to vindicate His Majesty's name."

Jake could only nod.

"I assume you will join us."

"What do I get if I join?"

"Besides preserving your country and winning back
your land? I would think those enough for a man of
honor." Busch's displeasure was brief but genuine; he

had already formed an opinion of Jake, and the expression of material interests conflicted with it. "You will get a bounty of fifty pounds, legal money, besides pay, and the return of your land when the insurrection is ended. Is that good enough for you?"

"I would fight for my king without reward," responded Jake, "though in my destitute state I will be glad for any I can find. Where do I sign up?"

"Consider yourself recruited," answered the captain. "After tonight, I consider you the brother I never had."

Approaching hoofbeats echoed through the trees, and Busch took a fresh pistol from a holster on his horse's saddle as he guided the animal to the side of the road. Jake pulled his own animal around and waited opposite him, his own pistol in hand. The Segallas was reloaded and returned to its resting place inside his belt beneath his shirt.

The rider had approached from a long way off, and it took several minutes for him to arrive. Finally his horse's light trot was replaced by a soft whistle—two bars from the fighting song, "British Grenadiers."

Busch answered with a whistle of his own.

"Captain?"

"Approach," Busch ordered. He kicked his horse's side gently and the mount cantered into the roadway, meeting a rider. Jake waited until both men had stopped, then pushed his horse out behind the newcomer.

"Corporal Caleb Evans, I want you to meet a friend of mine, Jake Smith. He has just joined us."

"Smith, eh?" Caleb Evans was a pudgy man, the sort who sat on his horse like a loosely packed bag of onions. There was not enough light to study his face, but he wore an oversized beaver hat not dissimilar to the Quaker van Clynne favored. He greeted the newcomer with unveiled doubts. "Who are you running from that you have adopted that name?"

"My father gave it to me, as his father had handed it to him," responded Jake. "It is thought that our ancestors worked at a forge, though we ourselves are farmers."

"Farmers?"

"Or were formerly," said the patriot spy. "I was run off my land."

"He's with us, Caleb; he's made that clear enough already," said Busch. "He has spent much time in England, and he just saved my life."

"Indeed?"

"We were ambushed by two Skinners."

The corporal's skepticism evaporated into concern for his commander. "Were you harmed?"

"My coat has a hole in it," said Busch. "But Smith saved us from further damage."

"We can't afford to lose you, sir. Perhaps you should return to Stoneman's, and let me go on myself."

"Nonsense. Come, and make sure your pistols are charged and ready. Smith,"—Busch had already turned his horse away and was starting on the road east—"take this road three miles to the west. You'll find a farm that belongs to a man named Stoneman. A small force is gathering there. Present yourself to the sergeant. His name is Lewis. Tell him I have recruited you."

Jake would much have preferred to stay with Busch and his corporal. But before he could protest, the two Tories rode off. The only course open was to travel on to Stoneman's, and see what he could gather of the group's plans.

Six

Wherein, Jake finds that Liberty has not hidden her fire beneath a bushel, but rather seeks to increase its flames.

Jake rode north along the road as cautiously as possible, searching with one eye for any activity that would hint at his destination, and with the other for additional American patrols. His pistol was no longer in its holster—he held it firmly in his hand.

This part of New York was particularly difficult to travel through at night, even when the moon was full; hilly and densely wooded where it was not farmed, it piled shadow upon shadow. The trees, proud of their new coat of leaves, obscured much of the already dim light thrown off by the stars.

Such are the areas where ghosts are born, and Jake might have been forgiven for thinking the spark he noticed through the woods on his right was some specter in search of its lost corporeality. Cautiously he dismounted and walked his horse along the roadside, paralleling the light's movements. It was running downhill toward what seemed to be a peculiarly shaped group of hills. As his eyes studied the landscape, the formation transformed itself into three buildings. A tight path through the roadside scrub—the type of shortcut children take to church —opened in front of him. He walked down it and within a few yards found himself in a haying field.

Jake's boots were heavy and he felt as if with every step he and his horse were making enough noise for a regiment, though in truth they were as silent as the slipping of time through a man's life. The animal he'd taken from Johnson had adopted him as its true master, and mimicked his movements perfectly; he pulled his head down as if to show he could sink to all fours if needed.

As Jake drew closer, he realized the layout of the barn-yard, arranged with its back to the field he was crossing, favored his approach. He also saw that there was definitely a gathering in the barn, and noticed a pair of figures walking down a lane from the other direction toward the building.

The light he had seen had obviously come from a torch, but its bearer had not gone into the barn. Nor had he taken up station in the field to guard against intruders, or else Jake would have had to announce himself long before this. Whoever it was had disappeared around a corner of the building, and Jake had to walk some distance in that direction before the light reappeared.

Prudence as well as curiosity demanded an explanation. The edge of the field was marked by a run of short fruit trees and a split-rail fence; Jake tied his horse to one of the posts and crouched down to creep through the grass.

He was close enough to the barn for the hushed sounds inside to form a murmur in his ears, a kind of music to which the figure carrying the light danced.

Not danced, but worked, for the shadow was placing dried rushes, sticks, and branches against the base of the building. This was no ghost, nor a lackadaisical guard, but a woman, thin and hatless, who was strong enough to take a large pail in one hand while holding a torch with the other.

Suddenly realizing what she was doing, Jake jumped from the bushes and flew to her, grabbing her hand just as she was about to light the pitch she had poured from the pail.

"Not a good place to be starting fires," he said, forcing the torch from her grip. "At least not tonight."

"Let me go, you Tory bastard," she yelped before Jake could clamp his hand across her mouth. "I'll send you all to hell."

She was a cyclone of energy; Jake had to lift her off her feet and plunk her onto the ground to knock some of the fight out of her. Seventeen or eighteen at most, the girl wore the simple dress of a servant. The torch illuminated a winsome, spirited face; he felt an instant attraction, all the more so because she was on the right side of the conflict.

"You've got to close the front door before you set a barn on fire," said Jake, who had experience in such matters. "Otherwise everyone gets out. And look at this— you've concentrated your oil in one spot; the blaze will be easy to extinguish."

"You Loyalists are all so smug and sure of yourselves. I hate you."

"If you be quiet a moment," said Jake, deciding not merely to trust her but to enlist her as an ally of sorts, "you will discover that I am not a Tory, but a patriot like yourself."

Whether she would have believed him or not, the young woman was given no chance to reply—Jake clamped his fingers back across her mouth as the indistinct murmurings from inside the barn turned into the definite noises of someone being sent to investigate the disturbance. He stamped out the torch, but there wasn't time to escape—or dismantle the brush next to the barn.

Only one thing to do: Jake pulled the girl forward and grabbed her in his arms, planting a large kiss on her lips as two Tories turned the corner of the building.

"What's going on here?"

"Be with you shortly," he said as one laid his hand on his shoulder.

He was fortunate that they had not brought a candle with them, for otherwise they could not have missed the obvious signs of the aborted arson. The two men laughed and headed back inside for the meeting.

"Well, how was that?" said Jake as he let the girl go.

His answer was a smack across the face.

"I'm practically engaged," said the girl.

"Was my kiss that unpleasant?"

Rarely do words have such a direct impact as these— the girl broke out crying.

Jake once more took her in his arms, this time soothingly. "I am a patriot, and your friend. Tell me why you were going to burn down the barn, and I guarantee to help you."

His voice was so reassuring—and the kiss had been so gentle and warm—that the girl trusted him instantly. Still, it took her a minute to calm enough to talk again. Emotion had broken from her like a river rushing a dam; its pent-up fury was overwhelming once released. Finally her sobs subsided enough for her to tell her story.

Seven

*Wherein, Jake's suspicions of the Tories' plot are
confirmed, and new dangers encountered.*

The girl's name was Rose McGuiness, and contrary to
the evidence of her lush lips and well-shaped if thinnish
body, she was closer to fifteen then eighteen. She was also
a devout patriot, as was her fiancé-to-be. The same age as
Rose, the young man was a blacksmith's apprentice who
had been put to work forging the great iron chain across
the Hudson River north of Peekskill.

"It's all they talk of now, destroying the chain," sobbed
the girl, tugging at her reddish-brown curls. "They'll kill
my poor Robert, I know they will."

Rose's fiancé would be quite safe, Jake assured her.
Most of the craftsmen working on the chain were actually
ensconced in Poughkeepsie or New Jersey, their wares
transported after they were fashioned. The few who had
to work at the forts were well protected, and Jake mentioned breezily that the posts were nearly impenetrable to
attack.

She could not see that he had crossed his fingers, and
might not have noticed in any case. Her eyes had gathered that dewy glow that is the first warning of lovesick-
ness; her body, so sharp and rebellious not ten minutes
before, was now soft and compliant in Jake's arms. Indeed, her fiancé faced a considerably more potent threat
from this patriot than from the entire British army.

"Rose, I guarantee that we will not allow them to attack the chain," Jake told her, his voice as sincere as it
had ever been in his life. "But you must do nothing now.
Trust me when I tell you that I will deal with the Tories

sharply and completely. In the meantime, go about your business as if nothing has happened. It is imperative that they have no warning before our forces surprise them."

There was a look in his eye that no poet could describe, unless that poet were inspired by the muse Freedom herself. Determination was not the half of it; his soul had opened up, and his will flooded into the girl's. There was no chance for her to disobey his words.

But let us not get too fancy describing eye contact. Suffice to say that Rose nodded weakly. Jake gave her flushed cheek a kiss to seal the matter, then put on his best Tory face and walked around the side of the barn to attend the meeting.

As gruff and obnoxious as any noncommissioned officer in the regular army, Sergeant Lewis greeted Jake's story of his recruitment and subsequent ambush with a sneering grunt.

"I've got business to attend to. Captain Busch can sort yourself out when he arrives," said the sergeant, turning to the horses.

This would have been fine with Jake, except that the other Tories immediately took their cue from his contempt. The hostility escalated as their leading questions turned to outright accusations.

"I think I've seen you before," said a tallish bald fellow, twisting his words so that it sounded as if he'd spied Jake murdering a child.

"Where would that be?" countered the disguised patriot.

Instead of answering immediately, the man walked to the center of the barn and picked a sword off the table.

"In New York, at a rally for Washington," said the Tory ranger, who pretended to test the blade's sharpness with his finger.

"You're mistaken," said Jake. He folded his arms in feigned disgust. The inquisition was picked up by a fellow nearly as tall as he was, and half again as wide, who came and stood next to him, hands on his hips.

"Your story of being challenged by rebels smells a few days old," said the man. Like most of the others, he wore a dark green coat—the official uniform of a Loyalist ranger. "Where is Captain Busch if it is true?"

"Captain Busch met his corporal. He told me to come on alone," said Jake. "I have enough sense to follow orders."

"He has a rebel stink about him, I'll warrant that," said a third irregular. "Someone with a name of Smith—as likely as finding a pig wearing a dress."

"Your wife speaks ill of you as well," Jake said.

Finally an answer that was well received—all but the subject of the rebuttal laughed.

"I was told that this was a competent group," added Jake boastfully, "but I think the rebels would laugh the moment they saw your ill-fitting coats. Or is laughter your weapon of choice?"

"Best watch your manners," said an older man in the audience. "You're new here. A few of us are veterans of the war with the French, and our bravery is well proved."

"In that war, certainly," said Jake, who tempered his mocking tone. "But with respect, we're not fighting dance masters any more; we're after real game."

"And you're here to show us the way, are you?"

"I've come just in time. What have you done till now? Upset a hen house or two?"

"Wasn't it our information that set the raid on Peekskill?" said the older man cheerfully. "And who stole Old Put's own fodder from under his nose three times last month? If his troops are boiling their shoes for meat, it's us he has to thank."

"We could beat the rebels entirely on our own," said another. "We don't need the *Dependence* or any other help."

"What's the *Dependence*?"

"A fire-breathing dragon. To the rebels at least."

The group laughed even more heartily than before. No one offered further information, and Jake thought it best not to press. The *Dependence* must be a British vessel that supported the Tories on their raids.

The talk proceeded in like manner until after 4 A.M., with Jake pretending to doubt the rangers' abilities so he could gather information from their boasts. The men gradually warmed to him, and his manner likewise eased. To hear them tell it, they were a constant threat to the Americans, a half-victory away from routing Putnam's troops from the hills. While their claims were no doubt exaggerated, Jake had good reason to believe they had some level of competence, based on what he had seen of Busch and Evans. They were at least well armed—an assortment of weapons and cartridge boxes were piled along two tables at the center of the barn, well polished and waiting.

As time passed, the men began to grow somewhat anxious about their leader. Their speculation was studded with bits of information about Busch and his background, adding to the portrait Jake already had received. Here was a man, though not as well born or widely known, to rival the infamous Colonel Robinson.

Patriotic readers familiar with Dutchess and Westchester counties in New York will remember Robinson as having been born in the shadow of Sugarloaf Mountain in Philipstown. Denying his free birthright, he raised his own regiment for the British; the once-respected Tory loomed large in the imaginations of men on both sides of the war, and his defection to the lower party did more damage to the American forces than his troops.

Busch, too, had grown up in the area and was well known among the inhabitants of the riverside farms. His father owned considerable acreage, but it was unclear from the gossip exactly how much or where. The captain was single, and in his early twenties as Jake already had surmised; a youthful tragedy had claimed his sister's life and his mother had died soon afterwards. Many of the local inhabitants did not yet realize where his loyalties lay, and he had not bothered to enlighten them, knowing that ambiguity would aid his activities.

A major assault was planned within the next day or so, but whether or not it involved the chain Jake could not tell and dared not directly ask. The Tories made his job of spying simple with loose tongues and eager curiosity, but Busch apparently was very guarded with information about their pending mission; not even Sergeant Lewis, who was presently in charge, could answer the men's questions about it.

When Busch finally entered the barn, it was nearly dawn. He had lost his hat; his face was worn with fatigue and the corners of his eyes showed the first marks of age, worry tearing at his brow. But there are certain men upon whom Care bestows nobility, and Busch was one of them; he walked into the barn with such a forceful bearing that even Jake found himself jumping to attention.

"Johnson missed the rendezvous," he announced curtly. "Something has happened to him and the escort sent to meet him. Caleb and I were attacked by a second rebel force, this time militia."

Busch scanned the barn until his eyes rested on Jake. He gave him a quizzical look, and for a moment Jake worried that the Tory commander had somehow discerned he was responsible for Johnson's death.

"I am afraid Caleb has been captured," Busch said finally. He gave Jake a nod, and the patriot realized Busch was remonstrating silently with himself for not taking his brave new recruit along on the second leg of his night's mission. "The rebels were hot on our heels and I only just escaped."

There was a general outpouring of sympathy for the corporal; he appeared much better liked than the sergeant. A few men asked if they would rescue him.

Busch silenced the talk with an outstretched hand. "If he is captured, they will take him to the old church. Perhaps Johnson has been taken there as well. We will proceed as originally planned and hope the *Dependence* holds to its schedule. When we have completed our attack, we will come back and rescue them. Tomorrow, not today."

"We can't leave him there, sir," said one of the rangers.

"We won't. I guarantee that he will be rescued, but only after our raid. They are not in immediate danger. As for the troop Johnson was supposed to meet, they will have to see to their own safety."

"If the rebels take Caleb to Fishkill, sir, it will be difficult to free him," said Lewis.

"We will hear of it, I daresay, from our sources, well in

advance. In the meantime, we have more important problems to concentrate on. Johnson's loss means today's attack will be with less men. We will leave in an hour, no more."

The men began to murmur that they had not yet been told of the destination. Busch smiled.

"You see why I do not give out all of the details of our plans?" he asked rhetorically. "What if Caleb knew everything? We'd all be in danger. Not even Johnson knew all our plans, and he is a marine officer in His Majesty's service."

Busch paused for just a moment longer, adding to the drama. No regimental commander, it seemed to Jake, had a better measure of himself or feel for how he impacted on his men.

"Salem. We're going to attack Salem near the Connecticut border. It will be a profitable engagement, I warrant."

The pronouncement was met with general approval, Jake nodding along with everyone else. But the target baffled the American spy—the small hamlet of Salem was many miles inland, on the opposite end of the county from the river. If they were undertaking a raid with the help of a British vessel, as seemed likely from Busch's reference to the *Dependence,* why were they going so far away? Why would a marine officer be involved? And what of the chain?

But there was no leisure to contemplate these questions, or craft some manner of clandestine inquiry. The barn door burst open, and rather than the patrol of American militia Jake might have wished for, one of Busch's uniformed irregulars appeared.

"Captain, I've found Major Johnson's horse," he declared, sweeping his hand in a bold gesture. A Tory behind him led the gray-dappled stallion Jake had left near the road into the barn. "He was hitched to a tree at the edge of the woods."

Eight

Wherein, a gift horse is looked in the mouth.

*W*hile Jake was greatly pleased to finally have the mystery of Johnson cleared up—and to find that he had inadvertently harmed the British operation—his joy was nonetheless mitigated by the untimely discovery of his horse.

The gathering of Tories did not know he had killed Johnson, of course. Nor did they yet realize that Jake had ridden the horse here. He therefore had the option of denying everything merely by remaining mute, and bluffing the rangers with some story about having had his mount shot out from under him on the way to the farm.

But that path was fraught with eventual danger. For instance, he might have to explain why he had neglected to include the incident in detailing his other exploits that night. He would also be testing Busch's memory of the animal he'd been riding. So Jake plunged in a direction that offered immediate liabilities, but presented the prospect of safety once these were cleared.

"What are you doing with my horse?" he exclaimed with mixed innocence and alarm, rushing toward the animal.

"Your horse?" answered the soldier who had led the animal in. He turned to Busch. "Captain, I swear to you that this is the animal Major Johnson was riding last month when we met with him. I'd know him, sir, if I met him in a blinding snowstorm on the Boston Commons."

Now the reader will realize that no stallion in the continent is so distinct as to be unlike any other; nevertheless, the dark gray markings on the lighter gray field of this animal were relatively unique. Not only Busch but Sergeant Lewis examined the horse; both men agreed with the soldier who had led him in.

"How long have you had him?" demanded Busch.

"I acquired the horse from a gentleman a day ago," said Jake. "The terms were favorable, though he requested that I be discreet. He did not give his name."

"Explain yourself."

Jake described Johnson carefully, right down to the cravat haphazardly tucked into his shirt. They had fallen in together while traveling down from Wiccopee, and through certain signs Jake had been given to understand that the man was British or at least loyal to the king. Jake told him in confidence that he was "heading south"; the man claimed to be going in the same direction, but had to dally in the neighborhood a while longer. It would be most convenient, he hinted, if an arrangement could be made regarding their horses.

"He said at first that his horse was tired from its exertions. When I examined the animal I saw that he was in fine shape. I got the better end of the deal by far, though I sensed the man was in some difficulty."

"Sounds like a convenient story to me," said the Tory whom Jake had teased so effectively before.

Jake turned to confront the man—and found a cocked pistol pointed at the small space between his eyes.

He shrugged calmly. His survival depended entirely on seeming forthright. "You can believe me or not. Where would I come by such a magnificent animal? I am a poor farmer—or was, until the rebels chased me from my land."

The party looked at Busch to decide the matter. And Busch looked at Jake.

The two men exchanged a glance that measured the depth of their souls. Jake, having saved his life, already had won the Tory captain's trust once, and thus had a deep advantage. Still, this was a long and penetrating look, and a less practiced agent might well have crumbled beneath its burden.

How long they stared at each other, Jake could not tell.

Nor could he say what the other men might be doing in the barn around him. All he knew was that this Tory was a strong man with an iron will and a sense of himself that rivaled many a firm patriot's.

"Smith's loyalty is unquestionable," said Busch, putting his hand to the ranger's pistol. "He saved my life when we were ambushed by Skinners. He didn't know then that I was a ranger; in fact, he couldn't be sure of me at all. He is a bit rash, perhaps, but his heart is sound and his body strong."

As their captain told the story of the encounter, confirming and indeed enhancing Jake's tale, the men's attitude toward the newcomer clearly warmed. The hints of his stays in England, which showed that he was from a family of some means, were amplified with a few words from Jake, who noted—honestly, as it happened—that his uncle was in business there. Otherwise, the disguised patriot adopted the stance of a humble and reticent hero, the better to add luster to his shine.

From the moment they met in Prisco's, Busch had taken a strong liking to the good-looking and intelligent stranger. But this should not be held as a serious character flaw; so had many American generals, including the commander-in-chief himself.

"I expect big things from you, Smith," said Busch as he waved his audience to breakfast. "Don't let me down."

"I won't, sir." Jake's voice was so solemn that the king would have counted him among his closest supporters.

As Jake had hoped, Busch theorized that Johnson realized he was being followed, and had therefore traded horses to avoid suspicion. The inevitable conclusion at his missing the meeting was that the Americans had subsequently captured the British officer, which could also explain the increase in patrols and the subsequent capture of Caleb. While the temptation to attack the prison was strong—the church was located only two or three miles away—Busch reasoned that the Americans might expect such an action. Neither Johnson nor Caleb knew enough of their plans to give them away, and Busch interpreted the fact that the rebels had not shown up at Stoneman's as a sign that they had not cooperated in the least.

Like all good commanders, the Tory leader took these setbacks as an opportunity to push his men harder. They would carry on, he announced; their cause was just and victory within their grasp.

Jake, meanwhile, played the role of good Loyalist. He exchanged his brown farmer's coat for a dark green ranger jacket, bowing his head as he took the cloth with nearly as much reverence as the king used for his coronation. Then he feasted with the others on the mountain of nutmeg-flavored corncakes Stoneman provided for the rangers. Rose made a brief appearance with the farmer's wife, carrying the cakes; she took no notice of Jake and pretended not to hear the whispers of the Tories who surmised she was the girl he'd been seen outside with. That small incident added nearly as much luster to his reputation as his rescue of Busch, the men kidding him that perhaps Smith was not such a bad last name at all.

Immediately after breakfast Busch had the sergeant issue weapons to the newcomers. Jake received a musketoon or carbine—the two words describe the same weapon—and a regulation musket, along with a fine sword and a good supply of cartridge ammunition.

The carbine measured almost exactly forty-five inches from stock to barrel tip, far shorter than the musket, making it easier to handle on horseback. A peculiarity of this French-made weapon was its partially rifled barrel; these grooves, meant to improve accuracy, stopped about eight inches from the end of the gun. In theory, this combined the advantages of the musket—ready loading—with the advantages of the rifle—better accuracy. The reality fell somewhat short, but there was more chance of hitting a target at fifty yards than with a pistol.

The musket Jake was given was an older model Brown Bess with a shorter barrel than was now standard issue in the British army, the idea being either that it was easier to carry on horseback or provincials were second-class troops anyway and so could get by with obsolete weapons.

Readers who have heard of the fearsomeness of cavalry attacks but never experienced them may be surprised to learn that even the carbine was not meant to be fired from horseback. Pistols and swords were the weapons of choice from the saddle, and a fully equipped dragoon—or Tory ranger, for that matter—would carry two pistols in a saddle holster or else his belt. But these were in short supply, and none were issued. Jake had to make do with the single officer's pistol he had arrived with; the gun was a bit lighter than the excellent models Busch owned, but it was finer than most of the other hand pistols displayed in the barn.

The swords were long, well-sharpened, and balanced weapons that could slice the head off an opponent if the horse's momentum were used properly. They were not so ornate as was common among British officers, but they had come directly from a London armory.

In truth, Jake wished the blades were rusted and the guns fouled. Considerable destructive power was arrayed beneath these wide rafters; if it were used to only half of its potential, the American toll would be great.

While we have been describing their armament, the rangers have been mustered and mounted, with Captain Busch now dressed in his own dark green coat at their head. One of their number bears a light green flag as insignia, so drunken is their arrogance despite their location behind enemy lines.

But nowhere is their insolent gall more obvious than in their hats. While most Loyalist units wear some similar shade of green coat, the men had been issued a distinct uniform cap meant to instill unit pride, as well as offer some protection. The helmets had started as leather coverings, with a small beak at the front; a smart, thick piece of bear fur was crisscrossed on the top, tied down with a thick rope of horse hair and pinned by a small brass button on either side. At the back, the hair and fur were knotted in a red bow, an emblem, or so Busch declared, of their patron, the Earl Graycolmb.

Claus van Clynne, a connoisseur of headgear who had derided Jake's customary tricorner on several occasions, would have laughed at these beanies, but to a man the troop thought them rather smart. They pressed forward in single file formation toward the road, looking for all the world as if they were heading toward a King's Day parade. At the intersection with the road, Captain Busch swung his horse aside and signaled his two dozen mounted followers to fan out and listen to his speech.

We do not wish to alarm the weak-willed into fleeing the countryside, and thus will not repeat his fiery charge here. Suffice to say it was well formed, praising their benefactor, the Earl Graycolmb, who had made this troop possible, and denouncing the ungrateful American rebels, who had made it necessary. The speech touched on rival Tory brigades, including the famous Rogers Rangers (the original leader's occasional remarks in favor of the Revolution went unreported). It ended with a stirring invocation of the king's name, which resulted in a strong cheer that sent a deep chill down Jake's spine.

Nine

Wherein, Claus van Clynne engages in activities of value to the war effort and, not coincidentally, to himself.

The reader should not think that Squire van Clynne has been idle during this interlude; in fact, the good and portly Dutchman has been doing yeoman service in the name of the Cause, rising well before dawn with the vim and vigor of a man determined to serve his country, though if the full truth be told, he did not rise in a very good mood. Indeed, the Dutchman had even more vinegar about him than normal and was twice as irascible, grumping and growling through his morning toilet.

Had we the time, we might linger over the description of this morning preparation, for the Dutchman is fastidious to a fault, customarily rubbing not merely his eyes but his cheeks and nose with the frosty water that stands fresh by the innkeeper's kitchen door. He combs his beard five times through every dawn with his whalebone comb, and even takes this instrument once—gently—through the hair atop his head. He then spends another minute—or more—maneuvering his large and revered hat over his crown, until it finds its most striking position. Last but not least, he runs his hands over his many pockets, belts, and buckles, making sure his weapons, money, and passes are at the ready.

This morning these customary ministrations were accompanied by a litany of complaints directed at the injustice of his assignment, and the lengths he has gone to in the name of the Cause. It must be remembered that the Dutchman, whatever his other interests, is first and foremost a hearty patriot and a sworn enemy of all that is

British, with the exception of their ale. His hatred has been bred into his genes, and in some respects, he regards the Revolution as personal vindication of his attitude.

Thus, it is natural that his ego would suffer a great blow at being left behind while Jake proceeded on the adventure to rout the Tories; he feels that he has been treated, if not quite as a cowardly poltroon, at least as a hanger-on. Considering his role—or at least, his view of his role—in delivering the fake message to Howe, this new job is a considerable disappointment. To be given the task of riding unadventurously to Albany to meet with Schuyler—a Dutchman who prefers Madeira to beer and relied on a British model in constructing his home—well, Samson had not been taken down so far when his locks were shorn.

There are, naturally, more material concerns: the squire was counting on an introduction from Jake to General Putnam to smooth the way for future business dealings, which would be of benefit not merely to himself but to his country. Far beyond that, he realizes that his best hopes for regaining his family property rest almost entirely on Lieutenant Colonel Jake Gibbs and his influence with His Excellency General George Washington. If Gibbs were to forget him—or worse, if he were to somehow become incapacitated—van Clynne would have to return to his past regime of endless legal battles and sobfilled entreaties.

The Dutchman put aside his cares at his predicament to bid farewell to his beloved. He promised he would return; he told her she was the tulip of his garden; he told her she was the yeast of his bread. Jane gave the only response possible in the circumstance—she happily continued to snore, as his shakes had not succeeded in waking her. The Dutchman left her sleeping with her aunt, bid the rest of the dark house goodbye, and started north on the road to Pine's Bridge. He had the two dead Tories' horses hitched behind his own gelding, intending to deliver them to the nearest American post, or to Schuyler himself, depending on which promised the most advantage.

He also planned to do everything in his power to find Jake and smash the nest of vipers himself, without violating the letter of his commander's instructions to head for Albany. After all, the road network here was extremely tangled; it could take days to leave Westchester, if the proper route were found.

The lack of light did not impede his progress as much as the lack of food in his stomach; he had not gone a half mile when a gnawing sound presented itself, growing louder with each step his horse took. Within two miles, he started to look for an inn.

The first to present itself featured a sign with a man with his wife on the back, yielding the inn's *nom de drink,* LOADED WITH MISCHIEF. This was obviously a very new establishment, as van Clynne had not met it before. His curiosity aroused, he tied his horse to the front post and walked up the short run of red brick to the front door. A fresh coat of green paint had been applied to the thick, battle-scarred wood, confirming—in van Clynne's mind, at least—that the inn was new, though the house itself was a nondescript brick affair that could have been erected at any point during the past fifty years.

"The wife will be down shortly," said the sleepy-eyed proprietor, greeting him in the foyer. Glad for the business, he hustled van Clynne to a seat in the small front room to the right. "We'll have some coffee for you directly. I'm sorry I can't offer you tea—it's too dear in these parts to afford, nearly as much as salt."

The Dutchman fell to commiserating with the man, who though of German stock was not altogether unpleasant. He had seen no one answering Jake's description, and van Clynne thought it best not to ask too many questions; the man's accent was thick enough to indicate his arrival in America was recent, making his loyalties suspect.

The coffee was strong, and van Clynne soon found it worked wonders for his disposition. But it was not until he overheard the innkeeper's conversation with two men at the door that the Dutchman's mood truly lifted.

They were a peculiar pair to be up this early. Their white shirts were so yellowed they might not have been washed in two winters, and their black trousers—a modern invention van Clynne did not agree with—were as crumpled as a discarded page of Rivington's lying Tory newspaper. Neither man had shaved successfully for a fortnight, though their faces bore the evidence of several close attempts. An expert limner could not have painted a more convincing portrait of two thieves down on their luck.

But the Dutchman was no mere portrait artist. He was an accomplished student of human nature and, as he had told Jake ad infinitum, a good man of business. He immediately realized the men were not mere robbers but privateers strayed far from their ship. More accurately, they must be members of a recent crew who had traveled inland to sell off their share of the loot at a better profit than what they could make in port. As such, they were prime recruits of the good dame Opportunity's army, and she had decided to knock on Claus van Clynne's door with a vengeance.

"Any bushel you can find will fetch nine dollars at least," one of the men told the keeper. To judge from his companion's remarks, the man's name was Shorty, though in truth he stood much taller than average.

"They're paying ten at Newburgh," said the second man, who was nicknamed Fats. He was of far less than average weight—obviously the pair came from a part of the country where bodies or nicknames were deformed.

"Two dollars would be robbery," responded the innkeeper. "Salt was thirty cents not two years ago."

"The problem is the money. You can't count its worth," said Shorty.

"I have Spanish dollars, as solid as any."

"Fifty *reals* per bushel," suggested Fats.

"Two bushels for five *duros,* and not a *real* more."

"Can't be done. That's not even thirty shillings," complained Shorty.

"It's forty if it's a penny."

"Excuse me," said van Clynne, stirring from his chair to enter the conversation. "Perhaps if you used Dutch equivalents as a standard, your calculations would be easier."

"What business is it of yours?" demanded the inn-keeper.

Van Clynne gave him an indulgent smile. "I have over-come such difficulties many times. Perhaps if I offered my services as a negotiator."

"Just another profiteer looking to cut himself in," said Shorty.

"No, no, I am an honest philosopher, a follower of the good Adam Smith," said van Clynne. "As men of busi-ness, I assume you have read his work?"

"There was an Adam Brown with us on the *Raven*," offered Fats. "He was a mate."

"An amazing coincidence," remarked van Clynne. "Perhaps they are brothers."

"You owe me two pence for your coffee," said the keeper. "You may pay in legal tender and take your leave."

"Tut, tut, my good man," said van Clynne. "I wouldn't think of using English money in a good Revolutionary household such as this." He turned to Shorty, obviously the brains of the operation, such as they were. "I gather you are from Connecticut?"

"So?"

"I always like to know where my partners come from," answered van Clynne.

"Partners?"

"Obviously you don't want my services as a mediator, so I will have to get involved in this transaction directly."

"I think you'd best stay out of this business," countered the keeper.

"Business is my business," said van Clynne, extending his hand in a grand gesture of friendship. "Claus van Clynne, at your service."

"Shorty Stevens."

"Fats Williams."

"I have a suggestion that will make us all very happy," said the Dutchman. He held out his coffee cup for a refill. The innkeeper was clearly not pleased, but went and got his kettle.

"We're waiting, Mr. Clynne," said Shorty.

"It's van Clynne, actually," returned the Dutchman

mildly. "But no harm done—call me anything you like. You are men of the sea, I take it."

"How'd you know?"

"A lucky guess. It happens that I am going north," said van Clynne, "and for a small fee, will gladly stop by Newburgh. There I can sell your salt on consignment. We're sure to double or triple our profit, as salt is in great demand there."

"Why should we cut you in?" said Fats.

"Gentlemen, surely you understand the theory of mercantile trade."

"Oh, we understand all right," said Shorty. "The question is, how much will you pay for our salt?"

"I've already set a price," interrupted the innkeeper. "Five Spanish dollars for two bushels."

"It's possible that a sale might make more sense," said van Clynne. "But I think it would be robbery to pay less than three Spanish dollars, or *duros*, per bushel. Now, if we converted that to crowns—"

"I thought you didn't have British money," said the keeper.

"I said I wouldn't think of insulting a patriot innkeeper with it," corrected van Clynne. "These men, being citizens of the sea, will find some simpleton to burden with it in a foreign port, I'm sure."

"There are plenty of simpletons in foreign ports," answered Shorty. "But none here. I think four dollars per bushel a very fair price."

The innkeeper objected strenuously, and began resorting to the argument any good thief makes when he sees his profit washing away—moral persuasion. He had a business arrangement with these men, he had stood by them when no one else did, he had sheltered them from the British authorities in Connecticut, etc. His efforts were unavailing until he agreed to pay four *duros* per bushel.

"Well, sir, can you meet that price?" Shorty asked van Clynne.

"Regretfully, no," answered the Dutchman. "I am sorry, but there are travel expenses to be considered."

"Then we have an arrangement," said Shorty, shaking the keeper's hand.

If the man smiled at the seamen, he frowned at van Clynne. But Shorty gave the Dutchman a wink, and then bought him another coffee—even consenting to pay for the two van Clynne had already had.

"Three," said the innkeeper.

"Three then," said Shorty.

The keeper's mood gradually lightened; he would still make a sizeable profit selling the salt in the neighborhood. The seamen were also in a jolly way, spending a portion of their profits on a large breakfast. Even van Clynne remained happy—for he knew the transaction had not quite been concluded.

The squire stayed talking for a few minutes more before excusing himself. He went outside and gathered his horses, which had been tended to by the keeper's teenage son. Van Clynne took great interest in the lad's description of the animals' care, inspected each part of his mare's saddle and equipage, and otherwise delayed so that he was barely on the roadway when the two seamen came tumbling from the cottage after him, yelling for the "Good Mr. Clynne" to halt and walk with them a bit.

"What a coincidence that we're going the same way," he ventured.

"Yes, indeed," said Shorty. "And of further coincidence is some notion that just fell into our heads upon seeing you—we have a few more bushels of salt to spare."

"Indeed," replied the Dutchman. "How fortunate."

"Old Harold can never take more than three or four bushels of anything we sell," said Fats. "He's afraid his past will catch up with him if he's accused of profiteering. He was run out of Connecticut, you know."

"A timid soul does not make a profit, eh, Mr. Clynne?" winked Shorty.

"The 'van' is an important part of my name," answered the Dutchman, whose tone now was so abruptly different from before that both seamen looked about to see if they had fallen in with the wrong fellow. "What business are you in?"

"Why salt, of course!" said Fats.

"And other things," allowed Shorty. "But just salt, right now. We'll sell you a wagon load, eighteen bushels full, at three *duros* per bushel. And we have a sack of sugar cones for the same price."

"I have no need for the sugar," said van Clynne. "As for the salt, three dollars a bushel in Spanish currency is much too much. I could arrange for the equivalent of, say, three New York dollars for two bushels."

"You were just arguing that three was too little for one!"

"I did that solely on the condition of helping you. Think of it as a commission for this new deal."

"What!"

"If you gentlemen are not interested in disposing of your wares, I must take my leave. I have urgent business further north with a friend of mine. He's quite at sea without me—no offense."

"All of the Dutch are thieves," said Fats, who received a slap across the chest from his partner for his candor.

"He meant nothing by it, sir," said Shorty. "I have some Dutch blood in me myself."

"I could tell. If we were dealing in Connecticut warrants, perhaps I could give you better terms," suggested van Clynne.

"That would be inconvenient."

"Come now. I would wager you will be traveling that way very shortly."

The negotiations proceeded for ten more minutes, as the two sides maneuvered for the final few pence advantage. Van Clynne was willing to go higher with the Connecticut money since he found it grossly devalued in New York. Still, he got his salt for less than half what the innkeeper had just paid, a bargain that would bring a sizeable profit in a few hours when he met Putnam's quartermaster in Peekskill.

Not a dereliction of duty, surely—Peekskill is clearly en route to Albany. And a man with salt in such starved country needs no special introduction beyond a sample of his spice.

When at last the deal was struck, the men sealed it by spitting in their hands—a bit of non-hygienic fuss the

Dutchman ordinarily shied from. Considering the profit he was about to make, however, some sacrifices were warranted.

But such are the contingencies of business during wartime that one finds not even a good wad of spittle will set an agreement in iron. For there proved to be an important codicil to this arrangement—evidence that Shorty did indeed have some Dutch blood in him.

Van Clynne had assumed that the salt was in a storehouse or hidden somewhere along the highway, where he might direct Putnam's men once the second leg of the transaction was concluded. He could therefore proceed without the bother of bringing more than a pocketful of the substance with him. But the commodity was actually in a wagon, and the wagon was precariously parked in the middle of a streambed, positioned in such a way that water came nearly halfway up the wheels.

"We'll just toss it out and be on our way," said Shorty cheerfully. "Sure you don't want any sugar?"

"How much for the wagon?" grumbled van Clynne.

"I don't know that it's for sale," ventured Shorty.

But of course, everything has its price, and van Clynne was soon able to work a reasonable transaction: he traded the two Tory horses for the wagon and its ox, with the sugar thrown in to sweeten the deal. Hitching his own mare to the back, he proceeded north, grumbling loudly about the seamen's sharp dealing until they were out of earshot.

Ten

Wherein, a traveler's desires go unmet, with dire results.

*A*nother traveler was looking for breakfast at this hour, though his appetite was well beyond what could be satiated by the thick mince pie offered by the proprietor of the small ordinary along the Old York Road where he stopped. Major Dr. Keen had traveled north in his coach from the precincts of Manhattan, crossing off the island at King's Bridge. The British soldiers he'd consulted at the various sentry posts had supplied no useful information about his quarry; the Dutchman and his assistant Gibbs had succeeded in vanishing from the environs without visible trace.

In itself, this neither supported nor refuted Bacon's belief that van Clynne was an imposter. Keen endeavored to keep an open mind on the issue. While naturally inclined toward the hope that his prey would prove counterfeits—and therefore suitable for whatever designs happened to take his fancy—the doctor attacked his problem as he attacked all difficulties, from a scientific angle. Certain drugs included in the large store that he kept in his carriage would aid his inquiries greatly, once he succeeded in locating the Dutchman.

Keen had left behind the safety of the British lines about an hour before, traveling through the Neutral Ground in the thick neck of the land above Manhattan. The Old York Road was only one of many different routes northward. Keen had gathered from his driver—though not a native, Phillip Percival had spent several years in the country prior to the war—that this was the most likely route a rebel in a hurry would take. The doctor himself knew little of this land; he had been in the county only once before. A small cottage further north owned by one of General Bacon's many intelligence operatives had been placed at Keen's disposal; if circumstances allowed, he would use it as a base of operations. Otherwise, he would have to improvise.

The small tavern where Keen now stopped was not more than a mile from the spot where Howe had made his headquarters during his unsuccessful foray into central Westchester the previous summer. The establishment was small even by local standards, more a private hovel with food and a spare bed for travelers. It had barely two rooms on the first floor, with the hearth in the main room doubling as kitchen; the upstairs was a half-story attic-cum-bedroom. The thick, rough logs betrayed its early Dutch ancestry and bore witness to a significant and rare battle with the river Indians—but Keen was not much of a local history buff.

One of the difficulties of working in the wilderness—a man used to London found even the highly cultivated land hereabouts untamed—was that the inhabitants failed to properly anticipate a man's needs. For example, the serving wench who brought him his tea and pie had to make a trip back to her small sideboard to retrieve cream. Such stupidity would not be tolerated even in so primitive a place as New York City.

And another thing—the people responded to the simplest question with bewilderment.

"He is Dutch, with a beard, russet-colored clothes, and a large, round, silver-flecked hat," repeated the doctor.

"No, sir, I have not seen any such man," said the girl. She had a wholesome tint in her cheeks, and her hips were well-rounded beneath the very simple and worn flaxen dress. It occurred to Keen that she was just the sort of morsel whose parts were worth more than the whole.

"Do you know of him?"

"No, sir."

"Come closer, girl; I'm not going to bite." Keen tapped her bottom gently with his gold-topped walking stick.

In London, such a young woman would recognize the opportunity and jump into his lap; here in the backwoods the girl froze.

"I'll thank you to keep your stick off my wife," said the flushed proprietor, appearing in the doorway from the back room. Just past thirty years old, he was a large man and the threshold small—his head brushed against the lintel, and his stubby arms, set against his hips indignantly, crowded the side panels.

"Well, my good man, I would not have marked you for a cradle robber," said Keen, who gave her another playful tap before returning his cane to his side. "How old are you, girl? Fifteen?"

"Get into the back, Elizabeth," said the keeper as he took a step forward.

The man's wife cowered, slipping against the small fireplace and knocking one of the iron pots to the ground. Its top careened madly on the wide-planked floor; she grabbed it, dropped it again because it was hot, and then ran into the other room.

"I've no desire to harm you," Keen told the man as he picked up his tea. "But I would not be adverse to it."

"Out of that chair, you English snake. Pay for your breakfast and leave my house."

"Do I understand that you are declaring yourself a rebel?"

The man stood over Keen with barely controlled anger. The doctor had given up wearing a wig when he came to America; otherwise the strands of it would now be curling from the heat of the insulted husband's fury.

"Out! And take your fool with you," said the keeper, gesturing toward Percival, whose large frame had just appeared above the top half of the open Dutch-door at the ordinary's entrance.

"I shall not leave until I have finished my tea," said Keen, raising the fine porcelain cup.

The keeper swung the back of his hand against it, dashing what until now had been one of his most valuable possessions against the wall. In the next instant, he found his arm grabbed at the wrist, clamped as in a powerful vice.

He had not expected such physical strength in the gentleman at the table, who not only appeared to be a jack-a-dandy but was at least fifty. The keeper had earned much of his living before the war as a stone mason, but here found himself steadily and slowly sinking to his knees.

"Do you like flowers?" Keen asked. "Lilies, specifically."

"Let go of my arm, you bastard," said the man, whose voice betrayed considerably more fear than his words did.

The doctor smiled, and flicked his left hand to reveal a small handkerchief up his sleeve. He put the cloth to the man's nose, as if to wipe it.

The scent was pleasant. Keen suddenly released the man, who by reflex grabbed the handkerchief to his mouth.

The doctor watched with satisfaction as the puzzled expression on the keeper's face changed, the poison beginning to work. In a moment his eyes grew large and he began to gag. Keen stood as the man fell back, his chest heaving wildly.

"The pity is, that was my last bit of *Convallaria,*" Keen said as he stood. "I shall have to rely on other potions for the duration of my trip. But I suppose one must make do in the wild. Here—" Keen dug into a small pocket in his vest and retrieved a crown. "This should more than pay for my breakfast. I'd stay and chat with your wife, but duty calls. Besides, I wouldn't want to intrude on your wedded bliss. You can keep the handkerchief."

By now the unfortunate man had collapsed to the floor, his chest heaving in a spasmodic fit. Keen's words were well beyond him; he would spend at least another half hour in convulsions, and then steadily waste away. By evening, his young wife would be a widow.

Keen picked his hat off the wall post where he had left it and placed it on his head. The beaver was put up as a tricorner, folded in three places in a style quite common in the colonies; he fancied it made him look almost like a native. Steadying it on his head, he tapped his cane at the door and called to the girl who must still be hiding in the back room.

"If you see the Dutchman, tell him that Major Dr. Keen is looking for him. He'll come to recognize the handiwork, I daresay."

Eleven

Wherein, Jake and van Clynne meet on the road and have a salty time.

*T*here was nothing like the prospect of a quick and reasonable profit to motivate Claus van Clynne, and as his contemplated salt sale would not only benefit the American Cause but establish the basis for many more transactions, the squire goaded his newly purchased ox with whip and song. The latter was a ditty of his own creation, roughly to the tune of an old Dutch love song, built around the refrain:

> *Nothing moves a fighting man*
> *like a bellyful of salt,*
> *Except of course a kettle full*
> *of heavenly fermented malt.*

For obvious reasons the reader will be spared further description.

The Dutchman saw but ignored the clouds starting to gather on the horizon; though still miles from the encampments, he would have his wares unloaded and sold well before rain arrived. At moments like this, his patriotism knew no bounds, and he had entirely forgotten his anger at being treated as a mere subaltern by Jake. A less troubled disposition could not be found for many miles.

He was thus taken largely by surprise when the woods around him erupted with Indian war whoops.

Van Clynne's travels prior to the war had made the Dutchman something of an expert on the various sounds emitted by northeastern natives; none of these fell into any recognizable category. His puzzlement was cured di-

rectly, when the figures emerging from the brush proved
not to be Indians at all, but base imposters—Tory thieves.

"Halt!" shouted the leader, whom we already know as
Captain Busch.

"What's the meaning of this?" demanded van Clynne.
"And what is all this nonsensical shouting?"

"I arrest you in the name of George the Third," declared Busch. "Smith, get down from your horse and truss
him."

Smith, of course, was our Jake Gibbs, who was dressed
so oddly that van Clynne scarcely had a chance to recognize him as he swung from his saddle.

But recognize him he did. Jake saw the look in his face,
and realized the puff of breath the Dutchman took was
preparatory to an exclamation. He therefore thought it
expedient to wield his carbine—butt-end first—in a pre-
emptive strike. He smashed van Clynne in the stomach,
knocking the air out of him and sending him backwards
into his cargo.

"Don't curse King George, even under your breath,
you damned rebel pig!" Jake shouted.

Van Clynne gagged in confused response. Jake slapped
him across the face with his open hand. It was an authen-
tically fierce blow, and the Dutchman only barely held on
to his wits.

"Play along," hissed Jake as he reached an arm down
to van Clynne. "You don't know me."

"Sir!"

"Out of the cart, weasel, before I strike you again. I'd
show a dog more mercy."

The Tories were an amused audience as van Clynne
was unceremoniously kicked toward the dust. While some
part of him realized he must play along with this charade,
a greater part expressed indignation at having to take
even an ersatz Tory's orders. And so when Jake commanded him again to get on his knees and profess his
allegiance to the king, the Dutchman declined.

"Claus van Clynne goes on his knees to no man. Who
are you sir, and who are your band of bowl-capped pi-
rates?"

"We are loyal subjects of His Majesty," proclaimed

Jake. "Rangers of service to Earl Graycolmb, who has given us warrant and funds to operate here as an adjunct to His Majesty's Marines." His fellow marauders choked with pride at Jake's pronouncement, little realizing that his intent was to give van Clynne enough information to have them all arrested. "Treat us with papers that profess your loyalty, or we will treat you to the gibbet."

Any lingering skepticism about Jake's abilities were removed by this performance, and a few Tories were heard to remark that this new fellow was quite a comer.

"I would sooner give my papers to a pole cat than to someone with such ill taste as to dress in a green coat."

"Tie the rebel up," ordered Busch. "We'll take his cargo under tow. I know several farmers who would welcome it."

Now van Clynne became even more upset, objecting that the Tories had no right to take his goods. His words were met by a rope held at arm's length by two rangers, who used it to tie him to a tree.

"Take the sugar but leave me the salt," offered van Clynne. His magnanimous gesture was met by a titter of laughter. "You're making a dreadful mistake. I was on my way to New York City to deliver this salt to General Howe himself. I am a loyal follower of King George."

"A gallows conversion if ever I heard one," said one of the Tories.

Well, it wasn't actually a Tory. It was Jake.

"I expected better of you, sir," said van Clynne indignantly. "I trusted that—"

The end of the sentence was lost in the swallow of air that followed a fresh blow to the Dutchman's waist.

"I remember this man from the inn," said Jake. "He was trying to make love to the judge's niece."

"Not a crime, surely," said van Clynne weakly.

"Yes, I remember him, too," said Busch. "Why did you not come out to us if you were on your way to New York?"

"I . . ."

"You what? Speak up." Jake patted his back; to the others it appeared as if he were helping van Clynne catch his breath, but he chose his spots and his timing to produce the opposite effect—van Clynne's chokes became uncontrollable, his face now the shade of a beet after it has simmered in a Dutch oven for three hours.

"Perhaps he meant there were too many rebels around," said Jake, looking up. "I had that impression myself. Here, sir, you sound as if you're drowning on dry land. Let me loosen your waistcoat." He reached into van Clynne's jacket and quickly rifled through the folded papers he knew the Dutchman kept there until he found one marked with a red seal.

"A-hah! And what is this!" he exclaimed triumphantly, as if introducing the last piece of invented evidence before an Admiralty court.

As Jake knew from experience, however, the letter proved to be a pass from General Howe himself, admitting van Clynne into New York City. It was, like every other paper in the Dutchman's pockets, forged, but neither Busch nor the others had any way of knowing that.

"We'll have to let him go," said the captain, after examining the pass. "But we'll keep the salt and sugar. If he's truly a loyal citizen, he shouldn't mind donating it to the cause of king and country. General Howe won't miss it."

Van Clynne stifled his protest with great difficulty.

"I'd like his horse as well," said one of the Tories, who was riding a nag older than several of the surrounding hills. "It's a fine-looking animal."

"We can't just take a man's horse," said Captain Busch.

"Perhaps he'll donate it," suggested Jake, walking back to van Clynne. He was between the Dutchman and the rest of the party, and they could not see the wink he gave him.

Whether van Clynne actually saw this signal or not, he wasn't about to give up his horse voluntarily. "That animal has been in my family for many years," he objected, wincing as he prepared for another blow from his erstwhile friend.

"Meet me on the road just above Pine's Bridge tonight. Wait for me," whispered Jake under his breath, adding in a louder voice, "Perhaps a little close negotiation will help you arrive at a reasonable price."

"Leave off, Smith," commanded Busch. "You've no right to hit him. He has a legal pass, however he's obtained it. He can keep his horse. We'll borrow his ox and wagon—Sergeant, prepare a receipt." Busch turned toward van Clynne, who was still gathering his breath. "It can be redeemed from the quartermaster corps in New York City when you arrive there. You have my signature upon it. Tell me, have you seen a tall man traveling by himself in a brown coat, with fine black boots and a fresh Quaker hat?"

"Sir," said van Clynne weakly, "you describe half the inhabitants of the country."

"Describe your horse to him, Smith," directed Busch.

"Black, a bit wobbly but a faithful animal, nonetheless. Five years old, if a day." A nearly imperceptible shake of his head gave van Clynne his answer.

"I have seen neither," said the Dutchman. "Or I have seen them all—gentlemen, I assure you, the description could be applied to half the equine population of the colony, if not the continent."

"Untie him and let us be gone," commanded Busch.

"Yes, sir." Jake reached into his belt for his elk-handled knife and flashed it before the Dutchman's face before slicing his ropes. "Don't fail me," he whispered. "Have Old Put put the troops guarding the chain on alert."

"I will do nothing of the sort!" yelled van Clynne, looking back to Busch. "I would sooner kiss my horse than lick your boots!"

The whole company laughed and applauded as Jake gave the Dutchman one last kick and returned to his horse. Even Busch smiled as they rode off in train. Van Clynne was left to cough the dust out of his lungs and clear his eyes, which he did to the accompaniment of a loud chorus of Dutch oaths.

The bruises Jake administered were real enough, and if van Clynne had suffered far worse during his career, still it grated him that these had been inflicted by a supposed friend and ally. Indeed, it seemed inconceivable that a true patriot could strike another—perhaps van Clynne had misjudged his companion's allegiance after all.

As that would have involved a sizeable flaw on his part —indeed, it would be such a gross mistake in judgment that it was inconceivable *any* Dutchman could make it— van Clynne quickly dismissed it.

He straightened his coat and reviewed his situation. Jake had given him two specific tasks—the meeting, which was not to take place until tonight, and alerting General Putman. He had said nothing in regard to the stolen salt, nor his prior assignment.

Obviously, the job of journeying to Schuyler was now completely superseded, as there would be no way of reaching Albany and returning before evening.

But on the other hand, his compatriot—commander, if he insisted—would certainly realize that the two assignments, no matter how important, would not take up much time for an able operative like van Clynne; one was not even to be undertaken until an undetermined hour late tonight. This could only mean that the Dutchman was to use his energies to accomplish other tasks vital to the Cause. Obviously, Jake had felt it self-evident and unnecessary to mention.

No mission could be more vital than the retrieval of his salt, destined for the very general whom he was supposed to now contact. Not only was it critical to the survival of Putnam's men; there was no telling how it might inspire the Tories if left in their possession.

But how to arrive at a plan which combined its liberation and union with Putnam, without exposing his comrade? Van Clynne sighed deeply and scratched his beard, as he always did in such crises. Then he followed the next logical step—he turned his horse back in search of an inn, where a few strong whiffs of stout would prepare his mind for the job ahead.

Twelve

Wherein, Jake concocts a plan to spoil the Tory raid on Salem.

Jake undoubtedly would have had a different view on the direction van Clynne should take. Fortunately for the squire, he was not available for consultation. Indeed, Jake's thoughts were devoted exclusively to the Tories he was riding with, and their mission of harrying Salem.

He had not told van Clynne to have Old Put send men there because he suspected it might be a diversion, though its precise role in any overall scheme was still unclear. Nonetheless, even a diversion could injure Americans, and as Jake rode he searched his mind for some way of sabotaging the operation without drawing too much attention to himself, or damaging his chances at discovering any plans to attack the chain.

The rangers proceeded east in high spirits, for there is nothing like an early and easy victory to set the tone for a campaign. Busch could not have arranged a better mood-setter than the Dutchman, so easily bested; the men practically sang to each other as they rode.

Jake noted that their path had been carefully scouted and selected; though nominally in patriot territory, they had yet to come across a patrol or even find a straggler foraging for food. The "liberated" ox and wagon slowed their progress, but their commander did not seem upset by the pace, and Jake realized as they pulled down the lane toward a single farmhouse in a hollow that they must be well ahead of whatever schedule Busch had set. Salem was now only a few miles away; even with the wagon, it would take less than an hour to reach.

No one came from the small house when they pulled up outside. Busch nodded at the sergeant, who signaled to two nearby men and began a perfunctory search of the property.

"We'll rest here a while," Busch told Jake. "This has gone easier than I'd hoped. You were brave back there, Smith; the Dutchman might have had a weapon."

"Something about him told me I didn't have to worry."

"Appearances can be deceiving."

The American agent found it hard to disagree.

"Come into the house with me." Busch's words had the sharp cut of a command issued under fire—a bit too strong, it seemed, for the circumstances. Jake immediately feared the captain had overheard his whispered remarks to van Clynne.

Great is the power of imagination under the press of danger; left to its own devices it can manufacture a nation of demons and devils from a few chance words or the turn of a phrase. The only antidote is sheer willpower—though a loaded pocket pistol does not hurt, and Jake secreted his up his green-coated sleeve as he walked up the path of raked gravel behind Busch.

If it was a trap, it was an exceedingly pleasant one. The stone-faced room had been freshly cleaned, with a fine layer of sand raked over the floorboards in a swirling pattern. A Franklin stove stood in the corner, all fired up. A pot of water sat on the iron top, just a degree or two short of a full boil. The only difficulty Jake faced was the room's low ceiling—he had to stand with a slight bend to keep from knocking his helmeted head on the exposed joists.

"Our farmer friend arranged to be away this morning, in case some rebel should find us," explained Busch. "But he saw to our needs just the same. There's feed for the horses in the barn; the troop will rest here an hour or two before proceeding."

Jake nodded, still unsure whether he was being tested.

"When I found you at the inn, you thought you were completely without friends in this country, didn't you?"

"It seemed the entire territory turned against the king."

"Hardly." Busch inspected the pot and then stoked the fire inside the stove. "No more than a quarter of these people have ever been firm rebels. I would say a half of the continent's inhabitants would go either way. That is our great problem—the neutrals."

"Yes, sir."

Busch smiled at him. "There's no need to be so formal when we're alone. I told you, I regard you as my brother."

"That's kind, sir."

Busch laughed. "You're always on your guard, Smith."

"I haven't always been," said Jake. He walked around the room as if looking for a place where he could fit his head without stooping—and tucked the pocket pistol discreetly into the side of his belt when the Tory wasn't looking.

"You're a man of learning, I can tell," offered Busch. "You're not really a farmer."

"I am a farmer in that I owned a farm. But my family sent me to England to school. I attended Oxford."

This was actually true, as was Jake's subsequent admission that he had spent much of his time at school not at school. His education was not so wasted as he implied—indeed, he'd been among the top students—but his bashful admission brought a smile to Busch's lips.

"I dreamed of going to Oxford," said the Tory captain. "I dreamed of going to England. But only to visit," he added quickly. "My home is here and I'll fight to the death to protect it. As will you."

Jake nodded.

"I can see certain things in men," said Busch. "Tell me, can you swim?"

"Yes."

"Good." Busch took a canister from a nearby shelf and began fussing with some cups. There was not much tea.

"Are we taking time off for a swimming competition?"

"Not necessarily."

Jake suppressed an urge to grab the Tory and shake the details out of him.

"You must forgive me, Smith; it is a strong practice of mine to be careful with information; there are spies everywhere. You've impressed me, though—I'm sure you will be an officer yourself before long, once our commanders find out your background and you have a chance to show your mettle."

"I'm flattered."

"You're obviously capable, and of good birth."

"My mother was indentured."

Busch shrugged off the vague retort—it happened also to be true, as is documented elsewhere—and concentrated on preparing the drinks. When the tea was brewed, he handed his subordinate a cup. This unstated ceremony was an eloquent way of forming a bond with a man, Jake realized, a gesture intended to build confidence.

"I have long needed someone with me whom I can trust," said Busch as he sipped his tea. "Someone who can think on his feet. Drink up, man. It's not as hot as it looks."

Jake had not let a single sip of tea pass his lips since he'd landed in Boston more than two years before, and he did not intend to do so now. Ever since the Tea Party, the drink had become the symbol of all he hated.

In truth, few Americans, even firm patriots, would go to the lengths he did, especially in these circumstances. But a principle is a principle—a cough welled in his throat just as he brought the cup to his lips, and his lungs exploded in a burst that sent the liquid sailing across the floor. The choking fit was so strong his helmet fell off into his tea cup, sending the contents as well as the porcelain onto the sandy floorboards.

"Went down—went the wrong way," Jake gasped. An epileptic could not have had a more convincing fit. He nodded weakly when Busch suggested he should get some air.

Jake was just opening the door when he felt Busch's light but firm touch stop him. It was the same grasp he had felt on the porch at Prisco's, and while he was not afraid of the Tory, still a shiver ran through Jake's body as he turned to face him.

"You and I are not riding with the others. Our mission will be more perilous—are you prepared for it?"

Jake nodded.

"I have a few more items to attend to," said the captain. "We'll ride in a half hour, no more. Smith—"

Jake's eyes were once again caught in the Tory captain's powerful gaze. What a shame it was this man was on the wrong side of the war.

"Sir?"

"You won't fail me."

"No," managed the patriot, having more difficulty with this lie than many longer ones.

Busch nodded, silently dismissing him.

The same imagination that had created ambushes in the house was now double-timed into more constructive work. If Fortune had smiled on Lieutenant Colonel Gibbs by having Busch decide to take him along on the true mission back at the river, and maybe the chain—why else would he have asked if he could swim?—Jake still hoped to prevent the rest of the rangers from striking the unguarded town.

Being the son of an apothecary, the patriot spy had grown up on a wide variety of cures and potions. He was particularly fond of sleeping bombs, as the Gibbs's family pets—and a number of British soldiers—could attest. But those were impractical here for any number of reasons, starting with the fact that the necessary ingredients were lacking.

His studies had acquainted him with a variety of herbs and other natural medicines, however, and he began scouring the nearby woods for some ingredient that would incapacitate the troop. A few pieces of Fly Agaric mushrooms placed in their canteens would do the job very nicely—the plant produced an effect not unlike exceedingly strong rum. Though its results were variable, it could generally be counted on to intoxicate its victims for six or seven hours. It would also repel any horseflies in the vicinity.

Jake walked behind the house and down a gentle hillside leading into the woods, looking for the mushrooms. One of the homestead's previous occupants had been a midwife, and plenty of medicinal plants tripped at his heels—some peppermint, a few spearmint, even a creep-

ing strawberry plant—but no mushrooms. Undoubtedly,
van Clynne would have explained this via some disserta-
tion on the natural order of things and one of his Dutchman's Rules of the Cosmic Arrangement: whatever you
want most at hand is always furthest away, until you don't
want it any more.

Jake passed the remains of an old foundation and felt
his feet sinking in mud. The brush here became thicker,
and as he surveyed the margins of the swamp he realized
that the short, ground-covering shrubs that ran back up
the hillside might serve his purpose as well as any mush-
room. For the plants and their spiky green leaves appeared to be dog mercury, a potent herb common enough
in Europe but only an occasional import to America. A
few sniffs of their sour odor was enough to confirm his
find; Jake took out his knife and stripped several handfuls
of the leaves into his pockets.

Dog mercury could induce severe gastric distress if ingested; it had the added advantage of waiting a good
hour or so before erupting. Unfortunately, it had to be
eaten fresh, as the poison was easily diluted—and its
strong smell tended to warn people away from it.

People yes, but not necessarily horses, so long as he
could mix it with something that lessened the bitter taste.

Like a few mint leaves and some sugar.

"What are you doing, Smith?"

"Just helping myself to a cone of the rebel's sugar,"
said Jake as innocently as possible when the sergeant
caught him in the barn a few minutes later.

"I got m'eye on you," said the man. He emphasized his
point by spitting toward Jake's feet.

Jake broke off a piece of the sugar cone and handed it
to the man. His stubby cheek turned down with the force
of his frown, but he accepted the peace offering nonetheless.

"You served during the French and Indian War, I'd
wager," suggested Jake.

"Sayin' I'm old?"

"No, sir. Not at all."

"Hmmphh." The piece of sugar was nearly as big as the

sergeant's fist, but he shoved the entire hunk into his mouth like a five-year-old would.

Jake smiled and licked at his own piece. He needed privacy to finish mixing the herb with the sugar and mint, and then slip it into the horses' feed, but the sergeant didn't offer to leave. Lewis swished the sugar around in his mouth, as if he were chewing an overlarge piece of barley candy. Finally, he swallowed it with a gulp.

"Want some more?" offered Jake.

The sergeant frowned, then took the rest of his cone from him.

Jake shrugged and reached back into the wagon for another. Lewis grabbed his coat to stop him. "That's enough, now. The captain has plans for this. Say, what do ya have in yer pockets, Smith?"

"A few leaves for a tea," said Jake. "Want some?"

"What's this then, sassafras?"

"It's Indian pine," said Jake, inventing a new species on the spot. "It aids digestion. I have a problem with gas, and learned this cure from an old Algonquin woman. I take a bit every day."

"I've the same problem," said the sergeant, taking a new attitude toward the trooper.

Jake graciously offered to share some in a tea with the sergeant, if he would fetch the water while the leaves were prepared. In the time it took the man to round up a pail and find the well, Jake had mixed the batch and fed two-thirds of the horses, who were suspicious but glad enough of the sugar. He left his own horse alone, naturally, and was just debating whether to feed Busch's when he heard the door open.

"Captain says yer to leave directly with him," declared the sergeant. "Take his horse to him."

"I'll leave this for you then," said Jake, pointing to the small pile of leaves on the bench. "Drop them straight into the water."

The sergeant picked a few up and made a face. "They smell like farts."

"Have you studied the theory of humors and fluids, Sergeant Lewis?"

"What humors?"

"The general idea is that like will repel like." Jake's science was accurate enough, though it could not be applied here. "The smell is what makes them effective. To tell you the truth—if you really want relief, eat them raw."

"Raw?"

Jake nodded solemnly.

Had the sergeant boiled the leaves they would have been rendered impotent. Uncooked, they would have the same effect on him as on the horses.

Lewis made a face but picked up some of the leaves, chewing a moment and then swallowing with a hasty gulp.

"Try some sugar with it," said Jake. "That's how I like it."

Between the sergeant and the horses, the troop would be completely incapacitated within two hours.

And the area would be uninhabitable for months.

Thirteen

Wherein, Claus van Clynne falls in with the wrong kind of fellow.

As a general rule, Claus van Clynne would not have gone back to the Loaded with Mischief Inn for several weeks at least, long enough to let its proprietor forget his role in raising the price of salt. But as the tavern was the first to present itself and as van Clynne's thirst had reached powerful proportions, he consented to break his rule just this once. His reward was an outraged shout from the keeper, who directed his wife to swat the Dutchman on the back with her broom on his way off the premises.

"Tut, tut, my good man," said van Clynne, fussing with the large gold buttons of his coat as he eyed the woman's raised weapon. "Surely you can't be upset with me for facilitating your deal."

"Surely I can. You doubled the price."

"You bought your salt at a third what I paid for mine," said van Clynne, nodding at the inn's only other customer as he walked to the table. Van Clynne was not actually lying, merely neglecting to divide his cost across all of his purchase. "You'll make a fine profit off it, I suspect. As I see by your clock that it is just about noon, I'd like a mug of stout, please."

The keeper frowned heavily and considered the matter. It was one thing to hold a grudge; it was quite another to let that grudge prevent you from making a bit of profit. And so he directed his wife to disarm and went and fetched some beer for van Clynne.

"Do you mind if we set up an account?" queried the Dutchman when the tankard was set down.

The vessel was whisked back so quickly its contents did not have an opportunity to spill.

"Just a jest, my good man," said van Clynne, reaching for one of the purses he carried on a string suspended from his neck.

"Legal money," said the keeper. "You will use coins or you will find yourself sitting on the roadway talking to yourself."

"I had no intention of burdening you with paper," said van Clynne haughtily. "I have been looking for a way to get rid of this shilling for many months."

He dropped the coin so that it rolled across the table and continued onto the floor, making straight for the door. As the keeper dove to intercept it, van Clynne looked over and nodded at the customer sitting in the large armchair near the unlit fireplace. He was dressed in a powder blue coat with a brocaded yellow vest and very properly arranged hair. He sipped a thimble's worth of Madeira from a tiny silver beaker, undoubtedly one that he had brought to the inn himself. A walking stick crowned by a golden eagle stood at the side of his chair.

The reader has already made the man's acquaintance, for the stranger is the notorious Dr. Harland Keen, as he introduces himself—without the "notorious," of course.

"And I, sir, am Squire Claus van Clynne, at your service I'm sure. It is always a pleasure to meet a man of the medical profession. There are not enough doctors in this world, that's my motto."

"And what, sir, is your profession?"

"I am a man of the world, a traveler and a philosopher, a person who sees needs and fills them—in short, I am a good man of business. I am currently engaged in an enterprise involving a little salt," added van Clynne in a confidential tones. "Salt which has been separated from me. Stolen, in fact."

"Ha! It serves you right," said the keeper, who'd been eavesdropping on the conversation.

"I am looking for a troop of bandits," continued van

Clynne. "They were dressed in green coats and wore odd brown beanies, as if they'd caught some hideous cancer."

"Interesting," replied Keen, feigning not to know the significance of the coats. "And these were Loyalists or Americans?"

"Robbers, sir, no matter what flag they fly. These woods are filled with miscreants of every stripe. It is something about the air, I believe—the archbishop of Canterbury himself would think of lifting a man's purse if he rode here."

"It's the times, not the geography," replied Keen. "I have often thought that things have gone very much downhill since the Dutch ruled this land."

"Indeed, you're very right, sir. Most observant. You say you're a doctor?"

"I have passed the necessary examination."

"I could tell you were a man of great learning the moment I set eye on you. That is your coach outside, no doubt."

Keen nodded.

"Quite an interesting vehicle," said van Clynne, who naturally recognized it as having been made in England and had concluded that its owner was not only well-off but probably allied with the British. While this might shade van Clynne's attitude toward him, a man's allegiance was not necessarily a barrier to business in a time of crisis, especially as he showed proper deference to the squire's ancestry. "I have had occasion to deal with some similar carts in the past."

"I'd hardly call it a cart," said Keen quite lightly.

"True, I suppose you would call it a carriage, with the high wheels and all," allowed van Clynne. "Still, it is most impractical on these roads."

"Impractical? I find it handy indeed."

"It requires a driver, does it not? That's an added expense in these days of inflation."

"My driver is most useful," said Keen.

Van Clynne nodded, and turned to signal for another beer.

"I don't suppose it's for sale then."

"For sale? I think not. But perhaps we can do business on another front."

The Dutchman took this under advisement while he watched the innkeeper pour out a refill. Keen took a sip from his silver cup so slight that a bird would have been considered a guzzler by comparison.

"I am always ready to do business," said van Clynne when the keeper had gone. "Even with a British officer."

"Why do you think I'm a British officer?"

"Come, sir, let us be frank with each other. What rebel would dress as you, or display such wealth? And no Royalist could afford to be so bold."

"And your allegiance?"

"I am Dutch. My allegiance is my own."

Now the reader will realize that both men were jousting, each aware the other was more than he presented but not necessarily sure what that more was. Keen had the advantage, not so much because Bacon had told him of the Dutchman's strengths, but because while van Clynne was signaling the innkeeper he had sprinkled some dust from his hand into the bottom of the Dutchman's cup.

The active ingredient in the powder was largely distilled from jimsonweed, but a pharmaceutical analysis would fill several pages. More important to note was that its intended effect was as something of a truth serum; anyone who consumed a healthy dose found within a few minutes that they were amazingly agreeable and unable to dissemble. This condition lasted only a short time, for the belladonna at the formula's core tended to have a heavy impact on a person's consciousness, quickly delivering him into a state of extended drunkenness—or worse.

Except in this case. The scientist in Keen was quite intrigued by the Dutchman's apparent resistance to the drug, for his companion not only continued speaking coherently—if at enormous length—but drained the entire tankard of beer without any noticeable effect.

To keep the conversation going, Keen made up a story about wanting to buy wheat, but as he knew nothing about the prevailing prices made a suggestion so low that van Clynne quickly brushed the offer aside.

"If you see your way clear to triple the amount per bushel, we might have some grounds for discussion," said van Clynne, sliding his mug away and rising from the table. "But in the meantime, I have other business to attend to. And if that is your hat"—the Dutchman pointed to the folded beaver on the post near the door—"you would do well to get a sturdier one. It's quite ruined by your bending."

"Which way are you going?"

"Generally, north, though as I am in search of my salt, I could not say specifically." Van Clynne's suspicions had been raised by the low offer for the wheat—ordinarily British purchasing agents bid far too high. So he wondered if this man might actually be an American disguised so as to lure people of loose business ethics into a trap. Not that such a description would ever apply to him.

"Perhaps I can be of service," said Keen. "Would you like to ride with me?"

"Thank you, but I think not. With all due respect, sir, your wagon is quite a magnet for rascals of all sorts. I am best off sticking to my horse."

"A traveler who refuses hospitable company?"

"Surely, sir, I do not mean to insult you," said van Clynne, stroking his beard absentmindedly. "I am as great a follower of the etiquette of travel as any man on this continent, I dare say. But as I am currently on business, and on a sharp error, errand . . . "

"Is something the matter?"

"No, no, just a slight flutter in my eyes. It is nothing," said van Clynne.

"Here, let me take a look."

"I'll thank you to keep your hands to yourself, Dr. Quack!"

Blame the intemperate behavior on the late-acting drugs and van Clynne's natural aversion to the English. He pulled his lapels and strode to the door, fixing his large beaver on his head as he reached the threshold. Dr. Keen followed, and was by his side as van Clynne reached up for his horse—and fell straight to the ground.

Fourteen

Wherein, Claus van Clynne is left to complain about the inefficiency of thieves.

Major Dr. Keen had his driver load the incapacitated van Clynne into the coach and then climbed into the cabin behind him. The Dutchman's reaction to the drug was atypical, to say the least; he seemed to have skipped not only the suggestive period but the hallucinatory phase as well, moving right on to sleeping—unless the British doctor was confusing his convulsions for loud snores.

No, a convulsive would hardly have such a benign smile on his face. Keen directed Percival to proceed down the road and then fell to searching the Dutchman.

His immediate attention was drawn to the ruby-hilted knife secreted in van Clynne's vest. The blade was an authentic sibling of the weapon in Keen's own possession; unless the Dutchman had succeeded in besting another agent, he must be a member of the dark brotherhood.

Difficult to believe, though. Leaving his nationality aside, van Clynne did not cut the robust figure Major Dr. Keen took to be typical of the species. But perhaps that was his secret efficiency. Clearly he had some intelligence —he had quickly discerned that Keen was British, and knew enough to steer away from him behind enemy lines. It might even be that his reaction to the truth drug was the result of some far-reaching general antidote ingested prior to entering the inn.

If so, the doctor was highly interested—so far as he knew, there was no known remedy, even for a fatal overdose.

Van Clynne's coat and vest had a large number of interior pockets. All number of documents were deposited within them, mostly testimonials to his honesty and safe passages of conduct. It appeared he could go anywhere in the world he wanted and produce the necessary permission; here was a voucher from the King of Spain, here a recommendation from Guy Carleton, governor of Canada. The sheer number convinced Keen they must be forgeries, but all looked most convincing, and when the doctor compared a pass purported to have been signed by General Howe to an authentic one he owned himself, he could discern no difference in the hand.

The Dutchman also carried representative samples of the currency of every major legitimate nation in Europe and at least half the illegitimate ones in the New World. Indented bills from Maryland, Connecticut warrants, a note from Massachusetts, and leaf-inscribed papers from New Jersey were among the most plentiful. They were numbered where required and appeared authentic, or at least good copies—the quaint TO COUNTERFEIT IS DEATH warnings the notes boasted notwithstanding.

There was no counterfeiting the coins in his several purses. Here Spanish doubloons mixed with old British crowns, French money mingled with German, loose wampum lay next to a mysterious coin that looked old enough to be the Biblical widow's mite. If the rotund squire was not a spy then he was a veritable walking bank.

British gentlemen in general were so prejudiced toward their own racial superiority that most would quickly conclude van Clynne must be in their service, for the colonists could never manage to attract, let alone pay, such a man. Major Dr. Keen, however, was remarkably free of prejudices and blinding opinions. His entire nature rested on firm philosophical principles; he believed one must not jump to conclusions not directly supported by empirical evidence. And evidence as to van Clynne's loyalties, the knife aside, was lacking.

His snores were not, however. As a young man, Keen had spent some time traveling in the Levant, gaining ancient knowledge. He had witnessed a particular practice among Syrian tribesmen involving the butchering of a live bull ox. The animal's wails were remarkably similar to van

Clynne's, except that the Dutchman's were louder. The carriage shook with every inhalation, and the crushed velvet curtains at the sides flew fiercely apart every time he exhaled.

Keen flicked the two assassins' blades back and forth as he contemplated the situation. The most expedient thing to do was to kill the Dutchman and be done with him. Another dose of the truth powder ought to prove fatal, despite van Clynne's strange resistance to it; Keen could always claim it was an accident if it was subsequently discovered that the Dutchman was indeed a legitimate member of the Secret Department. On the other hand, this might deprive His Majesty of an effective if unusual agent.

Two, actually. Bacon's hint notwithstanding, such an "accident" very likely would be deemed unforgivable if discovered.

Besides, there was no art involved in killing a man who was already sleeping; a thief or coward could do that, and Major Dr. Keen was neither.

If this Dutchman did prove an imposter, he would be a fitting subject for several experiments Keen had long hoped to perform. The fact that all would undoubtedly prove fatal was unfortunate; it meant he'd only be able to perform one or, at best, two. In the meantime, a way must be found to discover his allegiance.

The ringed jewels on Keen's hand sparkled as he reached up and pulled the silk string near the coach door. The string rang a small bell near Percival on the driver's bench, and they immediately stopped.

"Help me with him," said the doctor as he got out. The two men had a difficult time retrieving the rotund Dutchman from his resting place and ended up half dragging him to the woods, where they tied him to a tree.

The only effect the ropes had on van Clynne was to make him snore louder. Keen wondered if one of those famous American moose might think this a mating call and come for an inspection.

"We'll let him untie the knots and escape, then follow along and see what he does," said Keen. "Sooner or later, his true nature will come clear. Since he still has the knife, he has not yet discharged his duty."

"How long will he be like this, Major?" asked Percival. The driver was well used to the sounds of torture, but these wails twisted his large, oxlike face through fearsome contortions.

"Ordinarily the drug wears off in six hours, but I've never seen it follow this specific course," said Keen, returning van Clynne's ruby-hilted blade to his coat. "Take a few coins from his purse to make him think it was a robbery. The big purse that's so obvious. Drop a few and he'll conclude we were startled away when he wakes."

Which proved to be the case when van Clynne came to barely twenty minutes later.

"Came to" perhaps does not correctly describe his mental state. He did come to something, but it was more like a dazed drunkenness. His inability to focus and the slurring of his thoughts into one another alarmed him in no small degree, though it must be noted that the realization he was missing money from one of his several purses sobered him considerably. Van Clynne immediately began cursing the downtrodden times; as his wits slowly regrouped, he realized that his hands were just loose enough to reach into the back of his belt where he kept a finger-sized razor.

"Rascals didn't even take the time to tie proper knots," complained the Dutchman as he undid himself. "And left coins on the ground. Does no one know the proper way to rob a man any more? They leave after rifling only one purse, and the most obvious one at that. In the days of Stuyvesant, a man was left penniless when he was robbed. Those were halcyon days, to be sure."

The grumbling picked up steam and within a short time the Dutchman's verbal apparatus had returned to normal. His vision, however, remained somewhat corrupted, and the communication between his head and feet had been scrambled to such a degree that he found it difficult to proceed. He stumbled from the tree, flopped into the dust, and spent a good ten minutes floundering on the ground. Regaining a vertical position, he steadied himself on a thick tree and took another dive toward the roadway, proceeding with all the stability of a wobbly top.

The Dutchman's unsteady progress was studied through a spyglass from a distance of several hundred leagues by Major Dr. Keen, who had secreted himself and his carriage in the woods off the roadway. The recovery from the drug astounded him; Keen found himself wishing, nay, praying, that the Dutchman would turn out to be a rebel so he could dissect his brain with a clear conscience and see what chemicals it possessed to ward off the belladonna and attendant drugs.

"Be sure to keep our distance," the doctor told Percival as he mounted the carriage to sit alongside him at the front. He reached beneath the seat and removed a large weapon that attached to a metal brace in the middle of the open compartment. With an oversized, ornate stock and a thick barrel, it looked like an antique blunderbuss, but was in fact a newly adopted naval swivel gun. A light canvas container with perforated sides held a collection of grapeshot; the devastating ammunition was quickly loaded, a fresh flint secured in the lock.

"Be a shame to waste this on our friend," the doctor confided to his assistant. "But with some luck we'll run into a rebel patrol."

"We can only hope, sir."

Fifteen

Wherein, Jake catches his first glimpse of the great chain stretched across the Hudson.

"*H*ave you killed many men?"

The question caught Jake so completely by surprise that he fumbled for an answer. "One or two."

"You are a poor liar, Smith, but that is in your favor at least," said Busch, patting his horse's flank as the animal picked its head from the stream. It was now well past midday; except for a brief lunch, this was their first stop since leaving the rest of the troop.

"I recognized that about you the moment I met you. It's at the center of who you are. You're all surface, Smith; you're no more capable of lying than that squirrel on the ground there. Consider it your defining virtue."

"Maybe it's a flaw," said Jake. He fingered his musketoon, its metal furnishings hot from the sun. Busch had his sword in his hand, and both men turned watchfully toward the road every few moments, guarding against attack.

"You proved yourself when you saved my life," said Busch, "but there is a quality about you—I would have trusted you even without such an obvious demonstration."

Jake said nothing.

"Better a brave man incapable of disguising his feelings than a cowardly deceptor," continued the ranger captain, remounting.

"I should have stayed and defended my farm," said Jake. "I was afraid then; I have to make up for it now."

"Fishkill is filled with rebels."

"My farm was nearer the Brinckerhoffs in Wiccopee than Fishkill."

Busch nodded. "I know them; they are hot rebels, all against the king. You did well to flee."

"I can't help but feel like a coward."

"Then you'll have to find the chance to redeem yourself. Let's go; we've got no time to brood."

The Tory captain prodded his horse back to the road as Jake boarded his own. They rode in hot fury for several miles, once more following an obscure trail that climbed upwards through the hills. Busch seemed to know this territory every bit as well as van Clynne, whose knowledge of farm lanes and city alleyways rivaled a bishop's command of church law. It was necessary that they ride in obscurity as well as with haste; their green coats and bearskin helmets made it clear that they were the enemy, and would give any Continental soldier a free pass to shoot at them. Yet Busch apparently felt it was a matter of honor to show the uniform, and undoubtedly would have anointed Jake honorary coronet and flag carrier if they had a second ensign for their unit.

Jake was thankful that the late Major Johnson had supplied him with such a powerful horse; his own stomach was starting to ache from hunger but the animal seemed to have not a care in the world, gliding through the narrow path with an ease that Pegasus would have envied. The route, climbing steadily upwards, appeared to have been worn from a crevice in the hillside, strewn with massive boulders and flanked by a succession of gnarled trees.

The country they were riding over was among the most beautiful in America. There are some philosophers who hold that Noah's Flood was precipitated by a vast melting of polar ice, which at God's call washed whole civilizations away in its path; if this is so, perhaps that same ice age carved away the canyons of the river, heaving apart the hills much the way the gap in floorboards is widened by freezing water during the winter.

Jake did not realize that they had reached the top of one of those canyon sides until the river appeared below him. The view was so shocking that he felt his breath catch between his ribs, and even his stallion stopped short.

In the first instant, he saw the strong blue ribbon of the Hudson and its frothing surface, the ancient arm of Nature reaching out toward her sister the Atlantic from the north. In the next moment he saw mankind's stubborn expression of power and will, an exertion borne of the proposition that all Americans should be free from tyranny, and a guarantee that Liberty would not be left to wither and die in the New World—the great iron chain that had been stretched across the river.

Let the reader forget everything he knows of chains and rivers. The impression of the scene may be properly formed only after the mind is a complete blank, with distracting preconceptions and mistaken notions banished.

Draw first the muscular body of water, foaming slightly at the edges with the great torrent of water that flows back and forth daily. Then sketch sharp lines of gray and black at the borders, angry boulders and rocks heaped among the bits of green and brown at the water's boundary. Add the taste and light smell of salt, for the river water here mixes with the sea.

Green—there is much green, since the hills are rugged and the population sparse—dominates the edges of the picture. Huge trees—hemlock and chestnut, oak, evergreen—form a tall brotherhood halfway to heaven, interspersed with smaller but sweeter maple, some birch, and the occasional willow.

Fort Independence lies well behind you and to your left; it cannot be seen because of the topography and trees. Two other forts lie across the river. To the left, there is Fort Clinton, which is not so much a fort as a series of earthworks with ambition. To the right across the Popolopen Creek (and connected by a barely discernible wooden bridge) lies Fort Montgomery. This is more substantial, as befits a place named after the Revolution's first hero, General Robert Montgomery. The general also happens to have been Jake's first mentor, and if one were able to turn back from the sights below and scan Jake's face, the smallest blush and tear might be seen, bare hints of the sad memory of his leader's death. Jake had watched him fall in the dark cliffs below Quebec; the impotence of that moment still rattled his limbs.

Follow the line of the water now, finding the low shoreline just above Fort Montgomery. There is a thick, dotted line drawn diagonally across the river, a large brown ink stain such as one finds on a student's crib sheet for Greek. The mark ebbs upward and downward with the tide. It is thick and muscular but unnatural, and at first glance it appears not to have been made by humans but by some ancient god, Vulcan perhaps, who has decided to upset the order of things.

Closer inspection reveals the line to be marked by sunken tree trunks, hewn into uniform logs. And staring a few seconds more reveals a darkness in the blue waves that links them, a black deeper than the depths, some strength beyond reckoning that can throttle even Vulcan's forge-strengthened arm, holding him in check.

That is the chain. That is the band of iron formed by hundreds of men working for more than a year, around the clock. That is all that stands between the massive British armada even now gathering in New York harbor, and the vulnerable middle country of the American heartland.

You are not fully impressed? Then stare at the banks until you realize that the small specks, the dots tinier than fleas scattered on the banks of the river near the terminal points, are not fleas but men. Wait until the sun's beams ricochet off the river to hit you full force, impressing not themselves but the dark iron barrier into your retina.

"Even though the rebels built it," declared Busch from his horse, "it's an ingenious defense. Not even the Romans could have done better."

"Can anything pass?"

"Nothing," said the captain. "Even to try would be suicide, at least while the forts on the opposite shore are manned. But it blocks the rebels as well as us. You have heard of our galley, the *Dependence*?"

"There was some talk of it at Stoneman's," said Jake, "but I wouldn't know it from Lord Howe's flagship."

"It was a rebel galley we captured in New York. The

ship is able to raid the shores below the chain with impunity, because the rebel sloops can not come south to stop it."

"The rebels have warships on the river?"

"At least two in Poughkeepsie. But they are blocked by the chain."

In fact, the patriot sloops were held back for other reasons—they were not finished, and they had neither crews nor prospects of attracting them. But Jake did not wish to correct the Tory's mistaken impression.

"Does the chain have any weakness?" he asked instead.

"That's what we're here to find out," Busch confided.

Worried a little that they were about to plunge straight off the cliff, Jake nodded. As Busch continued to scan the water below, Jake asked about the guard, making his voice tremble just slightly.

"The drop from the mountain is so severe here the rebels have not bothered to post guards at the terminal point. If we are careful, no one will see us." Busch looked at the sun, well on its westward slide toward the fading hills where Hudson's crew sleeps in final repose, then swung off his horse. "Come. There isn't much time before sunset."

"I don't mean to be impertinent," said Jake, dismounting, "but how in the world is an attack on Salem going to draw away the guard here?"

"So you're a tactician as well as a scholar?"

"I didn't say I was either," answered Jake as he followed Busch, tying his horse to a nearby tree.

"The raid at Salem is not intended to draw the rebels from here, only the troops that would be used as reinforcements. The shifting of their reserves will add to their confusion and make our task easier. Take your guns and sword," said Busch, lifting a saddlebag over his shoulder and starting through the rocky bramble. "Be careful with your footing."

"I thought you said there would be no guards."

"It's best to be prepared." Busch added more lightly, "Don't worry. The soldiers in the area are a ragtag collection of ne'er-do-wells and malcontents, who will run at their own shadows."

Though the ranger captain severely underestimated the personal bravery of many of the soldiers guarding the Highlands, it is true enough that the Continental and militia defenses of the area were not all to be desired. To adequately protect the Highlands, as well as wage war in the Jerseys and Ticonderoga, garrison Boston and Philadelphia, shadow Howe in New York—the reader can see by the verbiage alone that it would require an army several times what has ever been amassed by even the largest power on earth. And naturally, numbers alone will not suffice, as soldiers are only as good as their ammunition and supplies allow them to be.

As strategically important as the Highlands are, they had until this point in the war received somewhat scant attention. General Washington sought to correct this situation by installing one of his boldest generals, Benedict Arnold, to head the department. Arnold, because of that wounded pride that has been his Achilles's heel since the first day of the war, refused. Washington then turned to Old Put, the most experienced soldier of the war, to shore up the defenses and bring in reinforcements.

The task is enormous. At the very moment Jake and Captain Busch began picking their way past berry bushes toward the river, Continental units were marching down double-time from New England to help bolster the defenses. The county militias had been called to alert as well. These last are chronically short of men, having great difficulty raising soldiers.

We will not further interrupt the narrative to describe these problems in detail, nor will we pause to dissect such depressing problems as the small pox epidemic that is sapping the army's strength, for Jake and the captain have reached the edge of a promontory affording a perfect view of the forts across the river—and not quite a clear jump down.

"Is there a path," asked Jake, after they had slid a short distance between the thick gray rocks, "or are we catapulting ourselves?"

"We're doing neither. I only want to sketch the general layout of the battlements." Busch disappeared behind a tree branch, sliding down a small gorge.

Jake hurried after him, half falling, half climbing; he found Busch brushing the dirt from his pants on a small, narrow opening that stood like a platform built on the side of the hill. The view north was cut off by a large rock outcropping, which meant most of the chain could not be seen, but west and south were clearly visible. There were masts off in the distance toward New York—the patriot spy wondered if they were British raiders, waiting for word from Busch.

"We will go down via another route," said Busch, finishing the thought he had started before slipping. "I have to scout the area first. Keep guard." The captain reached into his bag and took out some thick artists' pencils and sketch paper, as if he were about to copy the Pietà at St. Peter's. "There were rumors that the rebels intended to place a boom here, but I do not see one. Can you? Are they building it by the shore?"

It was difficult to tell exactly what was going on near the far shore, and Jake would not have said even if he could tell. He posted himself a few feet away, his carbine ready—though if some Continental group approached, he planned to train it on Busch, not the patriots.

An old, misshapen elm jutted from the edge of the promontory like an overgrown bristle on a hairbrush. It was easy to climb, and Jake soon had a crow's nest overlooking the near hillside. The only thing patrolling the woods between here and the water seemed to be some hawks and a squirrel or two.

The smoke of various encampments to the east and south wended its way lazily in the light afternoon haze. Peekskill, where General Putnam's headquarters were, lay too far inland for Jake to see from here. Likewise unseen, Continental Village, with its munitions depot and barracks, was located further east over the mountain and a little south of their backs.

They were sitting in a perfect, hidden pocket, as isolated and peaceful as the Garden of Eden. The serenity was so tempting, Jake felt it would be easy to forget he was in the middle of a life and death mission, whose success could determine the outcome of the Revolution.

But even Paradise was disturbed after the Fall, and Jake was shaken from his complacency if not the tree by the echoes of angry shouts and thick gunfire.

Sixteen

Wherein, the source of the commotion is discovered, and Squire van Clynne is grossly insulted.

Jake's first instinct was to jump from the tree and seek safer cover. But he quickly realized that the loud volley of musket fire was not only directed toward the river, but had originated nearly a mile away. The sharp, loud crack that made it seem so close was merely a trick of the echo produced by the rock-faced hills surrounding the water.

The patriot spy climbed higher, the tree branches leaning over as he craned southward to get a better view. Busch came running up in the meantime, a pistol in each hand. He put one of the guns down and slid the other into his belt, climbing up after Jake.

From the straining elm, the pair could just make out a small battery of men gathered on the shore to the south, reloading for another volley. But what were they aiming at?

The answer came in the form of a thunderous roar similar to what must have been heard when volcanoes devoured ancient Pompeii. This was followed by a loud whistle, which ended in a tremendous thud, accompanied by a shaking so severe Jake thought an ax blade had struck the tree. A cloud of smoke on the river below the hills pointed the way to the source of the disturbance—it was the *Dependence*, the murderous galley Busch and his men counted on so highly.

The boat was a peculiar beast. Though double-masted with triangular lateen sails, it strode through the waves on a caterpillars' set of oars. At her bow sat a thick, immense pipe, which erupted with fire and black smoke a second time as Jake watched.

The pipe was a 32-pound cannon. Those unversed in the art of sea warfare will perhaps find a single weapon unimpressive. They should know first that, like land cannon, the rating of the weapon is rendered by the size of the shot it typically fires; a 32-pounder fires 32-pound balls, though it can be loaded with shot and other particularly nasty devices designed to obliterate masts, sails, and limbs. The average 32-pounder weighs perhaps 5,750 pounds, and measures a good ten feet. It is an entire order larger than the 24-pounder, which under the French Valliere system is considered the largest practical calibre for a land gun. The *Eagle,* the most potent ship in the British American fleet—and the admiral's flagship— could mount her 32-pounders only on the very bottom of the vessel; the massive ship quite shuddered when those guns spoke.

Small wonder the rangers at Stoneman's had compared the galley to a fire-breathing dragon. St. George faced easier foes.

Naturally, the British could not have designed and built such a successful and deadly vessel. The *Dependence*— then named the *Independence*—was captured by the perfidious English during their siege of New York. Refitted and manned by British marines as well as seamen, she roamed the lower Hudson at will. Just at this moment, she was raining her shells in the general vicinity of Peekskill, much to the consternation of the local militiamen.

Even though it was too far to see them, the soldiers' affiliation was obvious. They yelled and cursed aloud and fired volley after useless volley, never in unison, wasting their valuable powder and shot.

"Excellent," said Busch in a hushed whisper. "We're right on schedule. Major Johnson could not meet us, but his portion of the plan has been put into effect."

"Do you think he was captured like the corporal?"

"Most likely he'll be waiting for us aboard the *Richmond,*" said Busch. "You probably helped him escape."

"I'm glad," said Jake, who would have been happier

still had he been able to "help" Johnson before he'd arranged the operation.

The battle proceeded as if a stage play. The militiamen stopped shooting, finally realizing that their bullets weren't even reaching the river, let alone their target—or perhaps they ran out of powder. The battery at Fort Independence and several across the river had about the same effect. The *Dependence,* meanwhile, continued to give birth to a series of earth-shaking eruptions. The sounds of disarray—and retreat—echoed throughout the valley.

"They're going ashore!" yelled Busch, descending a few feet in the tree and then jumping to the ground. "Let's go, Smith; we've no time to lose."

We will let Jake and his Tory captain climb down from their trees as we travel several miles eastward, where we left the good squire Claus van Clynne attempting to recover from the effects of Major Dr. Keen's drug. The Dutchman has made considerable progress since we were last with him, managing to select the proper direction to return to the Loaded with Mischief Inn, where his horse was still tied.

He did not make it to the inn, however. Instead, he came upon a company of soldiers under the command of Colonel Israel Angell, members of the same unit whom Jake and the Dutchman had met the day before. The three Rhode Islanders forming the advance guard were more interested in finding food than enemy soldiers, and at first ignored what appeared to be the drunken shouts of a wayward madman. But van Clynne, even in a dazed mental state, is nothing if not persistent—he grabbed one of the young soldiers by the tatter of his worn coat and demanded to be taken immediately to his commander.

"Or there will be hell to pay. Hell to pay, and at a high interest rate!" thundered the Dutchman.

"We'll shoot you if you don't let go of Christian," said one of the privates as the main body of troops drew near.

"Shoot away!" declared van Clynne. "You will be killing as loyal a patriot as the war has ever known, but shoot! Shoot! Go ahead, do your dirty deed. I command it!"

He let go of the soldier and grabbed another's musket by the barrel, pointing it straight at his heart—or more accurately, the thick purse protecting his heart. The poor boy—he had not yet seen his sixteenth birthday, though he swore to his captain he was over eighteen—began trembling.

"I do not understand why you feel obliged to cockade your hats so," said van Clynne, addressing the captain after letting go of the gun. "My friend Jake Gibbs likes to do so as well. What is it about those corners that attracts you?"

Christian, the soldier whom van Clynne had first accosted, took advantage of van Clynne's momentary interest in hats to leap on his back, hoping to wrestle him to his knees. Acting purely from reflex, with no harm intended—he made a protracted point of this later—van Clynne flipped the private over into the officer in front of him, sending them both in a tumble.

"Stop now, or we'll shoot," commanded a sergeant.

"Please," said van Clynne. "I only want to be taken to your commander. It is of utmost importance. I have papers, I know the mark of the Secret Service—it is on my companion's money belt, a Masonic symbol. He's lost it now, but I would know it if I saw it. And of course, I am Dutch, which should leave no doubt as to my allegiance. I have lately spent some time fooling the English, and done an excellent job of it—take me to your commander, I say!"

"You promise to leave off attacking us if I take you there?"

"Attack?" Van Clynne whirled around suddenly. "Who is attacking us? Where? How? Man the battlement! Rally the troops! Protect the strongboxes!"

The confusion continued for a few minutes longer, as van Clynne fought off the lingering effects of the drug. In truth, his befuddlement was mild in proportion to the strength of the concoction, and should have been of great clinical interest to the author of the potion, Major Dr. Keen.

But Keen, who not coincidentally was witnessing this spectacle from the nearby woods, was interested in something else. For the Dutchman's shouts had made it quite clear which side he was on.

"An interesting adversary," said the doctor as the troop fell back. Keen brushed some brambles from his coat and walked to his carriage, only a few hundred yards away. The size of the rebel force meant he would have to postpone apprehension of the Dutchman, but he was pleased to have determined his loyalties so easily. The man's clever antidote, whatever it was, had only shortened the effects and placed them in reverse.

"We will have to construct a most peculiar way for him to die," Keen said to Percival, directing him to hide the carriage and follow along by foot.

"You're Dutch? Then how can you be on our side?"

"How could a Dutchman be on the side of the British, who robbed our birthright, stole our land, and contaminated our best ale?" protested van Clynne as he stood before Colonel Israel Angell.

A man of average build with a light face and auburn hair nearly hidden by a dignified white wig, the colonel stood straighter than a fresh ramrod as he interrogated the Dutchman in the small hovel that served as Second Rhode Island headquarters.

"No insult intended," said Angell, whose blue eyes and Roman nose gave him an almost Caesar-like presence. "But you must admit, if we were to use the Philpse family as an example—"

"The Philpses are imposters and traitors to their race," thundered van Clynne, who face turned bright red at the mention of the aristocratic family. "They stole the rights to their land from Jonkheer Van der Donck and his descendants in a most despicable manner. There is not a more criminal clan in all of New York. It grieves me to say this, sir, about a family purported to have Dutch blood in them, but if the Philpses have not made a pact with the devil, then the devil does not exist."

Van Clynne was so adamant in his denunciation that the amused Angell had to take a step backwards. A neutral observer might have found his claims somewhat exaggerated, though it cannot be denied that Frederick

Philpse had lately spent time in a Connecticut jail for his impudent support of the British cause. Two hundred and seventy families, along with thirty-one slaves, lived in medieval bondage to the rapacious family, whose main house lay near the intersection of the Saw Mill and the Albany Post Road near the Hudson—a shameful situation in a democratic land, van Clynne asserted.

The squire's ire cooled when Angell asked if he would like some ale. The colonel's experience had shown that a man who began angry could be calmed by drink, while a calm one would likely undergo the opposite effect. "We have some beer brewed by a local housewife," he suggested.

More magical words could not have been uttered, and van Clynne was soon not merely calm but in jolly form. The beer was a top-fermented ale that had a deep redness to it which under other circumstances van Clynne might have inquired after, since the only housewife in these parts who made such a brew was a certain Margaret Schenck. But business was pressing.

"You must send a detachment of soldiers to the Great Chain immediately," said van Clynne. "I have it on the best authority that the British are planning a massive attack on it this very evening."

"An attack? Who told you this?"

"None other than the Revolution's finest spy, my assistant, Lieutenant Colonel Jake Gibbs," said van Clynne. "I sent the good man out on a mission to break up a nefarious ring of Tory salt stealers, and he came up with this piece of intelligence for me."

The reader will be spared, as Colonel Angell was not, Claus van Clynne's narrative of his role in winning the Revolution single-handedly. While Angell realized he must discount by half everything van Clynne said, that division still left plenty of concern for the chain. And so on his authority two companies of men were mustered and sent marching triple time north to the river, told explicitly to brook no interruptions or diversion, and to fight to the death anyone who threatened the defenses.

Seventeen

Wherein, Jake is an unwitting guest at a brief family reunion.

Busch rode his horse at a quick pace through the woods despite the high undergrowth and looming rocks, plunging toward a narrow road on the northeastern foot of the mountain. He wove his way downward too carefully for his speed to be the product of mere haste or excitement; Jake, struggling along behind him, realized that Busch knew these mountainous woods better than most men know their own homes. The sun was now steadily sinking, and the slant of the landscape meant the ground before them was in heavy shadow. Nonetheless, the Tory's pace continued to increase until Jake lost sight of him. With only sound to guide them, horse and rider followed blindly, branches and bushes grazing their sides as they rode.

Busch was waiting at the edge of the road, his horse barely winded.

"We will have to trespass on a farmer's acres to reach the chain," he said. "He'll shoot us if he sees us."

"He's a rebel?" asked Jake, who was as thankful as his horse for the rest.

"It has nothing to do with the war. He's quite mad, and has been that way for ten years. This is the safest route, though, since the rebels avoid his land. It's a pitiful hard-scrabble farm, strewn with rocks and lying on a sheltered nick of the hillside. The ground is treacherous, and there are two vicious dogs. Be careful about your horse. Ready?"

"Ready."

"Let's go then," said Busch, and he set off in a gallop down the road. Jake's horse was more comfortable on this comparatively level ground and he caught up with Busch. They rode side by side until they came to a field on the west side of the road. Once more the Tory dug his heels into his horse's flanks, steering the beast toward the low fence to his left. The animal bounded the rails as if they were twigs on the ground. Jake followed, urging his mount to do the same; the pair were soon flying across the dimly lit pasture toward a small orchard that overlooked the river. It was here that Jake heard the farmer's shouts, and then saw from the corner two black streaks heading in their direction.

The reader is no doubt acquainted with Hercules, who during his many labors came face to face with the giant Eurytion and his two-headed dog. The animals chasing Jake and Captain Busch had but one head apiece, yet they were nearly as fierce, snarling and snapping as they ran. They were also extremely fast, and though the two horsemen had the advantage of a head start, the pursuers gained on their winded mounts with every step.

Jake pushed his stallion faster, flattening himself against the animal's neck and urging it onward. His helmet strap broke with the jostling and the wind groped at his head, swirling its tangled fingers through his hair. The horse's body had turned hot beneath him, convulsing with each footfall, nearing the end of its endurance and strength. Jake dove tighter to its neck, trying at once to soothe it and urge it faster. The pair went over a small hedge and into an open field, but still the dogs came on. Their yaps and growls mixed with the pounding of hooves and the rush of air in Jake's ears, as if hell itself were closing behind him.

All at once he felt himself flying forward: one of the dogs had thrown itself at the stallion's legs.

The ground came up before Jake could properly prepare for it; his chin bashed hard and he felt a floating sensation in his brain.

His horse tumbled over in a somersault. It broke both its neck and a leg in the fall, but managed somehow to cling to life, screaming its agony in a wrenching whine.

The dog that had thrown itself at its legs had broken its ribs and gotten its muzzle mashed, but its venom was hardly choked; it raked its front claws on the horse's vulnerable stomach, trying to inflict more damage, unfazed by the injured animal's weak kicks.

The other dog descended on Jake, who had just risen to his knees when the demon barreled into his back. Still dazed, he had just enough sense to fall forward, trying to protect his neck. The dog raked its snout back and forth across his head, looking for an opening. These were not teeth, they were the hot fire of a glass furnace, withering all before them. The fangs slashed at the side of Jake's neck, ripping through the fleshy part of his earlobe; he just managed to duck enough to throw off the dog's aim as it clamped down, so that the animal ended up with his ponytail instead of his throat.

The hound growled as Jake shook himself free momentarily, spinning the black, furious shadow to the ground. In a flash it had rebounded back at him, stronger and more furious than ever, and for a brief second Jake felt the cold, wet sensation in the pit of his stomach he had felt only once before—on the cold cliffs near Quebec, when a redcoat's ball had taken him through the leg and he feared it was his turn to die.

But just as the animal clamped its jaws into Jake's side, a shot exploded next to his ear. The dog let go and Jake rolled backwards and onto his knees, catching his breath and steadying himself, his body still shaking from the fight.

Busch's bullet had gone straight through the animal's head. What had been a ball of fury moments before transformed instantly to a supine ball of fur lying peacefully on the ground.

Because of the ferocity of its attack, Jake would not have been surprised to find that the dog was a vicious hound bred from the wild beasts of deepest Africa. The reality was considerably diferent; it appeared to be one of the breed used in Scotland and Ireland to help herd sheep, an animal normally well known for its tame attitude toward humans. The warp of tyranny is not limited to human beings; all living things are twisted so strongly by it that they may turn against their own nature.

Jake's horse was writhing in agony on the ground a few yards away. He took the musket from the saddle holster and dispatched it quickly; it was the only way he could repay the animal's fine service. The stallion's murderer lay at its feet, already dead; Jake could not stop himself from smashing its skull with the butt-end of the gun in a burst of mad fury.

"Hurry," said Busch. "The farmer will be on the way with his guns. Take your weapons and jump on."

Jake threw his pistol in the saddle pouch and slung it over his shoulder. He grabbed his carbine and sword and picked up the musket from the ground but then realized he couldn't carry everything and still hold on to Busch. Taking the bag and the carbine in one hand, he pulled himself up with the other, clinging to the captain's coat as they rode away.

Busch plunged down the hillside toward a stone wall. He followed that to a wooded path leading to the river. This he rode down a good distance before finally slowing, confident that the farmer was no longer following them.

"At least the bastard has lost his dogs," said Busch. "That's some consolation. Are you all right?"

"We're even now," said Jake. "You've saved my life, and I yours." In the rush of the moment, the American patriot spoke completely from the heart; he could not feel animosity toward the man, though it soon might be his duty to kill him.

"I told you," laughed Busch. "We're brothers beneath the skin."

"I hope the dogs weren't rabid." Jake winced as he felt around his torn earlobe. He was otherwise intact and not permanently harmed.

"The man looked after the animals like they were his children," said Busch. "The beasts were probably healthier than either of us."

"How do you know?"

"The man is my father," replied Busch.

*   *   *

Such a remark would seem to warrant an immediate explanation, but the Tory captain offered none as he guided the horse through the woods. It was clear to Jake that they had circled around the large mountain that guarded the eastern approach to the chain, so that they had landed behind it; they were now heading south toward the terminus.

The path became so narrow and the way so dark that the two men finally dismounted and left the horse tied to a tree. Using a torch was out of the question; the light would have drawn attention from the forts across the river and any Continental units nearby. Given the desolate hillside they were now approaching, even a half-sleeping sentry would realize anything brighter than a firefly was out of place.

"My sister and I walked this path many nights," said Busch, stopping suddenly. "We loved to sneak down to the river when the moon was out and take a midnight swim. My parents would have beaten us to an inch of our lives if they'd found out—that was part of the attraction, I suspect. Here we climb down the rocks. It's steep but it will save us considerable time. Can you handle this?"

"Yes."

"Leave your carbine. It'll only get in the way. There are no guards at the edge of the chain."

"Are you sure?"

"We were above here, see?" Busch pointed in the dark. "It was the first thing I looked for. Besides, a sentry would have a small fire. There's still a bit of light on the river, but the land is dark."

"Perhaps they're waiting for us."

"If they're that clever," said Busch, starting down, "they deserve to capture us. Come on now, be your brave self. You've passed the rough part."

Jake nodded. He as not going down unarmed—he quickly and carefully tucked his uncocked but loaded pistol in his belt at the front of his pants. The Segallas, meanwhile, was secured beneath his shirt; the elk knife lay in its sheath tucked into his boot.

As Busch had boasted earlier, there were no guards on the eastern terminus of the chain because the terrain was so nearly impassable. Certainly the only reason Jake was able to descend to the shoreline a few hundred yards upstream from it was the fact that he had a guide who had been slinking down this way since childhood. Even so, the last hundred feet to the river bank were nearly as frightening as the tumble on the ground under the dog's fangs. The rocks were wet and slimy, covered with spray as well as vegetation. Jake felt his foot give way, and only Busch's strong arms, grabbing Jake as he slid past, saved him.

"Don't fall," whispered Busch. "The rocks at the bottom are as sharp as ax heads."

It seemed beyond belief that children would come this way, but then in innocence everyone is brave.

"It's much easier if you have small hands and feet," said Busch, as if hearing Jake's thoughts. "You can poke them into the crevices. Takes longer, though."

The river was gently tickling the shoreline, eliciting a soft murmur from the rocks. Jake went slower and slower as his guide went faster and faster; the distance widened between them over the last twenty treacherous feet, and the disguised patriot reached bottom a full five minutes after his guide.

Bush was standing at the edge of the water. Just as Jake was about to apologize for taking so long, the captain waved his hand in front of his face and pointed out to the river. It was a moment or two before Jake could make out the shadow three-quarters of the way across.

It was a whaleboat, patrolling the water just north of the chain. The men inside were resting silently.

Busch and Jake stood like statues on the rocks for a minute that seemed like three hours. The night grew immeasurably colder in that time, dampness welling into the air. A fog began to form and the last hint of twilight disappeared. Jake's ears adjusted to the stillness so well he could hear the whispers of the soldiers in the boat, or thought he could; certainly he heard the order, "All right then, back to the fort." The oars slipped into the water and the shadow receded into the larger blackness.

"A last patrol as the sun finally sets," noted Busch. "Just before they light the watch fires, I suspect." He started picking his way along the bank. "That will be easy to time. Hold on to the tail of my coat. Be very careful."

The rocks were slippery, but twisted trees and other brush gave them handholds, and they soon were within a hundred yards of the chain. The logs holding it up creaked continually, moaning under the weight of the iron and complaining of the tide. The chain itself creaked like hinges on a door, except that the sound was multiplied many times; the effect was something like a team of waterwheels might make, if built entirely of iron and made to operate at an excruciatingly slow speed, each squeak and creak amplified by a succession of paper tubes.

The chain links had been finished and placed in the water the previous November. At first, the current proved so strong that they snapped and were pulled downstream. Finally, the engineer for the project, Lieutenant Thomas Machin, realized that with certain slight modifications, the chain would hold if placed on a diagonal from its western terminus, in effect running with the strongest current.

It happened that Jake had met Machin in Boston a few years before; the lieutenant had been among the "Indians" engaged in the famous tea party. Their acquaintanceship was extremely brief, and would not amount to much now—Machin was undoubtedly in a warm bed on the opposite shore, while Jake was starting to shiver with the cold on these rocks.

Busch stopped in front of him, and Jake realized he was studying something on the ground, unrelated to the chain.

"Come on," he said finally, pulling off his coat. "We shall see if the links are of equal strength and look for obstructions. We'll go out on the river."

Before Jake could protest, Captain Busch took off his boots and dove into the river, aiming for the heavy chain and its log support bobbing a few leagues out in the water. He moved quickly, as if afraid to dwell along the shoreline.

Jake would have much preferred to stay there, but saw no way to do so without being branded a coward. It

seemed foolhardy to swim out in the darkness and climb
aboard a fitful line of wheezing rafts. Yet had he stopped
and thought about it, he would have realized he'd done
many less rational things in the name of Freedom—Jake
quickly stripped to his breeches and shirt, leaving his guns
in his boots. Armed only with the knife, which he tucked
inside his belt, he got down on his hands and knees and
half-stumbled, half-swam off the rocks toward the dark
iron backbone of the Americans' river defense.

Three yards out and the water grabbed him with a sudden jolt, hurling him downstream at the obstruction.

"Keep your hands ahead of you," shouted Busch,
who'd already reached the chain. "Use your hands on the
logs."

Easily said, but as strong as Jake was, he had trouble
with the tricky eddy in the frigid water, just managing to
get his arms up in front of his body as he hit the raft
support about mid-chest. With a loud groan, he pulled
himself onto the logs, grateful to get at least part of his
body out of the sharp and icy current.

"Imagine the riptides further out," said Busch, standing over him.

"Thanks, but I'll leave that to you."

"Those must be the fire rafts," Busch whispered, pointing across toward Fort Montgomery. The hulking log
boats were framed in front of a series of sentry fires the
night patrols had just lit to keep themselves warm by the
chilly river.

"The fires make it difficult for them to see us," said
Busch. "And besides, who would suspect that anyone had
snuck out onto the river? We can rest here for a while.
Look at how thick this chain is."

"It seems very strong," said Jake, sinking his hand
down to feel around the iron. The metal pieces were just
under two inches thick, folded into links. "How are we
going to break them?"

"We'll manage," said Busch.

Jake thought of several possibilities—an explosive
charge, a hammer and chisel, an immense file. Each had
its difficulties—but none were impossible.

"At least the boom has not been constructed," said

Busch. "Come, there was a float damaged further out a month ago; let's see if it has been repaired."

As Jake followed into the vast hollow between the banks, his thoughts turned to increasing the chain's protection. The farmer's land could be occupied, and some way found to place a guard on the shoreline where they had descended. Instead of sending a rowboat out on a precursory inspection, several small boats would have to be posted on twenty-four-hour guard. A vessel should be stationed in the middle of the river, with lookouts on each side—and sharpshooters, too, so another mission such as this one would prove fatal.

The log rafts were spaced and constructed unevenly, so that even if they had not been shuddering back and forth, moving on them would have been haphazard at best. Nonetheless, Jake soon developed a method of proceeding that was a cross between crawling and swimming, and if it were not for the cold waves—while it was June, this water had originated high in the Catskill mountains weeks if not months before—he might have been tempted to enjoy his foray. The sensation of being nearly naked on the river, without boat or paddle, was like none he had experienced. He began to wonder if mermaids' calls to sailors might not be made out of their innocent bliss, for truly to float atop the water unfettered must seem like an ecstasy one could only wish to share with all around.

Busch had stopped ahead on a raft that had been used as a workman's station. He sat cross-legged with the water lapping at his thighs, as if he were some new species of waterborne Indian chief.

"There's a float just to our right that is missing some logs," he said when Jake arrived. His voice seemed far away.

"Will we attack there?"

If Busch heard Jake's words, he did not acknowledge them. "My sister died at the spot where we entered the water," he answered instead. "That is why my father became a madman."

His voice had a distant quality that made it sound as if

he were talking about something he had read, rather than lived.

"We came down here one night when my sister was thirteen. I was twelve. It was a brilliant harvest moon that night, and the water was warm. You would not know it from tonight, but the Hudson is often warm, most warm —you feel as if you are swimming in a bath.

"She slipped, and hit her head on the rocks. Her body came down all the way and fell into the river, but the current was not hard, and it washed up there, near where they have fastened the chain. If it were light we might even see the rock where I found her.

"I called for hours, hoping. When I found her body, I just . . . held her, hoping she would be alive, that it was a dream, a terrible dream."

Eighteen

Wherein, Jake and the captain return to shore, with poor consequences.

The two men sat without speaking, the sounds from the far shore drifting over with the wind. Jake heard the guards grumbling curses about the food and weak tea. Where was the rum, one man asked.

"My mother threw herself off the rocks six months later," said Busch quietly. "My father has been twisted ever since. It's a pitiful story, isn't it, Smith? A cursed man and a cursed family."

As strongly as he reminded himself that the man sitting near him was an enemy engaged on a mission aimed at the heart of his country, Jake could not help but feel a pang of pity and even regret. There must be some way of converting this tortured and yet worthy soul to the Cause of Freedom, screamed Jake's heart. His head answered firmly that no such chance could be taken. Soon, the circumstances would demand that Busch be killed, or if not killed, arrested, which would amount to the same thing—any patriot court would surely hang him.

He should be killed here, now; it would be a mercy.

"Come on," said Busch, moving toward him, "we must be getting back. Our mission here is complete."

The Tory captain touched Jake's shoulder, unaware of the argument raging inside him. Jake looked up and caught the reflection of friendship in his eyes, and that as much as anything decided him—if he did not act now, he might never do so. But as he was about to toss the Tory over the side of the raft, he realized he did not yet know when or how the attack would be launched, and just as the Tories had gone on without Johnson, they would undoubtedly go on without Busch.

Whether the argument would have held him back under other circumstances, it did so now; Jake silently followed Busch toward shore.

The night had grown even colder, and the patriot felt his teeth starting to chatter. A good bottle of rum would be most welcome now, or even some of his friend van Clynne's favorite ale.

The rafts rocked more violently the closer they got to shore. Now the dark shadows that loomed ahead assumed eerie shapes of children and women, long arms grabbing out toward them, hair floating in the murky water. Jake stumbled on the wet wood, and for a moment felt the cold grip of the night plunge its icy fingers inside his chest and grab at his heart.

He lost his balance and fell forward into the water, his head crashing against the stonelike hardness of the barrier. He struggled, but in the darkness he slipped beneath the logs, and now found his way to the surface barred. In the dark water he saw the faces of the men he had watched die: his friend Captain Thomas, Lieutenant Colmbs, Horace Brown, and a host of nameless fellow patriots and countless British swam in the river, their souls seeking the shore. He already had swallowed two mouthfuls of water when he felt a sudden force take him and thrust him sideways, as if God himself had intervened to save him and preserve the Cause.

Not God, but Busch. The Tory hauled him to the surface and then paddled on his back to the shore, dragging Jake behind like a helpless child.

"Thank you," the American spy managed after he had finally cleared the water from his lungs.

"Now you owe me a life," said Busch cheerfully. "Come, we've made a bit more noise than we ought to have."

They walked back along the shoreline to their clothes and boots without waiting for their breeches to dry. The path they had taken down was too treacherous to climb up in the dark; Busch took his pistols and prodded Jake to follow him as he walked northward.

The action of the tides here had produced a small ledge of sand along the waterside, punctuated by large boulders and debris. The way was not easy, and Jake worried that it would take so long he would miss his rendezvous with van Clynne. He wondered also if Putnam had increased the defenses, though he realized that the diversions and the geography would conspire to leave any simple multiplication of forces impotent against the Tory designs. Indeed, if the attack were launched from this direction, an entire army could be waiting south of the chain, with about as much value as a barnful of milkless cows.

"This will bring us out near the road, and we will have to sneak back through my father's orchard to get to the horse," Busch said when they finally left the shoreline. "It is in full view of the house, but he will be sleeping by now. In any event, he is much less fearsome without his dogs. Perhaps I should have killed them years ago."

Jake had hardly taken two steps before he sank in mud well over his ankle. If Busch was following a path through this swamp, he failed to see it, yet the Tory captain made quick progress, turning and stopping every few minutes to let Jake catch up.

"It's only a bit more through this," said Busch. "Then we have solid ground and a hill."

"Are we bringing the forces through this swamp when we attack tomorrow?" asked Jake.

"No, the attack will be on the water," confided Busch. "Only a small force will go against the chain itself; our rangers and the marines will land near Peekskill as a diversion. I will explain it all, in good time. Let's go."

Jake now had all the information he needed about the Tory plan, and no excuse not to kill Busch. But how could he murder a man who only minutes before had saved him from drowning?

Jake followed along quietly until he caught his foot in the muck and fell face first into the swamp. He was by now so cold his joints felt frozen solid. "I hope we will have some device that allows us to see in the dark when we attack tomorrow night," he said, righting himself.

"You are starting to sound like a complainer, Smith,"

said Busch. "What happened to the brave man I found at the tavern?"

"He got cold and hungry, and a good deal wet."

"We'll be by a fire soon enough," said Busch. "If we cannot find a hospitable inn, we've only to return to Stoneman's."

Finally they reached dry ground. The Tory captain started up the steep incline like an African monkey. Jake made better progress here, and found that the quick pace warmed him. They soon reached a lane, and began walking south once more.

"This path leads to the road in front of the house. The roadway is just around that turn," said Busch, whose steps started to slow.

"Do you ever think of confronting your father, and asking his forgiveness?"

"I have, many times," said Busch. "He does not seem to recognize me. Something in his head has broken, and he would as soon shoot as say a word. He has tried to shoot me, in fact."

The words were no sooner out of his mouth than they heard noises ahead. Busch put up his hand and motioned Jake toward the trees at the side of the roadway. They waited in the darkness for a moment, then began slowly creeping forward.

Jake now wanted an opportunity to leave Busch without arousing his suspicions; he planned to go to his rendezvous with van Clynne, then return to Stoneman's and sabotage the plans as a member of the troop. The noises were just the thing—Busch's father must have come out to avenge his dogs' death.

But Busch's father wasn't waiting for them around the bend.

Claus van Clynne and a detachment of Rhode Islanders were.

"There they are, men! Capture the Tory traitors so we can wrap them in tissue for General Putnam!"

"I see one!"

"Watch, there's a whole brigade of them behind!"

"Halt or we fire! Halt, I say!"

The reader undoubtedly will credit Claus van Clynne with great mental powers of prognostication for his ability to scope the precise point where Jake and his Tory captain would emerge from their spying jaunt. The Dutchman would do his best to encourage this, though the true story of his fortuitous arrival at this juncture of our story is less flattering. For Colonel Angell had grown tired of van Clynne's endless diatribe regarding the conduct of the war, and had sought to get him out of his wigged hair by assigning him and a squad of men to the spot along the river he felt least likely to be attacked. In fact, the colonel might have had some hope that old man Busch—well known to the patriot commanders, if only from a distance —might be provoked into taking several shots at the Dutchman. Not that Angell wished him any real harm, but van Clynne provoked in him that double reaction he so often had on people—on the one hand, his service to the Cause of Freedom was indispensable and undeniable, and on the other hand, he had a way about him so annoying even the mildest of Jesus's apostles might be tempted toward murder.

The soldiers who had accompanied van Clynne to the area seized the opportunity to attack the shadowy figures ahead at least partly because they had grown tired of the Dutchman's lecture on the possibilities of screw-fitted breech-loading rifles. Thus their attack was premature, and both Busch and Jake were able to duck back safely into the woods, escaping their ill-aimed fire.

Unaware that van Clynne was nearby, Jake ran next to Busch when the firing started, but gradually began to drop back. A bullet whizzed dangerously close to him in the underbrush, and he dove to his right, getting an armful of prickle weeds as his reward.

"Smith?"

"I'm all right," he hissed at Busch, rising to his feet.

"This way," said the Tory captain. "Go straight over the hill. I'll wait for you there if we get separated. Forget about the horse. I know where there are others."

Jake continued to stumble forward, letting Busch increase his lead. The fire from the Continentals—who surely could not see well enough to aim, except at the noise—was remarkably hot and dangerously close. He wanted to make his feigned escape attempt look convincing, but not so convincing that he was wounded, and so Jake found it necessary to run further into the woods than he otherwise would have wished.

At length, he realized he had lost Busch. But as there was no way of knowing whether the captain was hiding in the shadows just a few feet away, he had to arrange his capture carefully. He continued to move in the general direction the Tory had indicated, meandering as if lost. The troops, meanwhile, had brought up torches and spread out to search the woods. A throb from his knee, which had been injured a few days before, suggested a perfect plan—he would complain about the knee loudly when found, in case Busch should overhear.

If Jake was unaware of van Clynne's presence, the Dutchman was equally ignorant of his quarry's identity. He had been left alone by the roadside, without even a flint to light the wood gathered for a fire, when his troop first ran to investigate the noises in the woods.

"Probably just a raccoon," grumbled the Dutchman to the darkness. But when it became clear that his men weren't returning, he decided to set out after them. He was quite surprised when he found the company—or one member, at least—almost immediately, walking straight into the soldier and knocking him to the ground.

Or would have, except that the man was bigger even than van Clynne, and so it was the Dutchman who found himself floundering in the dust, propelled there not merely by the surprise of having walked into the man but by a sharp blow as well.

"You idiot, I'm on your side," said the Dutchman. "Help me up. Come on, be quick about it."

"Do as he says, Phillip. After all, it would be too easy to kill him here."

The voice had a sickeningly familiar ring to it, instantly recognized by van Clynne. It belonged to Major Dr. Keen.

Nineteen

Wherein, Jake becomes acquainted with the inside of a patriot jail.

*I*t took the Rhode Islanders nearly a half hour to find Jake in the dark underbrush. By that time, he had decided to take off his green coat, following the theory that a real Tory would have done so, trying to escape as a civilian. Still fearful that Busch was hiding nearby, Jake not only groaned about his knee but noisily protested that he had done nothing wrong. He submitted to a search, which turned up his pistol and elk-handled knife, though not the Segallas, thanks to Jake's loud complaints that he would freeze if made to turn over the waistcoat where it was hidden. Eventually, he was allowed to keep the vest, and led from the dark woods in his damp breeches.

At the roadside, his hands were bound and a long rope attached to his leg so he could not run without dragging half the company with him.

"Where is the rest of your troop?" demanded a short corporal, whose cheek had been seared some time ago by a sword or bayonet point.

"What troop?" responded Jake.

"The troop you were intending to assault the chain with, Tory."

"I have no troop," said Jake. "I was not assaulting the chain."

"What were you doing here then?"

"I am a traveler, on my way to White Plains. I had no money to stay at an inn, and tried sleeping in the woods, until you assaulted me. There is no law against that yet."

The reader can well imagine the contempt with which

the corporal met this story. Jake nonetheless stuck to it loudly, and embellished it slightly for their lieutenant, a thin rod of a twenty-year-old who soon appeared from the woods. Without a uniform, the officer must treat Jake as a civilian and hand him over to the civil authorities—or decide he was a spy and shoot him on the spot.

Fortunately, the man seemed inclined toward the former, and Jake kept up his charade as he was marched up the road, in case Busch was still in earshot. The Rhode Islanders were rather pleased with themselves for having captured a man they assumed would eventually be judged a Tory criminal. They celebrated by prodding and pulling him along, greasing his way with epithets and curses, along with a good number of promises of what would become of him if their commander dared to turn his back a few minutes.

Under other circumstances, this show of spirit would have warmed Jake's heart, restoring his high opinion of the Continental army, or at least these troops, who had been mustered at the state's expense. Just now, however, he could have done with a little less enthusiasm—despite the torches, the path was dark and their pace brisk, which meant that he was continually in danger of falling; the soldiers' bayonets had been well sharpened, and pricked almost as sharply on the back of his neck as the dog's fangs had.

After they passed the hillside where Busch had told him to meet, Jake decided the time had come to reveal himself as an American officer. He had left the small glass token identifying himself as a messenger back at Prisco's for safety during his adventure; there was little chance the common soldiers would have realized what it meant in any event. His only hope was to persuade them to take him to their colonel, who would recognize him immediately.

But he must do all of this discreetly, in case the Tory leader was still hiding nearby. Jake stumbled in the dark and rolled on the ground as if he had fallen. Prodded by a pair of bayonets, he groaned about his knee. "Get the lieutenant," he whispered between the louder complaints. "I have to talk to him. Quickly."

The soldiers answered him in a loud voice that he must get to his legs himself or be run through.

"The lieutenant, quickly," hissed Jake. "Pretend to hit me, so that I lie unconscious. I have to see your colonel."

"We'll hit you for real, Tory!" shouted one of the men.

The other added threats and insults of his own. Jake got to his knees.

"I'm a patriot, you idiot," he hissed.

The soldier responded with a heavy curse which would undoubtedly have elicited a like response from Jake—had he heard it. For one of the guards had decided he had suffered enough lies that night from the Tory villain, and smashed Jake across the back of the head with the butt of his rifle, sending him to Sleep's lush vale.

Jake awoke with a start as he was dumped unceremoniously on the dirt from the back of a wagon the Continentals had commandeered to transport him. He had been unconscious for nearly two hours, during which time the soldiers had taken him to a small hamlet east of Continental Village and north of Cortlandville. Largely ruined during a side skirmish related to the Battle of White Plains, the hamlet had once included a church, two stores and a small mill, set up on the creek. All but the church had been destroyed, though the wooden-planked bridge in front of the church's graveyard lately had been restored.

Besides the church, a large barn nearby remained intact; it was now used as common property by the few inhabitants who remained in the three or four houses across the creek on the main road.

While the area was familiar—Jake realized as he shook his head clear that he had come this way searching for Stoneman's farm—there was no time to wax nostalgic. His hands still bound behind his back, he was lifted from the dust roughly and dragged to the church.

His mother would have expressed no surprise over this, but he was not on his way to a service. The building had been appropriated by the Committee Against Conspiracies to be used as a prison for suspected Tories; the guard at the door received him with a ceremonial curse and a threat against his person if he did not comply with all the rules and regulations of the jail.

Still groggy, Jake protested that he was innocent.

"Save your story for Mr. Jay," said the jailer. "He'll hear your case next week. In meantime, you'd best watch your manners inside. As big as you are, there's them who are bigger."

And with that, the man put his foot on the disguised patriot's back and propelled him inside the open door, to the great amusement of his escorts.

When it had been used for services, the interior of the church had been simple, its most lavish ornamentation a thick red carpet that ran down the center of the austere wooden rows. A small lectern was mounted at one side of the altar, itself made of wood. Now that it had become a jail, its decor was plainer still. The furniture was gone, except for a few pieces gathered in a pile at the side of the interior. The carpet remained in place, dividing the room in two; even in the dim light supplied by some candles in buckets at the side of the room it was still a dark if soiled red, and gave the impression of a tongue resting in a mouth.

The long, narrow windows had been filled by boards that ran nearly to the ceiling. A pump organ, once the pride of the small congregation, still stood in the choir, but the door to this balcony was boarded and nailed shut. Heaps of bare hay were scattered along the walls, each topped with a ragged blanket—beds for the accused. A tumble of basins and pipes—amazingly, they seemed to be some sort of still, and perhaps accounted for the sweet, sick odor—stood at the far end of the altar area.

The church's original congregants had been Loyalists, most of whom fled the neighborhood after the Battle of White Plains. They had now been replaced by a mixture of mild Tories waiting examination, and more difficult men, ruffians and thieves whose allegiance belonged directly to the devil. One of the latter, a large, broad-shouldered fellow with a crooked nose and a strange stench about him, approached Jake menacingly, and said he would cut off his binds for a price.

"How much?" Jake asked, wondering to himself if his pocket pistol was still hidden in his vest.

The man leered without answering. He reached for Jake's hands and sawed through the braided rope as easily as if it were a woman's mending thread.

"I'll take your boots in payment, for starters," said the ham-handed brute. "We can work the rest out as we go."

No blow on the head, no matter how severe, could have made Jake acquiesce to such bullying. He saw that he had a large audience, and recognized at once that all were awed by the Tory giant. They would sooner plunge into a volcano than help Jake.

"These boots will never fit," he answered. "You're a bit fat in all the wrong places, beginning with your head."

The brute gave him a quizzical look in response, not quite sure that he'd been insulted until one or two of the bravest men in the church let their stifled guffaws escape. His lungs began pumping like a pair of hot bellows, forcing his chest larger. His shoulders puffed up as well, and his face turned so red it seemed to glow in the dim light of the church.

"You'll do as I say, or you'll suffer the consequences."

"Where did you ever learn such a big word?" Jake took a half-step backwards, preparing himself.

"I will teach you!" shouted the villain, slashing at Jake. He cut only the air—the patriot spy had dodged backwards. The brute swiped again and Jake retreated once more, this time falling against some members of the audience—who promptly tossed him back toward his tormentor.

Jake dove into a somersault, bringing his foot up to kick the giant in the chest and knocking him backwards. Rolling back over to his feet, the patriot launched another kick but missed; he fell onto his back. The brute dove at him blade first. Jake managed to roll away, sparks glinting from the knife as it scraped into the slate floor. A sharp punch staggered his attacker and sent his weapon to the ground, but the man was built like Goliath and quickly recovered. He managed to catch Jake's boot as he aimed a flying kick at him and hurled the American spy back into one of the onlookers.

Jake had no time to thank him for breaking his fall. The bully grabbed him up with both hands and hurled him again in the opposite direction. Once again a Tory was fortuitously placed, but Jake realized he could not count on such luck a third straight time. He pretended to be stunned until the villain reached down for him in a rage. Then Jake leaped with all his might into the man's chest, knocking him over. Two sharp kicks to the brute's groin ended the fight.

It also initiated wild applause from the onlookers. The man, whose name was Charles Wedget, had tormented them for days, lording it over each of the twenty-odd men here and taking their possessions. Each now took his own kick at him, spitting on the prone body and laughing at its agony. Wedget was quickly tied with the remains of the ropes that he had cut away not only from Jake but his other victims. His fetters increased the animosity toward him, as it could now be vented without fear of rebuttal.

Once he caught his breath, Jake stepped forward to stop the slaughter, saying it was not fair that an injured man be attacked by so many. That argument proved of little deterrence, and it was only when Jake suggested the guards would hear the commotion and investigate that the men began to lower their voices, if not the strength of their blows.

"You're damn awful noble," said a voice from the back shadows.

Jake couldn't quite place the familiar voice until he saw its plump owner step forward.

"Caleb Evans," said Jake. "We feared you were dead."

"It would take more rebels than are gathered in the province to kill me," declared the ranger corporal heartily.

"I'm glad you're alive," lied Jake, clapping him on the shoulder. "We're to be rescued tomorrow. Captain Busch has already planned it."

"Word has reached us," said Caleb. "One of the boys who brings us food is the son of a friend to our cause."

"I wonder," said Jake, picking up Wedget's knife and tucking it into his belt. "Is there a man named Johnson here?"

Caleb shushed him. "All of these men are loyal, but under duress, I doubt most could be trusted. Do not reveal yourself to them; say nothing you would want reported to the rebel courts." In a lower voice, he added, "Johnson missed our rendezvous and I fear he must be dead."

Jake nodded solemnly. No better actor could have been found on a London stage.

"Will the attack on the chain be called off?"

"You don't know Captain Busch very well," said Evans. "Though he talked for an hour about how you saved him."

"He repaid the favor tonight. Twice."

"Then how were you captured?"

"We were surprised afterwards. He escaped."

Caleb nodded, and realizing that some of the others were watching, turned his attention to the fallen bully.

"Take that, you bloody bastard," he said, kicking him.

"You, sir," said one of the Tory prisoners to Jake. "What is your name?"

"Jake Smith."

"We all owe you a debt of gratitude. Come on, share a drink with us."

Now the celebration flew into high fury—the paraphernalia in the corner was indeed a still, built with the tacit approval of their jailers. The men had used a good portion of their rations to brew a repulsive-smelling swill so potent that Jake began to feel dizzy the moment a cup was poured for him. He was given the honor of the first sip, and reacted by coughing violently, much to the amusement of the other prisoners.

They, apparently, were well used to the stuff, and proceeded to drink it as easily as if it were pure stream water. Within half an hour the entire lot of them, Caleb included, were falling down drunk. Even Jake, who took nothing after the sip he spit out, felt the inebriating effect of the spirits.

Watching quietly from the corner as his fellow inmates passed out one by one, Jake began to feel great sympathy for the man who had started out to fix a rotted floorboard in his house and ended by constructing a brand new structure. Not quite twenty-four hours before, he had decided to forfeit a few hours of sleep to best some Tory rangers; he'd ended up discovering a major British plot against the key defense on the Hudson, then worked his way deep into it as much by accident as design. He was now a prisoner of his own cunning: none of the jailers would believe his story, and while John Jay certainly would—he and Jay had met twice before the war—the judge wasn't due for many days, by which time not only would the chain have been attacked but Schuyler would undoubtedly have concluded Jake's mission to fool Howe had failed. The general would have no choice but go ahead with his plans to abandon Albany and cede upper New York to the enemy, essentially surrendering the middle of the country to the king.

Which all in all might not be a bad idea, if Jake didn't find some way of stopping the Tories from destroying the chain.

Twenty

Wherein, Claus van Clynne discovers a cure for the common cold.

The effects of their homemade concoction were devastating—inside an hour the prisoners had melted into haphazard piles on the ground, as dead to the world as if run through with bayonets. Jake resolved to find the man responsible for the formula, and put him to work for the patriot cause.

Tomorrow. For now, he had things to do.

The plan was simple—sneak out, double back down the road to the point where van Clynne was waiting two miles away, tell the squire everything he knew of the scheme against the chain, and then come back and rejoin the sleeping prisoners. "Rescued" with them in the morning, he would be united with Busch just in time to sabotage his plans personally. That would still leave Jake three whole days to return to Albany with his message for Schuyler.

Jake's Dutch companion knew of a cosmic law to the effect that the simpler a plan sounds in outline, the more difficult it is to execute. Fortunately, van Clynne was not there to spread this particular wet blanket, and Jake was free to concentrate on the first leg of his plan with as much optimism as could be mustered in a room full of snoring drunks. He rose quietly, and made some movements he meant as decoys; finding no reaction, he walked to one of the piss buckets and relieved himself, taking a circuitous route back with still no sign that anyone else was awake. When a short burst of "Yankee Doodle" failed to raise a reaction, he decided it was time to leave.

How to go? The boards on the side windows were secured with enough nails to lay ten good-sized floors. The choir window, on the other hand, had been left open, and provided an inviting avenue of egress, except for the barricaded doorway to the loft.

Even standing on two buckets, the six-foot-two patriot couldn't quite reach the choir's bottom beam. Jake jumped, but his fingertips just barely grazed the wood before he fell back down to the ground. A second jump ended with similar results, except that he began to feel a little tenderness in his knee.

Two attempts launched with a running start got him closer, but it wasn't until he placed a discarded board from the corner on the buckets as a kind of reverse diving plank that he managed to grab hold of the thick piece of wood running along the bottom of the loft.

Jake rocked himself back and forth, building momentum for a swing over the four-foot railing. He had to let go of one hand to get enough of his body over; when he did so, he hung for a moment, his weight imperfectly balanced between his leg and his right arm.

Had the light been any better, he surely would have fallen, for he could have seen how precarious his position was. But there are certain times when it is best to operate in the dark, or at least semidarkness, and this was definitely one of them. After a breath to renew his strength, Jake pulled himself up and over the choir; he rolled as if a log clearing an obstruction.

And clanged his back on the organ chair, while simultaneously pricking his abdomen with Wedget's knife, which was tucked into his belt. How he managed to stifle a foul curse at that moment remains one of the great mysteries of this tale.

Having attained the choir and assured himself that his wounds were only temporary if painful annoyances, Jake confronted a new problem. The window was devoid of glass, and passage through it could be accomplished as easily as one might walk through an open doorway—except that in so doing, one would fall twenty feet, directly into the lap of a sleeping sentry.

Not for the first time in his life, Jake wished for wings.

He looked upward from the window, hoping to find the roof within grasping distance. It was, had his arms been fifty feet long. Nor were the branches of nearby trees any closer. But further examination presented him with another escape route—the facade itself.

Any reader who ever has an option in this regard should choose to be shut up in a church built of stone or brick, instead of one made of wood. Wooden churches can be made to look considerably more fetching, but their sides do not present many hand- or footholds, making it difficult to climb down from the second-story window.

Which is what Jake now proceeded to do. We will not increase the suspense by telling you precisely how many times he slipped, nor mention that the sentry stirred momentarily just as he stepped out the window. It is probably of only passing interest that Jake's hands became unbearably sweaty about halfway down. But perhaps it is not completely irrelevant that his waistcoat snagged on the clapboard edging when he was but seven or eight feet from the ground, just at the moment he was pushing off the facade to jump and run for the woods.

Jake swung around crazily, caught at the middle and dangling over the ground, hanging by the barest thread in a pose more than a little reminiscent of Icarus's the second before he crashed to earth.

He nearly yelled aloud, cursing the splinter that had caught him, and asking that God himself look down and free him.

No one enjoys being left hanging, especially when it is by one's vest some feet off the ground. But how much less enjoyable is it to be suddenly freed from that position? And so one must always be careful what one wishes for—as Jake discovered in the next moment when the well-worn threads of his waistcoat gave way.

The sentry posted at the front of the church was representative of the many green recruits who made up Putnam's army. Most were brave and patriotic lads, ready to make the greatest sacrifice possible in the name of Freedom. But sacrifice on the battlefield was one thing, and discipline behind the lines quite another. The fact that he was sleeping on duty was, sad to say, typical not only in his unit but much of the service. The only thing unique about it was that he had chosen to sleep in so conspicuous a place.

And a fortuitous one, as far as Jake was concerned. For his tumble took him right into the poor man. If not nearly so cushy as a featherbed, he nevertheless broke his fall. Jake's foot struck the poor man on the side of the temple; his sleep deepened several degrees, but except for a change in the tone of his snores, there was no sign he noticed.

Jake didn't bother to ask. Quickly looking around and seeing that there were no other guards in sight, he leapt up and made a dash for the woods. Undoubtedly the other two or three militiamen who would have been posted to guard duty had chosen better places to hide while dozing—in this instance, dereliction of duty was of great service to the Cause.

We will leave Jake hurrying through the countryside while we check briefly on the man whom he is racing to meet, Claus van Clynne. The reader will recall that the Dutchman was last seen being hoisted to his feet by Major Dr. Keen's driver, Phillip Percival. In the interval, he was guided into Keen's coach at gunpoint and driven away in the opposite direction of the troop he'd led to intercept Jake.

They were now riding hastily southeastwards, toward a small cottage owned by a man named Marshad. The fellow, a country lawyer before the war, was now in General Bacon's employ as a British agent, and the house had been placed at Major Dr. Keen's disposal.

The doctor had developed a certain fondness for van Clynne, which expressed itself in the great care he took in making sure the ropes binding the squire were just tight enough to cut off the circulation to his extremities but not do any lasting harm.

He wanted that bit of fun for himself.

"One of the difficulties of operating in the wilderness is that one finds himself having to make do with expedient substitutes instead of the proper tools," Keen explained to his prisoner as they drove. "Were we in London or even New York, I might be able to offer you a proper torture. Here, I'm afraid, we'll have to lash some make-shift thing together."

"It's quite all right if we skip it entirely," said van Clynne. "I have some business to conduct, and would just as soon be on my way."

"What sort of business would that be, exactly?"

"It has to do with salt."

"Still worrying about your stolen salt? I suppose it's good to have something to divert the attention with." Keen smiled and reached down to a worn brown leather valise beneath the seat. Opening it, he examined several small bottles before settling on one shaped like an elongated teardrop. He then took a syringe from the case. The instrument consisted of a long, tapered glass tube with another inserted into the middle; a rubber piston could be used for creating a vacuum and drawing liquid out of a standing pool—or a bottle in this case, as he filled the cylinder with the liquid.

"I see that you've taken my advice and gotten rid of the hat," said van Clynne approvingly. "Now perhaps you will work on a more sensible coat. That blue is suited only for cities."

"I'm going to squirt this up your nose to achieve the most rapid effect," Keen replied, testing the pump. "It will tickle at first, but you'll soon grow to like it."

"I suppose it would be too much to ask that the experience be delayed until my head cold clears."

"Oh, this will remedy any blockage, I assure you."

Van Clynne turned his head away and tried to resist, but being bound there was only so much he could do. The liquid shot into his nasal cavity despite his efforts.

Keen sat back on his seat, watching his subject with great interest. The drug he'd administered was a particularly potent incapacitating agent, but given van Clynne's reaction to the jimsonweed dust and its belladonna, the doctor was not at all surprised that it failed to take effect immediately. His patient sniffled and wheezed, and then gave a great cough that shook the whole carriage.

"You seem to be right, sir," declared van Clynne, whose voice remained surprisingly chipper, given the circumstances. "I can breathe much more clearly. You have chased away my cold; I congratulate you fully."

With that, the Dutchman promptly fell off into stone unconsciousness.

Twenty-one

Wherein, Jake finds reason to be disappointed in friends as well as acquaintances.

Providence had provided Jake with a straight and narrow path from the jail to Pine's Bridge, but he wasted little energy rejoicing as he trotted toward his rendezvous with van Clynne. The Dutchman would have been waiting an inordinately long time, undoubtedly filling it with complaints about the unpunctuality of American agents.

That or snoring. Of the two, Jake preferred facing the complaints, though if the squire were snoring there was at least the advantage that any vicious animals in the vicinity would have been driven miles away.

But van Clynne was doing neither. Jake searched the creekside as well as the nearby woods, stumbling and cursing in the dim starlight, his opinion of Dutch reliability suffering a severe reassessment. His anger exploded in a torrent of curses loud and strong enough to wake the dead; fortunately there were no corpses in the vicinity— nor van Clynne either, for had he appeared at that moment he might have been made into one.

This uncharacteristic (and, it must be admitted, somewhat unfair) display of temper soon ran its course, and Jake began plotting his next move. It was already far past midnight; if van Clynne had intended on meeting him he would have arrived hours before. Jake could not risk going to Putnam himself, as his absence when the Tory prisoners woke would raise serious suspicions.

Still, he must find someone to carry what he knew of the plans to General Putnam. Justice Prisco or some member of his family—the plain but patriotic Jane, per-

haps—would be perfect, but Prisco's inn was more than
ten miles south, too far to walk even if Jake could count
on borrowing a horse to get back on.

It took only a few moments more for his thoughts to
turn to the girl he had met at nearby Stoneman's farm:
Rose McGuiness. A woman would be allowed to pass
freely through the countryside, and one as clever—not to
mention pretty—as she would have an easy time getting
to the general's headquarters at Peekskill. Rose had been
prepared to burn down her master's barn in the name of
Independence. Surely she would take up an errand such
as this.

There was, naturally, one slight complication—there
was a good chance the ranger captain as well as the troop
had returned there by now. But those were just the sort
of difficulties one needed to keep the blood circulating
against the cold.

Stoneman's was under a mile away, and Jake ran nearly
the entire distance, loosening his vest buttons but otherwise making no concession to the exertion. Despite the
faint light afforded by the new moon, the way was clear
enough, and in a short time he had reached the woods
near the side of the farm.

His luck now took one of its rare turns against him.
The patriot could see from the road that a large fire was
burning in the barnyard. He could hear nothing as he
snuck closer, but he was so distracted by the fire that he
didn't realize there was a ranger sentry guarding the
woods until he was almost upon him. Jake threw himself
down the instant he made sense of the tall shadow and its
bayonet-tipped musket; the man heard the shuffle of
brush in the woods and took a few tentative steps forward
to investigate.

It was Jake's friend and one-time mentor Dr. Franklin
who had suggested that the American forces be equipped
with Indian bows and arrows, noting that not only were
the materials plentiful but the weapons were simple and
dependable. Jake could have added another benefit—
they were nearly silent, and at a moment such as this an
arrow would have been a godsend. As it was, he found

himself sprawled forward between a row of skunk cabbage and prickle bushes, barely daring to breathe, his only weapons the Segallas pocket pistol and Wedget's knife, both of which were tucked safely—as far as any adversary was concerned—inside his vest and boot, respectively.

Any movement would give him away. Jake lay on the ground, hoping the shadows were thick enough to guard him from the sentry's vision.

They nearly were. After the man passed by, the patriot spy rose to his feet slowly and drew his knife. But even as his fingers closed around the crude handle, the guard suddenly swung back around, advancing with the speed of a frigate before a hurricane wind.

"Who goes there?" demanded the Tory.

"It's I," said Jake, hoping the man's vision was as clouded by the deep shadows and brush as his.

"I who?"

"Caleb Evans," lied Jake, taking a step to his right, away from the guard.

"Caleb, where have you been? We're supposed to be rescuing you in the morning."

"I've just escaped from the Americans." Jake took another step as the sentry reached the spot where he had first stood. They were three yards apart, perpendicular to each other.

One leap, and Jake could fall upon him. But the gun might go off, and bring the others.

"Where is Captain Busch?" asked Jake, ducking and moving as silently as possible. He aimed to get behind the man, killing him before he could alert the others with a shout or gunfire.

"We're waiting for him," said the guard, confused and turning to see where his fellow was. "We returned just an hour ago—our day and evening have been a shitten disaster!"

Jake's careful plot was almost undone by his laughter. "Why?" he managed, stifling himself with his arm and moving back, continuing to circle through the brush and trees that separated them. The two men were barely six feet apart.

"We never made it to Salem." The sentry twisted again. It would be nearly impossible to get behind him.

Jake knelt but made no other noise, deciding to change tactics.

The Tory took another step forward.

"All the horses got sick on the road a mile away, and Sergeant Lewis as well. It was hours before they recovered. We had to walk the animals back, and the sergeant is in as foul a mood as ever I've seen. Where the hell are you, Caleb?"

"Right here," said Jake, springing forward. His blade cut a quick, deep hole at the Tory's throat; the only sound the sentry could make was a surprised gasp as his body surrendered its soul.

Jake pried the musket from the dead man's hands and dragged him a few feet deeper into the woods. Taking up the loaded Brown Bess, he crept to the barn, listening to see if the Tories had heard anything. If so, no one stirred —the troopers must have sought sleep as a salve for their disappointments.

For a brief moment, he considered whether it might not be a good idea to lock the door and carry out Rose's earlier design of burning down the building. He dismissed the idea, albeit reluctantly; even if he succeeded in killing the entire group, he might not stop the British attack on the chain.

Jake tucked the musket beneath a bush where he might find it if necessary and sneaked back along the edge of the woods to the house. The rear door was barred against easy entry, as were the windows. Finally he took Wedget's knife and tickled the 12-pane panel that threw light into the summer kitchen; it shot up quickly and Jake half wondered if Rose had greased it against his approach.

The room he climbed into was so dark it suggested another possibility—an entire company of rangers could have waited in ambush without Jake seeing them. Fortunately, there was but a solitary guard, whose presence Jake detected only by stumbling onto its tail.

The poor kitten yelped and scurried for the hallway, its eyes much better adjusted to the lack of light than Jake's. He followed its lead, proceeding as quietly as possible across the wide floorboards. Stoneman must have been a fine carpenter as well as a rich Tory, for the boards were so well constructed not a single one creaked.

But perhaps he hadn't done the work himself. Stoneman was no simple farmer; while it was too dark to make out his furnishings, his house's size alone spoke of great wealth. Large and rectangular from the outside, on the inside it seemed a series of rooms opening into one another and backing around like an English garden maze. Finally Jake found his way to the hall, which ran along the center of the building and featured two large stairways upward.

Whether she slept with other servants, the family girls, or alone, a female servant would be housed upstairs. Jake began creeping up the rear stairwell, staying close to the banister.

He'd gone a little better than halfway when he heard the slight but distinct sound of someone walking above him.

Rose?

Jake went up another step and saw the faint yellow illumination of a candle shaded by a hand. He took another step—just in time to catch sight of two thick legs dressed in boots and ranger trousers, coming his way. Jake ducked and waited as the man walked awkwardly by on his tiptoes, then crept up to watch from the staircase as the man proceeded down the hall toward the rooms at the front of the house, his attention apparently focused on his planned assignation.

Jake was somewhat surprised when he realized from the plumpness of the shadow that it must be the sergeant; he could not imagine any woman finding the gruff old goat attractive. But his wonder turned to something considerably more depressing when, after the sergeant knocked on the door at the end of the hallway, Rose's face appeared, illuminated by the Tory's candle.

Twenty-two

Wherein, the old opinions about the virtue of flowers are proven to be true.

"**W**ho are you looking for?" asked Rose.

"I came for Mary," answered the sergeant, to Jake's great but unspoken relief.

"She's gone south to New York with the family this afternoon."

The sergeant cast a furtive look down the hallway; had he not been so preoccupied, he might have caught Jake spying in the shadows near the banister.

"You'll do," he said, putting a hand on the door as Rose tried to push it closed. "Easy girl, my stomach has given me a load of trouble all day."

"Mary's not here! Out!" said Rose sharply.

"There's no one here to answer your screams," said the sergeant, pushing his way into the room. "I'll tell anyone who asks that you invited me in, wench." He kicked the door closed behind him.

Jake leapt up to the landing and went down the hall as quietly but as quickly as possible. He bent and eased the latch downwards, slipping his other hand to his boot for his knife. Then he swung the door open and sprang inside —just in time to see Rose's own solution to the dilemma: a fully loaded chamber pot, which crashed with great and instant effect on the sergeant's head.

"You drunken bastard," Rose was telling the unconscious interloper. "I would sooner go to bed with the devil than let a Tory kiss me."

"I'm glad to hear you still feel that way," said Jake. "You!"

"I thought you needed rescuing. Obviously I got here a little late."

"Don't get any ideas yourself," said Rose, clutching her hands in front of her nightgown.

There are few more beautiful sights than a patriotic woman whose breasts bulge the top of her white cotton gown and curls flow softly from her loosely-tied night cap. But Jake could not afford even a brief interlude tonight—besides, there might be another chamber pot lurking beneath the bed.

"I need your help," he said. "Are you still with us?"

"I'd give up my life to help our Cause."

"Get dressed and take anything you value with you. I'll wait in the hall."

"What should I do with him?"

Jake leaned over and inspected the sergeant. "If the smell doesn't kill him, he'll sleep for a couple of hours. We'll both be long gone by then."

The Mary whom the sergeant had sought was the farmer's wife, a fact Rose found great pleasure in relaying once she was dressed. Mary Stoneman had lectured the family's "girls" often on the need for virtue, and had especially hounded Rose when her attachment to the apprentice was hinted. The unmasking of her hypocrisy was therefore a victory on the order of Washington's at Trenton, and Rose found it difficult to control her enthusiasm as she led Jake down the stairs to the front hallway. She had dressed in a fine blue robe dress with white petticoats —obviously not her everyday dress, and one Jake suspected quite rightly had once belonged to the woman she was criticizing.

The outfit was mildly hooped, attractively showing off the sway of her hips. A knit shawl—prepared by her own hand—covered her shoulders, and a puffed mobcap sat atop her fixed curls. Jake now realized a second chamber pot would not have been discovered had he decided to dally, but Liberty rarely brooks delay.

Even as the crow flies, it was at least a dozen miles from Stoneman's to Cortlandville and Old Put's headquarters beyond. With time so critical, Rose needed some

way of traveling other than her legs, as shapely as they
might be.

"We need a carriage or a wagon," Jake told her, lighting a second candle off hers. "Where does your master
keep them?"

"The family took all the wagons when they left for New
York City," she told him. "They ran away and left me to
tend to these Tory thieves."

"Can you ride a horse?"

"Sir," she said indignantly, "do I look like a city girl? I
can ride a horse as well as any woman—and I would bet
as well as you."

"You may get a chance to prove that bet," said Jake.
"Come, let's steal a pair from our friends."

His plan was simple. There had been no guard posted
in the barnyard, the Tories deciding to concentrate their
resources on the perimeter. All one had to do was walk in
very quietly, untie a pair of likely looking horses, and
walk out.

Jake led Rose to the bush where he had stashed the
musket. Her grip when he gave it to her made him think
the young woman had taken militia training.

"You stand at the doorway—fire it only if they wake."

"We should kill them all while they sleep," said Rose.

"Trust me," said Jake, patting her shoulder before putting out her candle with his fingers.

The Tory troop had arranged itself in symmetrical fashion against the barn wall to the right, sleeping on field
cots in apparent contentment. Undoubtedly they had
been tired by the march back from Salem, during which
they'd had to walk their bloated horses.

The effects of the herb had worn off by now, the
horses' overstimulated digestive tracts having worked all
afternoon to evacuate the poison. They did not seem to
bear any grudge toward their tormentor; indeed, the first
animal he approached nuzzled against him, apparently
remembering that Jake had given him sugar earlier in the
day.

The stallion's reins were looped over an iron ring at the
side of the stall. Jake placed the candle on a post next to

three freshly oiled saddles and quietly prepared the animal to be ridden.

He had just rubbed the neck of a second horse in an attempt to persuade him to accept his role as a Revolutionary gracefully when a loud voice outside challenged Rose.

"The sergeant needs you in the house," he heard her say. "There are American thieves afoot."

Jake did not hear the reply to this, if there was one, for it was drowned out by the report of a musket. Cursing, he jumped up on the second horse's unsaddled back, grabbing at the reins of the first animal and kicking his mount toward the door.

As the horse leaped into action, Jake lost his grip on the other's rein. But his lunge brought his hand to the post where the candle was, and a sudden stroke of inspiration made him swat the candle to the ground. It fell against a pile of straw which had earlier sopped up some of the excess wax used on the saddles. Worn by the breeze, the candle's flame fluttered, unsure whether to exert itself. Then it remembered its patriotic duty, bucking itself up like a private enlisted for the duration—bold yellow tongues shot up to the rafters.

"Fire!" yelled Jake as he prodded his horse toward the door.

Confusion erupted with the flames. The horses screamed; men fell from their beds shouting. Jake held tight to the neck of his mount as he followed his instincts, plunging toward the barely opened door.

They had just crossed the threshold when a dark shadow leapt at his side. Jake turned to push it away—then realized it was Rose.

"You took your time," she told him curtly, pulling herself up behind him. "I thought I would have to hold off the entire troop."

"You'd have beaten them, I'm sure," yelled Jake as he hunkered down on the horse and headed for the road.

"The Tories may realize something's wrong if I don't make it back to jail quickly," Jake told her when they finally stopped two miles up the road. "We'll have to split up."

"Be off then. I know my way to Robinson's Bridge where the Continentals are camped."

"Old Put's house is in the village of Peekskill," said Jake, slipping off the horse. "It should be obvious from the guards. Remember everything I've told you. And if anyone stops you—"

"I'm not a simpleton. A child could deliver your message successfully."

"Putnam won't believe a child," said Jake. He reached into his shirt and drew out his Segallas. "Show him this pocket pistol as soon as you arrive. He'll know it's mine. There isn't another one like it in the colonies."

"The general knows you that well?"

"The old man and I have sung a few songs together at Fraunces tavern. His 'Maggie Lauder' is quite good." Jake looked down the road. The Tories had not mounted a pursuit, undoubtedly concentrating their efforts on saving the barn and their horses. They seemed to have been successful—the telltale glow such a great fire would produce was notably absent.

"A Dutchman named Claus van Clynne was to meet me on the road tonight and failed to turn up. It's likely he's still with Putnam. You'll know him if you see him— he's as fat as a pregnant sow and complains twice as much. He has a red beard that fills much of his chin and chest besides; he pulls it whenever he thinks over a knotty problem, which is often. He's a good man, though; you can trust him."

"I doubt I would ever trust a Dutchman."

"Trust no one else," said Jake sternly. "If you do meet up with him, tell him to go to Albany immediately. He'll recognize the gun as well."

"You've sang with him, too?"

"That is an experience almost too terrible to imagine," said Jake. A dim twilight was starting to invade the darkness; he could see her face clearly.

Would she succeed? A great deal depended on her getting to Putnam. Jake would do his best to sabotage the Tory efforts from inside their camp, but the guard must be alerted in case he failed. Her information would aid them greatly, especially as it foretold when the assault would be launched, and warned Putnam to guard Busch's farm, where Jake thought the assault would be launched from.

Freedom often calls upon common folk to play a noble role in Her struggle. Had it not been for the war—had it not been for her fortuitous meeting with Jake—this young woman would have spent her life as a simple housewife, bearing life's commonplace dangers with her quiet courage.

Now she would have to prove herself the equal of Paul Revere's midnight army, the fifty or sixty anonymous men and women whom the silversmith had rallied to save Concord and Lexington. Jake reached up to give her a kiss of encouragement. While he meant to aim for her cheek, she turned her lips toward him; they met in a warm, lingering moment fired by the passion of a shared cause.

"Hurry now," he told her, patting the horse's bare back. "Don't fail me."

"I won't," she said, spurring the steed away.

Twenty-three

Wherein, Jake finds it necessary to rout the American forces.

Jake proceeded back to jail at a half-trot; even so, the going took longer than the coming. By the time he arrived it was little more than an hour before dawn.

Along the way, the spy pondered the pending operation to liberate the Tory prisoners. It was bound to put the American soldiers standing guard at risk, and could very well prove fatal to them.

The greater good of protecting the chain must be served, of course, but Lieutenant Colonel Jake Gibbs was not the sort of officer who could make cold calculations of human lives so blithely. He therefore decided to try to find some way of removing the militia guards from harm's way before the assault was launched.

Given the circumstances of his escape, Jake had hopes that whatever guards had been posted would still be sleeping upon his return. This would make his course an easy one—each man could be trussed and trundled off to the woods while still dozing, assuming Jake could find their nap nooks.

Alas, an officer had made the rounds of the watch sometime after Jake's departure. As he cut through the barnyard across from the church, the patriot spy saw that the sentry whom he had landed on was now wide awake and pacing angrily in front of the church. The fellow's previous companion, Sleep, had been replaced by a much younger man shouldering a musket. The pair were grumbling loudly about their lieutenant, complaining about his threats and suspicious nature.

Jake retreated to regroup. His mental processes received a sudden jolt when, turning the corner of the barn, he smacked into another soldier, a short, frailish fellow of fifty-odd years who fell back in surprise.

"Excuse me," said Jake quickly, extending his left hand to help up the poor man—and then smashing him across the face with his right.

He grabbed his musket and hunkered down as he heard footsteps in the road; the distance between the church and barn was only two or three rods, and even the most precursory march could cover the twenty or thirty yards in a few seconds. But the guard did not come around the back, and Jake soon heard the steps walking the other way.

The fact that these militiamen had no set uniform, save the simple white straps crossing their chests and holding up a sack apiece, meant it would be easy enough to impersonate one. Jake took off the older man's straps and bags, then grabbed his powder horn as well. But he decided against stealing his long coat, as it would most likely have left the pallid-looking militiaman to face the rest of his call-up without one. Tying the soldier's hands with a piece of rawhide he found in the sack, Jake pulled off one of the man's boots, intending to gag him with his sock. But the sight of the bare heel and toes peeking out from the torn material moved him to pity, and he replaced the boot and pulled the man to the edge of the woods instead.

As far as Jake could discover creeping around the barn, the only other soldiers in the vicinity were the two fellows in the front of the church. Their patrol was haphazard, serving mostly to vent their emotion at the officer whose scolding had kept them from a good night's sleep. The man Jake had jumped earlier now expressed the opinion that the lieutenant had thrashed him on the head and shoulders before waking him, and cursed the man for denying it.

The men's oaths suggested an easy ploy—Jake would arrive cursing as well, and claim that the lieutenant had ordered him to replace them. But he worried they might not take the bait, and having neglected their duty before, might seek to make up for it now by asking a copious amount of questions. He therefore decided to launch a supplementary plan to draw their attention away—a barn fire. Given that he had recently worked that ploy to advantage at Stoneman's—intentionally or not, one couldn't fuss with the results—the patriot spy felt somewhat confident it would work here.

The only inconvenience was the poor design of the structure, which concentrated all openings at the front of the road, in full view of the soldiers.

Jake waited until both men were turned in the opposite direction and then scampered into the barn through a narrow doorway without being seen.

Almost without being seen. For he had no sooner ducked from the dim twilight of the roadway to the utter darkness of the barn's interior when he heard a shout from the street.

Somewhat indistinct, the words were followed by the more definite sound of a pair of boots running in his direction. Jake took a step backwards into the bowels of the large structure, only to feel something sharp and pointed in his back. Instinctively, he dropped the musket and put up his hands—then ducked in a flash, diving to the ground in case there was a loaded gun attached to the bayonet that had stuck him.

Not precisely. As he rolled over to kick his assailant, Jake looked up into the puzzled eyes of a large but tranquil ox. It curled its tongue with a question, yawned, and shook its head. Two dozen of its fellows swung their tails in sympathy.

Jake scooped up the old man's musketpiece and pushed his way between the animals as the militiaman arrived.

"Out, you thief, I know you're in there!" called one of the guards. "You Tory cowboys won't be stealing any of the town's oxen tonight, I promise you."

The men murmured in consultation outside, revealing their names as Harrold and Daniel, but otherwise offered little that was useful to Jake. He slipped to the back of the ox pack and waited for the guards' next move.

A sound at the large center door alerted him to their

plans, and suggested a counterattack. By the time the door swung open, Jake had the oxen mustered and pressing forward.

A stampede it wasn't. But the soldiers had their hands full trying to contain the large, lumbering creatures, and found it impossible to close the door before three or four escaped. This engendered some arguing as the men found it necessary to split up, one entering the barn and the other going after the beasts. It also gave Jake the opportunity to climb to the second floor loft.

Leaving his musket in the straw, the patriot jumped down onto Daniel's back as he came into the barn, thinking to ride him to the ground and quickly knock him out.

Jake would have had a better chance with one of the oxen, and in fact, might be forgiven for thinking he had landed on one. Daniel Higgins was an immense nineteen-year-old, and his first reaction to Jake's assault was a non-committal shrug, as if he did not realize he'd been tackled. This was followed by a violent shake and shudder, as Jake grabbed hold of his throat with one arm and pummeled the side of his head with the other. The man began screaming for help—Jake would have been justified in making a similar plea—and pitched forward so quickly that the patriot spy flew forward onto the ground.

The blow did not hurt him, though the smear of ox dung on his face when he landed was nearly incapacitating. Jake just barely rolled out of the way as Daniel charged forward, and watched with some satisfaction as the man slipped on the flattened ox turd himself.

It took two kicks to the side of Daniel's head to knock him senseless. Jake had just picked up the man's musket when he heard a sound behind him. He swung around and saw the other militiaman entering the barn, rifle in hand.

There was a split second of opportunity before the man could bring his gun to bear. But Jake could no more shoot a member of his army than he could shoot himself, even for the greater good of the Cause. He threw down the weapon and stood away from the fallen soldier.

"What have you done to Daniel?"

"Set him to dreaming what he'll do after the war," said Jake. "But otherwise he's fine."

"Don't be smart." The militiaman pointed his rifle at him menacingly. "Move away from the gun, you coward."

"Coward? I thought it took a lot of bravery to throw down my gun. I could easily have killed you, Harrold."

A confused expression grew on the militiaman's face. "Who are you?" he asked.

"I don't look familiar to you?"

"Not at all."

"Would you know your own brother?" Jake took a step forward.

The militiaman pointed his rifle in the approximate direction of Jake's heart. "You're not my brother."

"I asked only if you would know him. Sometimes, the circumstances of our surroundings can be so different that the familiar appears strange."

"This is a trick."

"A trick? Why do you think I didn't kill you?"

"You have your reasons, I suspect." Harrold watched as Jake slowly circled around toward the barn door. "I'm not going to let you run out of here."

"You really don't remember me? Not at all?"

"Are you that old countryman who deserted the unit when we were called last month?"

"Do I look like a deserter?"

Harrold hesitated, but then shook his head. In all this time, he had kept his finger firmly on the trigger, and for all his confusion, had not quite dropped his aim. A sudden noise, even a sharp movement, might cause him to fire—and shorten Jake Gibbs's career considerably.

"You're not in our militia."

"Think back, Harrold, think back to your youth."

"You run out that door, I'll shoot you, I swear."

But Jake's object was not to run out the door—it was to slap it closed and send the interior into pitch-black darkness. He dove against the heavy door the way a child jumps into a snow pile. The long irons hinges creaked in anger, but swung back nevertheless, shutting out the dim twilight.

As Jake hit the ground, he heard the stinging bee of the bullet pass over his head.

"You shouldn't have fired, Harrold. First rule of warfare, never shoot at what you can't see."

But Jake's eyes were no better adapted to the dimness than the militiaman's. He rolled forward, abruptly bouncing into a wall. As he got to his feet, he realized Harrold had gotten a bead on him and charged forward; Jake just managed to jump away as the militiaman lunged.

The crack Harrold's head took off the wall must have been severe, but it didn't stop him—he flailed with his rifle, using it as a club, and caught Jake in the side of the head. Jake ate straw and dirt for a moment, then caught a sharp blow to his ribs before managing to roll away.

This was just the sort of impromptu contest the American militia did well in. Put them in line and drill them until the corn sprouted, and no more than a third would follow the commands during a set-piece battle. But give them an ambush, let them show initiative, and they were strong foes indeed.

Unlike General Percy, the man who led the redcoat retreat from Lexington and Concord, Jake was not about to play into the militia's hands by retreating. Instead, he began a spirited counterattack, pulling at Harrold's leg and catching him off-balance. He knocked the fellow to the ground, where they began to wrestle for an advantage amid the legs of the cattle, who every so often added a kick of annoyance at being disturbed.

Now the reader will recall that Jake Gibbs is a tall, strongly-built man just past twenty-three; in his stocking feet he stands two inches beyond six feet, and every inch of his frame is well supported by muscle. His opponent, in his stocking feet, came no higher than Jake's collarbone; he liked to tip the bottle at night, and in truth had shied away from brawling ever since receiving a bloody nose as a nine-year-old. But here was a man who was fighting for his country; Jake would have had an easier time grappling with a German giant brought across the ocean to pay his prince's debts. Certainly he wished he was, for then he might have fought with a freer hand. Here he had to fight hard enough to stop the well-motivated patriot, yet not so hard that he would cause him permanent harm.

Harrold grabbed Jake by the throat and refused to let go, even as Jake rolled him onto his back and began pounding his head against the hard-packed floor. The man's grip tightened and tightened, and Jake began to fear that he would have the fellow's brains splattered across the floor before winning his freedom.

Finally the pounding took its toll, and Jake felt Harrold's grip loosening. He gave one more smash and jumped up, half expecting the militiaman to bolt up after him. But Harrold finally had been knocked senseless; his troubled breathing foretold a severe headache when he awoke.

Jake quickly went to the door; there were no reinforcements in sight. He tied the two unconscious militiamen up with leather straps and hauled them to the far wall, fastening them to a ring there. The oxen, confused by the activity, were pulled back inside their pen, and Jake found five seconds to tuck his shirt in his pants before returning to prison.

Twenty-four

Wherein, Claus van Clynne is guest of honor at a bloodletting, and Rose unhoops herself.

Claus van Clynne was generally known as a punctual man, at least as far as business was concerned. He was therefore greatly grieved that he could not arrive on time for his appointment with Jake at Pine's Bridge.

To put it more accurately, he was greatly grieved that he could not be anywhere other than his present location, a small house near Colabaugh Pond. The effects of the drug Major Dr. Keen had administered had worn off not long after midnight, now nearly four hours gone; the Dutchman was therefore in full possession of his senses—which meant he not only could watch as Keen snapped the lid off the large, coffinlike box his assistant Phillip Percival brought into the cottage, but he fully understood that the collection of jars inside contained particularly loathsome leeches.

Under normal circumstances, a bloodletting can be most beneficial when one's bodily humors are out of balance. The efficacy of the treatment has been documented for centuries, and one need no more fear a good medicinal leech than worry about being somehow poisoned by tobacco smoke. But these were not ordinary circumstances.

Nor were they ordinary leeches. Imported from a river in South America, each filled an entire two-gallon jar by itself. The black on the upper portion of its body was complemented by a tawny red on the belly, coincidentally the exact color of dried blood. Rows of small pincers shaped like tiny, vibrating daggers protruded from the elongated belly, stretching out like Howe's army marching up Manhattan after the debacle of Kipp's Bay.

Keen handled each animal with great care, grabbing the tail end with a long set of wrought-iron pincers and using a pointed rod to keep the head in line as he approached his patient. He wore a thick set of leather gloves that rose to his elbows, stiff riding boots, and a leather apron such as a glassblower might wear, sturdy protection should the massive worm test his availability as a target.

Stripped to a small loincloth that had been cut from his red flannel undersuit—Percival had taken great pleasure wielding his knife to slice away the material—van Clynne attempted to employ a special mind techinque he had learned from an old Huron Indian. Confronted by a host of Iroquois eager for his beaver pelts, the Indian had concentrated his will, flooding his opponents' minds with frightening hallucinations designed to make them run away empty-handed.

In this case, the Dutchman conjured a portrait of the most grievous beast he could think of—an irate Dutchwoman cheated of the proper price for a cow, coming at Keen with a large butcher knife.

The trick worked about as well for van Clynne as it had for the Indian—Keen used his black metal prod to guide the leech's head around the Dutchman's right ankle, whereupon the animal's instincts took over and it wrapped itself around the rest of the bare leg, up to the knee joint.

The sensation was something like what might be felt if a hundred kittens took their tiny paws and stuck them into the skin all at once; it was more a light tickle than a sharp pain. Far worse was the gentle slurping sound that accompanied the pricking.

"Well, sir, it was just about time for my monthly bloodletting," said van Clynne as cheerfully as possible. "I suppose this will cure me of the headache I suffered from your last potion."

"This will cure you of many ailments," said Keen. "Though I must say I have never liked bloodletting as a general therapy. My experimentation has proven it rather ineffective."

"Well then, perhaps we should desist. I wouldn't want to prove the exception to the rule."

"We must always seek more empirical evidence," said Keen.

The second leech was a bit rambunctious when released from its jar; Keen had to bat its head several times before getting it under control. But the creature was quite happy once it found van Clynne's left leg; it wrapped itself around even more tightly than the first, uttering a contented slurp.

"Tickles," said van Clynne.

"Good."

"I wonder if this might be the proper time to inquire as to what you have done with my money."

"Really, I hardly think a few odd pounds would occupy your thoughts at a moment like this."

"Actually, sir, it was more than just a few odd pounds. Not that I wish to question your mathematical abilities."

"Your paper money is on the bench there," said Keen, pointing as he opened another jar. The interaction of the glass, air, and alkaline solution produced a peculiar *pffff* sound when each vessel was first breached. "As for the real money—"

"I do not carry counterfeit, sir. My paper currency is all genuine."

"I am holding your purses myself for safekeeping. These woods are filled with miscreants, and I would not want your coins to fall into the wrong hands while you are otherwise occupied. My assistant Mr. Percival shall issue a receipt, of course."

"Perhaps there is the possibility of a business arrangement," suggested the Dutchman, eying the third worm.

"Quite late in the game for that," answered Keen.

The third leech was as big as the first two combined, and Keen had to ask Percival to help retrieve him. The assistant used a glassblower's wooden-handled stirrer to keep the worm's midsection taut as they walked the creature across and applied him to van Clynne's arm. The leech squirmed violently as it positioned itself around the ropes and the arm of the chair where the Dutchman was held. Its body exerted greater pressure than the last two; van Clynne felt as if a powerful vice had been applied.

"There is one piece of information of some interest to me," said Keen. "I wonder where you got your ruby knife."

"Which knife was that?"

"This one," said Keen, slipping the blade into his hand —and from there, into the floorboards directly at the Dutchman's feet.

"Oh, that knife," said van Clynne. "I'm afraid that is a very long story."

"I suspect I have more time to listen than you have to tell it," said Keen, opening the next jar.

However accomplished Major Dr. Keen was in other arts, he was not such a good time-teller as might be supposed. For as he was aiming his next leech, Rose McGuiness was approaching along the road at a goodly pace.

While Jake had impressed the importance of the mission on her so severely that she would have wrestled Pluto himself had he tried to delay her, she slowed and then pulled over to the side of the road near the cottage for three reasons, the first two of which were related: first, she was struck by the extremely odd sight of a fancy city carriage on this country highway. Second, she hoped its equipage might include some rein or rope she could use to keep herself from falling off her horse, as she had resorted to gripping the poor but patient animal's mane for the several miles she'd ridden thus far.

Last but not least, her hoops were killing her.

As the author has only a passing acquaintanceship with the intricacies of female accoutrements, the description of the cause of her discomfort necessarily will be brief. Jake had told her to take anything of value with her; being that the girl was not from a very rich family, the only thing worth more than a pence or two besides her affections were her clothes.

Lacking a satchel, she could only take one set, which she naturally wore. Her fancy dress had been given to her by her employer but a week before, with a stiff corset and hoops. She was only too happy to leave the corset behind, substituting a much more practical unboned jump, which performed the same function with considerably less poking around the ribs. But not being completely unmindful of her appearance, she had kept the hoops, putting them to their usual use beneath her dress. This proved to be a mistake—while they did not come close to approaching the dimensions of the more fashionable city attire, they were nonetheless stiff enough to cause distress as she rode bareback through the countryside.

Spotting Keen's coach thus provided a good reason to stop, as well as cover to remove the annoying barrel beneath her waist. The house appeared occupied, and light escaped from the cracks around the shutters, but the yard was empty and the shutters blocked anyone inside from seeing out as effectively as they kept anyone outside from looking in.

Rose coaxed her horse to a stop behind the carriage and slipped off. The animal was well trained and placid, standing still as she reached her hand to a lash dangling from a rear compartment. In a second the leather rope had been placed into service as a makeshift rein, tied gently to the horse's neck; the stallion was not pleased with this new arrangement but stoically refused to complain.

Rose's next priority was to liberate herself from her portable prison. Once free of the whalebones, she cast her eye over the elaborate coach. It took no imagination at all to conclude that it must belong to a Tory—no patriot could afford such an elaborate rig. She resolved to do the Cause a favor by freeing the team of horses, and sprang forward to do so—stopping short when she saw the shadow of the large gun mounted at the driver's bench.

Before Rose could climb up and examine the gun, however, she heard a loud groan from the house. As quietly as she could, she crept to the window. Climbing atop a battered old tree trunk for a better view, she pressed her face to the dusty glass. The crack between the interior shutters gave her a view of Keen and his assistant wrestling with their leeches. Her eye followed the worm to the rotund body before them; with its bearded face, it could only belong to the Dutchman Jake had described.

Just as she realized this, the rotted tree trunk gave way, sending her in a noisy heap to the ground.

If she had moved quickly before, she nearly flew now as she threw herself back to the carriage and onto the driver's station. Though she was no expert on weapons, she quickly saw that the miniature cannon was loaded and ready to shoot. The firing mechanism was in all the important ways exactly similar to the lock on a regular rifle, with which she was fully familiar. The swivel mechanism was perfectly balanced, and so it took no great strength for her to maneuver the business end of the weapon and sight it at the front door of the cottage.

A good portion of van Clynne had been covered by leeches, whose black bodies were not only rapidly swelling but had begun to take on a sheen. The animals jostled lightly against each other as they fed, grudgingly admitting newcomers as Keen continued to pack them tightly against the Dutchman's skin. There were still some reddish pink blotches of flesh poking out between the worms at van Clynne's prodigious waist, however, and the doctor expressed the fear that he might not have enough to properly complete the job.

"What a shame that would be," commented van Clynne. "So you won't be able to kill me after all."

"Oh, these aren't intended to kill you," said Keen, hoisting another leech from its jar. "This would be much too pleasant a way to die."

"I had begun to worry about that myself," said van Clynne.

Keen's assistant Percival grinned in satisfaction at the door. He still had his poker under his arm, but as the largest animals had been applied already, his help was unnecessary.

"So, are you ready to tell me about the knife, or will you wait until I have the leeches applied to your eyeballs?"

"I have been ready to tell that story for a half hour or more," conceded van Clynne, who was somewhat thankful when Keen applied the worm to a spot on his chest instead of his face.

"Go ahead then."

"Well, it began several years ago, when I was a young boy on business in South Carolina. A man named Bacon, I believe—a dour-faced fart, but then so are most British gentlemen, present company excepted—approached me and asked if I should like to earn a few guineas by doing an errand for the king. Naturally, I thought he was referring to the Dutch king."

Keen's laughter at the improbable tale was cut short by sounds outside. He listened for a moment as the horses began to whicker.

"Go see what's wrong with them," the doctor barked at Percival.

Keen turned back to van Clynne and placed his tongs on the Dutchman's nose as Percival went slowly to the door. The doctor was just starting to give a sharp twist when the front of the room exploded with warm shot.

Twenty-five

Wherein, Claus van Clynne is liberated and the road forks portentously.

Claus van Clynne had rarely had such an occasion to celebrate an explosion, for the shower of hot shrapnel and splinters abruptly ended the nose-twisting being administered by Major Dr. Keen. Though his body was covered with the most hideous leeches imaginable, there is nothing a Dutchman fears more than having his nose twisted; it signifies bad breeding and a certain facial inferiority.

A large piece of the shattered door caught Keen in the side of the head and knocked him down. Van Clynne bulled his chair over and began crawling toward a large shard of broken glass. The engorged leeches cushioned the fall, and though still bound to the chair the Dutchman quickly reached the glass.

He had just gotten his arms untied and had started working on his legs when Keen recovered from his momentary daze. Van Clynne distracted the doctor's charge with a cannonade of fattened worms; they tickled as he pulled them off, drunk on his blood.

But there are not enough leeches in the world to stop a man such as Keen. Determined to send the Dutchman to his grave and then deal with whatever force had blown up the front of the cottage, the doctor threw himself forward and struck at the legs of the chair. Van Clynne was caught off balance, and found himself being pushed backwards through the debris like a wheelbarrow, as helpless as a beached turtle bound for the soup pot. Splinters of glass and wood tangled in his hair as his head was battered against the broken chestnut floorboards.

This new torment was cut short by a feminine voice at the door, which ordered Keen in rather salty language—we shall leave the exact collection of Anglo-Saxon to the reader's own imagination—to put up his hands and stand away from the chair.

"I will shoot you, sir, if you do not," repeated the voice, and Keen decided he had best comply.

The doctor knew the explosion had been caused by his own swivel cannon, and realized, too, that his minion Percival must have been the principal target of the charge. But he did not criticize himself for the arrogance that had led him to leave the coach unguarded; he would not have survived his many difficult scrapes by wasting valuable time upbraiding himself. Instead, he let go of van Clynne, promising to return to him as quickly as circumstances allowed. Taking a step backwards, he turned slowly and faced his opponent.

Who turned out to be a thin girl all of fifteen, with naturally curly hair and a smart blush upon her cheeks, holding a small though admittedly pretty pocket pistol on him, the likes of which were rare even in London.

Keen realized this must be the four-barreled pistol Bacon had made such a fastidious point of describing when detailing van Clynne's assistant. He told himself that Fate had once more turned in his favor—all he had to do was unarm this fetching creature, and she would undoubtedly lead him to the gun's owner. His entire mission would be wrapped up with her pretty yellow bow.

"Come, child, you don't expect me to be scared by a mere pocket pistol."

"Fired into your face it will be quite fatal," answered Rose. "And at this range, neither shot will miss."

Keen smiled, but kept his hands half raised. "Where did you get such an interesting gun? I don't believe I've seen its like in any of the colonies."

Rose ignored him. "Are you van Clynne?"

"The one and the same," said the Dutchman, hurrying to undo his legs and get himself up from the floor. He, too, had recognized the gun, and expected that its rightful owner was outside seeing to some minor detail of the operation. "Your arrival was most precipitous. Please excuse my dress; I was occupied in medical matters. Where is my friend, Colonel Gibbs?"

"He's busy," answered Rose.

"What a shame he couldn't join us," ventured Keen, trying a half step forward.

"Stand back," Rose warned him as van Clynne whisked up his outer clothes. "If you charge me I'll fire."

The doctor smiled and retreated meekly. Rose was not so naive as to interpret this as a sign of surrender, and endeavored to keep her eyes on him—especially as van Clynne's naked and leech-bitten extremities were hardly pleasant. But Keen needed only the slightest moment to launch his attack, and when Rose turned an eye to check on the Dutchman's progress, he flew into action.

As the British have made such a habit of doing, he greatly underestimated the strength of the American force before him. Though he knocked a candle over into a pile of shavings as a distraction, Rose was quick enough to fire two shots from the four-barreled pistol as she dodged his grasp. The first bullet missed, but the second struck Keen hard in the buttocks.

The assassin yelped with the pain. Rose grabbed the barrels, ignoring the heat to flip them around and prepare the second round of fire. Van Clynne in the meantime grabbed the poker from the floor, wielding it before him like a bayonet.

Temporarily outnumbered, and believing that the Dutchman's assistant must be approaching with reinforcements—surely he wouldn't have relied solely on this reed of a girl—Keen decided to beat a temporary retreat. He dove through a nearby window before Rose had the gun ready to fire again.

Van Clynne continued his charge across the room, sweeping up the ruby-hilted knife and a pistol the British villain had taken from him. He could not fit through the window, however, and by the time he picked his way across the debris at the front of the cottage all he saw of his tormentor was a shadow disappearing into the woods. He fired anyway, and while he would later swear he hit the figure, his subsequent search discovered no evidence of this. Further pursuit was discontinued when he looked back through the trees and discovered tall red flames rising from the cottage—where all of his paper money lay.

A Dutchman in unstoppered mourning is a pitiful thing to behold. His cheeks sag, his clothes droop, his beard—ordinarily the light red color of leaves tinged by the first blush of autumn—blackens. Even his brow is dark with the color of grief.

Or at least with soot, as Claus van Clynne had run back to the cottage and succeeded in beating back the flames with the aid of a large blanket, though not before they had ravaged the pile of currency Keen had placed on the bench. All that remained was a single, charred quarter of a New Jersey warrant, which van Clynne picked up gingerly from the floor. As he studied it, tears began to form in his eyes; at that moment a light breeze fluttered through the half ruined cottage and caught the brittle remains, dashing them to pieces.

It was the nadir of Claus van Clynne's earthly existence. He stood before the world landless and penniless, bereft of all possessions.

But do we not exaggerate? After all, the Dutchman is known to have stores of money throughout the province, and considerable credit besides. True, he has a considerable pile of bills owed to lawyers and others, all connected with his thus far unsuccessful attempts to win back his family property. But the assets of the van Clynne clan have never been measured in mere financial terms. Forget the rings around his fingers, or the silver buttons—disguised by cheap gold paint—on his vest and coat: the true worth of Claus van Clynne can never be measured by his money, but by the fertile workings of his Dutch brain. For who else in the entire province could turn such a catastrophic loss so quickly into a potential for further gain?

At least that is how he consoled himself when he hoisted himself aboard one of the carriage horses and trotted behind the determined young Rose, who had resumed her mission to General Putnam.

* * *

"I would say that your arrival was timely, indeed, but I would not go so far as to say that it was essential to my well-being. In fact, I would posit that had you not arrived when you did, I would right now be concluding my inter-rogation of my captor on several points of interest."

"And what would those be?"

"With all due respect, young miss, I do not think mat-ters of high intelligence should be blabbed about on the common roadways where anyone can hear. It is but a few minutes to dawn, and I expect the entire countryside is already awake around us."

Van Clynne shifted uncomfortably on the horse. He did not like riding without a saddle and the beast seemed to like it even less, shaking its head and hesitating even though the pace was an easy one.

"You were covered with leeches when I arrived. You would have bled to death."

"Hardly. As a matter of fact, the bleeding was quite a tonic," said van Clynne. "I have been feeling too san-guine of late."

"You said you were feeling ill a minute ago."

"A good portion of my fortune has vanished in those flames," said van Clynne. "But there is no need to sulk. I intend on pressing my claims before General Putnam for full reimbursement, as the money was destroyed by en-emy forces while I was engaged on a lawful mission for His Excellency General Washington—"

"Piffle."

"A lawful mission and I am entitled to full recovery, as designated by congressional act and amply illustrated by precedents dating to the Romans. I shall call on you to testify; it is the least you can do, given your role in my personal disaster."

"I saved your life! You are an ingrate!"

"I am not ungrateful for your exertions," said the Dutchman. "I am merely pointing out that they did not come without a price. As you are young, and therefore open to impressions, I have endeavored to give you the full picture of the situation, so that you may hereafter improve yourself. It is called learning, and a child such as yourself should be thankful for it. Now, if you were Dutch—"

"Dutch?"

"A Dutch girl has a certain education from the womb. I do not mean to criticize your parentage, since it is not a manner of choice for the most part. And I have had stout ale brewed by an Irish housewife that ranks with the best of them," added van Clynne. That was near the highest compliment he could pay, though of course Rose did not know it. "But on the whole, on the average that is, the Dutch—do not take this wrongly, but a Dutch girl in your place would not have let my notes lie burning on the bench, for example."

Rose pulled her horse short and turned to confront her new companion. "I will take this abuse no longer," she warned.

"Abuse?" Van Clynne was not used to being addressed in such a tone by anyone, let alone a waif of a girl. Still, he was in a most generous mood—the bloodletting had removed many of the heavier humors from his body. "Dear, I am afraid you misunderstand me. I am not criticizing you, but praising you."

"Colonel Gibbs said you would complain about everything from your horse to the weather. But he did not say I should stand still for personal attacks. Remember I am armed, sir, with his own pistol."

"Have you heard me utter one word of complaint the entire time we have been together?"

"Hardly," she said satirically.

"I rest my case," said the Dutchman, prodding his horse to continue.

Van Clynne could not stay quiet, of course, but he turned his discourse to more neutral topics, settling on the state of the roads. He explained they had grown considerably more dusty since the British took stewardship of the area from the Dutch, and indeed were now in such an advanced state of ruin the wilden would hardly consider them cleared sufficiently for a planting of corn.

"Here we are," said van Clynne as they reached a fork. "To the right."

"No, this is the road to the general's headquarters," said Rose.

"Obviously in the dim light your tender eyes were momentarily clouded. Blink them twice, and follow me on the proper path."

"Your way heads east, mine is west. The Peek Skill Creek is west, is it not? And the general's headquarters in the village that lies near it?"

"The general's headquarters is indeed in the village near the creek," said van Clynne. "But we are not fish. My road will lead us to a shortcut and thence to another and a third. We will arrive in an hour at most."

"This will take us back to the Post Road," countered Rose. "And even a flying horse would take two hours to get to the general."

"Indeed. And we will be here all morning if you do not respect your elders and do as I say. Come." The Dutchman kicked his horse for the first time since he had boarded. The animal was so surprised he turned his head back to see if perhaps he had gotten a new master.

"My way," said the girl firmly, starting down it.

Now if there is one thing Claus van Clynne is truly and justly praised for, it is his knowledge of the road system of the province of New York. Indeed, the Dutchman has an almost encyclopedic knowledge of the highways and byways of the eastern half of the continent, and could find his way from Georgia to Vincennes with little difficulty. He especially prided himself on his intimate familiarity with shortcuts; if there was a way to cut five minutes off a route, he not only knew it but could point to an alley shaving another two.

Nor was his ability failing him here, though he might have admitted under different circumstances that Putnam's headquarters could be reached from the left as well as the right fork. But, aside from the sour mood inflicted by the loss of his walking-around money, Rose's manner put him off. She had been somewhat disagreeable since their first acquaintance, and hardly acted with the deference his station as leader of their delegation demanded. He stuck his nose into the air and declined further comment, riding on and expecting Rose to come galloping up behind.

She did not. In fact, she decided to let go of the carriage horse she had tied behind her own so she could increase her speed northward to General Putnam. She was not only sure her way was the right one, she was happy to be free of the Dutchman and his laggard pace. Her heels eagerly found her mount's ribs in an effort to make up lost time.

Loosing the horse was a critical mistake, though there was no way she could have known it. Had the animal not been left to stand idly at the intersection, the shadow lurking on the road half a league behind would have been forced to give up his chase, as the pain from his wounded rump had not responded satisfactorily to the cures he had administered. This was due in no small part to the aggravation caused by trotting behind his quarry.

But presented with a horse, Major Dr. Harland Keen saw the prospects for the swift completion of his mission improve greatly. Before climbing onto its back, he took two small bottles from the brown leather satchel he'd removed from the carriage. The contents of one were smeared as a salve on his wound; the other was divided between himself and the horse, man and animal taking an immense gulp.

The effects of the second bottle hit Keen more quickly than those of the first. His head lightened, and he felt his heart pounding in his chest with new energy. He boosted himself up on the animal's back, and found the mare as frisky as a two-year-old Arabian. The horse actually rose on her rear legs, anxious to run.

But before he could set out, he faced a choice—which road had they taken?

Keen had been too far behind to hear their arguing, and so had no way of knowing that either path would lead to one of his enemies. He decided to head down one until he reached some town or settlement; if he could find no trace of the fat Dutchman and the undernourished girl, he would retrace his steps and try the other.

There was no doubt in his mind that he would eventually find them, deliver his revenge, and then move on to apprehend the Gibbs character. In fact, Keen might be fairly said to be driven by the prospect of revenge, especially against the girl, whose actions at the cottage had catapulted her to the head of his list of likely candidates for experimentation.

Left or right?

He chose the left fork, for no other reason than it seemed to be the one his horse preferred, its nose already aimed in that direction.

Twenty-six

Wherein, Jake becomes a Tory leader, for the good of the Cause.

The sun's advance rays were just tickling the horizon as Jake secured the door of the barn where he had tied up the militia guards. He had little time to celebrate, and bare seconds to catch his breath. The American spy feared one or two of the Tory prisoners inside the church might fight off the effects of their late-night drinking and notice he was gone.

Deciding to reenter the church through the choir window, Jake took two long pieces of rope from the barn and knotted them together. After listening at the door for any sound inside—none yet—he knotted a large circle in the rope, stood back and threw it up, hoping to hook around one of the wooden staves that stood in the bell tower window above. Two tries and nothing; by the third Jake was working on a story to explain his coming through the front door. On his fifth try, he caught a metal spike in the ledge. He was up the side and in the church so quickly that the parson would have applauded, thinking that only a soul bent on salvation—and enamored with his sermons —could move so quickly.

Jake found the choir loft empty as before. Leaving the rope dangling outside, he crept to the balcony, his eyes adjusting to the dim interior. When he saw the coast was clear he retrieved the rope, coiling it in the corner, then slipped over the choir rail and plummeted to the floor.

This was not a particularly quiet operation, and in fact he cursed aloud, echoing his knee's complaints. He proceeded to walk noisily through the church, carelessly kicking pieces of wood and a man or two lying on the floor. A complete circuit brought him back to the front door, where what began as a cautious knock soon developed into a very loud bang.

While their homemade hootch had rendered the prisoners nearly unconscious, Jake by now was making enough noise to wake the dead. Of course, the dead might have woken with less ill-effect—his pounding echoed and amplified the pounding between their temples, and the first reaction Jake heard behind him was a collection of groans and undisguised threats.

"Smith, Smith, what the hell are you doing?" called Caleb Evans, stumbling toward him.

"There's no one guarding the front door. Help me."

"What do you mean?"

"Come on." Jake stepped back and took a running jab at heavy wooden door, pounding against it with his shoulder. The hinges barely creaked.

Caleb watched in bewilderment as he tried a second time. "Are you sure?"

"Don't you think the guards would be pounding on the other side if they were there?" Jake was so caught up in his role that he was out of breath. He wished he'd had the foresight to remove the strong board placed as a block across the door outside; as it now stood they would need several men rushing against it at once to break it down.

"The boy said the attack would come two hours after dawn," said Caleb, looking up at the soft light filtering into the church from the upper windows. "That's still a long way off."

"I was watching from the loft when the militia guards left," said Jake. "They ran off down the street with their weapons and haven't come back. Who knows what sort of trick Captain Busch is playing on them—we shouldn't wait to see if it fails." Jake took another run at the door, wincing as he rebounded. "Are you going to help me?"

Caleb's brain was still muddled by the effects of the drink. He continually blinked his eyes, as if focusing them could sharpen his thoughts.

"The boy said they would come for us," he said finally.

The words were somewhat slurred. "I think we should wait."

"Were we supposed to stay in the jail after we were rescued?" argued Jake. "They've obviously made whatever decoy attack they were planning, and we're supposed to take care of the rest."

By now most of the other men had gotten up from their straw beds and staggered forward. The majority were simple farmers, and while their sympathies were with the king, until their imprisonment they probably would not have considered themselves active combatants. Still, their jailing had hardened their opinions, and they were anxious to escape. Those with families were very concerned for their safety. So Jake did not have to provoke them too hard to get a consensus: there was no time like the present to leave.

The first rush at the door nearly reversed that decision, as the six volunteers were repelled not so much by the wood but the fierce pounding of blood against their brain pans. Fortunately, the barrier had started to give way, and Jake was able to organize a second posse, which split the lower panel in two. He kicked through the wood and was able to upend the wooden bar with his hand; one more bounce against the door with his shoulder and the metal lock snapped free.

He glanced at Caleb, then cautiously stepped through the portal—there was always the possibility the commotion had drawn reinforcements.

The street was as empty as a village clerk's office five minutes to supper time.

"Let's go!" he shouted from the porch. "Everyone out."

"What about Wedget?" asked one of the Tories inside.

"What about that bully bastard?" responded another. "I say, leave him to his fate."

"We ought to kill him. Damn rebels'll prob'ly set him free."

Once more Caleb and Jake exchanged glances. "I don't think that's wise," said Jake. "I think we should take him along, same as everyone."

But the sentiment was strong against him. Caleb finally

shrugged—as the bully was not part of the ranger troop, he did not care to exert himself in his defense.

"Well, come on then." Jake led the group down the street, past the barn and in the direction of the bridge where he had hoped to meet van Clynne last night. He was struck by a sudden fear that he might meet the Dutchman now; the squire had a tendency to involve himself in the worst situation at the least opportune moment.

Jake need not have worried, for van Clynne was hurrying in the opposite direction, determined to show the upstart little girl that his path to Putnam was indeed shorter and faster.

Perhaps the word "hurrying" is not entirely accurate. It could be used to describe the initial stages of his journey, as he prodded his horse along the road, grumbling about the fact that children no longer showed the proper respect for their elders. He shared his theory as to how this had come to happen with his horse; in abbreviated form, it had to do with their parents allowing them to wear shoes at a young age.

The horse, who had worn his own shoes from early colthood, did not make much comment. Nor did he respond to the Dutchman's requests to avoid hitting the ruts in the road as he traveled. But the animal was only too happy to comply when van Clynne loosened his makeshift rein and let him take a slower pace.

A considerable amount of time had now passed without van Clynne having acquainted himself with food. While one might think that his experiences with Major Dr. Keen had vanquished his appetite for good, the exact opposite was true. In fact, the Dutchman's voracious nature had been stoked beyond its usual capacity by the previous afternoon and evening's activities. The more van Clynne thought about it, the more he concluded that his way of getting to General Putnam's headquarters was so much faster than Rose's that he could easily afford a short respite from the ardors of the journey, and still beat her.

As it happened, he knew of a very accommodating innkeeper who lay a short turn off a minor detour not a quarter of a mile up the lane. With the imagined scent of bacon tickling his nose, he shook his lead and encouraged the horse to pick up his pace.

Twenty-seven

Wherein, the narrative ventures to the Loyalist side of the story, where the perspective takes a darker turn.

While Jake was doing his best to let himself be captured several hours earlier, Captain Busch was trying equally hard to escape. Busch had to sneak through the dense underbrush for several miles to avoid the Rhode Islanders who had ambushed them. When he reached the highway without any sight or sound of them, he took off his green coat and hat, realizing he'd increase the odds of surviving by doffing signs of his alliance.

Still, removing the coat felt perilously like striking the flag, and the ranger captain suffered a pang of regret as he stuffed the green badge of his honor beneath a rotted tree trunk. He went out onto the roadway, and paced in the dusty rut along the far side back to the south, hoping Smith would appear soon.

Busch walked back and forth like that for nearly an hour, willing his man to rush out of the woods with his cocky attitude and declare he would sooner fight the entire rebel army than surrender. When that didn't happen, Busch began to fear Smith had been captured. He trusted the new man like few others he had ever met, and knew he would keep quiet about his mission. But that alone might provoke the American rabble into killing him, especially if Smith were still wearing his uniform.

Reluctantly, the Tory admitted he must leave his subordinate temporarily to his fate. Smith had at least one chance of salvation if captured—before leaving the farm near Salem, Busch had given Sergeant Lewis strict orders to carry out the attack on the rebel jail within two hours of dawn, even if he himself hadn't returned by then. He had reasoned not only that Corporal Evans and possibly Johnson needed to be freed, but that he and Smith might be among the internees by then.

The rebels were likely to think the spy they were chasing would head back toward British lines in the south, so Busch temporarily headed north, intending to turn west and double back as soon as possible. Still wet from his swim, the Tory leader alternately walked and trotted through the darkness. He had grown up here, and knew the countryside intimately, but much of it seemed foreign to him, as if he'd been plunked into a far-off country. He could not fathom why so many of his neighbors had allied themselves to the revolutionists. Without the stability of the crown and the order of law, he reasoned, men were no better than a pack of dogs in the woods.

Busch's mood lifted a bit when he came to the property owned by Horace Fiddler. Now retired and near seventy, Mister Fiddler had been for many years a teacher—his teacher as a matter of fact, and he flattered himself that the old man had even taken a shine to him. Tiptoeing onto his land, he recalled a morning many years before when Fiddler had praised his ciphers. He remembered the moment fondly, and used it to justify his temporary rental of the old man's horse.

With a whispered promise not to harm it, he led the old mare from the yard to the road, waiting until he was out of sight of the house to board her. The animal was not used to being ridden—Mister Fiddler hitched her to a small kittereen or two-wheeled light carriage for his travels—and turned her neck in amazement at this unfamiliar task. But Busch persevered, gently goading the animal, and was soon riding at a steady if slow pace.

As the safest path back to Stoneman's lay over Pine's Bridge anyway, Busch decided to meet up with his ranger troop as they assaulted the jail. He got off the horse as the sun dawned; by then he was no more than two miles from the small crossroads hamlet where the church was located.

Had he stayed on the horse and continued riding, even at an easy pace, he would have gotten there just in time to see the last escaping prisoner kick a bit of dirt back in the direction of the church before running to catch up with the others. But wanting to keep the borrowed horse from accidental harm, he stopped and tied her by the side of the road in front of a house he knew belonged to another former student. The man—a carpenter whose politics were radical but who was otherwise honest and fair—undoubtedly would recognize the mare and see that she was returned.

Folding his arms across his vest, Busch walked on toward the prison. It took a little over a half hour for him to arrive at the neighboring creek. From the small bridge he could see that the church door was open and there were no militia guards in sight; he walked on cautiously, realizing the operation must be over.

His plan to slip through the hamlet and continue on toward Stoneman's was ruined, however, when a man and woman emerged from the barn across from the church shouting. The two militiamen Jake had tied up earlier followed them out, and Busch saw that the entire population of the hamlet—counting children, this came to nine people—had been alerted and were running back and forth, shouting alarms.

Another person, indeed, nearly any British officer, would have faded into the woods. But Busch was a highly conscientious leader, and trusting that he could talk himself out of danger if confronted, he decided to step briefly into the church to make sure all the prisoners had escaped.

The building was deserted, except for the bully, Charles Wedget, who remained tied in the corner. Wedget had formerly been apprenticed to a tubal-cain or iron founder several miles north; Busch recognized him and knew he was a Tory sympathizer.

He also knew the oaf well enough to realize why he'd been left behind. He frowned and spun quickly on his heel.

"Free me, John Busch, or I'll give you away."

Wedget had barely closed his mouth when Busch was upon him, pistol drawn and held to his head.

"Prepare to die, then."

Tears welled in Wedget's eyes as his bully's facade crumbled like the ruins around Rome. "Save me, and I can help you. The escape was planned."

"I planned it myself," replied Busch. "Those were my rangers you saw."

"There was no troop of rangers. The guards had all disappeared. It is a rebel plot. Please," pleaded Wedget.

Busch was still considering what to do when two citizens with rifles entered the building.

"They beat this man up because he was a patriot," he said quickly, pointing at Wedget. "Apparently they're planning an attack on White Plains."

"One of them locked the guards in the barn," said the plump man in front. "We've sent for a troop of Massachusetts men."

"I'm with the Committee on Conspiracies," said Busch. "I'll go on south and alert the forces at White Plains."

"You look familiar, sir," said the man as the other untied Wedget.

Busch thrust out his hand. "John Busch."

"Are you from this area?"

"Further west, near the river." Busch turned quickly. "Myself and this man will take the road south; send someone north to General McDougall. Hurry, man; John Jay will have my head if these villains get away."

Busch's mention of the well-respected Jay—besides heading the Committee on Conspiracies, he was a member of half a dozen other patriot committees and a state judge besides—set aside any doubts and got the locals into motion. Busch was able to commandeer two horses; he and Wedget were heading for Pine's Bridge and Stoneman's beyond it before the citizens had even stumbled across the third guard tied in the woods.

At the intersection of the road to Stoneman's, Busch wheeled his horse to a halt and confronted Wedget. The bully's face immediately clouded; Busch kept his hand near his belt but realized his pistol would not be needed to gain more information.

"What was it you meant to tell me?" asked Busch. "Make it quick, man."

"Everyone got drunk last night on some squeezings we'd made."

"Everyone but yourself."

Wedget nodded. "And one other man, brought in late by the militia. He said his name was Smith, and a more suspicious lurker could not be found anywhere in the country."

Busch betrayed no emotion at the mention of his comrade, though he was glad he was alive—and not surprised Smith had withstood the temptation of alcohol. Nor did he think it unusual that such a man as Wedget would misjudge his character. But as the tale of Smith's mysterious disappearance from the loft continued, Busch felt the sharp pang a bullet makes when it enters the gut. The pain took a crooked path, wrenching much of his insides, and though he endeavored to keep his face motionless, Wedget was encouraged by the turn of his lip to embellish his tale.

"When this Smith returned," said the bully, "the guards were gone, and all of the prisoners walked free from the jail. Something had been arranged; I heard this Smith whispering outside."

"How could you have done that when you were tied in the corner?"

"I did, sir," said the bully. "The door was broken from the inside, to make the escape look genuine. The man is a traitor and a rebel, this Smith. You can tell by his eyes."

Busch took his pistol from his belt.

"Where did they go?"

"D-don't shoot me."

"I will if I find you've lied. Where did they go?"

"They were talking about a farm over the bridge."

"Come with me," said Busch, uncocking his pistol. "And pray to God my guess is right. For if I'm wrong, I'll kill you."

Wedget struggled to keep up as the Tory captain, filled with regret as well as rage, turned his horse toward Stoneman's.

Twenty-eight

Wherein, Jake matches wits with Sergeant Lewis in a less than fair fight.

Though he might have understood them, Jake was not aware of the Tory captain's strong emotions, nor did he know he had reached the church. In fact, Jake suspected that Busch was waiting at Stoneman's, and spent most of the journey from the jail to the Tory hideout rehearsing an account of his capture that might sound somewhat plausible in the commander's ears.

The motley parade of Tories encountered no resistance. Caleb and the others seemed content to let Jake take the lead. The American secret agent kept the irony of his position to himself.

When they reached Stoneman's, they found the remnants of the ranger force in disarray. The clouds gathering overhead were but a hint of the dark mood that had descended on the supposedly unflappable irregulars. The captain had failed to return, and the attack on the jail had been forgotten as they attempted to regroup after last night's ferocious assault.

The details of what had happened were sketchy at best, and varied depending on the teller. The story gaining the most currency was that no less than three full regiments under General Alexander McDougall had overrun the corps as it slept. The rebels were said to have been beaten off by a determined counterattack, the rangers' only ally the attackers' inherent cowardice. Even so, the barn had been set ablaze, several horses lost, and a sentry killed. In addition, one of the servants seemed to have been carried off as a war prize.

Sergeant Lewis was wearing a bandage that swelled his already large head to twice its normal size. He was in a dismal, cranky mood, and not even the news of the bloodless escape from the rebel jail could cheer him.

A pugnacious sort who wore his ranger beanie far forward on his head when it wasn't injured, Lewis had just the kind of bravery for which Tories are known. While his commander and the British were nearby, he strutted back and forth in his fine boots, tugging at his green jacket with all the pride of an Italian prince. But under the pressure of the night's difficulties, his fine facade had crumbled. He was now a testament to indecision, inclined to wait at the farm for Busch to arrive, even if that took the rest of the war.

"Well, ya made sumthin' of yerself, at least," he said to Jake after hearing the erstwhile ranger's report of the adventure. "Ya might as well see if ya can scrounge up some breakfast. The girl's run off—or was carried away, whichever. We'll be here a while."

Jake realized that Busch's absence would make it considerably easier to sabotage their plot. He also knew that the longer they waited at Stoneman's, the better the odds he would show up. And so he endeavored to encourage the troop to leave for its rendezvous.

A rendezvous had been planned, hadn't it?

"Keep yer shirt on," said Lewis. "I'm the one what knows the plan, not you. It's me that's in charge."

"I don't question that," answered Jake. "But we should leave before the rebels find us."

"Why? We don't have to be aboard the *Richmond* until 3 P.M. Our horses will get us there within an hour."

"Given the problems of yesterday," said Jake, acting as if he had known the plan all along, "I suggest we should leave immediately."

"What do you know of the problems of yesterday?"

"One of the men told me the horses got sick."

"Yes, well, they're better now," said Lewis stubbornly.

"Even so, the rebels will be searching the countryside for us, sir."

The sergeant garumphed, and cast an eye toward Caleb. As corporal, he should have led the breakout from the jail, or at least the march south. Now his authority had been usurped by the uppity Smith. Would the sergeant's post be next?

But Jake was well used to dealing with a man such as Lewis, and proceeded to praise the sergeant for his leadership and rapport with the men. His words sounded so sincere that Lewis was somewhat softened.

"I wonder, Sergeant, why you were not actually placed in charge from the beginning," assayed Jake. "After all, you are considerably closer to the men than Captain Busch. And I don't believe what the others have whispered."

"Tell it to yer bunter, not me," said the sergeant. While the expression implied that Jake should seek the services of a woman whose loose morals would make her believe anything, there was nonetheless a hint of wounded pride in Lewis's face.

"As I said, Sergeant, I didn't believe it."

"Who said it? Who?" Lewis's cheeks screwed up like an angered puffer fish.

"I would not," said Jake, "turn traitor on any fellow in this troop."

Lewis's hand jutted forward as he prepared to demand an answer to his question. But the rush of blood to his head so increased the pain in his wounds that he had to stop and put both hands to his skull, as if it were about to explode.

"Listen, fool," he said after calming somewhat, "when ya've gone through the hells that I've been through, then ya can talk of courage. Anyone can stand up to a salt merchant on the road, or break out of jail."

Sergeant Lewis spit into the dirt and took a step away, debating with himself. Surely the rebels would launch a search for the escaped prisoners, and that could complicate things. He didn't like Jake Smith, but if he ignored him, Smith was exactly the sort of eager beaver fellow who would stir up the others.

It was probably Corporal Evans who had gone around whispering. He was just the type.

Well, the sergeant could deal with both of these bastards in one blow.

"All right, get your horses!" he thundered to his men, his voice trailing off because of the pounding in his brain. "We ride in five minutes—less, if possible. Smith, find yourself a new uniform from the pile there. We have no more helmets.

"You, Caleb—take Smith and round up these citizens and lead them south to New York. Hurry, before the damn rebels or their Skinners make an appearance."

But Jake had no intention of leaving the main column.

"Begging your pardon, Sergeant, but if Captain Busch doesn't show up—"

"I'm in charge now, Smith. I'll not have my orders questioned."

"I merely wanted to point out that I know the layout of the defenses around the chain, which I presume is our target."

"It might be," allowed Lewis, who in fact had only a hazy idea of the shape their mission would take once they reached the *HMS Richmond*.

"Then perhaps it would be better if I came with you to the ship, where my knowledge may prove useful."

Smith, the sergeant reluctantly conceded, had a point.

"Caleb, choose another man in his place," he said. "The rest of you, look sharp!"

"Perhaps six or seven men might be better," suggested Jake. "There are many rebels about."

"Don't push it, Smith. If yer gonna have a comment every time I give an order, ya'll soon find yourself swingin' upside down from an oak tree, no matter how important ya are."

Even so, the sergeant did add a few more soldiers to Caleb's force, leaving the ranger complement at a bare two dozen. He boarded his horse—to say "jumped on" would imply more vigor than his bandaged head allowed —and got his troops in motion. A few of the rescued Tories came up to him as he was about to leave and protested that they would prefer to go back to their homes in place of the city.

"Yer homes are as good as burned down now," he told

them. "Ya better do as I say and get yourselves south. Come tonight, the rebels will be getting what they deserve, thanks to His Majesty's Navy. And Earl Graycolmb's Doughty Rangers."

Twenty-nine

*Wherein, the virtues of the so-called weaker sex are
extolled, far too briefly.*

*H*ave we yet paused this narrative long enough to make
proper note of the contributions of the female portion of
our population to the great cause of Freedom? Have we
noted the unparalleled bravery, the sacrifices of the dis-
taff of our society? Or forayed into the differences of
women bred unto this New World, bolder than Eve herself, veritable mothers of Liberty?

Alas, if we have not had time to do it until now, we will
lose this chance as well. One of those brave women—nay,
she is barely a girl—was last seen riding hard in the night,
heading northwards for General Putnam's headquarters
to alert him and save the country from ruin. Her ride is
every bit as important as Paul Revere's, and should she
achieve her goal before daybreak, undoubtedly her name
will be mentioned in every sentence that praises the Boston silversmith.

Unfortunately, she is not to reach her goal, though this
is not due to any failing on her own. She rides her horse
as swiftly as possible, and while Squire van Clynne might
beg to differ, her route is a good one. But—and here is a
serious "but"—she is being pursued by one of the most
accomplished members of the British Secret Department,
a ruthless man who justifies his personal deprivations
with the rubric of philosophic experimentation, indeed, a
man whose polished demeanor hides the ferocity of a
wounded lion.

Rose McGuiness drove her horse hard once she was
free of van Clynne. But the poor animal, stolen from the

Tory rangers, had been left in a much weakened state by
the poison Jake had fed it the day before. The stallion
quickly tired, and within three miles simply stopped in
the road, near total collapse.

Rose slipped from its back and patted the animal's
heaving side. She realized it would die if pushed any further, but her mission could not afford a long delay. So she
caught the ribbons of her bonnet and tied them firmly
around her neck, pulled her cloak tight against the rising
wind, and set off on foot up the road.

The sun tickled the Connecticut hills to her right,
struggling to break through the ever-increasing layer of
clouds. Rose aimed to approach the first homestead she
came to and persuade the owner to lend her a horse to
proceed north on.

She had gone no more than a quarter mile when she
heard hoof beats coming up the road behind her. Her
first thought was that the fat Dutchman she had rescued
finally had realized his mistake, and was now coming to
make amends. She put her hands on her hips and continued walking without turning back, smug in the knowledge
that her path had proven the correct one.

But the lesson of Pride and its inevitable downfall that
Rose had so recently delivered to Major Dr. Keen was
now to be visited on her, with great severity. For the person approaching was not van Clynne but Keen himself.
The doctor spurred his drug-stimulated horse, the lingering flicker of pain in his rump where Rose's bullet had
buried itself an extra incentive. Hunkered down on his
horse like an English riding champion—which indeed he
had been during his youth—he plucked her from the
roadway with no more difficulty than if he'd picked up an
injured bird.

Freedom's partisans are not so easily vanquished. Rose
punched and kicked at the side of Keen's horse, forcing
the doctor to slow the animal and concentrate on his
steering. As she felt Keen's pressure lighten, Rose sunk
her teeth viciously into his thigh, which had an immediate
effect—he dropped her on the road.

The girl was barely able to get her arms out to break
her fall as she tumbled against the hard clay and rocks.

Spilling in a heap, she righted herself and flew for the woods, losing a shoe and her shawl in the process.

Keen cut her off, pulling the horse around and riding quickly to the edge of the path. Rose turned and darted back and he was before her again, flashing his sardonic smile. The flickering rays of the early light glanced off the rings on his fingers as a golden beam slashed from above and caught her on the neck.

Rose yelped in pain as she fell down on her back, hurt by the blow from Keen's cane. She remembered the Segallas tucked into her sock and reached for it, only to feel the heavy pressure of Keen's shoe on her hand.

The doctor flicked his cane and a long blade of silver shot from the tip like the tongue of a serpent's mouth.

"A very pretty face," he told her. "What a shame if I shall have to cut it severely."

The point of the knife brushed lightly on her cheek, and suddenly Rose felt incredibly warm, as if she'd been placed next to a fire. Indeed, she was convinced that had happened—for her conscious mind fled, and she lapsed back against the ground in dark limbo.

Keen examined the small slice he had made on her cheek before hauling her aboard his horse. It was a superficial wound, though it easily accomplished its purpose—the introduction of a sleeping drug into her blood system. The effects ordinarily would last a full hour, but given his experience with van Clynne, the doctor took no chances now. He threw her over his horse and returned quickly to the animal she had abandoned; the horse's ties served as hard restraints against her wrists and ankles. He then took a small envelope from his satchel, and mixed it with a few drops of a blue liquid contained in a dropper bottle; the doctor had to use a spoon to complete the operation and the mixture was crude and inexact. Nonetheless, he could tell from the scent—a light mixture of chamomile and licorice masking a more medicinal flavor—that the proper reaction had taken place. And the drug had the correct effect: after Rose was forced to swallow, her body suddenly bolted upright, eyes wide open.

Rose was both a bold and strong young woman, a fine

example of American breeding. But she was no match for Keen or his formula. Her throat burned with the hot liquid, then she began to feel dizzy.

Keen, standing at her side, began to make suggestions to help the process of the drug along. Though her limbs were clamped with tight straps, he told her she was free. He suggested that her arms had been changed to wings; he could tell by her smile that she believed she had escaped him at last.

"Who is the eagle flying near you?" Keen asked in a level voice, as if he saw the vision he was introducing to her mind. The technique had been taught to him by the African necromancer who gave him the drugs.

"Colonel Gibbs," replied Rose.

"Your lover?"

She shook her head. "My fiancé Robert is working on the chain. Colonel Gibbs is going to protect it. He'll peck the Tories' eyes out. I must fly to General Putnam, and tell him. The fat Dutchman will help. The Tories plan to attack tomorrow night. I—must—go."

Keen let her body collapse back onto the ground as the drug's more useful effects wore off. She could now be expected to sleep for several hours, and would wake with a terrible headache—assuming, of course, that Keen decided to keep her alive until then.

The doctor faced a minor dilemma, in that the girl had revealed that this Gibbs character was trying to sabotage a British military operation. While his own mission naturally took ultimate priority, he was nonetheless bound to thwart them, especially since the British target was the chain, which he properly understood to be the key rebel defense on the upper Hudson. He would have to alert his fellow countrymen.

There was only one ship on the river this far north that could serve as a command post for such an operation, the *HMS Richmond*. Keen's best course of action was to find the ship and its commander, inform him of the plot, and continue with his business.

This was not necessarily a detour, he realized; it might very well lead him directly to his two targets. Nonetheless, he was annoyed, for it meant he would have to postpone his dissection of the light sack of flesh he hoisted in front of himself on the horse.

As Keen turned the animal back toward the cottage where his carriage had been left, Rose murmured something. Still in the last throes of the suggestive phase of the drug, she repeated it at Keen's request: "Just let me catch a wink of sleep, darling."

"Oh yes," chuckled the doctor, patting her cheek as he set off. "You'll need your rest."

Thirty

Wherein, Captain Busch is too late, Squire van Clynne is too poor, and Lieutenant Colonel Gibbs too quick.

The rangers had been gone from Stoneman's for nearly an hour by the time Busch arrived. But there was still plenty of evidence that they had found hot action there—the captain quickly noticed the damage to the barn, and then saw the crude grave of his soldier. He jumped from his horse and knelt at the tree-limb cross, convinced by some unworldly sense that the man below had been killed by his nemesis, Jake Smith. It was as if the knowledge was contained in the soil he rubbed into his fingers.

"Damn you, Jake Smith," he cursed as he rose. "I don't know what your true name is, but when I find out it will be sung in infamy throughout the land."

"Infamy!" repeated Wedget, still sitting on his horse. "Kill Jake Smith!"

"You!" shouted Busch. "Off the horse."

"But—"

"Off, I say!" Busch took two strides to his horse and grabbed his pistol.

In that short distance his stature seemed to double. Wedget slid off the horse quickly—only to find the captain standing before him, pistol in hand.

"You gave me your word you'd save me," cried the former bully.

"I did nothing of the sort," said Busch. He cocked back the lock as tears rolled down Wedget's face. "Off with your shoes."

"But my feet are swollen inside."

"I will shoot them off, if you wish."

Wedget yanked away at the boots with all his might. It was plain that he was speaking the truth; his feet were in horrible shape, filled with pus and bleeding besides. Busch realized no further precaution was necessary against his being followed.

"A word of any of this to the rebels, a word of me or any citizen loyal to the Crown, and I will search you out and pull the tongue from your mouth with my own fingers," promised Busch. He pointed the gun back up the road. "That direction will take you to New York, if you're lucky."

"B-But I want to come with you."

Busch's answer was only to point the pistol at Wedget's face. The bully took a step backwards in fear, and then the man who yesterday had proclaimed himself complete despot of his squalid domain lost control of his sphincter.

So may it be with all bullies, and especially that one most pernicious, King George III himself. Busch shook his head in disgust, then leapt to his horse and galloped off in pursuit of the damnable Smith. Wedget remained sitting in the dust for a long while, sobbing softly to himself.

Claus van Clynne, Esquire, had by now had a sufficient breakfast to find himself in a relatively forgiving and generous mood. This spirit extended itself toward the upstart young woman whom he had rescued earlier from Dr. Keen's clutches—for so the story formed itself in his mind, now that he had time to arrange it for proper dramatic effect—and most certainly would include any enthusiastic patriot who found it within his heart to extend him credit in the name of the Cause.

"No matter what your politics, you'll pay me for the meal you've just had," said the innkeeper where he had breakfasted. "I don't give an owl's hoot for your feelings toward me, one way or another."

"Come, come, my good Jan. How long have we been acquainted?"

"An hour too long, by my reckoning," spat the keeper. "Claus van Clynne, I've never known you to travel without three bags of silver coins tied to your waist, and twice that number hanging from your neck."

"You may search me, sir, if you do not take my word," said van Clynne, sweeping his hands out in a great gesture. "Though the day a Dutchman does not trust a fellow Dutchman—well, that is a sad day for us all, is it not?"

"I'd trust him as far as I could throw him," said Jan's wife from the doorway. Missy Lina had always been a disagreeable woman, as far as van Clynne was concerned.

"I hope you are not seeking to search me as well," he told her. "There are certain proprieties, even among friends."

"Come, Claus, stop this nonsense and pay up," said Jan, holding out his palm.

"I tell you, I have been robbed. First of my salt, then of some paltry coins—mostly clipped, fortunately—and finally of all my warrants and true currency. I am as penniless as the day I was born. My wealth perished in a fire several miles from here."

"What about the notes you keep in the heel of your shoe?"

Jan turned and looked at his wife in amazement. Van Clynne blustered again that all his purses had been stolen.

"I'm amazed that my integrity is called into question," he said. "I am penniless and you will find no coin in my possession. I am searching for my friend Jake Gibbs; surely you can wait until I find him or he comes here himself, for he will be glad to pay you from the sum he owes me. He has blond hair, stands just over six foot and is often seen in a contemptuous three-cornered hat. Despite his poor taste in headgear, he is a personal confidante of His Most Excellent Excellency, General George Washington, and therefore should be dealt with accordingly."

"Stop trying to change the subject," said Jan's wife. "Pay us with the money in your shoe, smelly as it may be."

"Surely you do not expect me to part with notes that were given to me by my dear, departed grandfather."

"Your grandfather passed on before they were printing bills on paper," said Missy. "Besides, he took every guilder he had to the grave."

With a vigorous complaint, van Clynne reached down and amid much huffing and puffing pulled his leg across his lap. He stopped suddenly and asked if there was no longer such a thing as modesty abroad in the country.

"Pay up or we shall teach you about modesty," warned Missy, who in the end condescended to turn her back while van Clynne took off his shoe and worked a trick screw on the heel. The continental note—his last emergency money, he swore—was more than enough to compensate for his meal.

The Tory rangers, meanwhile, were making steady progress toward the river. Sergeant Lewis rode at their head, next to a private deputized as ensign and carrying their trifling green pennant on a long halberd. A British chronicler might well find pleasure in describing the image of their green coats passing in thunderous parade down the road, their bear-fur bonnets proclaiming doughty resolve and righteousness before man and king.

We, of course, shall have none of it, turning our attention instead to Jake. Decked out in a fresh new ranger coat—a bit short in the sleeves, but otherwise serviceable —and armed with a musketoon and light sword, he rode at the rear, urging the last stragglers onward. The troop moved off the main road near Pine's Bridge to follow an obscure Indian path in the forest.

Jake realized their route had been chosen to lessen the odds of a chance meeting with American patrols. He also suspected that Busch himself had set it out for the sergeant, as he was much more familiar with the area than Lewis.

Would he follow it then if he arrived at Stoneman's after his troop had left?

Surely an easy question to answer, and Jake looked for some method of precluding that possibility. Now that Busch was out of the way, he wanted him to stay there; the British forces would be formidable enough without the captain to help them. With luck, Old Put had already captured him and was preparing a nice surprise at the chain, thanks to Rose's warning—but Jake knew better than to count on luck.

Could he count on the caltrops he'd taken from the barn's arsenal, however? Multi-spiked iron snowdrops or nails, caltrops are often used by cavalry units to slow pursuit. Properly deployed, they put an iron bramble in the path of mounted troops, whose horses must step smartly if they are not to be stung and lamed.

Jake did not have enough to blanket the path. Instead, he scattered them clandestinely, dropping them randomly when the other rangers were not watching. He hoped that a traveler in a hurry—as Busch would be—wouldn't notice the iron prickles until it was too late.

"What the hell are you doing, Smith!"

Stunned, Jake looked up into the face of the sergeant, who had stopped at the intersection of an old Indian path and waited for his men to pass him.

"I was just dropping these in case we were followed," Jake explained, tossing his last handful.

"Stop wasting time. No one is following us. Now, down this path and look smart—I don't like stragglers."

"Yes, sir," said Jake, kicking his horse.

Lewis was wrong, and in fact the group was being hotly pursued—by Captain Busch. The Tory urged his horse onward, succeeding in getting it to gallop—only to be deposited in a heap when the stallion stung its foot on one of Jake's caltrops not a quarter of a mile from the place where Lewis was bawling out his rear guard.

Cursing, Busch gathered his wits as he dusted the dirt from his clothes. He examined the horse and found the poor animal sufficiently injured that it could no longer be ridden.

Had the circumstances been different, he might have shown the poor animal more compassion. Indeed, he was a great lover of horses, and realizing that the animal's wounds would soon heal, he did not shoot him. But neither did he take the horse with him as he struck out through the woods toward a small inn where he believed he could secure—or steal, if necessary—another.

The tavern was owned by a Dutchman known to be sympathetic to the rebels, though his wife seemed a better judge of character. Not that it would matter much if they tried to stop him—Busch made sure both pistols were loaded as he ran the half mile to the house.

Thirty-one

Wherein, Squire van Clynne falls in with a group of patriots inoculated with the love of Freedom, among other things.

Refreshed from breakfast, Squire van Clynne set out with new vigor, though his pace was even slower than before. The chafing of his posterior against the horse's back was so severe that he would have gladly reopened his heel for the purchase of a saddle, if only one were to be had. The country here, rolling hills and forest, had not been adequately developed, in van Clynne's opinion. It was given over entirely to apple farms, and even these appeared to have been abandoned for a considerable length of time. Thus the conveniences of modern life—like saddle shops—were not at hand.

Nonetheless, he made steady progress, prodded by the knowledge that General Putnam was empowered to issue a certificate that would compensate not only his financial losses but his efforts to the Cause as well. Indeed, an even greater plan took shape in the Dutchman's mind as he rode. He would ask—nay, he would demand—that the general appoint him to the lead of a squadron of men, bold soldiers whom he would take against these Tory scoundrels, foiling their attack on the Great Hudson River Chain and, not incidentally, recovering his salt.

And very possibly, his coins as well. His exploits would be proclaimed throughout the continent—he knew newspaper owners in every city of consequence—and General Washington would volunteer to restore his estate. The Congress would demand it, for the population would have his name on its lips: "Claus van Clynne, the man who saved the nation. The man who saved the Great Hudson River Chain."

The Great Hudson River Iron Chain—that had a better ring to it. An iron-willed Dutchman who saved Freedom. Why, he could hear the minstrels celebrating his victory already.

Actually, now that he listened more closely, the music sounded remarkably like "Yankee Doodle." Van Clynne turned his head in the direction of the song and spotted a small wooden house not far off the road. A makeshift banner fluttered on a slender twig stuck near the doorway; van Clynne concluded that the red dots on yellow background were a company marker, designed to give the unit pride as well as identity. The owners were all inside, obviously celebrating a recent victory over the British—for the song, once sung in derision of the American army, had been turned around and appropriated as the boldest curse possible against the British regulars. The young voices sang with such joy and emotion that the roof was shaking, and van Clynne suspected that though the sun had only just risen, the men had gone through their daily quotient of rum.

Providence had sent him his soldiers!

Why not enlist them now, foil this damnable plot against the chain, and present himself to Putnam as a hero instead of one more worthy citizen who had been robbed?

Any reader who thinks van Clynne would have paused to answer such a question, rhetorically or otherwise, does not recognize the true nature of the Dutchman. In a thrice he had crossed the small stream separating him from the house and hitched his horse outside. Without bothering to knock, he walked straight inside and immediately fell in on the chorus of "Yankee Doodle."

There were a dozen young Connecticut continental privates crammed into the room, all in spirits jolly enough to ignore his frequent sour notes. They passed him a cup of cider and continued their song, venturing into a verse the good Dutchman had scarce heard before:

Heigh for old Cape Cod
Heigh ho Nannatasket

Do not let those Boston wags
Feel your oyster basket.

The ribald play on words—the interested reader should ponder the image contained in the last line—had a curious effect on the Dutchman, whose recent pursuit of love had made him curiously chaste. He turned red and momentarily lost his voice. Nonetheless, he soon fell back in tune as the men swung into a rousing version of "Free America," Dr. Joseph Warren's ingenious revision of "The British Grenadiers."

The accompaniment was provided by a pasty-faced man of twenty or twenty-one, who worked his fiddle with such fervor that his face blotched with red dots and smears of exertion. Every man kept beat with his shoe, and one or two blew tin whistles instead of singing.

Van Clynne was moved by the evident patriotism and spirit of this group; Fate could not have provided him with a better troop to win his fortune back.

"Gentlemen, gentlemen," said van Clynne, moving to the center of the room as the song ended. "Please, listen to me a moment. Who is the commanding officer here?"

"There's the colonel, sir, John Chandler," said one able young man, a great strapping lad barely out of his teens, if that. "He's up at headquarters, though."

"In this cottage, who is in charge?"

"Well, there's no one in charge exactly, sir. We're all equals, being free men of Connecticut."

Van Clynne nodded his approval; these were men inoculated with the spirit of Democracy from the very cradle.

"Excellent, excellent. Whom do I have the pleasure of addressing?" asked van Clynne with great flourish, determined to commit every detail of this entire episode to memory, so as to provide a careful account for future chroniclers.

"Private Martin, at your service," said the young man, who promptly stuck out his hand and shook van Clynne's.

"My name is Claus van Clynne, gentlemen. I am a special agent assigned in the service of His Excellency General Washington"—not a great exaggeration, surely, if one follows the logic that Jake Gibbs was Washington's man, and van Clynne his coequal assistant—"as well as a roving member of the Committees of Correspondence, Safety, and Ale Tasting." Ever mindful of his audience, the Dutchman was well aware that these young men would respond most fully to the last. "My rank as a hereditary commissioner of the New Netherlands authority as vested under the Treaty of Amsterdam is the equivalent of captain-general, triple-cluster."

The privates were somewhat stupefied by the speechmaking, and while looking for any excuse for action—they had been confined here for some time—did not know precisely what to make of their visitor.

"Begging your pardon, sir," said Martin, seeing he had been designated their spokesman. "With all respect and honor, we've heard of lieutenant generals and major generals and even general generals, but never captain-generals. Where exactly does that fit in?"

"Captain-general, triple-cluster," van Clynne corrected. "Unclustered, it would correlate precisely between my brother generals, the lieutenant and major. But the clusters are indeed multipliers, as I'm sure you recall from your school days. If we turn to the table of threes . . . "

The reader by now is familiar with the sort of logic and tactics of persuasion the Dutchman habitually calls on, and thus will not be presented with the bulk of his argument as to why the (admittedly) hereditary rank was in (more than) full force at the moment. It should be noted that he was careful at all times to use such words as "equivalent" and "correlate," so that he could not technically be charged with impersonating an American officer, though in spirit he was certainly leading these poor young men to think he was as authorized to direct them as Old Put himself.

The soldiers, naturally, began very doubtful, but a twenty-minute lecture from Claus van Clynne on nearly any subject will weaken the strongest will. And it must be remembered that his speech, if based on premises that were somewhat false, was aimed at an end wholly true—the defeat of the British.

"I won't bore you with my other titles and authorities, gentlemen," said van Clynne, after he had indeed bored them at length. "Suffice to say that we have a mission of vital importance ahead of us. Take your weapons and follow me!"

"Begging your pardon, sir, but follow you where?" asked Martin, who alone among the group had tried to work out the logic of the speech.

"There's no time to lay out the entire mission, son," said van Clynne. "We've no time to lose."

The Dutchman, intending to lead by example, stepped to the door and opened it without waiting for the others. He was surprised to see a bored soldier facing him at thirty or so paces, on the other side of the creek, musket with bayonet fixed in his arms. The man motioned with annoyance that he ought to close the door.

Van Clynne took the action any army commander does when faced with something he does not immediately comprehend—he ignored it, and stepped through the doorway.

"Let's go, men. The Tories won't spend their morning waiting, I warrant."

"Get back inside," said the guard. The man was a Massachusetts private, and as such, not given to much chatter.

"Who do you think you are addressing?" demanded van Clynne. "This troop is now under my direction."

"I don't give a bent penny for whose direction they are," responded the guard. "Get inside and close the door. You're infecting the air."

Van Clynne turned back to his men, determined to lead them onward despite the obviously addle-brained soldier outside the door. "Let's go, boys! The man outside has attended to one too many cannons, since he forgets what side he's on. Try not to harm him."

None of the soldiers moved.

"Come, then, you're not cowards are ye!" thundered the Dutchman, his voice elevating. He knew instinctually that these small trials must be overcome manfully, or the bigger ones will be lost before they are met.

"We're not cowards, no sir," said Martin. "But—"

"But nothing, man! Let's go!"

"We're confined to barracks, sir," ventured another of the soldiers.

"What crime have you committed?" asked van Clynne. "Come now, confess; I'll arrange a pardon straight away."

"No crime, surely, sir," answered the man. "We've been inoculated for the small pox, and are under quarantine."

Thirty-two

*Wherein, Claus van Clynne moves the poxed soldiers to
their duty and his glory.*

*H*ow sturdy is the human spirit, how unflappable in the
face of pending ruin and destruction. Present it with the
proper motivation, and no enemy will loom too large, no
problem will seem insurmountable.

Granted, the difficulties faced by Claus van Clynne at
the moment were legion. There was the infectious pox—
which having stepped foot in the room he was powerless
to escape. There were the damnable British, and the heinous Tories. There was Dr. Keen, deprived of his leeches
and his assistant, but in possession of his considerable
wits and the squire's innumerable coins. There was the
plot to destroy the chain, which van Clynne must foil if
his beloved Cause was to survive. Then there was the
mission to Schuyler, which while annoying would nonetheless help him toward his ultimate goal of retrieving his
lost patrimony.

But what are these against the strength of a Dutchman's will? How do they measure against his wisdom, or
his tongue?

"Gentlemen," van Clynne began, addressing the Connecticut soldiers, "hear me well. For what I am about to
tell you, I swear upon the Bible, is the truth without exaggeration. You may think—"

Here he was interrupted by a member of the company,
who announced that he had a Bible, and the Dutchman
was welcome to use it.

Van Clynne swore twice—the first time under his
breath—before continuing. "My friends, as you know,

there is a huge iron chain stretched across the Hudson not ten miles from here, a barrier that protects all of northern New York, and thereby all of interior New England, from the British Navy and her marines, not to mention whatever troops her ships could ferry northward. As we stand here, confined to our barracks for an ailment no more serious than a sniffle—"

"Excuse me, sir," said Martin, stepping up to the Dutchman. "But the small pox is not a trifling disease. Many of our friends have died from it."

"A trifling disease that is no more than a hiccup to stout young men as yourselves—"

"But, sir, the doctors say that we must be confined to barracks for two weeks at least. Just three days ago most of us were abed, and some of us are running fevers and—"

"Enough!" thundered the Dutchman, and in his voice was an echo of that great and noble warrior-cum-governor, Peter Stuyvesant, bad leg and all. His round red cheeks grew rounder and more red, his beard twitched with emotion, even his brow furrowed as he exhorted the men not to let a scratch on their shoulders keep them from their duty. They could stop these heathen Tory pigs, but they must act quickly; they must move now. They must gather their weapons and march from the barracks to meet the enemy with all haste and speed.

"Let the pox be our secret weapon!" thundered van Clynne to a rapt audience. "Let us infect the bastards, as Freedom has infected us! Let the fever of Liberty singe their skins and boil their souls!"

Even so great an orator as Patrick Henry might have been pleased at van Clynne's wondrous performance, if not his exact metaphors or grammar. If his success was due largely to the soldiers' innate love of Freedom and their overwhelming boredom at having been locked up for nearly two weeks, certainly the result could not be argued with—van Clynne managed to rally the entire company to him, and proceeded out the door to confront the poor Massachusetts man assigned as guard.

Now as far as the Massachusetts regiment keeping

watch over the inoculated soldiers was concerned, there always had been some question as to whether they were protecting the sick men from attack, or keeping them from running away. Indeed, General Putnam—who was actually opposed to the inoculations but in this matter found himself overruled by the commander-in-chief—believed his most formidable enemy to be desertion, not disease or the redcoats. All manner of men were constantly leaving his army, most to go home, though a number to rejoin and claim extra enlistment bonuses and a few, it must be admitted, to join the enemy. Thus the Massachusetts man who now found himself confronted by two dozen troops, unarmed but certainly infectious, can be forgiven if he thought he was confronting a mutiny.

Van Clynne intended to win this man to his small army in the manner he had won the others. But when he lifted his arm and pointed his finger as a necessary precursor to making his point, Private Martin and a few of the others misunderstood, and rushed at the soldier. The Massachusetts man stood his ground as they approached, right up until the moment he heard a few of the soldiers begin to cough. At that moment he decided there was no honor in catching the pox from a fellow American and ran for his health, if not his life. The Connecticut troops responded with a laugh, boasting that this was an omen of the easy time they would have with the egg-laying Tories their general had promised to take them against.

They led van Clynne to a barn on the farmer's property where they were camped. Here they liberated their weapons, a healthy supply of ammunition, rations for the march—and a pipe of rum, to help speed their progress.

The inn that Busch headed for after his horse pulled up lame was in fact the same establishment so recently darkened by Claus van Clynne. Indeed, the somewhat smelly odor of his folded dollar bill still hung in the air, midway between the chestnut floorboards and the white-washed ceiling.

Missy Lina was hard at work scrubbing the floor with

the aid of some fresh sand when Captain Busch stepped inside.

"John Busch, I never," she said, standing. "We thought you'd gone and joined the Tories."

"Not quite," said Busch, deciding on the spot to play the rebel for this old acquaintance. "I had forgotten this was your inn, Missy. Is your husband at home?"

"He just walked up to Elmendorff's to sell some eggs for me," she said, wiping her hands. Missy gestured at the square table to Busch's right. "Sit down; I'll fetch you dinner."

"I haven't time," said Busch. "I'm pursuing a rogue." He caught himself, just barely, from saying 'rebel.'

"A Tory thief?"

"Yes," said the ranger captain, who realized that by embellishing his lie he might win a horse with no trouble. It is not difficult to cobble a falsehood from the truth. "His name is Jake Smith. He stands six-foot-two, with very blond hair. Have you seen him?"

"He sounds quite a lot like Claus van Clynne's friend," said Missy. "Which would certainly make him a rogue."

Busch nodded, not knowing whom she meant but definitely wanting to encourage her. "He's my age or a little older," said Busch. "He gives his name as Jake Smith. He has the accent of a man from Philadelphia, and I daresay he is a clever sort. We must capture him directly."

"That is exactly the man Claus described," said Missy. "But he said his last name was Gibbs."

"Jake Gibbs? And who was this van Clynne?"

Missy had never liked the squire and now gave full vent to her feelings. "As fat a Dutchman as any sow in the city of New York streets, I'm sorry to say."

As her description continued, Busch realized that she was describing the man Smith—make it Gibbs—had harassed on the road, the man from the inn whose salt they had stolen. Suddenly the entire plot unfolded before his eyes: everything had been cleverly arranged to deceive him.

No wonder they had been surprised above his father's farm. But the fact that his fat Dutch compatriot was searching for him must mean some part of their plot had gone awry. The rebel army must not yet know of the plan against the chain; if Gibbs could be captured quickly, they would be thwarted.

"I've never heard of Claus being partial to the British," continued Missy. "Still, he is capable of almost anything."

"I need a horse," said Busch. "Quickly. I think I know where this Gibbs fellow is headed."

"Claus went north," said Missy hopefully.

"A horse?"

For a moment, the mistress of the inn hesitated. She and her husband had only one horse, and lending it to Busch, even for the good of the American Cause, entailed a severe sacrifice. Busch was just slipping his hand to his belt to retrieve a knife and force the issue when Missy set her jaw and shook her head so vigorously her kerchief slipped.

"If it will help foil a Tory, I'm sure Jan would gladly lend it," said the woman.

Rose had told van Clynne that the rangers used Stoneman's as their camp. The Dutch squire therefore decided to strike there immediately, rather than waiting for them to attack the chain. He knew the farmer—an old countryman, barely six years removed from England— and was quite satisfied that his low opinions of him had been borne out by this perfidious association with the British forces.

The distance from the inoculation barracks to Stoneman's was at least ten miles, even with the several shortcuts the Dutchman led his men over. This was an immense march, given their condition, and van Clynne found it necessary to keep up their spirits with a variety of exhortations and, in a few instances, complaints. Mounted on the fine carriage horse stolen from Keen— now equipped with a proper rein and saddle from the supply barn—he rode up and down the column cheering and chiding his troop. He made wild promises of success, and gave out not a few hints of fantastic rewards if only their pace could be accelerated.

The result was severe disappointment when the men, formed into a picket line and charging through the

woods, burst onto the grounds and discovered
Stoneman's to be practically deserted. The only occupant
was the former Tory and now ex-bully, Charles Wedget.
The man sat on the ground between the barn and the
house, picking at his unshod toes, lamenting his fate.

Wedget took no notice of the Connecticut soldiers as
they assaulted the place. They, in turn, were inclined to
dismiss him as inconsequential, until they realized he was
the only enemy they were likely to find here. They surrounded him and waited while their commander trotted
his horse back and forth across the barnyard, in the forlorn hope of having somehow missed an entire company
of rangers.

By the time Private Martin flagged him down and
asked what should be done about Wedget, van Clynne
was in his habitual mode of complaint, grumbling about
the fact that no one in the country was ever where they
were supposed to be anymore.

"We have a prisoner, sir," said Martin, breaking van
Clynne's litany.

"A prisoner! Excellent work. Lead me to him." The
Dutchman slipped from his horse and the animal gave a
whinny of gratitude, not because its physical burden had
been eased but because the Dutchman's grumbling had
begun to weigh on its nerves. "Is he armed? Has he barricaded himself in some makeshift fortress?"

"Not exactly, sir. In fact, he is sitting alone in front of
the barn, without a weapon or even shoes."

"We will be on guard for some sort of trick," said van
Clynne, approaching the knot of soldiers in front of the
barn. "Reinforcements may be nearby. Search the rest of
the farm." The Dutchman glanced over the crowd at the
prisoner. "What is he doing?"

"He appears to be talking to his toes, sir."

"Do they answer back?"

"Not that I can tell."

"That's something, at least," said the Dutchman. He
took up a spot and observed Wedget a moment. The former bully had stopped playing with his feet, and was
frowning toward the rest of the company in a somewhat
threatening manner. But he made no sign to get up—

wisely, as half a dozen muskets were pointed in his direction.

"Well, sir," said van Clynne, stepping forward, "it seems we have finally met." Van Clynne bent to Wedget and extended his hand. "I have searched the entire countryside looking for you."

"Run back to your hole, rebel. I have no idea who you are, and you won't trick information from me. I have sworn an oath."

Wedget clamped his mouth shut, refusing to speak. Considerable beard stroking and even some hat preening followed before van Clynne decided on a new tactic. He sat in the dust with the man, then asked a variety of questions in the friendliest tone possible. None drew a response until he happened to ask if the man had met a Jake Smith, the name his companion had been using when he was last seen among the Tory rangers.

"I'll kill him! I'll kill him! And any of his friends!" Wedget launched himself against the Dutchman's throat. Taken by surprise, van Clynne had everything he could do to avoid being throttled. It was only after two soldiers came to his aid that he was able to free himself.

But the sudden outburst represented Wedget's last stand as a Tory. As he fussed against the two men holding him—they were able to bring him under control only by stomping on his wounded feet—van Clynne realized the man would now answer anything put to him.

"What happened to your shoes?" he demanded.

"Captain Busch took my shoes and left me here because he didn't want me to follow," answered Wedget.

"Where did he go?"

"To the river. There are men there. Jake Smith is a traitor and a rebel."

"Where along the river? Do you know?"

Wedget shook his head. Tears welled in his eyes.

"Which road did he take?" asked the Dutchman.

Wedget shook his head. "He was going to the cove and boats."

"Which cove?"

Again Wedget shook his head.

"Should I twist your toes?" threatened the Dutchman.

"They're going to the *Richard,* a boat or something."
Wedget erupted into tears, and van Clynne realized his
usefulness was at an end.

"That might be the *Richmond,*" suggested Martin. "It's
a British ship off Dobb's Ferry or thereabouts. We've
heard talk of it."

The mention of the word ship brought with it the necessary association of water, and van Clynne's cheeks momentarily paled. He turned from his soldiers and began
calculating the number of coves on the river between
Peekskill and Dobb's; the number ran to the hundreds.

But you would not need a cove if you rode to Dobb's,
or any place where wharfs and docks would make boarding boats a routine matter. So van Clynne decided to
eliminate Dobb's and the vicinity. The cove in question
must be either in Tory hands or sparsely settled country,
which would most likely place it above Tarrytown; while
there were many Tories still on the old Phillipse ground
thereabouts, the patriots were strong enough to alert
American troops and might be expected to take some
action against a force of rangers.

One by one, van Clynne eliminated potential landings.
While all of this mental process was severe work—several
beakers of ale would have been of great assistance—he at
last concluded that there were two likely candidates, both
a few miles north of Tarrytown, and both formerly used
by certain Dutch merchants to avoid the complications of
British taxes. Van Clynne was just trying to decide which
to try first when a shout came from the barn.

"We've captured an entire wagonload of salt, General," one of the soldiers declared. "There's enough here
to keep the countryside in beef for a year."

Thirty-three

Wherein, Claus van Clynne proceeds toward the river, as does his nemesis, Major Dr. Keen.

So was Claus van Clynne reunited with his salt. This development greatly cheered him, as he interpreted it as a sign that Providence would reward him for his efforts. Indeed, he went so far as to believe that his luck had improved severalfold. Not only would he save the chain and get his land back, but the name van Clynne would be celebrated with the likes of Adams and Washington.

While van Clynne was engaged in these flights of optimism, the Connecticut troops he had appropriated to his command were busy scouring the grounds for additional supplies and items that might help them. They discovered a half-keg of explosive powder and a few fuses, and a large and lengthy rope. This was no ordinary string, as it stretched over thirty yards. It seemed to have been constructed of fine Asian hemp and was particularly elastic. Being the George Washington of ropes, the men insisted on taking it with them; you could never have enough string in an emergency.

Four horses had been left at the farm. The Dutchman now discovered himself at the head of a mounted column —three privates apiece on the horses, with the rest of the men crowded atop the salt wagon, pulled by its ox and a horse. Several large white canvas sheets had been tied over the contents of the cart, for the sky looked threatening, and the Dutchman did not want to lose his salt a second time.

While overall the arrangement might seem a bit motley, it promised better progress than on foot. The soldiers clung to their various stations with good cheer, happy to be freed of the boredom of their quarantine. The easy victory at Stoneman's fired their optimism and bravery; they sang as they fell in behind their leader, (hereditary) Captain-General, triple-cluster, Claus van Clynne.

No general (hereditary or otherwise) was ever prouder of his men. The only thing the Dutchman lacked was a proper insignia of rank, and as he proceeded he tried to decide if their route would take them near any place where he might find a sword or epaulette.

While these thoughts may seem a diversion from his true task, in fact they helped spur van Clynne along. For had he been left to concentrate solely on the next stage of his mission, the good Dutchman might have severely faltered.

The reader will recall that Achilles's mother Thetis, wishing to make him invulnerable, dipped him in the River Styx, with the result that his entire body became invulnerable, except for that small part of his heel which was not immersed. A somewhat different result had occurred when, as a small child, Claus had been dunked in a barrel filled with water and kept there near to drowning.

While he had overcome his severe aversion to the sea in order to accomplish his last mission in New York, he was far from cured of this affliction and wished strongly to avoid anything to do with water. Had he contemplated the possibility of missing the Tories at the cove, and drawn the next logical conclusion—that they must be met on the river, aboard the *Richmond*—van Clynne's haughty tone and fearless direction surely would have faltered. Indeed, he began to hiccup uncontrollably as the column drew in sight of the Hudson.

Aside from two or three lost seagulls, the shoreline of the first cove was empty, and showed no sign of having been visited by the Tory party.

"They must be at von Beefhoffen's," the Dutchman said hopefully. "Quickly, men—I know a shortcut that will get us there within a quarter hour."

* * *

As van Clynne and his followers were hurrying down the valley, another traveler was proceeding in somewhat the same direction.

Major Dr. Harland Keen carried Rose on his horse to the charred remains of the cottage where he had tortured van Clynne. His carriage was still out front. Except for the fact that it had been ransacked by van Clynne in a futile search for his coins, the vehicle was in fine shape, its many concoctions and paraphernalia intact.

The same could not be said for his dead driver, whose battered body still lay before the ruins. The fire had burned a portion of his face away; even the hardened doctor felt some tingle, some shadow of grief as he dragged the dead man into the woods. A pair of ravens sat in the high trees nearby, undoubtedly angry that their morning meal was being stolen.

Percival's brief but valuable service had earned him a proper burial, but Keen did not have time to supply it. Instead, he threw two blankets retrieved from the ruins over him, vowing that the proper dignities would be accorded at some point in the near future, if not by Keen, then by forces he would direct hither.

After dressing his own wound and procuring a fresh jacket from the coach, Keen took Rose down from the horse. Her eyes remained tightly closed, her mouth agape, her reddish brown curls hanging in a tangle to the ground, as if she were Guinevere under some spell of Merlin's. Placing her on the carriage seat, he put fresh iron cuffs on her wrists. Rose slept the entire time, so heavily drugged that what should have been an expression of alarm and concern on her face was instead a vague smile.

Keen, tempted by the thin folds of the dress bunched up to reveal her naked leg, considered taking at least a portion of his revenge immediately. He forestalled himself, realizing revenge was best extracted at leisure, and after giving her a rough pat and fixing her clothes as if worried about modesty, ran to the woods and retrieved van Clynne's coins from their hiding place.

As he placed the pouches beneath the coach's rear seat, he caught a reflection of himself in the eyepiece of a small spyglass he kept there. His hair was disheveled, his cheeks were flushed, and his eyes—his eyes had that wild character so many of his critics had used in London as proof that he was mad. Truly, he told himself, they had confused genius with madness, high intellect with insanity —but nonetheless he paused to fix his hair, then took some paint to daub his cheeks and soften his brow. Finally, he retrieved a thin green vial from his store of medicines in the back; bracing himself, he uncorked it and drained the contents, forcing the liquid down against the natural reaction of his throat and gullet.

He only barely prevented himself from retching. Keen clamped his teeth together tightly and fought against the reaction; his fingers swung tight on the carriage wheel, holding on for support as tremors ravished his body. One hundred and seventy-six seconds of hell, and it was over; he felt the effects of the drug immediately.

The ill-tasting potion was his greatest discovery, made from a long list of expensive and difficult to obtain herbs and vapors. The slightly modified Egyptian formula promised immortality. While he doubted it could live up to that claim, Keen knew that each time he survived the bitter taste and reactions, he emerged refreshed and invigorated, and looked as if he were in his mid-twenties, despite his white hair.

He picked up his cane and leaned inside the coach door to tap the supine girl on her leg.

"Perhaps, my dear, I will give you a taste of this elixir. Eternal life would suit you—after we make a few other amendments to your constitution."

Keen laughed aloud and climbed up into the open driver's seat. He did not have a map, nor did he know the area. But the river surely lay to the west, and if he went in that direction he eventually would find a place where he could hire a boat and have himself rowed out.

Despite the thick clouds obscuring its path, the sun had already reached its meridian point in the sky when "General" van Clynne dispatched an advance party of his troops to scout the defenses of the second cove. As he waited with his main force, the Dutchman found his thoughts beginning to wander. He thought of his favorite gelding, left at the Mischief Inn; he thought of his companion Jake Gibbs, undoubtedly still disguised among the ranger troop.

And he thought, alas, of the river, and the dangers of traveling upon it if the Tories had been missed.

For a moment van Clynne wondered if it might be prudent in that case to hold his assault off until dark, when he would at least have the advantage of not seeing the waves before him.

But then a voice spoke in loud tones to his inner ear. It was so cantankerous, so cranky, so dour, that it could only belong to one person—Grandfather van Clynne.

"Listen to me, you no-account youngster, and listen good. This is your chance to win back our homestead. Get your fat arse out on the river or I will kick it there. Fail me, and never call yourself a van Clynne again!"

"Sir? General van Clynne?"

Van Clynne shook the apparition out of his brain and looked across at Private Martin, who had addressed him.

"General?"

"Hereditary general, remember," said van Clynne. "Captain-general, triple-cluster."

"Whatever you say, sir," said Martin. "There are horses and boats by the river, but only one guard," continued the private. "Should we attack?"

"Stealth, my boy, that is our strategy," said van Clynne. "I remember advising my good friend His Excellency General Washington the same thing on the eve of Trenton."

"You were at Trenton with General Washington?"

"Well, not precisely at the time," said the Dutchman, turning to his men. "You two execute a flanking maneuver from the roadside, you three come up the shoreline. The rest of us will give you a five-minute start, and then we will descend on them all, shouting like wilden."

"Wilden?"

"Indians, lad, Indians. Honestly, how long have you boys lived in this country?"

Whether van Clynne had actually been in the vicinity of Trenton—and the reader would be well advised to consume the full contents of his salt wagon before accepting that statement at face value—his plan here worked perfectly. The lone ranger guard was surprised and routed without firing a shot. While the man at first refused to give any information, van Clynne's direction that he be tied to a tree with a bonfire started at his feet soon changed his opinion.

Unfortunately, he knew nothing beyond the fact that the rangers had arrived here two hours before and taken boats out to meet the British warship, and that Captain Busch had arrived in a frenzy fifteen minutes ago, searching for a man named Smith or Gibbs.

The North River swelled and roiled angrily as the Dutchman turned to face it. With a gulp, he turned back quickly to shore.

"What I wouldn't give now for a cold pewter cup of nut-brown ale," sighed the Dutchman.

"There's bound to be some waiting aboard ship," said a voice that sounded suspiciously like his grandfather's.

Thirty-four

Wherein, Jake and the Tories reach the Richmond.

We shall turn back time to briefly summarize the actions of the rangers during the last two hours, as we have missed some coming and going while attending Claus van Clynne and his brave group of Connecticut men.

Earl Graycolmb, the villains' sponsor, would no doubt have been proud of the way the rangers rallied from their humiliating trials to arrive in grandeur at the obscure river landing west of Clark's Corners at midmorning. Their spirits had been quite restored, and even the sergeant felt his headache lifting slightly—until he dismounted.

A half-dozen large whaleboats had been secreted near the shore. The Tories needed only three, and even then could have fit several more men aboard each. After leaving a single man to guard the horses, they set out for their waterborne rendezvous. Though they were several hours early, they soon spotted a small boat headed upriver in their direction. Two volleys from the rangers were answered by a single pistol shot, and the sergeant quickly directed his men toward what proved to be one of the Richmond's boats.

The inexperienced rowers had difficulty coordinating their strokes at first, earning various shouts of derision from the midshipman in charge of the Richmond's craft. Finally, they began to make progress, and within an hour spotted the frigate, which lay south of Dobb's Ferry, a Tory stronghold.

The frigate Richmond was smaller and lighter than the

immense ships of the line that stood at the head of Britain's naval might. She carried only thirty-two cannon and was designed to be manned by just over two hundred men; even a smallish third-rater would have twice as many guns and more than twice as many men, sitting a full deck higher in the water. Nonetheless, the *Richmond* was impressive in the comparatively narrow confines of the river, lording it over her escort the *Mercury,* a 20-gun craft with a checkered career whom she had captured earlier in the year off Antigua.

The rangers approached behind the lead of the *Richmond*'s boat, rowing alongside the ship where a series of shouts and odd whistles welcomed them to climb aboard. Their weapons were ordered left behind; they would neither require them aboard ship nor be missing them very long, the boat's mate declared.

Jake leapt to one of the manropes and walked himself up the side of the ship to the entry port. This was a bit harder to do in practice than in theory, as the river was moving with particular vigor, rocking the ship back and forth. Jake mistimed his first leap, catching the painted yellow hull with one boot and one knee; unfortunately, this was the knee he had hurt several days before. His ligaments promptly reminded him he had not kept his promise to go easy on them.

Aboard ship, a sailor greeted the rangers with a contemptuous sneer. Obviously some sort of petty officer, though just as clearly not a gentleman, he had a brace of pistols in his belt and a thick naval cutlass hanging from a shoulder baldric that could have been stolen from a regimental drummer, given its ornate design and incongruity with the rest of his dress. This consisted of striped trousers that appeared loose enough for harem duty and a white shirt that had more stains than the average dishrag. If Jake were not playing the role of a Tory he would have found it difficult to maintain a straight face.

There was, nonetheless, a primitive efficiency about the man, as well as an air of toughness that perhaps owed more to the tavern district of the city where he had been recruited than life at sea. Jake nodded at him, and joined the other rangers loosely mustering at the side of the deck, next to a large, long crate covered by a canvas sheet. The identity of the item or items was concealed by the tarpaulin, which dominated that quarter of the deck and was guarded by two marines with loaded weapons.

A handful of other lobster-coats milled in the general vicinity, but they left the rangers to themselves, as if some native disease might infect them if they got too close. The sailors in the meantime went about their business without giving much notice to anyone, indiscriminate scowls pasted to their faces.

When the troop was all aboard, their sergeant attempted to muster them into order behind the tarpaulin. At that point, two officers approached. Had their feet not touched the broad deck planks they could scarce have had less authority about them. Nor was this air due solely to their elegant, long blue coats or the immaculate white knickers and vests. Their long, confident strides carried them quickly across the oaken deck, and the two marines assigned as their guard had to practically trot to keep up. The sailor who had shown the rangers aboard turned up at their right and announced in a loud voice that he had the honor of presenting his lordship Earl Graycolmb's Doughty Rangers to Captain John Lewis Gidoin and the honorable, if still somewhat young, Captain Sir George Valden.

The men could have been presented to King George himself with less fuss. The ranger sergeant, clearly awed, stepped forward and saluted.

"Captain. Captain. I am Sergeant Robert Lewis, t-temporarily in charge of Earl Graycolmb's Loyal—"

Captain Valden did not wait for Lewis to finish before demanding to know where in shitten hell—and worse—Busch was.

Lewis was not exactly a choir mouse, and had heard stronger language even on the Sabbath. Nonetheless, the spew of curses that emanated from Valden's mouth in connection with his question took the sergeant by surprise. In his view of the world, British gentlemen—and most especially anyone to whom the word "sir" was ascribed as an adjective—spoke in words that wouldn't flutter the meekest butterfly.

"Well, speak up, you arse. What the shitten damn hell happened to Captain Busch?"

"He's been detained, sir," said Jake when the sergeant was unable to speak.

"Detained where?"

"We were ambushed by the river during our mission to spy on the chain."

"And the sister-rogering turd rebels captured him?"

"No, sir, he escaped, but was unable to make it back to the rendezvous." Jake thought it wise not to mention his own adventures in jail, though that meant suppressing a desire to hear what new concoction of curses the inventive British captain might cobble together in his honor.

"See what comes of working with goddamn catch-fart Americans," Sir Valden said to Gidoin. "Mr. Washington undoubtedly knows the entire operation by now."

"Begging your pardon, sir," said Jake, "but General Washington is many miles away in New Jersey."

"Mister Washington," Valden corrected. The accordance of honor to the American general was a touchy subject for many British officers.

"How do you know where he is?"

A not inappropriate question, Jake thought to himself before telling Gidoin that it was common knowledge. "Even the farm waifs keep track of their hero," he added cheerfully. "It's a sport for them, just as many Londoners watch the king."

The parallel was not appreciated. Gidoin and Valden moved back a few paces to discuss how to proceed. More than Busch's failure to arrive, they were bothered by the disappearance of Major Johnson, the disguised marine officer who had been sent to help coordinate the operation. Johnson was supposed to have sent a second ranger group to the ship for the mission; both he and the Royalist had failed to show up as scheduled last night.

"Begging your pardon, sirs," said Jake, overhearing. "Our captain believed that Major Johnson was captured by the enemy. He was pursued and involved me in a stratagem to escape, but has not been seen nor heard from since. Our captain did not care a wit for him; we proceeded beautifully without him, and I daresay we will continue to do so."

Jake's voice was confident, and he spoke almost as if he were bragging about the Tory group's exploits. But he fully realized that the British officers would pay attention to the substance of what he said, not the style. He could thus fan their caution while seeming to boast of his group's fearlessness.

Sergeant Lewis, angry at being usurped and somewhat over his shock, stepped up to join him. "Sirs, begging your pardon, but my men and I are quite ready to proceed without Captain Busch or this Johnson fellow."

"Yes," added Jake. "I can supply all the intelligence we need about the chain. I walked out on it myself. There are no more than two dozen batteries concealed along the eastern shore north of Anthony's Nose, and I doubt that any of the American ships we saw are much bigger than this."

"How many ships?" asked Gidoin.

"I couldn't say precisely, sir, as it was dark and the masts tended to blend together. They were cowardly in any event, hiding upriver."

To every question the British commander asked, Jake replied with a boast and well-turned lie, making light of the defenses on the one hand, while greatly multiplying them on the other. His was the work of the greatest alchemist, his tongue a veritable philosopher's stone, creating from whole cloth—nay, from discarded wool—an army and navy several times the size of the largest force available on the continent. To order an attack against it, the British commanders would display a degree of stupidity unusual even for their breed. Even the marine guards accompanying them shuddered with Jake's description.

Jake continued on blithely, as if unaware of the effect of his words. Indeed, he stated quite clearly that he was ready to lead the force himself, and volunteered to command a vanguard of forlorn hope that would launch itself in rowboats, swim the thirty or forty leagues to the chain under fire from the shore batteries, climb past the two rows of raft obstacles and dive on the twelve-inch-thick chain, sawing it in half with the files they'd carry between their teeth.

"We already have a bloody-damn-well-conceived plan," said Valden in a withering voice.

"And what is that, sir? I stand ready to take my commander's place at the head of the column."

The ship's master cast a cautious eye toward the sky and bade Valden step away for a private consultation. They began discussing not only the defenses but how the bomb canoe—Jake heard the words but as yet could not make sense of them—would perform if the storm kicked up.

"I'm in charge here," muttered the sergeant to Jake under his breath. "Best remember your place."

"Captain Busch chose me to go with him to the chain, not you," said Jake defiantly. "I'll not back down before you, or before General Washington and his horde of rebel thieves."

Five more minutes of this, the patriot spy thought to himself as he folded his arms over his chest in mock satisfaction, and they'll pack me off to Bristol to recruit regulars.

Gidoin and Valden broke off their conference. They stepped forward and addressed both Jake and the sergeant, much to the latter's consternation. "In light of the situation," said Valden, "we are going to delay the attack until tomorrow evening. In that time, perhaps Major Johnson or your Captain Busch will reach us."

"Begging your pardon, sirs," said the sergeant, desperate to boost his image, "but why should we wait for either of them? I am ready to lead the way."

"Johnson planned the diversionary assault on Peekskill," said Valden. "It's his to lead. I'm not committing my marines to a donkey ass plan under the command of goddamn colonial half-wits."

"I know Peekskill as well as any man born here," said Sergeant Lewis, fired up by the insults.

"And as for the chain—"

"Let me go against the chain," declared Jake.

"I don't think—"

Jake turned quickly to the men.

"Who will join me?" he thundered. "Who will come with me for the honor of God and king? Who will defy certain death at these bastards' hands, face down their guns, and defy their bullets! I have seen their defenses and I don't care what the odds are—I say death is a noble thing in the name of our cause!"

Not surprisingly, no one stepped forward.

"Then I'll go myself!" he declared boldly. "I'll swim there if necessary and beat the damn Americans with my bare hands."

"Brave words. I could hear them halfway across the river."

All eyes on deck turned toward the entry port, where a man in shirt sleeves had just hauled himself up. His hair waved in the breeze, and his cheeks were flush, not with the exertion of hauling up the side of the ship but with anger.

"Arrest him," said Captain Busch, in his voice a barely controlled fury. He jabbed his finger at Jake as he walked across the deck. "The man is an American agent."

Thirty-five

Wherein, Jake's true allegiance is revealed, and he gets all choked up about it.

"**Y**ou damnable bastard," said Busch as his short but rapid strides brought him to his enemy. "You are as evil a traitor to king and peace as any man in this land."

There was a moment of shocked stillness on the deck, perfect quiet as the rangers, the ship's complement, even the birds and animals of the surrounding shores, all stopped what they were doing and stared at the accused. Busch, whose fury welled so greatly that he was unable to continue speaking, moved his hand to slap Jake across the face. But Jake's reflexes were too quick for him, grabbing the arm and stopping it mid-air.

"I treated you as a brother," said Busch as he broke his hand free. "I trusted you."

The glare between the two men was as palpable as an iron rod. As yet, Jake had made no comment, offered no defense. He had faced such difficult moments before, and knew the best strategy was to continue the bluff through. But never had the impulse to throw off his disguise and declare his proper allegiance been so strong.

"What the hell is this about?" demanded Sir George Valden.

Busch's glare of scorn momentarily mixed with a hint of regret before he turned to Valden.

"I am Captain John Busch of His Lordship Earl Graycolmb's Rangers," Busch said. "Arrest this man as a traitor."

It was the sergeant, of all people, who spoke in Jake's defense.

"He led a prison break, and helped get us here." The sergeant's eyes went back and forth, from one man to the other. "How can you be a traitor?"

"The prison break was arranged," said Busch. "A man named Wedget told me all."

At that, the rangers began to murmur, and a few even to laugh, saying they knew of Wedget, and believed Caleb and Jake's story that he had been left behind for bullying the others. Busch put up his hand to silence them. "He has cleverly arranged everything, including an attempt on my life. His name is not Smith, it's Gibbs."

Until that moment Jake had been undecided on his course, content to let Busch state his case so it might be more easily refuted. But as Jake saw the British officers eying him suspiciously, he realized that even if they hadn't been by nature inclined to prefer a captain's suspicious word above the faith of an army of privates, they would certainly detain him for further investigation. Inevitably he would be found out.

And so, sensing that the locks about to be slapped around his arms were held by Fate herself, Jake decided he would go to his death as a man, not a rat shrinking in the corner. Along the way, he would do what he could to preserve his mission, which now depended on van Clynne and Rose, and General Putnam's troops.

"I did not arrange for an attempt on your life, nor did I work with others," Jake said solemnly. "Chance put us together. I admit I took full advantage of it."

Jake undid the buttons on his green coat and threw it to the deck, kicking it away with a disdainful push of his boot. "I am Lieutenant Colonel Jake Gibbs, a member of General George Washington's army. I demand to be treated as a prisoner of war, as I am entitled."

"You are entitled to nothing," declared Valden. "You came aboard as a spy."

"You betrayed your country and your king," said Busch.

In waistcoat, bareheaded, unarmed—save for the elk knife still concealed in his boot—Jake addressed the entire ranger troop, speaking as boldly as old Sam Adams would have.

"It is you who have betrayed your country. You would give up your birthright to a man you have never seen, and who regards you as a farmer regards the ants beneath his feet."

Busch spit on the deck. "You are beneath contempt, aligning yourself with criminals."

"It is your allegiance that puzzles me," said Jake, his voice a mild, calm rebuke. "A man with as much intelligence and courage as you ought to be fighting against the people who would make us slaves, not acting as their lapdog."

"The Devil speaks with a golden tongue," said Busch, his words equally soft.

The reader should not misinterpret Jake's next actions as the ship's captain and Valden did. For when two marines stepped up to grab him, Jake meekly let his arms be taken, and did not offer more than token protest as his hands were slapped in a set of iron cuffs. Before being searched, he volunteered that there was a knife in his boot.

The patriot spy surrendered so easily not because fighting would have been futile—certainly he would have been overpowered eventually, but by grabbing a nearby cutlass he might have taken a half-dozen Loyalists and perhaps one or both of the officers before being slain. Jake gave in because he wanted to turn his surrender to the patriots' advantage. He went easily to the captain's cabin, and gave a full if utterly false accounting of his operations, saying that he had been assigned by General Washington to spy in the area, though he had as yet been unable to report. He studiously avoided giving any impression that Old Put knew there was a plot afoot, hoping that the details he had already given Rose would be enough to foil it.

Jake said he'd been due to make a report the previous night, but had been unable to reach his contact in Dobb's Ferry. He named a prominent Tory there—a man he knew was loyal to the king, not the Americans—as his contact. He also took full credit for Johnson's disappearance, deciding that it was best to solve that mystery for the British before they complicated things by trying to do

so themselves. When Captain Gidoin asked who his accomplices were, Jake had a simple reply: "If I had assis-
tants, would I have been so easily found out?"

Busch, confident now that he had squelched the rebel
design to foil him, attended to his plans with Valden and
the captain of the *Dependence*, Lieutenant James Clark.
Clark had been a mate on the *Phoenix* in December when
the galley was captured, and as customary with the navy,
given command of the prize.

The rangers were still shocked by the announcement
that a man they had looked toward as a leader had been
discovered a traitor. Taken together, the events of the last
two days had greatly undermined their faith in the British, and while they found themselves now committed on
this path, they could not but fear they had chosen un-
wisely. Nearly every soldier, even when reminded of the
bounty offered for his allegiance, would have sworn on
three Bibles that he would have preferred the war never
happened.

Not so their leader. Busch emerged from his conference and strode across the deck to his men with firm
resolve, projecting the strenuous image of a leader with a
full grip on Future's throat. If he reproached himself for
having misjudged Gibbs, there was no sign of it. If he felt
betrayed—if indeed some part of him wanted to hear
from Gibbs that he was indeed the man he'd taken him
for—no one would have guessed from his manner.

A company of marines was mustered alongside the
rangers behind the tarpaulined supplies, waiting for their
commanders to give them their last instructions. As
Busch walked forward, he caught a glimpse of Jake being
led from the captain's quarters under guard. He swung to
his right, pulled his hands together at the hips of his
green ranger coat, and addressed a knot of sailors standing near the main mast.

"I need a strong man who is not afraid of becoming a
hero to posterity," said Busch without blushing. "You,
sailor, what is your name?"

The man, a tall fellow from Devonshire, smirked a bit

before answering. It was obvious he thought the colonial
captain full of himself. "Able Seaman Williams, sir."

"Can you paddle a canoe?"

"I've never tried, sir."

"Never?"

"I've stroked an oar in a ship's boat many times, if that
counts."

"Are you brave, Williams?"

The hard look in Busch's eye caught the seaman off
guard, and he took an involuntary step backwards. His
face turned as red as the sun that sets over the Indian
Ocean.

"Well?"

Williams pulled his chest up. "I am as brave as any man
in His Majesty's Service, sir."

"Excellent. I have need of a volunteer I can count on.
Come with me."

Williams fell in without so much as a glance at his comrades. Busch—who stood a full six inches shorter than
him—had transfixed the man by some innate power.

Jake, watching from near the cabin, could not help but
smile. The show had undoubtedly been put on for his
benefit, but that did not make the figure strutting across
to the knot of red and green coats any less impressive.

"We will board the boats shortly," Busch told the
troop. "We will proceed with the *Dependence* to the far
shore, where we will wait until twilight. When the shadows are long enough, we will move ahead and engage the
rebels directly below their fort near the Peek Skill Creek.
The sergeant will coordinate the attack on land, and we
will have the support of Lieutenant Clark and his craft.
Myself and Seaman Williams will proceed upriver once
the assault is launched. We will arrive just after their patrols have retired; I timed it myself the other day.

"You see the canoe lashed there on deck," he added as
two sailors pulled back the canvas before them to reveal
the odd-looking but deadly craft. "It will be a surprise for
the rebels, I warrant."

The vessel was a cross between a native dugout canoe
and a pregnant Franklin stove. A cone made of tin and
painted black covered the entire front half of the canoe,

its leading edge shaped into a triangular wedge like a rounded pyramid. The second half of the canoe was more familiar, though a little wider than normal, apparently to add extra buoyancy.

The tin cannister at the front contained a massive amount of gunpowder, which would be set off by a special waterproof charge contained in a glass tube. It was this charge that was to do the work against the river's iron chain; Busch would lash the canoe against the floats and set it off. Once the cable was broken, the British fleet would be free to proceed upriver at its leisure.

Jake surmised from the fact that only a small ship and not the entire fleet was anchored behind the *Richmond* that there was a certain degree of skepticism about the plan among the British command. Nonetheless, they were happy to let some Loyalist rangers take a crack at it, especially since their contribution amounted to landing a few marines ashore and running a captured galley under a few ill-aimed cannon.

But it was just the sort of bold, unexpected attack that would work best if the fleet stayed away. A full mustering of ships in the river would have put the entire countryside on alert. And more troops, no matter how well trained, would not increase the chances of success.

Busch turned from briefing his troops and walked back toward Jake, who with his marine guards was still waiting for the captain to finish some other business.

"I would have taken you with me," Busch told him. "You would have had the glory instead of this simple sailor."

"It would have been your greatest mistake," said Jake. "I would have stopped you."

"I doubt it."

"I'll stop you still."

Busch laughed. "You'll be hanging from a noose before I'm halfway there. I'm only too sorry that I can't stay to see that."

Jake shrugged bravely as the Tory went to supervise the crew struggling to get the bomb canoe into the water. Aided by a block and tackle, they finally lowered the vessel to the water, where it was tied to another canoe, and then rowed to the *Dependence*. Both small boats would be towed upriver behind the galley.

The *Dependence* herself looked oddly benign. Her sails gave a taut rap as the wind continued to pick up, the sheets fluttering against their rigging. The massive pipe in her bow was quiet, covered with a loose black tarpaulin that from a distance looked like a casually deposited blanket. Her sailors, in their striped jerseys and black trousers, exuded the nonchalant but busy air of men working an admiral's pleasure cruise, bustling about as if preparing for one more dalliance before the weather broke. The ship took on a load of marines and then her complement began working the oars, galley slaves like ancient Athenians.

Busch's company, again under the sergeant's command, descended to their whaleboats after the marines. Their captain had buttressed their emotions, though here and there a face betrayed great doubt.

Even taken together, the British landing force was many times smaller than the several hundred men that had harried Peekskill a few months before, but it was more than enough to draw attention from the chain while Busch and his sailor set their charge.

Jake busied his eyes with an appreciation of the rugged tree-lined shore to the north. His focus blurred as he gazed northward, as if he could somehow spot the iron and wood floating in the water. By now, Rose and van Clynne would have delivered his messages to Putnam; the general would be waiting.

The patriot spy bit the inside of his lip, wondering if his decision to admit his identity had been the correct one.

Some reflection on the choices of his life, both immediately past and those of long standing, were inevitable given the circumstances. The ship's crew, having gotten the raiding party safely off, now turned its attention to the traitor. A gibbet party was a rare treat, especially on so disciplined a ship as the *Richmond,* and the very ad hoc nature of the arrangements added to the excitement. Jake's situation was not unlike that of the first few Christians to be eaten by lions in the Forum, before the Romans truly got the hang of things. There was genuine excitement and anticipation, and even Captain Gidoin, who had witnessed executions of many different varieties, exhibited some jitters, which he disguised by striding back and forth as the rope was readied.

There was some discussion of whether the condemned man ought to be allowed the privilege of climbing up the mast to the spot where he was to be pushed off; this would require his binds be loosened if not completely freed, and it was decided Jake had forfeited such a right by rebelling against the king. Besides, there was some question of whether he might then be able to jump off of his own free will, and what the consequences of that would be; there was a heavy superstition against suicide aboard ship, though the doctor argued that a man who jumped under such circumstances could not be properly considered a suicide.

"You're not going to make me walk the plank?" asked Jake lightly.

"You've been reading too many rebel journals," said the captain. "This is a ship of the Royal Navy. We do not allow such barbarities."

"No, you merely hang people without proper trials."

"Gag him," said Gidoin firmly. "Then haul him up by the neck. If that doesn't kill him, drop him and repeat the process until it does."

Jake's curses were stifled by a stiff cloth that forced its way between his teeth. A rope thick with the toil of the sea was pulled around his throat and the knots adjusted while the other end was tossed upwards. Just as Jake felt the pressure beneath his chin, the ship's captain put up his arm and stopped the proceedings.

Merciful God, thought Jake to himself, at last justice prevails. I will have a trial in New York City, where at least I will gain some fame from a speech before being condemned to death.

"I'm forgetting myself," said Gidoin. "I'll not have a hanging without some passage from the Bible."

A collective sigh of disappointment at the delay rose from the sailors. A lad was sent scurrying to the doctor's cabin. Jake felt the light prick of raindrops on his face and looked up into the pregnant clouds. He wondered how wet he would get before being hanged.

"Ahoy! I say ahoy!"

So many of the ship's complement ran to the side to see who was yelling at them that the *Richmond* began to list.

"Help me up! Come now, I haven't all day! Toss me a line, lubber your yards, move your masts, I have important business and news for the captain!"

Frowning, Gidoin walked to the side. Without saying a word, he motioned with his arm and a half-dozen sailors flew into action. In a thrice, a rotund Dutchman in a black-gray beaver and old-fashioned clothes unceremoniously toppled through the entry port onto the deck.

Thirty-six

Wherein, Claus van Clynne has a salty time taking custody of his prisoner.

"*A*llow me to introduce myself," said the Dutchman after he righted himself. "Claus van Clynne, Esquire, counterintelligence agent par excellence, at your service. And—"

Suddenly the squire's complexion, which had been shading toward a deep green, changed to beet red. "There you are, spy!" he shouted. "I arrest you in the name of His Majesty the King! You shall not escape me this time, you cowardly bastard—you are my prisoner!"

Van Clynne advanced on his man like a first-rate warship bearing down on the enemy line. His arms flared, his neck telescoped; were it not for a smudge of mud on his russet socks, he might have appeared the personification of a heavenly avenger. Indeed, his thundering voice and sharp manner brought the entire ship to attention, and a few superstitious souls believed that Old Man River himself had come aboard, aiming to stop a deed that would cast bad luck upon the boat and all who sailed through this stretch of water.

"You there," van Clynne said to a marine. "Take charge of the prisoner. Get that ridiculous necklace off him and double the ropes on his hands and feet. You don't know who you're dealing with. Move!"

The last sentence thundered against the hills loud enough to wake Hudson's crew.

"Belay that," said Gidoin, stepping forward. "Who the hell do you think you are?"

Van Clynne swept around and doffed his hat in an aris-

tocratic gesture that would have impressed the dandiest
macaroni. His voice changed instantly from brimstone to
sugar. "As I was saying, sir, my name is Claus van Clynne,
and I am engaged on a mission for the king to rout out
treacherous traitors."

"The king?"

"Through Sir Henry Bacon," said van Clynne, letting
the name drop like a piece of fiery shot on the deck. "You
have heard of General Howe's intelligence chief, I assume."

"Don't insult me."

"I wouldn't presume to," said van Clynne, "and I expect similar respect."

Gidoin eyed him suspiciously. "Captain Busch warned
me this man had several accomplices."

"Do I look like a rebel, sir?" Van Clynne stuck his nose
into the air. "Here you, marine—double his binds, I tell
you. This man is not only clever, he is a thief. He will
steal the very ropes you tie him with if they are not heavy
enough."

As van Clynne fussed, an assistant followed him
aboard. Wearing the somewhat tattered clothes of a
country bumpkin, the man—we have met him before as
Private Martin, though he now wears even less official
markings than previously—saluted his commander and
informed him that all was ready.

"Bring it aboard then," said van Clynne. "Must I issue
a specific order for every stage of this operation! I tell
you, sir," the Dutchman confided to Captain Gidoin,
"there was a time when subalterns showed their own initiative. You could count on them to take the proper actions and get where they were going without having to
wash their linen for them."

"Excuse me," said Gidoin loudly, "but just what do you
think you're bringing aboard?"

"Salt," said van Clynne. "A dozen barrels of it, and at
bargain prices, too. Lord Howe will be overjoyed."

"We are not a supply ship."

"Admiral Lord Howe will be pleased to discover your
high opinion of yourself," said van Clynne in a withering
voice. "Dump the salt overboard!"

Captain Gidoin was an able seafarer and a competent captain, but when van Clynne was in the middle of a streak like this, no mere mortal could resist him. The references to Black Dick Howe, the navy commander whom Gidoin answered to, were particularly potent. The captain grimaced and belayed the latest command, waving two men to help hoist the barrels aboard.

"You thought you saw the last of me, I warrant," said van Clynne, addressing Jake. "Thought you'd escape me by giving yourself up here. Ha, I say. You'll not get away so easily."

"We were just about to hang him," said one of Gidoin's lieutenants, Justin McRae. "Not set him free."

"Oh, surely you jest. Excuse me, sir, but hanging is the least of his worries now. Hanging would be pleasurable. Come, take him to my boat. He must be punished suitably—hanging will follow his being burned at the stake, which itself will come after his being drawn and quartered. The only question is when he will be shot."

Gidoin put his arm up and the two marines who had taken Jake's arms halted. "Do you have any proof that you are who you say you are?"

"What sort of proof do you require?"

"Some insignia of rank or paper."

"A spy who carries proof that he is a spy? Let me ask you, sir—have you been at this business very long?"

"It is difficult to believe that a Dutchman could be employed in His Majesty's service," said McRae.

"Excuse me, but what is the name of the river we are floating in?" demanded van Clynne.

The officer looked at him as if he were a simpleton. "The North River."

"Is it not called the Hudson as well?"

"What's your point?"

Van Clynne accented his dignity by puffing his belly—an awesome sight. "My point, sir, is that this Hudson fellow belonged to which country?"

"He was an Englishman."

"Precisely. In the service of which country?"

"And what do we have here, an exchange program?" asked Gidoin.

"Well, sir, if that is the tone you're to take with me, I'll be off. Joseph," he said to Martin, "see to the prisoner for me. Find some coat for him; I wouldn't want him catching cold in this drizzle."

"Excuse me," said Gidoin, "but you won't be taking him anywhere until he's been hanged properly as a traitor and a spy. And you'd best provide yourself with some proof of your identification, or you'll suffer the same fate."

"Well, now, there's a complication," answered van Clynne, thoughtfully rubbing his cheek and placing his hand into his pocket. He retrieved a pass from Admiral Howe, another from his brother General Sir William Howe, and a long Dutch pipe. "Would anyone have a match?" he asked after handing over the papers.

One of the sailors fetched a light for him. The rain was not yet coming down hard enough to extinguish the flame, but the Dutchman was careful to shelter the bowl and take no chances. After a pair of puffs, he offered it to the captain but Gidoin declined.

"Now, as I understand it, you want me to take a dead man back to General Bacon for interrogation," said van Clynne, snatching his documents back. "Well now, I fear he would not be overly enthusiastic about that."

Gidoin frowned.

"Perhaps you know the general better than I," said van Clynne. "I will give him your regards."

The Dutchman's bold step toward the edge of the ship was arrested by Gidoin himself, taking hold of his arm. During all of this time, Jake had kept quietly to himself—not difficult to do, considering that he was bound and gagged and had a rope around his neck. His hopes of rescue had alternately soared and soured. Was this all van Clynne had planned, a simple bluff?

Fortunately, the rag in Jake's mouth was thick enough to choke his curses.

"Wait," said Gidoin, his hand on the Dutchman's coat. "Perhaps I'm being too hasty."

There was no need for van Clynne to conceal a smile at this late victory—the view of the pitching waves had quite vanquished any trace of optimism from his face. In fact, he was starting to feel a little woozy—Dutch courage could only travel so far.

"Are you all right?" the captain asked.

"Yes, yes," said van Clynne, sinking against the barrels.

The sailors recognized the problem and started smirking among themselves. Gidoin tapped his foot impatiently, wondering how England would ever conquer the damn colonies with men such as the fat Dutchman in its employ.

Jake did nothing, though this was not precisely his wish.

"I wonder," van Clynne asked, "would it be possible to get something to wet my thirst?"

"Seaman—a cup of water," said the captain.

"No, not water. Anything but water," answered van Clynne.

"Not used to being on a ship, are you?" said McRae, glad that the Dutchman's weakness had been so easily discovered.

"The sea is a dreadful place."

"We were discussing who would have custody of this prisoner," said Gidoin.

"You can have him," said van Clynne.

"What?"

"Take him, he's yours."

Jake's reaction could not be properly chronicled if we had eight hundred pages. Gidoin's was somewhat less severe, though the word "shocked" does not quite convey the half of it. But as he was about to question the Dutchman further, he was interrupted by miscellaneous shouts and whistles and piping and perhaps even an orchestra of drums welcoming a new man aboard ship—Major Dr. Harland Keen.

Thirty-seven

Wherein, Squire van Clynne's plot blows up.

Was the prodigal greeted with such shouts of joy as van Clynne received from Keen? Did Columbus respond with greater happiness as the king and queen of Spain met him at the dock?

Without question. Nor did van Clynne seem willing to put a single metaphor to the test. His body drooped, his arms hung down as he leaned back, practically draping over the nearest salt keg.

Jake's fury simmered. He did not know that van Clynne and the doctor were previously acquainted, and could conjure no explanation for the Dutchman's sudden and obvious—though as yet unstated—capitulation. Nor could he see, from his vantage, that van Clynne's pipe was not quite dangling aimlessly. For the good Dutchman had indeed come aboard with a plan that involved more than mere bluff—he'd fashioned a bomb inside the salt barrel where he was sitting, and was endeavoring to light it.

"Well, is not this my old acquaintance Squire van Clynne?" said Keen. "What a coincidence!"

"Yes, yes," said the Dutchman, fumbling to light the fuse without being detected. Why was nothing ever where it was supposed to be?

"You're looking quite pale, my friend. I hope you've recovered from my blood treatment."

"Superbly," said van Clynne. Worried that Keen would see what he was doing, he turned his head up to attend to him—and silently cursed as the pipe slipped from his hand.

"What are these barrels?" asked the doctor, pointing the eagle-handle of his walking stick. He had not replaced his hat, but otherwise looked as fine and fresh as the day he strode off the ship into the New World.

"I found my salt."

"Ah, very good, very good," said Keen. To this point, the British agent had ignored all the others, playing his moment of triumph for all the drama he could squeeze from it. In truth, the doctor had a thespian streak that would have impressed even Mr. Jonson.

"You are Gidoin, I assume," said Keen when he finally turned to the captain. The doctor knocked his stick once on the deck for emphasis, and then consulted one of his watches, as if concerned about the time.

If Gidoin had taken an immediate dislike to van Clynne, his feelings toward Keen were even worse. "My name is Captain John Lewis Gidoin, master of this ship," he replied tightly. "And whom have I had the pleasure to meet?"

Keen reached into his vest and retrieved his ruby-hilted knife—and with a sharp flick of his wrist, sent it sailing to the deck between the captain's feet. "You will do precisely as I order you to."

Gidoin froze. While he did not know all that the blade implied, he realized from conversations with his father, a former admiral, that it was a signifier for the Secret Department attached directly to the king, and that its bearers were not to be jostled with. In the least.

Reacting to the knife, two of Gidoin's marines took a menacing step toward Keen. The captain immediately commanded them to stop—though the withering glare from the doctor might have accomplished the same on its own.

"What do you want?"

"The Dutchman and the other man are my prisoners," said Keen. "I require a proper boat. I had to induce a few of the rabble to get myself out here, and I fear they may be unreliable."

Gidoin looked over at van Clynne, who had gone to his hands and knees in order to retrieve the pipe—and use it to light the fuse. He was just about to grab it when one of the marines, acting at McRae's nod, took hold of his coat and hauled him to his feet.

"Unhand me," blustered van Clynne. "Captain—arrest that man," he shouted, pointing at Keen. "He claims to be a British operative, but he is only a thief. He stole my money, under the pretense that I was a traitor."

"It was no pretense," said Keen, walking to Jake and ignoring van Clynne's continued protests. "General Bacon took an interest in you," he told the trussed spy. "He mentioned something about a dinner appointment he hoped you would keep. I wonder if that meant he wanted you returned alive?"

Jake's eyes displayed no emotion, save fierce hate.

"Alas, it's too much bother," said Keen. "Hang him quickly."

Finally, something the sailors agreed with. They hopped like children at a May Fair to comply.

The reader will realize that the disguised Private Martin has quite gotten lost in the recent chain of events, so rapidly progressing. For he has followed the foot-soldier's motto: "When in doubt, keep your head down."

Or more specifically, duck behind the salt barrels and pray that no one sees you.

There is no underestimating the ingenuity of a Connecticut man, nor can his initiative under fire be truly assayed until the moment in question. Martin saw the pipe on the deck boards and realized that General van Clynne was no longer in a position to light the fuse. He therefore came to the fore, crawling on his hands and knees while the sailors took up Jake's rope and the rest of the ship's company turned to watch the entertainment proceed.

"I think you should reconsider," van Clynne said, producing his own ruby-topped knife for the bewildered master of the *Richmond*. "I, too, am a member of the Secret Department, and Mr. Gibbs is my prisoner. General Bacon will be very angry when I tell him what you've done."

"You will not live to tell him," answered Keen curtly. "Pull him up!"

Jake felt the pressure on his neck and decided to make one last, desperate try at freedom, coiling his legs beneath him and gasping for a breath. As the sailors prepared to give the first pull, he bolted upright, tensing his shoulder muscles and leaning against the rope, so that his neck became a swivel. It was an awful, wrenching motion, but it allowed him to kick his boots against the mast and swing back into the sailors, sending them into a tumble. The rest of the ship's company erupted with laughter.

Lieutenant McRae began shouting at the men; Gidoin cursed; a marine grabbed Jake from the deck where he had fallen and yanked him upright.

Van Clynne, his guards distracted by Jake, took a sniff at the air and made a perfect dive into the oak boards, landing at Gidoin's boots.

All eyes turned toward him.

"What the hell are you doing?" thundered the ship's captain.

At that moment, the disguised salt keg exploded with a loud and very spicy bang.

Not even Homer could describe the scene that followed with proper accuracy. Martin, aware that the fuse was very short, had taken his chance to dive overboard the moment van Clynne fell. The explosion threw splinters and salt in a large circle, small cakes of the mineral acting much the same as pieces of shot. Keen was bowled over by a barrel lid, and knocked unconscious to the deck. Gidoin escaped serious injury, but was blown against a spar and also knocked unconscious. And Jake—

Jake would have been struck through the heart by several pounds worth of exploding salt were it not for the marine who had manhandled him. The unfortunate redcoat acted as a human shield; in an instant, the back of his coat turned a much darker shade of red.

Now was Claus van Clynne's greatest moment. He had chosen his trajectory not merely to escape the impact of the explosion, but to be in a position to grasp the red-handled knife Keen had thrown down earlier. Rocks were still flying through the air as he rolled to his feet with his blade in his right hand and Keen's in his left. He reached Jake and sliced through the hanging rope with a bold stroke of his right hand, while plunging his left into a marine's belly. Van Clynne then hauled Jake's body upon his shoulder and courageously proceeded to the side of the ship, where he cursed King George III in a loud and bold voice, ignoring the pistols and cutlasses of the crew. Flashing his small dagger, he took a manrope between his teeth and slid gently to the boat where Martin was already waiting, making good their escape.

At least, that was the story the Dutchman would tell upon reaching shore. From Jake's point of view, the action proceeded in somewhat different fashion:

Tossed to the deck with no warning, the patriot managed just barely to stay conscious. The blast severed the halter rope, though its long strand remained attached to his neck. His arms and legs were still tightly bound, and he could not walk freely. The explosion had rocked the ship severely, and Jake found himself able to roll and crawl toward the fallen van Clynne and McRae. Spotting Keen's ruby knife in the smoke was not difficult, but pulling it from the wood—the doctor's throw had buried the sharp blade nearly to the hilt—took all his strength, and he worked it back and forth for what seemed like forever.

Fortunately, the crew members who were not wounded by the explosion immediately set to saving the ship, which listed severely to port. All manner of men ran back and forth around him. Smoke from two small fires filled the air, and the general din was rent by several wretches whose limbs had been severed by the blast. This was more than enough distraction for Jake, who finally succeeded in pulling the knife from the wood.

He had to twist to slice the rope around his hands, but eventually sawed himself free. As he pulled himself up, Jake felt a sharp tug on his neck and he fell backwards on the deck. Twisting around, he saw that McRae had grabbed the severed end of what was to have been his death rope and tied it around his waist.

The lieutenant held the rope with one hand. His other flashed a thick, heavy cutlass.

"The one consistency in everyone's story is that you are a damnable traitor and a rebel," said McRae, whose cocked hat had been knocked crossways by the explosion but was otherwise unharmed. "I shall take great pride in ending your life."

"And I yours," said Jake, managing to grab the rope as McRae tugged. He lurched forward even so, and was just able to force himself sideways, escaping the swing of the blade.

A naval cutlass is a heavy weapon created for hacking an opponent to bits. It is unmerciful in its blows, its weight multiplying the momentum severalfold. But that advantage brings a problem to the man using it, for it lacks the finesse of a lighter sword.

McRae had used a cutlass to maim his share of opponents, but in his enthusiasm now found his slashes somewhat haphazard. Still tethered, Jake was able to retreat to a point where he could use a large, upended sea chest as a barrier between them. When McRae charged to the right, Jake slipped quickly to the left, and vice versa.

As the lieutenant took his charges, Jake worked more and more slack between his neck and the rope in his hand. This was naturally very dangerous, as it shortened the distance between the two men. But it also allowed him enough room to slip the thin but sharp blade of the Secret Department against the rope without McRae seeing. In a wink, the blade cut through.

Jake didn't let on. Instead, he waited while McRae collected himself for another lunge. As the British officer picked up his cutlass, Jake let go of the rope and dove to the right, falling below McRae's outstretched arm. The sword sailed down, slamming into the deck; in the next moment Jake was tumbling head over barefooted heels, kicking upward as he passed.

He aimed for McRae's face but missed. He hit the officer's hand instead, which was good enough—the smack sent the cutlass flying to the deck, and it slid away as the ship rolled.

McRae was too maddened to retreat. Instead, he reached to his belt for a knife—then fell forward, pulled off balance by van Clynne, who had grabbed his ankle from the deck nearby. Jake's knife quickly put an end to the English officer's career.

"Over the side," the patriot shouted as he pulled his Dutch companion to his feet.

"Easy for you to say," grumbled van Clynne, who wobbled from obstruction to obstruction before reaching the rail. There, one look at the deep blue water—the very deep blue water—and its rolling waves was enough to give him pause for reflection.

The fire was now almost under control. While sailors were still rushing around, some of the marine guards had appeared on deck with their muskets armed. One fired in the general direction of van Clynne, which cured his contemplative mood. He lifted a foot tentatively—then felt himself flying toward the dark, hideous waves, propelled by a quick shove from Jake.

Thirty-eight

Wherein, the river proves more crowded than expected.

"There are no good fuses to be found any more. The first business of Congress once peace is established ought to be the propagation of proper fuses. Imagine if the situation had been dire."

"I can't imagine it more dire," said Jake, working his long oar fiercely. He and Martin had hauled van Clynne aboard the whaleboat and were now rowing furiously up river, away from the Richmond. At any moment he expected the frigate to send a broadside their way, or launch boats in pursuit. Their comparatively empty boat rode high in the water, except at the stern where the Dutchman was stationed by the tiller.

"You were never in any danger," replied van Clynne. He guided the craft with one hand, using the other to clear the light rain from his face. As proper steering demanded he look at the water, the boat's course tended to wander. "We were ready to take you off at any moment. When Claus van Clynne and his men appear on a scene, you may rest easy."

"Turn the tiller to the right! Your right!" said Jake. "I will admit that things are always interesting when you are involved," he added, conscious that despite the thick bruise on his neck, the Dutchman had indeed saved his life. "For the moment, we'd better concentrate on making our escape."

"You are rowing wonderfully. The *Richmond* has been severely hampered by my charge, and is in no position to harry us further. I envision a long period in the repair shed for her. They may even take her out to sea and shoot her, as is done with a horse."

Van Clynne had no sooner made this prediction than the air was rent by a dozen or more cannon. Fortunately, the ship was listing severely and could not be maneuvered for a proper aim. Only one ball came close enough to send a spray of water near them. Jake and Martin nonetheless pushed their oars with renewed vigor.

"How many troops did Old Put send to the shore with you?" Jake asked van Clynne.

"Well, none, exactly."

"None?"

Van Clynne's answer was drowned by the reverberation of a second cannonade. The gunners had compensated somewhat for their ship's handicaps, and the whaleboat took some water from the resulting waves.

"Has Putnam sent his entire army to watch the chain?" Jake asked.

"If the truth be told, I never reached the general," said van Clynne. "I was waylaid by that scoundrel Keen, who tortured me nearly to death."

"Did a girl named Rose meet you?"

"She did indeed, but I decided it would be most efficient if we divided our efforts, taking separate routes," said the Dutchman. "I sent her by the shortest route possible, while I meandered on a side road. I have no doubt that she reached the general, and that the entire army of the Highlands is presently on alert."

A fresh broadside whizzed through the air, and the three Americans found themselves in a cloud of steam and hot waves. When it cleared, Jake saw a cutter emerging from the far side of the *Richmond*, beginning its pursuit. The boat was manned by oarsmen and had a sail besides, and moved toward them with the speed and deadly purpose of a bloodthirsty shark.

"Throw your body against the tiller to steady it," Jake shouted at van Clynne. "Take us to the shore. It's our only chance."

"We only have to get around that bend," said van Clynne, pointing ahead briefly before closing his eyes to steady his stomach.

"We don't stand a chance on the water."

"We have a surprise waiting for the British bastards," said Martin. "General van Clynne is quite clever."

"*General* van Clynne?"

"Captain-general," expanded Martin, with only the slightest hint of impishness, "triple-cluster."

"It is a hereditary title which I seldom use," said van Clynne. "Row, man, row."

Jake's response was drowned out by yet another round of cannon fire from the ship. Fortunately, this proved to be a rather half-hearted attempt at striking them, and only one ball came near enough to present a threat.

It was also close enough to send van Clynne's beloved beaver hat sailing into the water.

The hat had been in the Dutchman's possession since he was a small lad, and had been constructed from pelts hand-selected for him by members of a small Iroquois Indian band who had befriended his father. And so van Clynne's reaction was natural—momentarily forgetting not only his duties as helmsman but his phobia of the waves, he threw himself across the gunwale and snatched it from the water.

His effort came exceedingly close to spilling them overboard, and it was only with the greatest effort that Jake and Private Martin were able to keep the craft afloat. All forward momentum was lost, and the cutter was able to make significant progress toward them—so much so that a marine in the bow felt he was close enough to stand and fire.

His shot splintered a piece of the gunwale between Jake and van Clynne, but its main effect was to rally the Americans back to action.

"Push the tiller to your left, to your left!" ordered Jake as he struggled to get them moving again. "Take us in to shore!"

"I'm trying," answered van Clynne, his face a mixture of determination and nausea. The cove he had launched from was nestled like the mouth of a funnel between two large outcroppings of rocks and fallen trees; it seemed to have moved three miles in the few hours since he'd left.

By the time they made the turn, the *Richmond*'s boat

had closed to within thirty yards. As Jake pumped his oar, he watched the sharpshooter place another cartridge at the top of his gun barrel, then ram it home with a deliberate and determined motion. The churning current threw off his aim, however, and the bullet sailed well overhead.

No matter. He calmly prepared another shot.

The cutter had been put under the direction of a senior midshipman, whose shouts and curses echoed against the banks. When he saw that the whaleboat was turning toward shore, he trimmed his vessel for a sweeping turn that would protect against a possible feint and run for the north. There was blood in his voice, and undoubtedly he hoped a successful action would play heavily in his quest for an officer's commission.

The cannon and gunfire had one positive effect, considered from the American side—the Connecticut men on shore were well prepared as their "general's" boat rounded the rock outcropping and slid toward the cove.

Which meant that they were nowhere in sight, an uncomforting fact for Jake as he pulled with all his might. Poor Martin two benches before him was exhausted and ready to drop; only the danger of their situation kept him upright at his post, the doughty private struggling on pure willpower alone.

As the cutter cleared the rocks behind them, the sniper prepared another shot. His boat pressed to overtake the Americans before they reached the shore, and angled between the rocky shore on the right side and sunken tree branches on the left. The distance between the two boats shrank steadily from twenty yards to ten, until finally they were within spitting distance. The cutter continued to gain as it neared the submerged tree trunk on the left, a mere twenty yards from shore.

Jake had just realized they would not reach the pebbly beach when a shout went up from the rocks. In that instant, the water in front of the cutter rose up mightily and the ship was upended, marines and sailors flying in all directions.

"This chain of yours gave me an idea," said van Clynne as Jake put down his oars in astonishment. "A rope can be made to serve the same purpose, if it is a thick, fine rope levered with trees and stout men. The van Clynne of ropes, in fact."

The rope was that magnificent weave of hemp discovered earlier in Stoneman's. Those same stout men who had pulled it taut at the last possible instant now emerged from the woods, muskets loaded with double shot. The water perked with good, American lead, well aimed; a froth of blood quickly covered the surface, and the whine of stricken Englishmen soon filled the air. Jake, Martin, and van Clynne were pulled ashore, and the Connecticut company gave a shout of hurrah as the survivors of their ambush quickly surrendered.

But there was no time to celebrate.

"Gentlemen, you've done good work here, but our battle is just beginning," declared Jake as the troop reformed. His officer's voice hit full stride as Freedom herself perked up his timbre. "The province's safety, and perhaps our whole country's, relies on the integrity of the Great Chain thrown across the Hudson north of here. Even as I speak, a force of despicable Tories and British marines are mustering against it. The Continentals who have been alerted may not realize where the real danger is, and so it is up to us—we will have to stop them. We will have to kill the Tory bastards with our bare hands if we have to! Get the horses and follow me!"

"Begging your pardon, sir," said one of the men respectfully. "But Captain-General van Clynne is our leader. He has taken us this far."

"That reminds me—"

"Gentlemen, I turn over my command to Lieutenant Colonel Gibbs," the Dutchman said quickly. "He has a tactical sense of the situation that I could not possibly challenge. When we have finished this next phase of our assault, I shall, er, resume my rightful position."

Jake was in too much of a hurry to scold van Clynne on his shameless self-promotion. Nor did he note tartly, as he might have, that the Dutchman was coming up in the world, having progressed from a landless squire to a general of fantastic rank.

"Take the horses and follow me," Jake shouted, running to the animals the rangers had tied here. His boots, still sodden from his brief plunge in the water before boarding the whaleboat, felt like squishy lead bars, but he nonetheless managed to leap atop the biggest horse he saw. "Claus, the best road north along the river. We need to reach Anthony's Nose before nightfall."

"Less than an hour," grumbled the Dutchman, heading for his horse. "They are not making days as long as they used to."

Thirty-nine

*Wherein, certain matters of strategy and geography are
laid out as the two forces race northward.*

*A*s they raced northwards, Jake was somewhat surprised to find that van Clynne, contrary to his usual habits, not only galloped along every bit as fast as the rest of
the company, but hardly uttered half his usual complaints
against the roads, the weather, or the British. He didn't
even open his mouth to show them shortcuts, merely
pointing the way to country paths that sliced off precious
moments from their route. Perhaps the mantle of leadership agreed with him.

Jake realized Busch's plan had a major flaw—the Tory
would be highly vulnerable once he separated from the
diversionary forces and the *Dependence*. The trick for the
patriots would be to get around the screening ranger
force and avoid the *Dependence*.

The woods of upper Westchester were heavy with shadows, and the leaves crinkled with the ever-growing rain.
Jake put up his hand to halt the column and let it catch
its collective breath while he consulted with van Clynne.

"Where can we get boats along the river near Peek
Skill?" he asked the Dutchman.

"During peaceful times I would direct us to Lent's
Cove," said van Clynne, "as we are only a few miles away.
But Annsville Creek further north will be much surer.
Francis Penmart's Dock is near the road to the King's
Highway, and inevitably there will be boats idle."

"Can I get to the chain from Lent's Cove?"

"In almost a straight line north," conceded van Clynne.
"But if they are attacking ashore, the British will most

likely land at the cove and move northwards, as they did at the end of March. I know a man named Green who lives on the cove," added the Dutchman, twirling his beard. "He inflates his prices and his politics have been questioned. Now, on the Annsville, there is a good Dutchman who will rent his craft out for a few pence below the going rate, and they are a higher quality besides."

"Take us to Green." Jake glanced northward, as if he could see their destination through the thick trees and growing rain. It was almost nightfall; the attack might already be underway. "We'll risk whatever we must to make up the time. If we run into the rangers, I will go ahead to the river or wherever I can find a boat. You lead the men."

"But if we stay inland, our chances—"

"Come on, General, there's no time to lose," smirked Jake, picking up his horse's reins and getting the party into motion again with a good kick of his heels. "I would think a captain-general would not waste a moment when the enemy is at hand."

"It is a hereditary title only," mumbled van Clynne.

The Tories had proceeded upriver at a slower though nonetheless deliberate pace, shepherded by the *Dependence*. Their first test came at King's Ferry, which despite the name was held by American troops.

The *Dependence* fired a few shots from her smaller guns above the ferry at Verplanck's Point, which was lightly and in truth poorly manned. A few muskets answered from the primitive earthworks, but the British forces didn't tarry long enough to be bothered by them. The stretch of river north of Verplanck's was ordinarily a calm lake, lying placidly below Dunderbury Mountain; the *Dependence* and her accompanying boats made their way slowly along the eastern shore, conserving their strength for the coming attack as the weather steadily rose against them.

The river forms a V here, with the Peek Skill at the vortex. As the assault was launched, the *Dependence* would draw the attention of the defenders near the river-

side and inland at the camps near Robinson's Bridge that
have come to be known as Continental Village. The marines and rangers, meanwhile, would come ashore in the
relative calm of Lent's Cove, an easy landing area removed from the main rebel positions. This would allow
them to form up before proceeding inland. The strategy
followed roughly the same pattern taken during a raid
earlier in the year, and the marines could walk through it
with their eyes closed.

Busch and his bomb canoe, meanwhile, would slip upstream to the chain. He would have to stay as close to the
eastern shore as possible to avoid Forts Clinton and
Montgomery, which lay directly across the narrow neck of
the river from his target.

Lieutenant Clark, the master of the *Dependence*, inspected his vessel as they reached their staging area. Already the night was falling, and the pistol which would
launch the attack was loaded and stuck in his belt.

Busch, walking the long deck and scanning the empty
river, kept to himself. This day was the culmination of
many weeks of planning; now that it had come he felt a
certain stillness inside his chest, a quiet even more profound than his studied outward manner. He had no doubt
that he was about to strike a death blow to the Revolution; in so doing, he would also win much glory for himself. But his thoughts were not focused on that, nor even
on the difficulties of the mission ahead. For one brief
moment he looked southward on the river in the direction of the *Richmond*. Smith—or Gibbs, if that was his
true name—would be dead by now. A twinge of regret
wandered through the depths of the Tory's soul, for he
recognized that under different circumstances the two
men might have been good friends.

But Gibbs had made a fatal mistake, placing his own
ego before that of his sovereign's; all of these rebels had
done this in their hubris, and now they must pay for it.

Lieutenant Clark met Busch at the bow of the ship,
standing near the massive gun that made the galley the
most fearsome raider above New York. Even in the growing shadows and light rain it was an impressive weapon,
with a bulk that belonged to a living thing. The wooden

carriage that cradled it seemed a squat elephant, taken from the Hindoo wilds. The large iron pipe was a lion's prone body, coiled and ready to strike.

The deck around her had been cleared and made ready for action; the gun crew stood to one side, watching as the captain studied the far shore with his spyglass. Many of these men had been with Clark aboard the *Phoenix* when the galley was captured, and were the hardened salt of the sea, prepared to follow him up the River Styx if necessary.

The marines, bayonets sharpened and musket locks covered with protective cloth against the weather, stood midships, trying to pretend that they were not nervous about the pending battle. A supply of whale oil, as well as candlewood and kindling, had been stored in a row of casks; half the countryside would soon be on fire, if the weather allowed.

The rest of the ship's complement was at battle stations, straining their eyes to see if the rebels on shore had spotted them. There were no signs that they had, though they fully expected word of their arrival would have been passed by now.

"Are you ready?" Clark asked Busch.

"More than ready," said the captain.

"Then let's go."

He nodded at the gunners and the crew instantly sprang to work, readying their large cannon. As the match was raised, Clark handed Busch the pistol from his belt. The Tory captain smiled at the honor, and nodded in appreciation at the finely crafted gun—then fired. Instantly, the gunners answered with their own personal hurrah: the thick, throaty roar of the massive lion by their side.

Even before the huge ball struck through the roof of one of the homes along the river, the British boats had begun to strain for the western shore.

Though neither Rose nor van Clynne had managed to alert them, the patriot defenses were not idle. Even before the gunfire at Verplanck's, lookouts had spotted the *Dependence* and the other boats heading north, and had signaled an alarm with the aid of a series of tower signals and beacon fires that formed a chain of their own up and down the valley. The fires became more pronounced as the dusk approached, and before the British rangers had reached the shore near the creek, Americans as far north as Fishkill knew something was up.

But it was one thing to know an attack was underway, and another to meet it effectively. Twice this spring, the area around Peekskill had been attacked by well-coordinated raiding parties. While there were now more American troops and a new overall commander here, the general result was much the same. The mobility of the British force and the disposition of the American camps meant the shoreline was practically conceded to the attackers. The inland village itself was protected, but when the marines and rangers touched shore not a single bullet crossed their path. The *Dependence* and her round-bottom hull floated directly south of St. Anthony's Nose, in roughly the area she had been the day before when Jake observed the feint from the hillside. She switched her target from the houses on shore to the gunworks eastward at Fort Independence at the head of the Peek Skill Creek—though perhaps it inflates the post's strength to capitalize its name.

Van Clynne and the Connecticut men did a good job keeping up with Jake, and in fact were no more than a few rods behind him as he approached the riverbank near Lent's Cove. But the enemy army had been ashore for nearly a quarter hour by then—a fact announced to Jake by two small balls of lead sailing just above his head.

He dove off his horse to the ground just ahead of a more concerted volley. The Connecticut troops followed suit, van Clynne's curses ringing in their ears.

Jake's brain realized he was too late. Not only would Busch already have a head start but he now had to fight his way past a considerable force of rangers and British marines. But it was his heart that motivated him, pushing him through the bushes and the rapidly darkening woods, telling him he must not give up no matter what the circumstances.

Forty

Wherein, the British marines are met with a sharp counterattack, while the navy is serenaded.

The troops who were firing at Jake were marines, members of a small party who had stayed close to the shoreline to prevent a flanking maneuver. They were tough soldiers, well trained and battle hardened, but even they could not see very far in the darkening woods. They held a makeshift line in the trees just down from the road, inland from the cove. Jake reckoned there were at most a dozen of them.

He pushed through the brambles as quietly as possible, hoping to sneak to the riverside and find a boat. In an instant, he had given up hope of taking his troops with him; there was simply no time to waste, and the unflappable patriot was prepared to fight Busch single-handed if necessary.

Jake snuck south twenty yards before turning back to the east, and was in sight of the river when he came under fire from a picket behind a rock across a narrow ravine. He just barely found cover beneath a tree trunk as a shot parted the leaves above him. Now a second picket took up the cause, and a third; the patriot spy was pinned beneath the cross fire. He crawled forward a few inches on his belly, but then could go no further; even in the looming darkness he would be an easy target on the barren ground that ran down to a small rivulet feeding the nearby creek. The rain was still light but steady, and his face as well as his clothes were smeared with reddish brown mud.

Even as Jake began to curse the redcoats who had

trapped him, his salvation was at hand. Van Clynne and his men had overwhelmed a marine position and pressed their attack. The Dutchman grabbed an unfired British musket and pushed his way through the trees, grumbling and grousing like a bear whose hibernation had been interrupted. This drew the attention of a good portion of the force, and left the Connecticut men free to engage in a classic out-flanking maneuver.

The troops saw the gap open in the defenses and rushed it, and with a shout the fight erupted into hand-to-hand combat. The marines who had been sniping at Jake turned to hold down their flank, and the patriot spy ran forward, grabbing one of the lobster-coats by the neck as he reached for a new cartridge.

The Briton fell back against the rocks. The cloth of the cravat and collar he wore around his neck dampened some of the fierce force in Jake's fingers, but no coat would protect against the weight of his blows. As the marine continued to struggle, Jake grabbed his fallen musket and slapped him in the mouth with its stock; a more substantial blow to the forehead finished the struggle.

The Connecticut men in the meantime had begun rolling up the flank, sending the British into a confused panic northwards. There were shouts from the other side of the creek, and calls further inland as reinforcements began to take tentative steps toward a counterattack. But the growing night and the ferocity of the assault, as well as the woods, made the situation chaotic enough that a rally was impossible, and the Americans turned to mop up the stragglers.

Van Clynne, meanwhile, was operating more or less on his own, by now well west of the main troop. After discharging the Brown Bess musket into a receptive enemy body, he fell back on his favorite weapon, the tomahawk. The squire was as good with the hatchet as any woodsman alive, and had more than held his own during competitions with Indian companions, where a good showing tended to lower the price of proffered beaver pelts.

His showing now was applauded by a Connecticut soldier who found himself hard-pressed by a pair of marines.

Van Clynne's two axes made their marks in the oppressors' foreheads; Cain was not sent upon the land with a grosser sign of his perfidy.

But as the Dutchman advanced to retrieve his weapons, he was confronted by a marine sergeant, sword in hand. Van Clynne just managed to grab one of the hatchets and hold it up in defense; the sergeant's blade glanced off the blade head with a sharp clang. His weapon was severely dented, but the Dutchman was left in a worse position—the force of the blow knocked the tomahawk from his hand.

"I can tell by your breath that you've been drinking rum," declared van Clynne loudly. "And cheap rum at that."

"I'll send you to hell," answered the sergeant, launching the sword in a forward parry. The Dutchman was able to avoid it, thanks to the shadows and a young stripling tree he let fly into his attacker's face.

"Really, sir," said van Clynne as the marine whirled back, "I would have expected a bolder threat from a member of the British marines. Who is your commanding officer?"

While his patter was completely characteristic, it was not without purpose. The Dutchman meant to keep the swordsman off balance and with any luck flustered until help arrived or a weapon presented itself. He thus inquired into the sorry state of the British armed forces, desiring to know why they were equipped with swords that could not hack out a few paltry weeds.

The sergeant spent several strong blows against the bushes between them trying to disprove this theory. Van Clynne found it expedient to retreat from each—until at last his path was blocked by a large rock.

Even with the light fading, the glimmer of the British sergeant's eyes were unmistakable. The Dutchman was an inviting target; the most difficult task was deciding which limb to sever first.

The sergeant drew the sword over his shoulder, aiming straight for van Clynne's tongue.

"Perhaps, sir, we can negotiate a cease-fire," suggested the Dutchman.

The smirk on the sergeant's face changed to a grotesque death mask, blood spurting from a gash in his neck.

The rock van Clynne had backed up against was the same outcropping used earlier by a marine as cover against Jake's assault, and the patriot spy had found himself in the vicinity when the Dutchman began his commentary.

Those complaints were now renewed with great vigor, van Clynne concluding that, if the present army and navy were to have fought against the Netherlands for control of New Amsterdam, the lands here would still be Dutch and there would be no need for the Revolution.

"Think of it this way," suggested Jake, cleaning off his thin assassin's blade. "If you were alive then, you'd be dead."

"That is a most slippery form of logic, sir," declared van Clynne. "I believe it pure sophistry, and denounced specifically by St. Thomas. A live man cannot be dead, especially if he is Dutch."

"You're welcome," said Jake sarcastically.

"I was indeed about to thank you," said van Clynne. "You saved me a certain amount of exertion, though I would have defeated the heathen dog in due course."

"By talking him to death?"

"I would have thought by now, my friend, that you understood the brilliant subtlety of Dutch battle tactics."

Their conference was interrupted by Private Martin's arrival.

"All present and accounted for, sir," declared the private. "We've a few nicks and bruises, but no bullet holes."

The main British force had marched further inland and was fighting in the hilly area above, between the village and the creek, where it had met militia and Putnam's regulars. They were undoubtedly so preoccupied that an assault from their rear would wipe them out, but Jake had other priorities.

"Which way to our friend Green's?" he asked van Clynne.

"I believe that is his abode yonder," said van Clynne, pointing toward the settlement on the riverbank. "There should be a boat or two in the yard. If you knock on his door—"

"No time," said Jake. "Martin and I will find a boat. You take the soldiers and continue north across the creek. Advance up the shoreline as quickly as possible. Send a man to Fort Independence and tell them to direct snipers to the chain."

"Begging your pardon, sir," asked Martin, "but if the *Dependence* is on the river, won't we have a difficult time in our boat?"

"I wouldn't be surprised."

For a stretch of land under violent attack, the shoreline was remarkably peaceful. In truth, the few local inhabitants had wisely fled for their lives. With the British marines vanquished, Jake and Private Martin had their pick of the vessels beached along the cove.

Their pick of one, that is, which was perched precariously on a group of rocks overlooking the water. It was the only craft in sight, if one excepts the British whaleboats, which were too large for them to maneuver successfully, and the equally impractical galley well offshore.

As it happened, they would have chosen the boat even among a million others. For the craft in question was a birch bark canoe.

Were there more time to praise the construction of this genre of vessel, several pages could be filled regarding the sturdiness of the hull and the effectiveness of the very lightweight structure, which made the boat highly maneuverable. Jake lifted it without Martin's help and launched it immediately into the river, where the doughty private quickly joined him. The two men pushed their paddles into the water and the craft seemed to jump beneath them, hurrying northward as if its Indian maker had bestowed a supernatural spirit within its ribs.

The weak fires ashore, hampered by the drizzle, were now the only source of illumination. Behind them to the west, fierce Bear Mountain growled in the wet darkness, throwing fits and shadows across the channel as they broke into the open water.

A brilliant red and yellow flash lit the river above them,

and the waves reverberated with the sound of the *Dependence*'s 32-pound cannon unleashing an awesome missile. The round iron ball groaned and whistled as it rent the air, and for a moment even Jake feared that the cannon had been fired at them. The dull thud of the projectile crashing harmlessly against rock and mud was not so much a reprieve as a warning; they had a long way to go before fulfilling their mission.

Fortunately, the British vessel seemed to be concentrating on Fort Independence and was busy maneuvering at the mouth of the creek below it, seeking to draw as much attention as possible. The current and the rising wind made it difficult for the galley to stay in position to fire.

It also made it extremely difficult for Jake and Private Martin to paddle upstream, as the rain now started to pick at their faces like a swarm of angry bees.

"Pace yourself with long strokes," Jake instructed his bowman. "Lean against the left side of the canoe and I'll compensate back here."

Martin did not answer, but Jake noticed a better pull. He hoped that the heavily laden bomb canoe would find the going several times as difficult.

Their small boat shook with the reflected reverberation of another round from the *Dependence*. Jake looked up and realized that the vessel was considerably closer to them than he had thought—and in fact was speeding south on a collision course with their canoe.

"Stroke, Martin, stroke!" commanded Jake, going at the water like a grave digger in the last moment before Armageddon.

The private responded not only with strong strokes, but with a cheery hum meant to revive his sagging spirits.

The song, naturally enough, was "Yankee Doodle."

Before Jake could order the private to keep quiet in hopes the enemy might miss them, an alarm rose on the *Dependence*. As a swivel was manned and aimed in their direction, Jake took up the chorus of the song—and bent hard over the canoe, tucking the boat closer to the rocky shore.

The *Dependence*, which had been changing position to

cover the force that seemed to be under attack at the cove, came on strong. But Jake managed to slip the canoe to the side, escaping the collision and clearing the long arms of the sweeping oars.

"Fire, damn you!" shouted the master of the galley, barely ten yards away. "Sink that infernal boat and its blasted singing!"

Forty-one

Wherein, the chase proceeds in the dark currents of the North River, and even darker events transpire on shore.

Jake's guess about the effects of the wind and current on the bomb canoe was correct. Towed behind an ordinary dugout canoe manned by Busch and the sailor he had recruited on the *Richmond*, its bow was a heavy anchor. The craft kept sliding against its tow rope, trying to change direction; it was a struggle to make any progress at all.

Nonetheless, they kept at it. Busch's determined example rallied the hulking sailor at the rear of the canoe. The man, whom the ranger captain had chosen largely for the size of his shoulders and chest, began now to pay back the faith shown in him. A lull in the wind presented an opening, and they began a steady climb against the passion of the water. The chain, stretched across its wooden logs, lay ahead; at this slow but steady pace, it would take no more than a few minutes to reach.

"Come now," said Busch aloud to the sailor behind him. "There's a thousand guineas' reward waiting if we bull the rebels' iron in half."

"Why didn't you say so earlier!" exclaimed the sailor, redoubling his efforts.

At least one subject of His Majesty King George III did not need any hint of pecuniary reward to fire his energy on this dark night. Major Dr. Harland Keen had all the motivation he needed—indeed, one might say he was overmotivated, with a surfeit of evil energy burning at the core of his twisted soul.

The blast of van Clynne's salt barrel had knocked Keen against one of the ship's masts with such force that he lay unconscious on the deck for several minutes. During that time, the rebels escaped and the *Richmond*'s crew went about the business of securing the vessel with no attention to him. His prostrate body was treated much as a broken and discarded spar might have been; indeed, the lumber might have received more concern, as it would have potentially played some role in the operation of the ship.

There were many wounded men aboard, but the victim whose injuries were most important was the ship herself. She leaned badly to port, where the explosion had sent a jagged finger downward to yank at the keel, cracking the boards badly enough to allow water to flood the lower gun deck. The sailors worked madly to seal this breach, which was as severe and deadly as any inflicted by a warship in battle.

While they were at least not subject to bombardment as they worked, the circumstances of the blast, the peculiar shape of the resulting wound, and the disruptive effect on the boat's entire structure presented problems that would have challenged even Admiral Drake's hand-picked and battle-hardened crew on the *Golden Hind*. The approaching darkness and gathering storm clouds, which kicked up the wind and the river's waves, added to their difficulties. The few ill-aimed rounds they threw at the rebels were mere tokens, and the small force they sent in the cutter was the most Captain Gidoin could spare to preserve British honor without losing his chances of preserving his ship.

The *Richmond* had been ripped from her anchors by the blast, and drifted for some time before she could be brought fully under control. The vessel was not the biggest in the British fleet, nor the strongest, but still she had her pride. With great creaks and groans she pulled her timbers together, aided by the ministrations of her retainers. She had been well engineered and manufactured; her breeding finally won out over the grievous hurt that had been inflicted.

By the time Keen had regained enough of his senses to

push himself upright on the deck and wipe his brow with his hand, the master of the *Richmond* felt reasonably sure his ship would survive. But several more hours of close work remained before it could proceed south to New York City and permanent repairs.

Keen had no desire to go with her, much less help tend the wounded around him, though since he was a doctor such might be considered his moral duty. His entire concern was the Dutchman, who had managed to outwit him.

Keen's enmity for the squire reached apocalyptic proportions, and incited in him a positively artistic hate. He saw himself flaying van Clynne alive while turning him on a spit, the fire fueled by the oozing strips of human fat. He envisioned the construction of an elaborate apparatus that would sustain the squire's heart while his legs and arms were sawed off. He foresaw all manner of hideous tortures that would have put the storied Borgias to shame.

"I will have a boat," he said to Captain Gidoin once he recovered. The ship's master started to object, but the unworldly look in Keen's eyes warned him off. He quickly gave the order to have the major rowed ashore, even though he could ill afford to spare the men.

Keen stood in the bow of the small boat as it was rowed toward the spot on shore where he had left his carriage. There was an immediate obstacle to his plans for revenge—he had no idea where van Clynne was.

He could, however, make certain assumptions, the most important being that the Dutchman would endeavor to thwart the operation against the chain. To do so, he would undoubtedly enlist the assistance of the main American forces in the area, under General Putnam. Putnam, or one of his officers, would therefore know of his whereabouts.

Keen had observed that van Clynne was steadfastly loyal to his underlings—he had risked a great deal to save this Gibbs. How much more would he do to rescue the pretty young Miss McGuiness, bundled in the rear of Keen's carriage? Could she not be used to lure him to his fate?

Rose did not answer when the doctor put the question

to her. This was largely due to the fact that she was still unconscious; the Chinese sleeping concoction he had administered before setting off to the *Richmond* would render her senseless for many hours yet.

The doctor took a lingering look at her body, limp and untrussed on the seat. Her legs were spread carelessly and she looked for all the world like a garden nymph, caught asleep beneath a lilac bush.

With great resolve, Keen forced himself to concentrate on his goal of revenge and closed the door to the coach. Without a clear plan yet, he began driving north toward Marshad's cottage; ruined as it was, it was the only spot in the area he knew.

Indeed, his ignorance of the country now worked against him. On his journey from New York he had relied exclusively on the knowledge of his driver. It was easy enough to find the river from the shore; one kept trying roads that headed west until it was reached. But finding Marshad's, especially in the growing darkness, was another story entirely.

And so the reader will not wonder that Keen was soon lost, and he realized he must enlist some native as a guide. This person could then be put to a second use—he would be dispatched to Putnam's headquarters, and told to find van Clynne.

Keen did not construct this scenario all at once; indeed, it took his fevered mind nearly a half hour's worth of travel before he conceded to himself that he was indeed lost. By that point, the chances of haphazardly coming across someone who would know the way to Marshad's—indeed, the chances of coming across anyone —were very limited. He therefore decided that he must stop at some inn or similar establishment and enlist aid there.

The inn he happened on was Prisco's.

Keen's clothes had been rent in the blast, and his face covered with bruises. But a few daubs of paint on his forehead and a fresh jacket—he chose brown, mindful of van Clynne's earlier remarks on local fashion—restored some dash to his appearance; when he walked into the inn he looked no worse than most of the patrons. Indeed, he outshone them all, as this was a particularly slow evening for the Prisco establishment—its only customers were the two uncommunicative checkers-playing gentlemen Jake had met earlier.

Keen gave the proprietor a polite smile when he greeted him at the threshold, and allowed himself to be shown to a Windsor-style chair that stood in front of a round hickory table arm's length from the fire. Prisco allowed as how he had some very fine rabbit stew left in the kitchen; Keen nodded and asked for some Madeira with which to wash it down. The order was taken up cheerfully —the good keeper made a nice profit on his wine sales.

"My niece will take care of you," said Prisco, retreating toward a back room.

The doctor saw his course fully developing; he would take this girl as a guide to the countryside, keeping her for his own pleasure once he had succeeded in luring his nemesis to destruction.

The second portion of his plan was abandoned as soon as Jane entered the room with a fine leather bottle of wine in her hand. As the reader has already seen sweet Jane described, there is no immediate need to amplify. It will be granted by all—with the natural exception of her true love, Claus van Clynne—that she is not, in any conventional sense, beautiful. Even the word "plain" is stretched somewhat to describe her.

But her instinct and intellect—now those are handsome indeed. Jane immediately realized that the stranger had some evil design in mind, and so she was on her guard as she approached his table.

"Thank you, my dear," said Keen, beaming a smile at her. "I wonder—do you know who General Putnam is?"

Jane looked at him oddly. "I doubt there is a person in the country who doesn't."

Keen smiled. "And you know where to find him?"

"At his headquarters, I suppose." She leaned down to pour the wine, deciding that the man before her was a harmless simpleton. But the guest's next question showed her first instincts had been quite correct.

"I wonder, could you tell me the way to Marshad's cottage?"

"Martin Marshad?" she asked, endeavoring to keep her voice neutral. "The lawyer?"

Keen nodded.

Marshad was a notorious—at least in her mind—Tory and spy; her visitor had just declared himself a perfidious skunk. Jane decided in an instant that she would alert her uncle, who as a member of the Committee of Safety and the local justice of the peace could have him arrested. Something in her manner gave her away; as she poured the wine into Keen's glass, she suddenly felt a cold hand clamp onto her arm.

"Do not scream, my dear," said the doctor. "I require your services as a guide and as a messenger." He smiled, and nodded with his head toward his left hand, which held Jake Gibbs's Segallas, stolen from Rose. "This weapon has two bullets left, so that after I shoot you, I can kill your uncle without bothering to take a second pistol from my belt. Let us get your cloak; I wouldn't want you to catch your death in this rain."

Forty-two

Wherein, the shortcomings of birch as a naval material are briefly but thoroughly surveyed.

As glorious and adaptable as the birch canoe may be, it was not designed to withstand the grapeshot of a swivel gun, let alone the heavier calibers of cannonball. Jake and Private Martin were well aware of this defect, their joyful chorus of "Yankee Doodle" notwithstanding, and they paddled away from the *Dependence* with all they were worth. The galley, meanwhile, was engaged in several battles at once—besides the pesky singers passing off its side, the ship was firing at the shore to support its troops and maneuvering desperately to avoid the rocks close to shore. Given the darkness of the night, the confusion, and the wind that began to whip up, it would be but a mild surprise to find that they missed the little canoe entirely.

Alas, one cannot always count on surprises, mild or otherwise. The second blast from the nearest swivel gun was followed by a light patter somewhat similar to the sound rain makes on shale, assuming the rain is several degrees hotter than boiling and the shale much thinner than paper. The bark of the canoe literally disintegrated in a puff of steam and smoke. Martin fell face first into the water, striking his head with such force that he was knocked senseless. Jake was able to stay upright and hold onto his oar, which provided some comfort if not protection as a wave dashed him into a large and not very soft rock. He clambered onto it, then saw Martin's distress; he dove back into the river just as a sailor aimed the *Dependence*'s swivel at him.

The bullets ricocheted off the rocks and sent up a pronounced splash, but once more the patriot spy had escaped harm, his impulse to save the soldier proving his own salvation. In two quick strokes he reached Martin and hauled him over his shoulder; Jake found a sandy spot on the shore and pulled him up to safety.

By now the galley was too concerned with its other problems to waste time bothering with shipwrecked singers. Jake quickly propped the unconscious Martin against a tree, then began racing north along the shoreline, heedless of the sharp rocks and cragged roots beneath his feet. Within a league, the soles of his wet boots were sliced through, his ankles swelling from the severe pounding against the uneven terrain. His lungs were near bursting and his knee was sorely strained.

How much further he could have gone before collapsing—even Lieutenant Colonel Jake Gibbs must have his limits—will remain an unanswered question, for Providence had decided in her generosity to provide him with a small, open rowboat, a fisherman's craft complete with oars and tackle, placed directly in his path. Jake jumped into the boat with great haste, more sure than ever that God was on the side of the Revolution.

The Creator undoubtedly is, but if He placed the small boat there, He is not without a sense of humor. For Jake had gotten only a few yards out from shore when he noticed water lapping against his sore ankles; a few more strokes and he realized the water was now to his calves. He put his back into the oars and hauled with all his might, hoping that he might somehow avoid or at least lessen the rush of water if he could move ahead quickly enough. But the river was relentless, and before he had gone a half mile his thighs were nearly submerged. Jake continued to row, but within a few minutes realized that his progress was slowing to a crawl.

The glow of fires from Fort Montgomery on the west bank illuminated the river ahead like the flickering flames of a stove in an empty house. Fits of yellow light played out like water spirits across the Hudson, and dark, lumpy shadows sat before him, gargoyles guarding the cathedral of Freedom. Except that one of those shadows must be

Busch, as determined to reach the chain as Jake was to stop him.

His boat was no longer of much use, but Jake feared he would have a difficult time swimming against the river, roiling with the growing storm. There seemed no other option, however, for his short pause had allowed the water to lap over the gunwales. He made sure the ruby-hilted assassin's blade was secure in his belt, removed his sodden boots and socks, and tossed off his vest. Throwing one of the oars ahead of him to help as ballast, he dove into the icy cold water.

The Hudson's current is a varied thing, depending not only on the time of day but the location and perhaps Nature's momentary whimsy. Jake found it suddenly veering in his direction, but that was little consolation. As he looked up from the water, he expected at every second to see a brilliant flash of red: Busch's canoe igniting with the Tory's terrible wrath.

Jake had not lost hope that Rose had notified Putnam, and at every second prayed patriot patrol boats had been strung like a necklace in front of the chain. For a brief moment he was sure the shadow he was nearing was one. But as he reached for it, the hulk darted back against the shoreline, and he realized it was a trick of the reflected light. The rain was dampening the poor illumination and blurring his eyes, and now the river's strange sounds began crowding into his head, thrusting him into a Hades-like maze.

Jake kicked with all his strength, but his energy was nearly gone; he feared he would lose this battle. He let go of the oar, deciding that it was slowing his progress. Stroking ahead, he determined to make one last lunge for the dark line that protected his young country's fate, or drown in the attempt.

A moment later, he noticed a thick shadow ten feet away that seemed different than the others; while it too moved away and changed shape, it did so slowly. With another stroke, he realized it was a real, solid object, with another ahead, and now he could pick voices out from the chaos—Busch giving orders, the two boats knocking harshly against each other.

And then he heard the hard creaking of the iron chain against its log supports ahead.

The slap of the bomb canoe against the hull of his own craft sent Busch's heart to his stomach. While he knew that theoretically the charge could only be activated by the fuse, he did not want to test that theory here. He pushed the vessel off with his hands and found himself straddling the water, his legs still in the lead canoe.

For a brief moment he felt a twinge of panic, fear shaking his grip. Then he caught hold, and used his arms to bring the bomb canoe close again. As his assistant steadied their craft, the captain climbed aboard and took up the paddle he needed to propel himself the last league to the chain.

The rain was now sufficient to have soaked entirely through to his skin. But he welcomed the growing storm as an ally, for the more difficult the river, the greater his chance of success.

While the scene was dim and confusing to Jake's eyes, Captain Busch interpreted the fires on the bank below Fort Montgomery as being considerably brighter tonight than when he scouted the chain, even with the rain. Busch believed a good lookout would have spotted him by now, and undoubtedly alerted the patrols on the shore. Indeed, a whaleboat loaded with soldiers had been dispatched and was hurrying across from the western terminus.

"There," he said, pointing to a dark froth still protected by the shadows of the cliffs. "That will be one of their patrols coming for us."

"I'll hold them off, sir."

"Just draw them away," said Busch. "I only need a minute to reach the chain. The bomb will explode within ten minutes, once the fuse is set."

"Won't you have trouble with the fuse in the rain?"

"It's all mechanical," Busch assured him. "Just hold these men off and our success is guaranteed. You can do it; you're worth ten of them."

Busch didn't hear the response, if there was one. He was already paddling hard. While working the other canoe had been difficult, moving this one was practically impossible, with the immense dead weight of the bomb acting against him.

It's a few yards, no more, Busch told himself. I must do it, and I shall.

The British sailor let his canoe drift momentarily with the current, waiting for the whaleboat to approach. Had someone told him the day before that he would sacrifice himself against the rebel rabble, he would have laughed heartily—after punching him in the face. But this ranger captain had somehow filled him with pride, and shown him that the destruction of the chain was not merely his duty, but an enterprise that would rank with Drake's defeat of the Spanish in the Channel. How much greater would the fame be, when two men alone took on the rebels, and broke the Revolution's back in a single night?

And so the Devonshire native waited grimly for the whaleboat. Though his orders were to lead it away, he was determined to put up enough of a fight that the damn Americans would be close enough to feel the flash of fire from the explosion—a mere taste of the reception that waited the bastards in hell.

The man's attention was so focused on the boat making its way to his left that he did not hear Jake's breast strokes to his right, nor realize where the true danger lay until Jake's hand was on the side of his canoe. By then, it was too late, for summoning all his strength, the patriot yanked the boat out from under its occupant, sending the seaman tumbling over him into the Hudson.

The sailor's foot kicked Jake's head as he went over, hitting him in the eye and raising a welt. More importantly, the blow knocked the ruby-hilted knife from Jake's hand, throwing it into the river and leaving Jake without a weapon save his own battered hands and legs.

The patriot pushed the canoe forward, attempting to board it, but was grabbed around the waist by the Briton, who flailed not only for king and country, but life itself. Like many sailors in His Majesty's navy, the man could barely swim.

Jake smashed his elbow against the man's face twice

but could not loosen his grip. The canoe slipped from his hand and the two men plunged downward into ice cold blackness, their arms and legs tangling against each other like a pair of maddened octopuses, each blinded by the other's ink.

The suddenness of the plunge made Jake swallow water into his lungs, and his chest began to explode. The sailor's grip tightened as they sank; though Jake kicked upwards with his feet, the man was as heavy as a howitzer, and about as buoyant. Jake reached his hand toward the sailor's face, trying to jab at his eyes or throat, anything that would provoke him into letting go. The patriot's own right eye was swollen shut; while that was not a handicap at the moment, since the left, open, could see nothing in the pitch darkness of the water, it added to a general feeling that bordered on despair. His lungs were now close to bursting, and his limbs were showing the full effects of fatigue.

Ah Liberty, how swift you are to inspire those in most desperate need of your charms! For how else to explain the suddenness of the idea that knocked on the door of Jake's brain and won ready admission: if you can't get to the surface, sink.

Sink like a stone, and let the other man's instinct for survival take over. Jake ended all effort to escape, curling his legs together and making his arms go flaccid, as if he had given up the will to live.

It took the brute, in his panic, a moment to realize what was happening. In the next, he let go of Jake and kicked desperately upward.

The moment he was freed, Jake coiled himself into a spring and shot to the surface. The air that filled his lungs was as welcome to him as the Greek shore was to Odysseus, and the rain felt like a refreshing warm shower in Circe's cave.

The sailor also had found the surface of the river and was trying with awkward strokes to reach the canoe.

Jake got there first. The boat, though it had taken water, had righted itself and sat high enough on the river to block him from the sailor's view. As the Briton reached his arm for the boat, Jake shoved it away, and kicked his leg forward in the water. Though the blow was not severe, it caught the sailor by surprise.

The spirit Busch had inspired drained with that kick. The man began blubbering and crying that he was going to drown; he prayed for salvation and cursed the king.

Jake took him by the neck and hauled him to the boat, bending his shoulders over it before climbing aboard himself. Dazed but conscious, the sailor clung to the side, the fight gone out of him forever.

As Jake fished a pair of oars from the bottom of the craft, he heard a challenge directly to the west—the whaleboat of Americans rowed up belatedly.

"Take this man," Jake shouted. He slid an oar into the sailor's hands to keep him afloat until they arrived and pushed him off the side. "Then quickly follow me to the chain!"

The Americans' answer was drowned by an enormous peal of thunder as the sky overhead was illuminated by a vast sword-stroke of light.

Forty-three

*Wherein, Nature is tested and overcome, leaving only
Liberty to fling Herself against her foe.*

The storm clouds vied in a brilliant show of electricity,
clattering against each other like oaken ships determined
to batter themselves to oblivion. The rain turned to tor-
rents, falling with the stink of burnt air. But Tory Captain
John Busch was so focused on his goal that he noticed
none of it. He lifted his heavy arms again and again
against the fierce river, driving himself as the ancient
Irish hero Cuchulain had against the waves. Despite the
weight of the bomb before him, despite the force of the
water and the wind that kicked spray in his face, he was
able to reach the wooden floats that supported the heavy
barrier.

Busch found the weak point of the barrier he had spotted the previous night. The thick chain lay nearly two feet
below the water here, and if it were not for the alterations
and the weight of the front of his craft, he would have
been able to pass right over it.

Busch felt the bow of the canoe scrape the top edge of
the chain. But he could not ground the canoe on the float
as he had initially hoped, and so was forced to fall back to
his secondary strategy, tying the bomb boat to a nearby
raft.

To do this, he had to first paddle the canoe parallel to a
log and hold it there while he grappled with a stiff rope
and hook. The river's current turned violently against
him, pushing him away while the rain spit in his face.
Busch made his first try with one hand on the oar, trying
to hold himself in place; the toss was pathetically short.

By now his arms were so weak he could hardly lift them to pull the rope back in. The river sent him too far away for a second try without more paddling. He moved nearly to the tip of the raft before trying and missing again.

The hard flashes of lightning threw distorted shadows to harass and confuse his aim. It was as if all the elements had conspired to stop the Tory, Nature herself taking a hand in saving the Revolution.

"You will not beat me," he shouted when his third toss failed. "I will succeed."

As Busch was battling the will of the elements, Jake struggled with the canoe he had taken from the British sailor. Dug out from an old pine tree, it was too long for one man to handle easily in the river at night, especially in a thunderstorm. The patriot's eye had not reopened, and his arms and legs were badly bruised from the sailor's batterings. His lungs wheezed with the river water he had swallowed. The wind blew straight into his face, and the thunder punched at his temples like the sharp blows of angry boys.

When he realized he was moving southwards away from the chain instead of north, he despaired of reaching the barrier in time. He dug into the water harder with the oar and changed direction, worried he would be caught in the explosion and die a useless martyr's death.

Jake had no compunction against giving his life in the name of his Cause, but he wanted it to be a worthwhile sacrifice. And so Death himself drove him onwards, the hoary specter swinging his scythe with abandon at his back, his hot, relentless breath warming Jake's spine.

A particularly wide burst of lightning sparked its jagged insignia but a few yards ahead, and in the short instant of illumination, Jake saw a figure stand in a misshapen canoe not more than ten yards ahead.

Destiny had delivered him to his opponent.

Though it actually struck the side of St. Anthony's mountain, the lightning seemed so close that Busch involuntarily ducked. He caught himself, and with a cry as severe as the archangel will use at the end of the world he gripped the grappling hook with both hands and hurled it forward. Rage renewed his strength, and the forged metal and its rope sailed beyond the barrier and its rafts; with two quick pulls he caught the back of one of the floats and began hauling himself forward.

The canoe twisted with the current; Busch put his feet against the side and tugged at the rope, letting the back of the craft become the front but still moving toward his target. With every pull he gave a loud groan and cursed the rebels, swearing that tonight King George would have his victory sealed.

The chain was no more than three feet away when suddenly the hook slipped and Busch fell back against the bottom of the boat. His head rebounded off the deck with an agonizing smash. His senses returned in the next instant as he was yanked to the side of the canoe—the iron had slipped from the log and grappled on the chain itself, and as he had twisted the rope around his hands, he was literally being pulled out, the canoe trying to run with the river's flow.

He nearly broke his elbow against the side of the boat, but managed to stop himself; then swinging his feet around for leverage he managed two great heaves and crashed onto the deck of the sunken chain support.

In that moment, the energy drained from the storm. The rain softened to a fine mist. Though the lightning continued, the flashes were now confined to the clouds above, the thunder rolling up into the northern hills.

Busch secured his rope against the canoe gunwale and then reached down and touched the iron links. They were cold, as cold as the snow from the worst day of winter, and somehow brittle against his hand. In that moment he felt the great triumph of his victory; the rebel defense was pitifully inadequate compared to the great force the bomb in his canoe promised.

The device that would set off the charge was as ingenious as the canoe itself. The spark would be provided by a flintlock encased in a glass jar for protection against the hard elements; it had been tested successfully in a downpour twice as heavy as this. Loaded by a large, wound spring, the sort of mechanism the Swiss have perfected

for their watches, it was set by a large brass rod inserted
in a pitch-covered wooden box. The rod's hole was keyed;
only the specially designed brass wand could be rein-
serted to defuse the weapon. Once removed, Busch had
only ten minutes to reach safety.

The plan had been for him to board the other canoe
and paddle off to safety. But with the sailor busy with the
rebels, Busch was on his own—he would run along the
floats as quickly as possible, counting the time to himself.
With luck, he would reach the shore, or at least be close
to it, when the bomb went off.

Without luck, he would die where his sister had so
many years ago.

There was a fitting irony in this; Busch paused ever so
briefly to consider it, then stood and pulled the long pin
from the bomb.

Jake flew at him as he did.

He landed across Busch's back, and both men tumbled
forward onto the sunken raft next to the canoe, their
heads and bodies smashing against the heaving blocks
and metal of the barrier.

Busch crawled away, forcing himself to the next float,
dragging Jake with him. The patriot had the advantage;
he had taken his enemy by surprise, was on top of him
and stronger besides. But Busch had already removed the
brass pin and started the timing device; without it, Jake
could not prevent the canoe from exploding and destroying the chain.

As Jake got to his knees and grabbed his arms behind
him, Busch pitched the rod. It landed on the float only a
few feet away, teetering on the edge but remaining on the
wood. Busch cursed himself, then sprawled forward as
Jake grabbed at his waist. The two men struggled against
one another, reaching for the rod, the patriot realizing
from Busch's struggles that it must key the explosives'
trigger.

Busch grabbed the metal, but as he tried to slip it over
into the Hudson, Jake caught the other end. Busch
wrenched his elbow back and flung himself forward, curling around the metal as if he were a kitten attacking a

fallen piece of wool. He managed to slip it out of Jake's grasp; in the next second, he let it fall into the depths of the river.

Instantly, something in the side of his neck cracked under the weight of Jake's fist.

He smiled nonetheless.

"I've set the bomb already, traitor," he said. "It will go off in seconds. Your rebellion is doomed."

Jake threw a second punch and let go of the Tory, stumbling backwards toward the canoe. Tied firmly to the chain, the vessel heaved with the waves that wrapped themselves around his thighs. Jake struggled to reach it, walking, swimming, with no thought of how he was moving.

As his fingers touched the gunwale, he felt a hand grip his shoulder and pull him back; Busch had recovered enough strength to try and stop him. Jake shoved him back like a small dog. The Tory draped himself on his side, but Jake ignored him, crawling into the boat arms first.

As his hand found the wooden floor, his side suddenly warmed. Then he felt a scrape against his rib—Busch had a knife in his hand.

Jake only just managed to duck away from a swipe at his neck. He fell back against the black bombworks as Busch steadied himself to deliver another blow.

"Your death warrant is already signed," said Busch, slashing the air in front of Jake's chest.

Jake held his breath as he fell to the rear of the craft. The darkness and the injury to his eye made it nearly impossible to see Busch, let alone his knife, even though he must be no more than six feet away.

"You're a brave man," Jake said. His voice was sincere, though his intention was to get a response—anything—to help him find his enemy. "I was being honest when I said you belonged on our side, not the king's."

"I won't listen to your treachery anymore," shouted Busch, lunging at him.

Jake pulled himself to the side but was unable to escape the knife, which plunged deep into the flesh just above his hip. At least there was no longer a question of where Busch was—Jake grabbed his arm and wrenched it back across his body. The Tory let go of the blade and twisted back, kicking at the same time. As the pair wrestled, the canoe rocked wildly, threatening to drop them both overboard.

Busch, with his smaller, slippier body, was able to spin around and grab Jake in a headlock. Within seconds, the patriot spy felt his throat beginning to close, compressed between his enemy's arms.

None of his blows against Busch seemed to have any effect. Pulling with his left hand against Busch's lower arm, he poked and punched with his right, trying his elbow as well as his fist.

Jake could feel his lungs crying for air. Powerless to stop choking, he felt his right hand fall limp at his side—

Against the knife, still lodged deep in his hip. As if he suddenly had been given a new supply of energy, Jake pulled it up and flailed backwards, sending the blade through Busch's cheek and instantly freeing himself. Even as his lungs gasped thankfully, he rammed the knife three times into Busch's chest.

A dim spark of far-off lightning framed the Tory's face with the last blow. Dark sadness mixed with surprise as Busch's eyes grew glassy. In the next moment he coughed blood, the fight over.

Even in that second, Jake felt genuine regret that this soul had been lost to the enemy. But it did not stop him from dropping the limp body to the floor of the canoe. He took the knife and looked down at his own hip, awash in blood.

It would have given his mother quite a fright to see him now, he thought.

Odd, to think of his long-dead mother at a moment like this. Her image flickered in his brain as he dropped to his knees along the side of the boat, fishing for the rope that bound it to the chain.

At every second, he expected to be immolated in a resounding blast. It may have been three seconds before his wrist struck something wet and warm; it may have been three hours. By the time his brain realized it was the rope, his fingers were already sawing the knife through it.

Suddenly he felt a gentle tap on his shoulder. He looked up in amazement. The only thought that seemed plausible was that he had died, and was being welcomed to heaven by his long-dead mother.

But Jake Gibbs hadn't died—not yet, anyway. The rope had merely given way, and the current snatched the canoe with such force it was as if a dozen teamsters had grabbed hold of the boat and pushed it downstream. The tap he felt was the lash of the rope; when it brushed by him he was already flying into the water.

Forty-four

Wherein, rocks fill the air and other signs announcing the approach of the Apocalypse are seen.

Claus van Clynne and his adopted band of Connecticut regulars had not been idle during Jake's heroic battle on the river. Indeed, the soldiers and their general—if we may stretch the term a little longer—had found themselves hard-pressed by the retreating Tory raiding force. The storm warmed van Clynne's heart if not his clothes, as he understood the disturbance to be the product of certain former members of Henry Hudson's crew, but this old story was too long and complicated to be explained to his men under the circumstances. Nonetheless, he rallied them with every encouragement possible as the combined company of rangers and marines fell against the American interlopers in their rear.

At first the British forces unloaded their weapons with great relish, whether they had a target in sight or not. Their enthusiasm at the chance to spill some enemy blood kept them operating more as individuals than as a massed group, which was fortunate. For so it is in warfare, that overweening energy can be as great a detriment as an asset; as long as the red- and greencoats stayed isolated in ones and twos and did not mass for a charge, the Americans caught between them and the shore were comparatively safe. Their officers soon realized the problem, and began trying to organize them into two brigades for a frontal assault, where their bayonets and not their weather-fouled guns would be the important weapons.

The galley *Dependence,* meanwhile, had realized something was amiss on shore. She came up with her cannons and swivels loaded, ready to provide whatever support her ground forces required. The captain gave one good flash of an 18-pounder—a heavy cannon under the circumstances, but a mere child's weapon compared to the vessel's main armament—to alert her troops that she was prepared to assist. The ball sailed a good distance over everyone's heads, landing with a thud in the hills.

Having completed some of his most successful business dealings in the dark of the night, van Clynne realized it would be difficult from the water to tell who was friend and who was foe. He therefore endeavored to convince the *Dependence* that her troops were those nearest the shore—a not unnatural assumption, since that was where she had originally left them. And so he answered the cannon shot with his own pistol, and called out, with his best British accent, that the Americans had overwhelmed the advance guard and were about to overtake them.

One hears many tongues and accents in the Americas; there is French and its many varieties, Dutch and German, various African languages, a multitude of Indian dialects. English itself comes in a cornucopia of styles and slants; it is not difficult to tell a Rhode Islander from a Virginian, nor would someone from Boston be confused with a Jamestown resident, once his mouth was open.

The Dutchman's shout from the shore had an accent all its own. Though it was based on what he imagined a British marine would sound like, in truth, he had not had so much experience with these fellows that he could easily mimic the voice. His own Dutch accent was strong besides; overall, the tone was quite peculiar, if not overly pleasing.

Fortunately, the mate aboard the *Dependence* who heard it took it for Welsh. More importantly, he interpreted van Clynne's words—"We are here, and the rabble is a hundred yards further inland."—as perfectly as if they were the king's own English. The *Dependence* immediately began firing its heavy weapons into the supposed rebels, breaking up the marine and Tory charge.

Another man might have thought this a pretty good night's work, and been content to lie low while the balls shot overhead. But the squire was just warming to the battle. Besides, his dislike of the water extended to everything upon it, and this galley and her monstrous gun were a tempting target.

Or would have been, had they anything to bombard her with. The impudent British, unaware that they were firing at their own men, proceeded right up to the shore, launching ball after ball. A youth with a slingshot could pick them off with his rocks.

Van Clynne grabbed one of his soldiers just as he leveled a musket in the galley's direction.

"I have a much better idea," said the Dutchman, glancing upward at the rocky edge of the nearby hillside. "Two of you men stay here and pretend you're part of the British landing party. When you hear our assault begin, run for cover—don't dally."

As van Clynne leads his men to a small but strategic path between the berry bushes up a short but not insignificant promontory south of St. Anthony's Nose, we will take a brief but critical detour of our own, joining Dr. Keen and his kidnapped guide, sweet Jane. They were at this precise moment hurrying in the doctor's coach to Marshad's cottage.

Keen, partly because of intermittent pain from his wounds, had been a perfect gentleman—assuming one makes the natural allowance for the fact that he held Jake's loaded Segallas next to Jane's throat. After permitting her to fetch a cloak, he escorted the girl from the inn to his coach, making a brief detour to borrow a horse from her uncle's stable.

The animal was tied to the rear of the carriage. Jane was then introduced to the coach's sleeping occupant. She reacted with an involuntary gulp—Rose's mother lived a short distance away from Jane's uncle, and the two girls had often played together before Rose was sent to the Stonemans' to learn the rudiments of caring for a house.

"This will be even easier than I hoped," Keen declared, taking Jane to the driver's bench and tying a long rope to her ankle. He suggested that, should she disobey any of his commands, he would kill not just her but her entire family. From that point on, the doctor sat back and let her drive to the cottage, brooding in silence while working out the details for her lover's ambush.

Keen did not know that there was a connection between this young woman and his enemy, else the course of our tale might be far different. Jane, however, had recognized the Segallas as belonging to her lover's assistant—one must forgive her for seeing the world through Claus van Clynne's eyes. She therefore had some confidence that she and Rose soon would be rescued. She was also comforted by the knowledge that the exceedingly sharp paring knife secreted beneath her boned corset would come in handy should her captor get fresh.

As they neared the heavily damaged cottage, the rain began to beat down fiercely. Jane pulled her dark woolen cloak up and hunched inside, as if it were a cave that could keep her dry. The doctor, meanwhile, seemed as impervious to the elements as a beaver.

Keen's coach was equipped with a pair of ingenious candle lanterns constructed with mirrors and metal in such a way that a goodly amount of light shone on their path. When the house was in sight, the doctor stopped the horses and unfastened one of the lanterns from its side post, using it to illuminate the ruins and the surrounding woods. When he was satisfied that there was no one else here, he set the lantern back down and reached into his coat. There he drew a long knife from a scabbard sewn beneath the arm.

Jane saw her life glow in the reflection cast on the blade as Keen moved it slowly toward her. She froze, the connection between her brain and muscles momentarily severed.

"Take the horse at the back of the coach and go to General Putnam," commanded Keen, slicing through the rope at her heel. He smiled, relishing the fear that had flooded into her face with the appearance of the blade. "Tell the general to send the Dutchman, Claus van Clynne, here immediately, or my captive will die."

"Claus van Clynne?"

"He must come alone—if there are any soldiers with him, she will be dispatched before they turn the corner there," he added, pointing ahead. "And then your family at the inn will die. And after that—yourself. Go. Now!"

Jane flew from the top of the carriage to the horse. Keen watched her leave with much satisfaction. He was not such a simpleton to think that Putnam wouldn't send a troop of soldiers, but the look on her face when he mentioned van Clynne convinced him she knew the Dutchman and would endeavor to send him here.

Keen would have ample surprises for them all.

The hill van Clynne and his men climbed stood over the sheltered bit of water where the *Dependence* had been maneuvering. The height was not great, but the elevation was more than enough to protect anyone who stood on the top from the awful 32-pound dragon at the mouth of the ship.

"What we need, gentlemen, are stones," declared the Dutchman as he huffed to the crown. "Not huge ones, mind, but ones you can throw readily. You see the ship; that is our target, and it is an easy one at that."

And so it was. The deckhands and gun crews on the British galley, who had already done well to cope with the rain, now found themselves inundated with much heavier material. It was as if God had opened up the sky and forced brimstone down upon them.

Well, not quite. The British quickly realized that the rocks were being thrown by mortals, and rebel mortals at that. But they found this new threat nearly impossible to counter. Only two swivels could be brought to bear, and the darkness made it difficult to see what they were shooting at. Had the Americans been firing muskets, the flashes would have given them away, but the rocks arrived suddenly, crashing on deck—or on a sailor's head—without showing where their authors stood.

The ship's captain was beside himself with anger at this new rebel ploy. He ordered the helmsman to bring the ship about, and yelled at his gun crews to send "the damned rebels back to hell where they belong."

The crew endeavored to comply. But the swirling rip-ides made it difficult to swing around quickly, and suddenly a loud crash signaled yet another problem—the keel had struck against a submerged sandbar, leaving the *Dependence* snagged in an even more difficult position than before. The rock throwers quickly realized the ship's plight, and responded with a hurrah—and a fresh round of projectiles.

As their confidence grew, van Clynne's troops steadily increased the caliber of their stones. Lieutenant Clark's curses reached a new fervor as he urged his men to row themselves off the rocks and retreat. The river roiled with fresh and heavy stones, and for a moment it appeared the great British terror of the Hudson was about to meet her doom.

Surely that would have been the case had the troop of American soldiers—two full companies of men, under the personal direction of Major General Israel Putnam himself—been able to fight their way past the last marines and rangers in a few minutes' less time. Their shouts as they reached the shore added to the confusion, and Clark felt a sinking sensation in his stomach he had never experienced while wearing the king's coat of service in the navy. But a roar from his 32-pounder succeeded in rallying his spirits; even more importantly, it helped loosen the ship from its snare.

"All hands—get us the hell out of here!" yelled the lieutenant, not caring how ignoble his words would sound to posterity. "Get us the hell out of here!"

Forty-five

Wherein, the Apocalypse arrives.

Free of the bomb canoe, Jake took two immense strokes and found himself back at the floating iron barrier. He climbed atop, pausing to cough as much of the river water from his lungs as possible.

Though the thunder and lightning had faded, cannon fire on shore and from the *Dependence* took up the slack. Pandemonium echoed around him, the gunshots joined by shouts and cries from the wounded. No longer hampered by the rain, fires broke out with vengeance all along the river below. It seemed as if he had swum from the Hudson directly to the mouth of the river Lethe at Hades' gate.

The bomb canoe was floating downstream, carried by the current. Jake had no idea whether it was still close enough to damage the chain if it exploded; indeed, he had no idea how long it would be before the bomb went off. Both matters were out of his hands—his best course now was to run like hell for the shore.

Under any circumstance, running along the chain, with its floats moving back and forth with the waves, would have been a daunting if not impossible task. Given the churning of the river due to the storm and Jake's tired and bruised condition, however, it was not even conceivable. He took one step and fell flat on his face, dropping his arms barely in time to break his fall. Groping forward, he managed to reach the end of one float and climb to another. He made the next one before slipping again, this time hitting his chin on the heaving iron. River water filled his mouth and he began coughing so hard he fell over. Some action of the river or the storm punched a link up into his ribs so severely that he nearly rebounded into the air. He began flailing about, as if under attack from some monstrous creature of the deep. For a moment, blinded by the pounding of the water into his face, Jake thought he saw the chain rise up and tangle itself around him, as if it were a giant ray or eel, trying to strangle him.

The monster Despair, more powerful by far than any denizen of the river or sea, loomed at his back, its icy grip pinching the strained muscles in Jake's neck. With a start, the patriot realized he had slipped off the logs and was completely under water.

He opened his good eye and thought he saw two figures below him, worm-eaten corpses with their arms extended to him, hair flowing in the current and dresses billowing with the river's movement. He muscled every last ounce of strength into his arms and pushed for the surface, kicked his legs and struck his arm on one of the barrier's supports; despite the pain, he used it for leverage and lurched away.

And then in a second the storm vanished completely, the wind finally pushing the clouds so hard against the surrounding mountains that they were drained of their liquid in one last torrent, and had nothing left. The Hudson in that brief moment went calm as glass, and Jake made strong progress toward shore.

Free of the chain, free of the monsters of his imagination, the patriot saw the dark outline of St. Anthony's looming overhead. In that instant it turned from demon to protector, a natural barrier that helped the Americans form their line against the British tyrants. The river and her eddies helped now, with a current that pushed him toward land. Jake felt a sudden burst of speed, and as he stroked for the riverbank shook his head clear of the mucus that had accumulated during his struggle.

And then the Hudson was lit by a fireball unseen since the Earth's creation.

The water was rent in two. Huge waves welled up in a massive tide, pushed by a force several times that of the greatest Caribbean hurricane. The air itself turned hot from the friction of the blast, rushing against the shore like the hard blade of a carpenter's plane, taking with it whole trees and immense boulders, while burning the unprotected flesh from men's faces. Jake was propelled a hundred yards directly upstream, and then sucked back by the rebounding waves. He was tossed like a cloth sack against the chain, landing directly atop a float.

The patriot barrier shook with the force of the blow, rebounding up and down all across its length as the strong rope of a hammock under the weight of a child jumping on it. But like such a rope, the boundary held—whether because of superior design and manufacture, some trick of the river's reflection, or even Providence herself, the reader may take his pick. An engineer would realize the orientation of the chain was such that it actually rode much of the shock wave, which was largely wasted in the open air.

Even so, the iron and logs groaned so loudly that Jake's first thought was that he had failed. He lay on his back against the logs for a long moment, dark dread once again filling his head. But he soon realized the wood below him was intact, and creaking against its fellows; he sat up and began shouting insane hosannas as if he had been deposited directly into the balmy waters of the Mighty Jordan, en route to heaven.

Forty-six

*Wherein, slight complications mar the otherwise well-
deserved joy of the patriot forces.*

Old Put pushed his stocky torso from the ground.
Frowning, he retrieved his hat from the bush where it had
been blown by the shock of the bomb canoe's blast just
upriver. The cocked hat had been fatally bruised; one
fold had been torn halfway through and the other permanently folded so that it hung down over his face. He
tossed it aside and began shouting at his men to look
alive, to take up their positions, to finish rounding up
their prisoners and rout any other Tory or Briton who
dared darken the surrounding woods with his presence.

General Putnam is among the most esteemed of American leaders, and certainly one of the oldest; while he
appeared as something of a rooster strutting around the
barnyard barking orders, still his commands were received with the alacrity one expects from soldiers re-
sponding out of respect for the man as well as the rank.

Except from the Connecticut men, who looked to their
own general for direction.

"Begging your pardon, sir," said one of the privates,
pointing to their adopted leader. "But General van
Clynne has taken us under his command, and as he is of
captain-general rank with a surfeit of clusters, we answer
to him, sir."

"Captain-general? Clusters?" scowled Old Put. "When
did Congress establish such a ridiculous rank?"

"It is a hereditary title from the Dutch, sir," said van
Clynne quickly, "one which I seldom invoke except under
the most dire circumstances, with which we were faced."

The Dutchman stepped forward and reached up to doff his hat. As it had been blown off his head, he came up empty-handed, but bowed nonetheless.

"What the hell are you talking about?" demanded Putnam.

"Surely Miss McGuiness told you about me when she arrived," said van Clynne. "She is a stubborn young woman, sir, but you must make allowances for her; her heart is that of a true patriot."

"What Miss McGuiness? What in damnation are you talking about? Speak clearly and quickly, or I'll have you flogged."

"Rose McGuiness. Didn't she alert you to the plot against the chain?"

"What plot?"

The general could not have realized how grave a mistake the question was, for it invited the Dutchman to launch into a full narrative of the night's adventures. Despite Old Put's constant exhortations to get to the point, van Clynne embroidered a lengthy tale of destruction and woe—with himself, naturally, at the center of it.

The general, tiring of the discourse and suspicious of the Dutchman, would have had him slapped in irons, except for the mention of Jake Gibbs's name.

"Jake is involved in this?"

"After a fashion, sir, after a fashion. We are a team, as it were."

Putnam was spared further details by the timely arrival of Jane, who rode astride the bareback horse much as a young lad would have. She dismounted in a flash, her heavy woolen cloak swirling around to reveal her homespun skirts—all soaked as badly as any shirt of Job's.

To Claus van Clynne, this was the most beautiful sight imaginable, the swish of a tulip petal loosened by the wind.

"My sweet Jane!"

"Claus!"

The two dear hearts came together with a crash that rivaled the recent explosion. General Putnam was about to take the opportunity to attend to more important matters, when Jane broke free of her lover's grasp and stopped him.

"General, please—I've ridden nearly the whole night to find you. A British spy has taken a young servant girl named Rose McGuiness hostage. She must be rescued—Claus, the man's name is Dr. Keen; he says you're to come to Marshad's cottage without any soldiers, or he'll kill Rose straight away. And then he'll start in on Uncle."

While van Clynne was confronting this new twist, his erstwhile partner was basking in the sweet calm that victory brings. Triumph makes all manner of injuries light nuisances, easily dismissed. The river was illuminated by fresh watch fires across the way; overhead, the stars fought through the fading clouds and glittered with all their might. Bear Mountain seemed to hunch his shoulders and proclaim his majesty, the Hudson lapping at his feet with a gentle snicker.

Jake might have been forgiven if, as he sat cross-legged, still half in the water, he thought this glorious show of Nature was all for his benefit. His exertions had left him near drunk with the afterglow of his body's fiery humors. The knife wound in his hip had stopped bleeding; his other wounds and bruises drifted away like memories of lost bets.

Some hoarse shouts nearby quickly sobered him. The patrolling whaleboat had been literally blown to splinters, and its soldiers were now clinging to the rocking chain as if it were a life raft.

"Make your way towards me," shouted Jake, gingerly going out to help them. The British sailor and one of their comrades had been lost in the confusion, but otherwise their injuries were light.

Jake pointed them back to shore and helped the stragglers. As the way became easier, his thoughts turned to his mission to Albany; he must leave tonight if he were to reach General Schuyler before his deadline. He also thought of the woman he had left there some weeks before, Sarah Thomas. She would welcome him gladly when he arrived.

Distracted by her image in his brain, he did not notice

the man with the rifle leveled at the shivering regulars who had reached shore ahead of him.

"Stand back," said the old man, his shoulders against the rocky crag on the narrow bank. "Stand back or I'll kill you all."

Jake knew who he must be at once.

"Mr. Busch—don't shoot at us. We're on your side."

"Side? What side?"

"The patriot side," said Jake.

"I don't know what you're talking about. You are all trespassing on my land."

They outnumbered him, and if they rushed him would surely overcome him. The rifle was loaded though, and even in the dim light he surely would not miss hitting someone.

"We've come to try and help you find your daughter," offered Jake. "We heard she was lost."

"Annie? Yes, I can not seem to find her. She and John have been missing since supper. It's John—the boy always gets into trouble. He is a rebellious scoundrel—if I told him to walk he would run."

"Mr. Busch, please put the gun down," said Jake, taking a step forward. His injured feet made him wince with pain, but at least his eye had opened and he could see normally. "It'll only scare your daughter when we find her."

The old man looked down at the weapon in his hands, as if confused at how it had gotten there. His attention was turned long enough for Jake to spring at him. But the gun was surrendered meekly.

"My daughter?" asked the elder Busch.

"She's gone. She died in the river. John, too."

"John, too?"

"Yes, sir."

The old man's face erupted with tears at the fate of his family, whether for the first or last time, neither Jake nor anyone else could tell.

"I feel it only fair to point out, my pumpkin, that had this Rose followed my directions, she would not be in this

predicament. This is what comes of questioning a Dutchman's counsel."

"Claus, you have to rescue Rose," said Jane. "You
must."

"Well, yes, I will do so without fail," said the Dutchman, who in truth was as interested in liberating his coins
as the girl. His opinion of Rose had shifted slightly because she was a friend of Jane's—but only slightly. "If the
general will lend me my troop back."

"Granted," said Putnam, who was prepared to do
much more to get the squire out of his powdered white
hair.

"But Dr. Keen said—"

"Tut, tut, my dear; one doesn't go into the lion's den
unarmed. Undoubtedly our doctor friend has some surprise in store for me, some stupendous-sized leech which
he plans to twirl around my head. My men here will
sneak through the brush and wait until I have flushed out
his plot. It will undoubtedly be clever," added the Dutchman as an aside, "but the inherent limitations of the British intellect will leave a large gap for us to proceed
through."

Jake and the soldiers helped the grief-stricken old Mr.
Busch up to his farm, comforting him as best they could
with the aid of some medicinal rum kept by the fireplace.
The lieutenant colonel had just finished wrapping his
wounds in bandages and taken a sip of the rum himself
when there was a sharp knock at the door. One of the
soldiers answered it to discover two men sent by General
Putnam.

"We were told to fish Colonel Gibbs from the river if
necessary," said one of the privates, "and return him before the general is drowned by verbiage."

"Do you understand those orders, sir?" asked the
other, whose face betrayed the fact that he himself did
not.

"Oh, absolutely," said Jake, laughing. "It means the
general has made the acquaintanceship of my good
friend, Claus van Clynne."

Jake borrowed some shoes and Mr. Busch's horse to

ride to the house on the Fishkill road where the general had made his temporary headquarters. Along the way he found Private Martin, who claimed to have been blown there by the bomb blast. While that seemed highly unlikely, the Connecticut private could not remember what had happened if not that. In fact, he could not remember much of anything at all, including his adventure on the river or his brief sojourn under the command of "General" van Clynne.

Nor did he remember having been among the privates that Old Put had routed from a New York City wine cellar on the eve of the British invasion a year before.

"I'm sure I would remember that, sir," muttered the distressed soldier as General Putnam questioned him about the incident. In Jake's opinion, that was the one thing he might well remember, his profuse head-shaking to the contrary.

"Well, what do you remember?" demanded the general.

"Being inoculated against the pox, sir."

At that, Old Put turned several shades of color. "Get back to the damn hospital then. Get!" The general turned to Jake as Martin vanished through the door. "These damn inoculations. Half my army is sick, and the other half is guarding the damn fools."

"Begging your pardon, sir," said Jake, "but the Dutchman?"

"The Dutchman?"

"Claus van Clynne. I understood from your message that he was here."

"I sent him off with some men to look after a kidnapping. Frankly, I was glad to get rid of him. This van Clynne—he claimed to be your partner."

"He has served lately as my assistant," said Jake. "He has his own ideas about his importance. He has saved my life now on more than one occasion, though I'm not sure I would admit it in his presence."

"I doubt he would give you the chance," said the general.

Forty-seven

Wherein, the despicable Dr. Keen makes one last display of his prodigious talents, to Squire van Clynne's great distress.

*V*an Clynne's plan for foiling Dr. Keen was a classic snare maneuver, during which he would offer himself as temporary bait while his Connecticut soldiers closed the noose. After positioning his men in the woods near the cottage, he snuck back to the roadway and prepared to proceed toward the cottage.

At this point, sweet Jane threatened to become a barrier to the plan, wanting to join him. Van Clynne had to turn his considerable powers of persuasion on her, assuring her that in the first place he was well armed—the red ruby dirk was hidden up his sleeve and two tomahawks were secreted at the sides of his coat—and in the second, she would perform a much more useful function by remaining here.

"Doing what?"

"Well, you shall be our reserve," proclaimed the Dutchman. "Ready to swoop in like winged Victory herself at the moment of denouement."

"That is not a job," said Jane. "Rose is my friend and I want to help rescue her. I can and I shall."

Van Clynne recognized the strong bent in her eyes and knew it was as useless to argue with her as to rant against the lingering thunder.

Not that he wouldn't try either.

"Well, then," said the Dutchman, "you must sneak into the coach and attempt to retrieve my coins, if that's where they are. You can already consider them part of our joyful estate. As the wedding proverb says, 'What's yours is yours and what's mine is yours,' or something along those lines."

The squire was in fact endeavoring to send her from harm's way, as he supposed the coach would be far from the line of fire. Jane nodded at his advice that she must postpone her advance until he had given her a clear signal—a Mohawk war whoop. He demonstrated once to make sure she knew the sound.

"That's not a Mohawk call," she objected. "It's Huron."

Van Clynne frowned and made a note to instruct her on her future duties as faithful wife when he found himself at greater leisure.

Had Keen not already detected the Dutchman's presence thanks to an elaborate system of strings placed further north on the highway, the war whoop would have fully alerted him. In any event, he was well prepared when van Clynne rode slowly down the road to the ruined cottage, glanced around the environs, and then entered the small building. The fire had taken away three-quarters of the roof and a good portion of the rear wall, but otherwise it was reasonably intact, if sooty.

Fully expecting a trap, the Dutchman examined the shadows carefully. Then he set a candle on the stump of a stool before the fireplace and lit its wick with a bit of flint. The rain had ceased, and the stars were making an effort to contribute some illumination, but even so the ruins were dark. Still, there was more than enough light to reveal van Clynne's purses on a charred table in the center of the room.

The Dutchman's joy at discovering that they contained all of his coins was interrupted by Keen's voice behind him.

"And so, Mr. Clynne, we meet again."

"The van is an important part of my name," snapped the Dutchman, tucking the money inside his coat as he turned around. Even the dim candle before the hearth had enough light to reflect off the polished barrel of the weapon Keen held—an ancient though apparently operative matchlock musket, whose smoldering fuse hung at its side. "You should not like being called Dr. 'En, I suppose."

"A man holding a gun on me can call me anything he pleases."

"That is an interesting weapon," conceded van Clynne. "I took it for a museum piece."

"Not at all. It is very old, but still exceedingly efficient."

"Of Dutch design, I suppose."

"Hardly."

"And the girl?" asked van Clynne, taking a short step to his right as he looked for cover. "What have you done with her?"

"She was having difficulty sleeping, so I prescribed some powders. They seem to have worked very well; I left her snoring on the bench of my coach."

Van Clynne took another step. His lighting of the candle had been a signal to his men that he was inside; they were to proceed forthwith to the attack, advancing with weapons drawn and bayonets sharpened. The Dutchman had only to pass a few light words with his quarry and the engagement would be his. In truth, rarely had victory come to him so easily.

"I see you have not yet replaced your hat," said the Dutchman. "But you have at least improved the color of your coat."

"I like to believe I can learn from my mistakes."

Van Clynne frowned to himself and wondered where his men were. This was the problem with using soldiers who were not Dutch—they might be filled with energy, but had no sense of timing or discipline. "Considering that you are a medical doctor, sir," he stalled, "perhaps you would consult with me on certain difficulties I have been having with my digestion. You worked wonders with your leeches."

"I don't intend on making that mistake again," said Keen, moving his left hand to the fuse.

Van Clynne threw himself toward the candle, dousing the light and yelling for his men to launch their assault. But he was not answered by the glorious sounds of a charging company of bloodthirsty Continentals. Nor did Keen fire in his direction. Instead, the night became day and van Clynne found himself not only illuminated but surrounded by a ring of bright phosphorous laid in a deep trail with several full pots at strategic spots in the ruins. The surrounding walls, which had been covered with a thin pitch, caught fire, becoming thick torches in the night.

At the same time, a dozen barrels placed in the woods ignited with a purplish powder that rendered anyone within twenty feet completely helpless—and so was van Clynne's army temporarily annihilated.

"You didn't think I would shoot at you in the dark, did you?" asked Keen. The doctor had concealed a small bomblet in his hand, and lit it off the gun's fuse before dropping it into a pile of the phosphorus. "I'm afraid I found it expedient to remove the brigade you brought here; I wouldn't want them interfering with our interview."

Van Clynne pulled himself up indignantly. "This is but a stage trick," he said. "What will we have next, dancing clowns?"

"If you wish," said Keen, pointing the gun at van Clynne's feet. "Dance."

"I will not, sir. I would rather die."

The bullet that ricocheted directly at van Clynne's feet did not change his opinion, but the second one did. The Dutchman hopped up immediately, and was still in the air when the third bullet whizzed by his toes.

The reader, not to mention the squire, will naturally wonder how Keen was able to accomplish this, when he was holding only one gun. The ingenious doctor had used his study of the writings of Marco Polo and certain Chinese scholars to construct a multi-tubed musket, whose lock end contained not one but three different firing mechanisms. Small balls and their charges were wedged into cylinders directly above the stock and ignited by the end of the fuse when it was touched against them.

Keen did not bother explaining the gun's genesis or operation to van Clynne. Out of bullets, he merely put down the gun and reached into his pocket for another weapon, this one considerably more familiar to the Dutchman—Jake's Segallas.

Van Clynne was not idle during this small interlude, reaching for a tomahawk and unleashing it in the doctor's direction. As he did so, it vanished into a wall of flames that suddenly shot up in front of him.

"I had some ambitions on being a stage designer when I was young," said Keen as the flare-up subsided. "I'm afraid I still have a tendency to indulge myself in theatrical bombast."

"I was indeed impressed by that trick, sir. I begin to feel humbled in your presence."

"If you believe in God, prepare your soul to meet him," said Keen, pointing the gun.

"I recognize your weapon, sir; it belongs to a friend of mine who will go to great lengths to get it back."

"Indeed."

"Its bullets, if I may say, are rather small." Claus took a cautious step forward. "They will sting, but they will not kill me."

"They do indeed sting," said Keen, whose own buttocks attested to their effect. "But I have taken the opportunity to add a treatment to them that will make them do considerably more than that. You have heard of the scorpion?"

"A delightful creature," said van Clynne. "Are you planning on following his example and cut your head off, now that I have you surrounded?"

"On your knees, pig."

"Jane—no!" shouted van Clynne.

His exclamation was completely in earnest, for Jane had managed to elude the ring of smoke and flames and slipped into the cottage to rescue her true love. Keen, however, interpreted the remark as a juvenile diversionary tactic, and so was nearly caught off guard when sweet Jane lunged at him with a large and heavy tree branch.

Nearly was not good enough, unfortunately. Keen leaped aside and tripped the girl, then swung and ducked van Clynne's second hatchet.

"Tie him up," the doctor ordered Jane, pointing his gun. "And be quick about it."

"I would sooner die," she replied.

"Then I will kill you both," promised Keen.

"Please, Jane, if you value our love, do as he says. I will gladly forfeit my life for yours."

What bravery from the mouth of a Dutchman! What sentiments of love!

And surely the sentiment was heartfelt and genuine—though it should be noted for scientific accuracy that van Clynne had spotted a familiar shadow approaching through the darkness behind Keen. Sweet Jane bent her head, and with a tear in her eye took the rope the doctor tossed her.

"Tut, tut, my dear. We shall be together for all eternity," said van Clynne bravely. "This is but a momentary nuisance."

"Prepare to meet your maker," said Keen, in a voice at once so evil and dramatic that Shakespeare would have taken him for Burbage.

"It is you who should prepare yourself," said Lieutenant Colonel Jake Gibbs, kicking away the short piece of smoldering wall that had covered his approach. "I would think the odds much higher of my rifle bullet finding you than your bullets hitting my friend."

So many events were crammed into the next second and a half that it would take several days—indeed, an entire trip from Westchester to Albany—to unravel them properly. Jake had enlisted a company of American dragoons to assist him; mustered upwind on the hill leading to the roadway, they suddenly flashed their weapons and charged toward the ruins. Van Clynne grabbed sweet Jane in his arms and dove with her to the ground. Jake shot square at Keen, and swore later he hit him in the side. Keen fired, but not at van Clynne or at Jake, nor at any of the soldiers for that matter. Instead he hit a specially prepared barrel, which exploded instantly, sending a dark powder into the air that doused the flickering phosphorous and blocked the stars and dim moon overhead.

Shouts, gunfire, screams—all mixed in the confused air. Jake grabbed a body he thought was the doctor's. Immediately a sweet odor filled his nose, somehow defeating the cotton he had placed there as a precaution against such tricks. He felt his grip inexplicably weaken. The mounted soldiers fell upon each other in the darkness. Horses wailed, a woman wept; by the time fires were lit and the smoke cleared, Keen and his carriage were gone.

Forty-eight

*Wherein, the story is temporarily concluded, loose ends
tied, and further adventures promised.*

Jake found Rose on the ground near where the carriage
had been, Keen obviously calculating that his escape
would be easier if he did not carry her along. The patriot
took her into his arms and brought her to the cottage
while the dragoons recovered themselves and set out after the doctor. Even as they mounted their horses, Jake
knew the odds were greatly against them—but he also
sensed that eventually he would meet Keen again.

While the patriot spy searched through the remains of
Keen's drug jars for something that might bring her
around, Rose came to on her own, slowly opening one
eye and then the other as the effects of Keen's potion
wore off. But rather than leaping up, she closed both eyes
and waited for her hero to return with a small bottle of
smelling salts.

He lifted her head gently into his lap, smoothed her
curls back, then waved the blue glass beneath her nose.
Despite her resolve to enjoy this sweet pillow as long as
possible, she immediately began coughing.

"There we go," said Jake, lifting her up and standing
beside her. "Are you all right?"

His question was answered by a swift and strong hug.

"Thank God you rescued me," she said, underlining
her gratitude with a series of kisses.

"You're welcome," said Jake, returning the favor. He
indulged himself a while longer—surely there are rewards
no man can ignore.

Van Clynne's harrumphs eventually interrupted him.

"I played a role in your rescue as well," he pointed out with great dignity.

Rose, after a nod from sweet Jane, gave the Dutchman a polite buss on the chin, then turned back to Jake, looping her arm in his.

"Robert will be happy to hear you're safe," said Jane. Her voice was not quite pointed, but there was no mistaking her meaning.

"Robert," said Rose, clinging to Jake.

"Yes, Robert," said the patriot, who nonetheless let her cling a little longer before gently freeing his arm. "He's quite lucky to be marrying a brave young woman like you."

"But—"

The patriot spy could not resist silencing her protest with a deep—and, dare we suggest, wistful?—kiss.

Several hours later, the patriot spy and his Dutch companion were once more on the road, the sun urging toward dawn and van Clynne deep into his favorite habit of complaint.

"And so, had his show included some such surprise as flying arrows entering my head, you would have let it continue for your amusement."

"Now, now, Claus, I had to wait until the dragoons were in position. You seemed to have things well under control."

"I should have liked to hear your opinion, were the roles reversed."

"They were on the *Richmond*. I had a rope around my neck the entire time you were aboard. You claimed I was never in any danger."

"It was an English rope, sir, and they are notoriously inferior. I have seen a man hanged for three hours before finally giving up the ghost."

"There's a consolation."

"I, on the other hand, faced down the most despicable criminal in all of Christendom," said the Dutchman, still working to shape the narrative of his adventures—and much more importantly, the writ to have his property returned. "I did so single-handedly and without fear."

"No fear at all?"

"Sir, the Dutch are different than other races. We are not constitutionally given to fear. Something in our blood prevents it." The Dutchman's horse—the gelding had been retrieved from the inn where van Clynne had first met Keen—gave a whinny, whether in wonderment or agreement, who could say?

"I thought Keen and his leeches took all your blood," said Jake.

"He endeavored to, sir, but he had not counted on the Dutch physique. It is a finely tuned, resourceful engine. The Romans found this out when they tried to take us over in the days before Christ."

"Your country was occupied for a thousand years."

Van Clynne suddenly stopped his horse dead on the roadway. His face turned white, and his manner sickly.

"Claus?"

"I have completely forgotten! I have the pox!"

"The pox?"

The Dutchman slumped on his horse like a dead man. "My soldiers were infected with it. I must have caught it. I ignored the danger of my disease to fight for my country, and now surely I have caught my death."

"What soldiers were infected?"

"Private Martin and the others. I found them in isolation. Poor sweet Jane will be left a widow, before she has even married! If I didn't infect her at the cottage with my kisses!"

"If the soldiers were inoculated, they're not infectious. The germs are too weak. You haven't caught anything."

The Dutchman gave his companion a wary look.

"I know my business," said Jake, shaking his horse's reins. "I did not spend every day at school whoring."

"I was merely testing your knowledge," said van Clynne, resuming his former posture and urging his mount forward. "There are so many quacks in the world today, one can never be sure of another's credentials. Henceforth, I shall refer to you as Dr. Gibbs."

Jake smiled. Under oath, he would have admitted that the Dutchman had done a fine job these past few days, and played an important role in defeating the Tory plot against the chain. And yet van Clynne's tongue had the effect of a powerful telescopic glass, magnifying his own importance so gravely out of proportion that it was comical.

Almost.

"It was a shame you had to lose your salt. General Putnam's men would have welcomed it."

"I did not lose it all, sir; just a small portion was needed to cover the tops of the barrels. The rest will find a welcome market with the general's quartermaster. Mistress Jane is even now engaged in seeing that small transaction to its proper conclusion."

"I suppose you'll make a profit."

"My investment will be recovered, that is all. Of course, the loss of my paper currency during our difficulties has put a strain on my situation. Fortunately, a proper claim has already been made to General Putnam, who accepted it quite readily."

"As a condition for you to leave off telling your story, no doubt."

Van Clynne smiled to himself, as Jake's guess was correct. Old Put's document could be redeemed at Kingston or Albany with any of several merchants he knew, and would more than compensate for his losses. And as he was once more equipped with his many purses, to say he was well pleased with himself would be to understate the case as surely as the Dutchman overstated his role in any victory.

Lieutenant Colonel Gibbs, battered, bruised, wrapped with many cloths and bandages, was nonetheless also in a light mood. What he had once seen as a brief diversion to while away an hour or so—a game or two of chess—had turned into a three-day adventure, during which he had thwarted not only a group of Tory rangers but the British navy, her marines, and a member of the Secret Department as well. Such sweet victories for the Cause—all the better to have been topped off with some sweet kisses from the remarkable young Rose.

The girl had been left with General Putnam, who promised to dispatch one of his men and arrange a reunion with her husband-to-be. Undoubtedly, the bounty he promised for her efforts would provide an extravagant wedding feast, even with the war. The general had even broadly hinted he would preside at the match—Old Put never lost an opportunity to join a celebration.

The Connecticut men who had proved so useful to the operation had been sent back to their barracks for more rest by Putnam. The commander promised to remember them with a choice assignment as well as leave. Jake feared that might not add up to much for the doughty soldiers, who'd shown their muster against some of Britain's toughest fighters, but that was the lot of the common foot soldier—always doing the dirty work, and never receiving much of the reward.

And Captain John Busch? Perhaps his fortitude and torment when alive had earned him a passage to bliss. Jake hoped this was so, for never had he found so worthy a man, let alone a Tory. Had circumstances been different —but one could just as well wish for two suns to rise instead of one.

The patriot spy had no doubt he would meet Dr. Keen again. At that point he might be able to retrieve his Segallas, stolen by the villain and worth ten times more to Jake than the lost money had been to van Clynne.

There would be time for that in the future. Now he had to ride north as quickly as possible to meet Schuyler.

And then get some sleep. Even his iron constitution needed rest eventually.

They reached a turn in the Post Road and the river suddenly came into sight, illuminated by the light pink of early dawn. From this distance, the Hudson was a peaceful lake, quiet in her majesty, silent and sure. The iron chain rocked against her restraints many miles to the south, protecting the upper reaches of the valley, and the nation.

The British would undoubtedly try again. Jake had seen that there were many vulnerabilities to the local defenses, and even such an accomplished soldier as Old Put might not be able to fix them. Yet this morning he was filled with an optimism that the country would endure no matter what the British did, and that the Revolution would succeed. So beautiful a river could flow only for free men.

"I don't think I've eaten a decent meal since Prisco's," declared Jake as the road turned away from the water. "Perhaps you can lead us to a good place for breakfast."

"There is a housewife who makes the most excellent cakes you have ever tasted but a short distance away," said van Clynne. "She will be happy to feed us, as long as you compliment her on her garden as soon as you meet her. She will talk nonstop," added the squire, "but it is the price we must pay for her excellent food."

"She's Dutch?"

"Could there be a question?" answered van Clynne, kicking his horse to pick up the pace.

AN HISTORICAL NOTE

The question of the historical veracity of the manuscripts upon which this series is based was addressed in *The Silver Bullet*, and hence won't be repeated here. A few points of note that apply specifically to this tale, however, may prove to be of interest.

No mention of the attack on the chain detailed in this book appears in any history that I know of, but then again, Jake Gibbs doesn't either. An iron chain *did* span the Hudson above Peekskill approximately where the Bear Mountain Bridge stands today, and it was intact during the period covered by this book. For a description of it, as well as the more famous barrier that spanned the river at West Point, interested readers should examine Lincoln Diamant's excellent book, *Chaining the Hudson*.

The first iron chain's strategic importance was every bit as vital to the American cause as the old manuscript indicates; alas, it was breached later that autumn under a flanking attack aided by a local Tory. Sir Henry Clinton led a small but fierce party of British soldiers northward; they burned Kingston and perhaps with reinforcements might have succeeded in rending the young nation in two. Fortunately, upper New York had been secured by that time, thanks to the defeat of Burgoyne north of Albany. The Americans were able to turn aside Clinton's threat, though not without considerable misery.

A galley called the *Dependence* operated on the Hudson during the time span covered by this story, as both American and British documents show. Even General

Putnam complained that his forces were impotent against it.

One of the best existing narratives of the Revolutionary War, and indeed the most complete by a "common" soldier, is the book published under the title of *Private Yankee Doodle*. Its author is Joseph Plumb Martin—which would seem to match the name of the soldier who assists Squire van Clynne and Lieutenant Colonel Gibbs in their operation. According to Martin's narrative, he was under quarantine for small pox inoculation at the time—exactly the condition of this book's Martin when he is called to greater duty by Claus van Clynne.

He does not mention the operation against the chain or the related adventures in his narrative. An oversight?

Perhaps further clues as to the authenticity and purpose of this private history of Jake Gibbs lie in the manuscripts I have left to work on.

One last thing: as I said in *The Silver Bullet*, once you start reading accounts from the Revolutionary days you quickly discover that it's best to take everything with a large grain of salt. It would probably be wise to follow that same spirit here.

—JD